RYAN O'NAN
WINDERS

BOOKS BY RYAN O'NAN

Winders

RYAN O'NAN
WINDERS

Published by JAB Books

SF

WINDERS
Copyright © 2021 by Ryan O'Nan
All rights reserved.
Published in 2021 by JAB Books
ISBN 978-1-625675-36-1 (hardcover)
ISBN 978-1-625675-37-8 (ebook)

Interior design by Lisa Rodgers
Cover design by John Fisk

JAB Books
49 W. 45th Street, 12th Floor
New York, NY 10036
http://awfulagent.com
ebooks@awfulagent.com

First edition: September 2021

Printed in the United States of America

0 9 8 7 6 5 4 3 2 1

For Lorraine Maxine O'Nan

Do I dare
Disturb the universe?
In a minute there is time
For decisions and revisions which a minute will reverse.
~ T. S. Eliot

CHAPTER 1

CHARLIE

My mother died twice.

This *fact*, and the brutal, relentless memories tethered to it, lock on to me once again like a familiar firing squad. Some facts are inescapable. Some are not. I've learned there's a difference. Some facts, with the proper motivation, can slip away: like a snake's tongue they can shoot out, taste the world, then snap back in the blink of an eye. But this isn't one of those facts. Not even close.

The memory always begins the same.

With the ugly, heartbreaking sound of leather hitting leather.

"Strike three! YOU'RE OUT!" the umpire boomed as hope drained from my dopey ten-year-old face. By the time the humiliation finally ebbed to a breathable level, I looked up and saw the two teams already shaking hands. Game over. We'd lost. By one.

Leading our side of the handshake line was Donald "Ducky" Jones, the young star of our team, as well as my best friend since we were three. Mere seconds before, Ducky had been poised on third base, waiting to race home and tie the game. He'd nodded to me in that last moment, attempting to beam confidence my way. Ducky was five feet tall, dark-skinned and well on his way to being seriously handsome. His good looks and daddy-longlegs body eclipsed the fact that he wore glasses and got good grades, which I'd always thought was pretty damn unfair. The least he could do was get mercilessly teased for *something*. Ducky glanced back, making sure I was okay. I could tell by his face that he was seconds from breaking out of the line to check on me, so I started moving. The second I began walking, I felt her eyes on me.

My mother never sat in the same spot at my games. She said she liked to keep me guessing, but I always knew exactly where she was—even before she started shouting things like "End that ball's life, kiddo! NO REMORSE! NO MERCY! YOU EAT BALLS FOR BREAKFAST!!" That last one was one of her personal favorites. I could hear the mischievous smile in her voice no matter how serious she tried to scream it.

People always loved my mother. There was a gravitational force to her that seemed to be universally understood—a kind of bees' sense of social order. I knew my mother was beautiful before I even knew what beautiful meant, because people were always instructing me on it: *"God, your mom is so hot, Charlie,"* Bobby Stugle's older brother had leaned in close to me and whispered at a Fourth of July party when I was six. *"You know, Charlie, some would say that your mother is proof there is a God"* had been my Sunday school teacher's take on the matter. I never thought of her like that. Not that I thought she *wasn't* beautiful…just, I guess, maybe if you were born and raised in the Sistine Chapel, you wouldn't be like, *How amazing is my ceiling?!* You'd probably be more like, *Why aren't I allowed to hang any of my posters up?*

My mother also did a lot of annoying, gross stuff, too: like announcing to me when it was "time for a good old-fashioned lady poop" (which, to this day, I honestly have no idea if there's an actual difference between a lady poop and a non-lady poop), or when she'd get nervous, she'd bite her fingernails, then casually slide the shrapnel under whatever she was sitting on. I'm sure she thought no one ever saw her. But I did. I saw everything.

She also loathed the status quo—especially the unwritten agreements about what constituted "normal" at my school. Unfortunately for me, the expression of her disdain usually ended with me being morbidly embarrassed. Like the Halloween when all the other mothers at the annual school Pumpkin Patch Picking Party came dressed as sexy cats, and sexy witches, and even one sexy hunchback, and my mother arrived looking like she'd been savagely attacked by fifteen werewolves. There was not a speck of her body not covered in blood and goo. When asked what exactly she was going for with her hideous costume, she had shrugged and said that *I* had dared her to come as a woman who'd been turned inside out. (If you looked closely, you could make out all of her hanging organs.) The other parents looked at me like I'd thrown the statue of David down fifteen flights of stairs. My mother belly-laughed at their reactions, because, of course, I hadn't dared her to do anything. She just loved to watch me squirm. She'd say, "We're a team, kiddo, and part of being a team is making sure we both stay scrappy and on our toes."

But that day, as she watched me skulk off the baseball field— the boy who had just shat the bed for his entire team—I could feel her wanting to stand in front of the shame bearing down on me. And knowing that made me not want to look at her. So, I didn't. I was too busy whispering one sentence repeatedly to myself—a sentence I'd heard Sawyer Siggafus whisper to Ducky last spring when he'd asked him for the fifth time to try out for our team. Sawyer put one of his freakishly long freckled gorilla arms on Ducky's shoulder and without even the slightest hesitation said: "Fuck baseball."

Ten minutes later, the sun had set and the pukey, golden light had all but died away. A few straggling parents were hanging around talking. Ducky's mom laughed at something my mom said. Mrs. Jones was a voluptuous, stylishly dressed Black woman who had one of those contagious laughs—the full-chested kind that made you feel like you were genuinely funny.

A car horn honked, and the power trio all waved at a big old burgundy battleship of a Lincoln Town Car as it carved its way across the parking lot toward the exit. Behind the wheel sat "Grams," Ducky's grandmother and the matriarch of the Jones family. Grams always treated my mother like a second daughter. My mother lost both of her own parents when she was in her early twenties, so she often turned to Grams for any kind of real mom-ish advice. My mother used to say Grams was the kind of woman who effortlessly commanded respect. One more honk and Grams turned out onto the main road, heading for the turnpike.

I sat alone at the far end of the bleachers, head hung, one hand picking at the shredded wooden bleacher underneath me, while in my other hand I still held the treasonous bat. By my feet, a small army of ants had covered a discarded popsicle stick, sucking at the dregs. *That's right,* I thought; *some get the popsicle, and some just get the stick. CLONK.* I let the aluminum bat tap against the wooden bleachers, and all the ants began scurrying in every direction. I let it hit again. *CLONK.* The frenzy turned into an ant riot—all clamoring for safety.

A tall, gangly shadow drifted over the chaos below. "You're making a lot of traumatized ants," Ducky said. "You got any idea the kind of funding it takes to provide mental health insurance for that many ants?"

A silence hung in the air. I wasn't in the mood. But I knew Ducky well enough to know that he had no intention of leaving. That's one of the worst things about Ducky: he's patient. Finally, reluctantly, I glanced up at him.

"…Like a dollar?"

"More like five. And who's gonna pay for that? Not *my* taxes."

"You sound just like your dad."

Ducky's face fell. "I'd take that as a compliment if my dad wasn't over there undressing your mom with his eyes, like, *right* in front of *my* mom."

I looked over and sure enough, Ducky's dad, a towering, former college basketball player, who had been forced to leave the sport at nineteen due to a knee injury, and who managed a bank in Morris County, was trying extremely hard to not look like he was staring at my mother's body as she and Ducky's mom talked. And he was totally failing.

"…So embarrassing, man," Ducky said, shaking his head.

I broke down laughing, despite my dark mood, despite my anger and frustration. Ducky laughed with me. More in victory for pulling me out of my dark funk, but regardless, it helped. And as my spirits rose, I instantly felt bad about the ants. *Sorry, fellas. Nothing like a crybaby giant, huh?*

Once my mom and I drove away from the park, night wrapped around us, making the New Jersey Turnpike feel like the last highway left on Earth. We rode in silence as I pulled at the stitching of my mitt. I was actually much better at catching than hitting. *Why does everyone have to hit?* I thought. *Can't there be an exclusion rule for kids who swing at the ball like a schizophrenic trying to club invisible birds?* My mother looked over at me.

"How you doing over there?" she asked, attempting to sound nonchalant.

"Great," I said, not looking up.

"You wanna get ice cream?"

"I'm not five, Mom."

"Is that a *no?*"

"I didn't say that."

She smiled at me. More of a smirk, actually. More of a "gotcha." The smile was crooked and mischievous, and for a moment I wondered what she was like at my age. Was she like me: shy at all the wrong times, vice-president of the Land of Awkward (that's right, not even president)? I couldn't imagine her being anything but the confident, striking woman sitting there smiling at me.

"Ducky said his dad was undressing you with his eyes."

She casually glanced in the rearview mirror at the minivan following behind us, containing Ducky and his mom and dad. In the side mirror, I could see that Ducky's parents were arguing. Possibly a shared theme was being discussed in both vehicles. My mother, who saw the same thing as me, grinned slightly.

"*Did* he?" she asked, but I could tell it was one of those questions that doesn't expect an answer.

But I wasn't just delivering compliments; I had an agenda. "Think you might start dating again any time soon? You know, you're not gonna look like this forever."

My mother looked at me, aghast, and for just a moment, guilt yanked at me. In my whiny little anger, I'd been too mean. I'd brought a machete to a needle fight. But then I saw the edge of her mouth curve upward. "Is that a fact?!" she said, giving me her best wounded outrage. "Thank you very much for that reminder. Wow. Did I ever tell you how charming you are?"

"No."

"Good!"

"Well?"

She paused. I waited for her inevitable comeback. But then the silence stretched out until I felt compelled to demolish the awkwardness. But she spoke before I could.

"I don't know, Charlie… It's hard to find a good man." Fascination tore into me. There was a sadness in her voice, which told me one thing: she was thinking about my father. At least, I thought that's what it meant. My father was something she very rarely talked about. I'd never met him. Never saw a picture of him. Didn't even know if he was still alive. But he definitely lived inside her in some way, and it was only in rare moments that I'd get a glimpse of the face I'd been trying to piece together in my mind. I know in my heart she didn't keep him from me to hurt me. But she still kept him from me.

"Why's it hard?" I asked, nonchalantly. *Keep cool and she might get careless.*

She went quiet again. I was sure she was going to drop it, but then…she didn't.

"I'm not sure… Men are always at war with their own fear, Charlie. You hide from that and you hide from life." She turned to me, and in her eyes it felt like she understood everything that was tumbling around inside of me like a trapeze swinger, and that maybe some part of her wished things could be different, and that there was something she could say to make things easier for me; but instead, she said, "Besides, I already have a man in my life. And he's *horrible* at baseball."

"Mom!"

She squealed with laughter.

"It's not funny!" I cried, trying to look angry, but it was too late; I was already laughing. Like thousands of others, I found myself utterly disarmed by her.

"Truth hurts. Don't it, kiddo?!"

We laughed our faces pink. Rolling laughter—the kind that ebbs, then relights off the tiniest spark. And in that moment, I loved her so much. More than anything. In that moment, I needed nothing else. Only her. And that's when I saw the headlights.

"Mom…" My voice cracked with alarm.

By the time she turned back, the truck was already in our lane, heading right at us. There was no time to react. The sound was so much louder than I could've imagined—having seen a million car crashes in movies. For the briefest of seconds, I focused on the ugly brown paintjob crushing in on us. The hood of the truck had a decal of a tornado on it. Later, I'd learn it was actually a whirlpool—that the owner of the truck worked for a plumbing company which he'd been laid off from earlier that day and had spent several hours prior to our meeting drowning his sorrows at a local bar. The name of our little league team was the Cyclones, and for that eternity of a second, my ten-year-old brain was convinced that it was some kind of dark payback for me striking out. *Maybe it was.* But if that were true, then why did the steel truck hit almost entirely on the driver's side?

My mother was crushed before my eyes. The air filled with a kaleidoscope of shattered glass and deranged high beams, as both our vehicles flipped over the side of the highway, turning end over end, until finally coming to rest at the bottom of a steep hill.

Thick smoke knifed into my esophagus, burning my eye sockets. Through the shattered window I could barely make out Ducky's family at the top of the ridge, screaming our names. They sounded so scared. Then I turned toward my mother. She must have turned her head right before impact, because half her face looked normal, while the other half seemed hidden behind some nightmarish mask. Blood streamed from her nose and mouth as her "normal" eye stared vacantly into me.

"Mom… No. …NO! …Please… Please! MOM!!!" I wailed. Sobs choked my clenching throat. The smell of gasoline was getting stronger and the smoke in the car was growing more opaque. But none of that mattered as long as my mother sat two feet away, hunched and lifeless. I clawed and stabbed at the truth, trying to force it back into whatever cesspool it had crawled from, but it just came at me again and again. With a passion and hatred and force I had never known, I cried out into the suffocating darkness, wrenching my little broken spirit like a sponge.

And then something happened…

THE WORLD AROUND ME BEGAN TO SHIFT.

DARK SMOKE HUFFED OUT OF MY THROAT. BLOOD SUCKED

BACK INTO MY MOTHER'S BODY. OUR CAR SPRANG TO LIFE, RIPPED
UPWARD BY SOME UNSEEABLE FORCE. IT FELT AS IF THE WORLD WAS
REWINDING ALL AROUND ME. OUR CAR SPUN THROUGH THE AIR AS
IT CLIMBED ITS WAY OUT OF THE DITCH AND BACK UP THE HILL.
MY EYES TRIED TO FOCUS AS OUR TWO VEHICLES LUNGED BACK-
WARD THROUGH THE BROKEN GUARDRAIL AND SKIDDED ACROSS
THE HIGHWAY. WE WERE LOCKED TOGETHER ONE SECOND, THEN
WE WERE APART. OUR CAR REBUILT ITSELF AS WE WERE YANKED IN
OPPOSITE DIRECTIONS ACROSS THE ROAD. HEADLIGHTS SLID EVERY-
WHERE LIKE PRISON-BREAK SEARCH BEAMS. And then it was over.

The world began moving forward again.

A high-pitched squealing sound—almost like guitar feedback—punctured the air (with no apparent origin). And through
the harsh noise, I suddenly heard her voice next to me… "Besides,
I've already got a man in my life. And he's *horrible* at baseball."

I whipped my head so hard to the left, I felt a muscle in my
neck pop, and there was my mother, sitting there, perfectly fine.
Not just fine—laughing her ass off. *It was a dream,* I thought. *Some
horrific nightmare. I fell asleep in the car, she noticed, and now she's
repeating her words just to mess with me.*

"Truth hurts. Don't it, kiddo?!" *I knew she was going to say that.
That's impossible! What is this?* My mind pounded. *Please, let this be
one of her pranks…*

And then I saw the truck swerve. Its headlights beginning to
aim in our direction.

"Charlie?" she said, sounding concerned by my lack of response.
"You okay?" She wasn't looking at the road. In a kneejerk moment,
I reached over and yanked the steering wheel. "Charlie?! What are
you doing…" She struggled to regain control. The headlights were
seconds away. I yanked harder. Our vehicle skidded, missing the
truck by inches.

I saved our lives, I thought. *It makes absolutely no sense, and I'm
probably totally insane, but somehow, I know I saved us.*

My mother slammed on the brakes, swerving toward the side
of the road.

I knew it was coming before I saw it. On some unconscious
level, as I turned to look back, it was the only thing that made

sense—*nothing for free.* The putrid, burning smell of our tires sliding across the broken asphalt filled my lungs as I watched the runaway truck plunge into Ducky's minivan. My mother covered her mouth in disbelief.

The convulsions came like a flash flood, shaking my body to its core as the veins on my face and neck threatened to burst.

"Charlie?!" my mother cried out, wrapping me in her arms. "What's happening?! CHARLIE?!!" Then I was enveloped by black as I hurtled into unconsciousness.

But the black seemed to last only a second, as if I breathed in darkness, then breathed out blinding light.

The emergency room was drenched in manic energy. Nurses slammed gurneys down a long corridor as doctors wove in between, searching for answers at breakneck speed. I was strapped down onto a gurney, wearing a plasticky-smelling oxygen mask.

"How many?" a doctor asked, racing next to one of the EMTs.

The hefty female EMT barked out facts, "Two adult males: DOA. One adult female: critical. Two children—"

"Where's the other child?" the doctor cut in, trying to sound all business, but the fear of seeing a dead kid betrayed him.

"Minor cuts and abrasions. Running a CAT just in case."

An audible sigh of relief escaped the doctor.

"Where's my mom?" I moaned.

"I'm right here, Charlie!" She rushed up next to me. I'd never seen her look so frightened. It made me twice as scared. A nurse tried to aim her out of the way.

"Ma'am, you're not allowed past here."

"I'm not leaving him!"

I howled for her not to leave me alone, but the merciless nurse held firm. "He's going to be okay. Let the doctors take it from here."

My mom swore she'd be close by as I was shuttled down the long hallway. Finally, I let my head rest, turning to the side. My cheek scraped against the starchy stiff sheet. Next to me on a separate gurney was Ducky's mom. She had a huge gash on her forehead, which was bleeding profusely. Her blank eyes stared into me. It was haunting, but I couldn't turn away. A guilt and sadness I could barely comprehend burned in me, stinging my nose as my eyes filled with tears.

Ducky's mom's heart monitor suddenly flatlined. Just like in every doctor show, there was that listless *beeeeeeeeeeeeeeep*, and then all sound went extinct—like my ears had simply had enough. As I was hustled down the mint-green corridor, I looked back to see Ducky's mom's body arching from the electric paddles over and over. I thought of Ducky. He wouldn't miss out on the stories that were read to him, or the day his dad taught him how to ride a bike, or the late nights sneaking into his parents' room after a bad dream—when he'd curl up next to their big, warm bodies and feel completely safe. He'd have all those memories tucked away into the crevices of his soul. But the future: the first loves, the teenage fights, passing his driver's test, prom photos, and a million seemingly mundane moments between him and the two people he loved most in the world—those moments would never be shared—all because I reached for that steering wheel.

I faced toward the ceiling and let the hypnotic, recurring overhead fluorescent lamps lull me into submission, pulsing... pulsing...pulsing.

The bus lurches to a stop at a traffic light, causing my face to smash into the seat in front of me, ripping me out of the dark memory. My stomach spasms, but truthfully, I can't tell whether it's my body trembling or the old Greyhound bus I've been stuck on for the last thirty hours finally shaking my insides loose with its monstrous, gargling motor. Slimy sweat coats the palm of my left hand from white-knuckling the pill bottle for the last five hours. *Why didn't I think about the bus? I hate buses! It was a bus that took me away in the first place. I should've done it afterwards. Got home first, then tried to kick this shit...* But some part of me knows that plan wouldn't have worked. I wouldn't have had the strength to do it later. If I had come home high, that's exactly where I would've stayed. I shake off a chill as it rushes through me, then look around, hoping no one's noticed my jerky weirdness. The last thing I need is someone to tell the bus driver there's an eighteen-year-old, junky psycho, dressed like a marine, having a seizure in the back of the bus. That would be bad. But what could they do? They couldn't send me back. A prison for boys can only keep you as long as you remain just that: a boy.

The bus moans and hisses as it finally spits me out onto the crumbling sidewalk of my hometown. New Brunswick, New Jersey. It's night. I didn't picture myself returning here at night. It was always day in the thousands of times I'd imagined it. The shadows around me feel hostile. I close my eyes, but the second I do, I'm back in that car, watching my mother get crushed. Then she's not. Then it doesn't matter—she's still taken from me.

I know it wasn't real. None of it. And I never told anyone but my mother what I thought happened that night, and even to her I only said it once. The look on her face told me it was a horrible thing to say, or to think, or to imagine. And by then, the coughing had already started. I had bigger fish to fry than wondering if I was crazy. My mother would be dead within a month. Cancer. Not the kind in movies, where you basically look the same, minus the hair, and maybe less makeup. The shitty kind. The kind where you get to see the person you care about most rapidly wither away like those videos of decomposing fruit played in fast motion. One day, she was my beautiful, tough, playful mother; then she was fragile and confused by the pain and her quick decline; then she was a living skeleton twisted in agony; then she was gone.

And I must have known. I must have heard the coughing before that night on that highway and pushed away its potential. It makes too much sense. My hallucination: the reeling mind of a young boy, terrified of losing his mother, imagines her destruction and gives himself incredible powers to reverse it. A great fairy tale. The metaphor is so pathetically simple, it's crippling.

So, here I am, back on this familiar street corner, staring down a place I once wanted to flee so badly—a land of ghosts—where everything reminds me of her. I sit down on the bus stop bench. My hand won't stop shaking. *I don't think I can do this.* I can't let them see me like this. They wouldn't want to see me like this. I don't want to hurt them. And this would. I know it would. So much easier to just escape.

Slowly, I reach into my pocket and pull out the bottle of pills, my last parting gift from Camp Lazarus—a military-style jail for minors convicted of violent crimes. Three years ago, I almost killed somebody. Put a kid in a coma. Now I'm back, and this next part is going to be really fucking hard. I don't think I can do it. I thought I could when I got on the bus, but now the thought of coming home feels impossible. I only know one reliable way to strip away all the depth and definition from these phantoms bashing around inside my head. I shake the little plastic pill bottle. Lots left. Plenty.

CHAPTER 2

JUNIPER

They're after me. I know they are. The roar of the subway car barreling through the station momentarily masks any approach I might hear from behind. So, I risk a look back. *Nothing.* I don't see anyone out of place—no one that doesn't belong—no one except *me.* Part of me expects every face of the crowd that I'm walking with to be staring at me—sensing the intruder among them. But not one of the weary black and brown faces emerging out of the darkness, trudging their way up the filthy concrete steps toward the exit, gives me even a glance. It makes sense. I look like them. My father's people came to this country from Haiti, while my mother's face could've been on the Scottish flag. Throw them in a chromosomal blender and you get me—just another thin, eighteen-year-old girl in New York City. I saw four different versions of myself just on my journey here alone. My dark green eyes might be a more identifiable trait, but no one's looking that close.

I pull my hands from the pockets of my black hoody and grip the straps of my backpack. Its contents bounce against my spine as I climb the stairs. Rain pours down outside the exit. People around me groan at the weather. The few that have umbrellas open them. But I know I'm lucky for the rain. Rain makes people lazy. Makes them try just a little less.

Others rush out into the downpour, getting it over with. An older man swears as he holds a newspaper above his head and reluctantly exits. I take a moment to check behind me one last time, then I walk into the wet.

Even in the harsh weather, this part of the city feels dangerous. To my left, drunken patrons stand under the awning of a seedy bar, smoking, laughing and shouting. Makeshift tents cover the homeless along my side of the sidewalk. Loud music blares from a speaker attached with bungee cables to a bicycle. A patchwork of faded stickers from the 2012 presidential election covers almost the entirety of the speaker. The bike is leaned under a bus stop where its rider, an obese man with a thick, black mustache, chats with an old woman in Spanish. I watch them both glance across the street to the black-and-white police cruiser. Their gaze moves up to the two uniformed officers standing under the entryway to a crumbing old apartment building, drinking coffee out of blue paper cups. One officer is tall and lanky; the other resembles a bulldog with his slouching cheeks and squat posture. *I wonder if they're ours.*

I feel the chipped brick wall against my back as I crouch in the shadows, getting more and more waterlogged by the second. I keep swallowing, choking back my gag reflex at the putrid, acidic smell of urine surrounding me. Apparently, I'm not the first person to find this hiding spot suitable for their needs. How are these people allowed to live like this? It's cruel. Not that we've done anything to help them. But to be so discarded by their own kind… I try to focus and breathe, then immediately regret the breathing part as the stench overwhelms me again.

This was a horrible idea. I feel stupid for coming here. *But I have to know.*

I maneuver myself closer, doing everything in my power to remain silent and hidden. I'm not sure how well-trained these two police officers are. I'm hoping for *not very well.* Now I can clearly hear their voices.

"Someone oughta burn this neighborhood to the ground," the short officer says.

The lanky officer looks over. "Didn't you grow up on this block?"

"Yeah. What about it?"

The lanky officer laughs and the shorter man smiles at having amused his partner. *They're not ours.*

"I'LL KILL YOU, BITCH!"

My body floods with adrenaline as my attention snaps toward

the belligerent scream. Under one of the bar awnings, two drunk women, their faces almost pressed together, yell incoherent profanities at each other. The heftier drunk shoves the other woman, who's covered in tattoos and wearing what looks like a hundred bracelets, out into the pouring rain. The wet, tattooed drunk comes back fast, swinging wildly. They slam into the small crowd watching them, and both get shoved back into the downpour.

None of this makes sense. What the hell were you doing here, Elijah?

The women tear each other's faces bloody using what's left of their long multicolored nails. Their complete lack of technique makes me feel like I'm watching two blind people fight. I might laugh if my impatience weren't bursting at the seams. To make matters worse, the police are just watching. *Cowards.* I've heard of things like this but never seen it with my own eyes. It's sad how little solidarity exists in the human world. I don't want to watch anymore, but I can't leave. *Focus. Count your breaths.* Slow in, slow out. The childhood habit calms me. I get to ten by the time the big girl gets Bracelets down on the ground. Fifteen when she starts kicking her in the stomach. Even in the storm, I hear the bracelets jingle with each impact. When I get to twenty-one, the two negligent officers finally toss their coffees and run toward the brawl. As they pass me, I slip behind them, making my way up the stone stairs and into the tenement building they've been impassively guarding.

Inside, the only sound is the dripping of my soaked clothes onto the grimy, cracked tile floor. *God, it smells terrible in here, too.* Not like urine, thankfully, but there's a stale, choked odor. Probably mold. A lot of it. A light flickers overhead, giving my movements the feeling of slow motion. I've barely taken ten steps into this coffin of a building and I already feel claustrophobic. The thought of encountering an adversary here terrifies me. *Just keep moving.*

Then I see what I'm looking for: yellow police tape blocks the stairs leading up to the second floor. I focus all my senses, listening up the dark stairwell, but I hear only the muffled drone of televisions inside apartments. This building may be old, but the walls are thick. *They must have been. They said there were no witnesses.* Hesitation grips me. *I'll be trapped up there if things go bad.* I tell myself I don't have a choice at this point, but I know that's not true. I could leave right now—save myself this last part. No one would blame me. That's not true; *I* would. And I would be brutal. I duck under the tape and climb.

The door I'm looking for stands ajar. I push it the rest of the way, ready for an attack. Nothing comes. The rundown studio apartment is completely empty except for a single occupant: a lone wooden chair. Lit by moonlight from a large window, the chair sits at the center of a trapezoid of yellow tape, surrounded by tiny numbered evidence markers. The tape says CAUTION over and over. *What exactly are you cautioning against? Your "crime scene" is an iceberg, and none of you can swim, so good luck seeing beneath the surface.*

But then I remember what brought me here in the first place. *Am I any less ignorant? I didn't get here by accident. Someone knows much more than me, and I need to learn everything I can—very quickly.* I force my eyes back to the chair.

They found you here, Elijah. "Broken," *I heard someone say.* "Shattered" *was my father's description. They murdered you. My Teacher... my friend. And where was I? Where were any of us?* They're calling it an assassination—possibly the Japanese or Swedish Chapter. Both have been bitterly vocal lately regarding our Chapter's trade policies. *But it doesn't matter what they call it; you're gone. And I want to hurt whoever did this to you.* I don't make friends easily.

I stare at the wide bloodstain on the wall. *Big gun.* Most likely a shotgun.

I step over the police tape, eyeing the brackish crimson gore behind the wooden legs of the chair. I'm careful not to step in anything. The chair seems to stare at me. Its stillness feels hostile. I take in every inch, swallowing the scene whole with my eyes.

My hand traces along the arm of the chair, fingertips probing tiny grooves newly carved into the wood. Matching grooves on the other arm as well.

Your arms were bound. Rope wouldn't have made these marks. Not handcuffs, either—there'd be bigger gouges in the wood—less symmetrical. Plastic, I think. Zip ties. It would've taken a while to cut into the surface like this. Why? What were they trying to get from you? Why did they need so much time?

And for a moment, I can almost see him there, Elijah Spencer, clean-shaven and handsome, his tender eyes edged with wrinkles from thirty-eight years of smiling his pale, Irish skin into crows' feet. And then I see him broken and bloody, zip-tied to the chair, struggling, needing help that will never come.

I shut my eyes against the image, then lower myself into the chair. The hard wood presses against my body. Through the window, I see a tall skyscraper in the near distance across the New York City skyline. Red lettering at the very top reads VALCORP.

They wanted you to know how close you were to home. But that means they had to know what ValCorp Tower really is: a sovereign nation. Father must be right; this was an act of war.

As I clutch the rounded ends of the armrests where Elijah's hands would've been holding on, I suddenly feel something. I get up and bend low, looking under the armrests. Scratch marks cut into the wood where Elijah's fingertips would've been curled under. *Just like when I first met you, Elijah. Too similar. You seemed so enormous then, so unbreakable.*

I was five and a half, sitting in that little white chair, facing the corner of my room. It'd been three days since my father told me my mother was dead. I don't know how many times my father turned my chair back around that day. Maybe the image of his little daughter facing the wall was too much for him. He didn't understand that it felt better to see less—to only have that long crease where the wallpaper bunched at the corner to look at—to have that crease be my whole world.

My tiny fingertips were raw, fingernails cracked. I'd clawed the wood into rivets under each armrest. I'd been at it for days. When I heard multiple footsteps behind me, I didn't turn around. My father, Cameron Trask, loomed above me, tall and elegant, his rich mahogany skin and big, golden-brown eyes heavy with grief. I remember he smelled like peppermint.

"You have a visitor, Juniper," he said.

My eyes didn't leave the crease. I heard Elijah set something down; then he slid a chair across the floor and sat down next me. My father quietly left the room. Elijah spoke with a light Alabama accent. His eyes were the purest blue I'd ever seen, and there was honest kindness in them.

"Hi there, Juniper. I'm a friend of your daddy's."

"You're from the Leadership Council," I said, softly. "I've seen your picture."

"That's right. I heard you've had a hard couple days." I said nothing, so eventually he continued. "I don't mean to bother you. I was just wondering if you'd do me a big favor. See, I've got a friend..." Elijah reached into the little plastic carrying case I'd heard him set down and pulled out a young cat. Not a kitten. About a year old. Grey, with orange-brown stripes in its fluffy, chaotic fur. It took me completely by surprise. I'm not sure I'd even seen an animal so close up at that age. I just remember staring at it in wonder as Elijah petted the creature on his lap. Every part of me wanted to reach out and touch it. It looked so soft but also so foreign. I hesitated. Then it looked up into my eyes, and I suddenly realized it was just as scared as me.

"...He lost his mama too," Elijah said, "and he needs someone to look after him."

I watched Elijah register the lack of emotion I'd managed to achieve. Even then, I was working to keep myself controlled, protected. Plus, he didn't know the truth. So, I told him:

"All things die," I said.

Elijah didn't look scared, or angry. He simply nodded. "That's true, Juniper. I wish it weren't, but it is." He looked contemplative. "But I like to think that maybe, as long as we get a little love along the way, maybe that part ain't so bad."

I looked at the cat again, then at Elijah, then spoke in a whisper, making sure my father couldn't hear, assuming he was listening outside the door. "They told us in training that weaker creatures die easier. Because they're less important."

He didn't say anything at first. I was afraid he wouldn't, and I needed to know if this was actually true. Because if it *was* true, then it explained a lot. Finally, he leaned close and whispered back, "Yeah, they told me that, too. But you know what? I got a feeling you're a little too smart for that. I read a book once that said the meek shall inherit the Earth. Wouldn't that make us all look a bit silly?" At five and a half, it was the most blasphemous thing I'd ever heard spoken, and I was completely floored—the idea that the strong weren't simply entitled to the world by evolutionary right.

Elijah slipped the cat into my arms. I didn't resist. In fact, as soon as I held it, I felt like I never wanted to let it go—like we belonged together. Letting my fingers gently slide through its gossamer fur, I felt how thin it really was beneath all that fluff. It began to purr. That little rumble filled me in a way I can't quite express.

"But here's the thing, Juniper," Elijah said. "This little guy's gonna need a friend. He ain't a baby, so he don't need to be treated like one; but he's had a pretty hard time, so he's gonna need someone strong. Do you think you could manage that?"

I thought about it. I didn't want to lie. Finally, I said, "I can do my best."

Elijah stood up and smiled down at me.

"That'll be enough. I'm gonna keep an eye on you two, if that's all right with you."

I gave him a little nod, not wanting to move too much and disturb the amazing creature contently purring on my lap. Elijah turned and left.

It would be two years before I saw him again. Seven years before he'd save me from myself for the second time.

Now, here, in this dank and filthy room, staring at the same shredded claw marks on this lonely wooden chair, my face burns with hatred. "Who the fuck tortured you, Elijah?" I hear my words echo in the hollow space.

From the pocket of my hoody I pull out a piece of damp, folded paper. I can see the words bleeding through. Two smudged, dark, hand-written sentences stare up at me:

Go to the place where it happened. There's another layer.

I have no idea who left the note under my chamber door tonight, or why; but I'm here, and if there's something to find, please let me find it.

I shove the note back in my pocket and approach the wall, facing the epicenter of the bloodstain. It's gruesome. But it's also purposeful. I lean in close, my face less than an inch from the wall, and inhale deeply. Beneath the ugly sour smell of decaying blood and tissue, another scent is very faint, but unmistakable. Bleach. This was *us*. This diorama of a crime scene was carefully curated—staged to look like a suicide—probably by shotgun—to even close examination (which it would never receive). It would've been reported; the information would have reached those of us working within the police department; then we would've been here first to shape the story. They went with suicide; a murder would've begged too many questions. I feel my clinical nature swelling to the surface again, divorcing me from my fury. *Good. I don't want to miss anything.*

I look for the edge of the mask, trying to peek at the skin beneath. Where the wall meets the floor, I find what I'm looking for: a tiny faded red dot. I scratch at it, but nothing comes off. There's no blood on the surface here, just a stain. It could be old. Maybe it's not even blood—spaghetti sauce, perhaps—remnants of a messy child.

Unzipping my backpack, I pray the contents haven't gotten wet. I pull out the camera device. From the front pocket, I withdraw a small tablet and attach them together. Both devices power up. I breathe a sigh of relief.

Police spray Luminol to discover hidden bloodstains. When it interacts with blood, it glows blue. But the kind of bleach used here wouldn't have left anything to be detected, or more precisely, the entire wall would've glowed blue. But the note had specifically said: *There's another layer.* I knew Luminol wouldn't work here, but there's no hiding from infrared. I aim the IR camera at the little red stain. On the tablet, I see patches of infrared imagery. It's definitely blood. *Blood that was there before our people cleaned up. So, what did they clean?* I slowly tilt the lens up and my heart starts hammering in my chest. On the screen, I see four words slashed across the wall in Elijah's blood:

MAY FATE BE RESTORED

My head jerks up, looking at the bloodstained wall. There's

not a trace of the hidden message. I look back at the screen. Dark, curdling thoughts slam into my mind as the truth about Elijah's killers hits me. Then I hear the voices coming up the stairs and my mind fills with panic.

"I ain't sitting out there in the goddam rain! It's 2014! Ain't no law says a cop gotta get soaked." I dodge into the shadows just as the two officers enter. *I'm trapped! So stupid! How could I let myself get so distracted?* "I think that bitch broke my goddamn pinky." The portly officer shakes his wounded hand.

"We could hang down in the car. I got some Oxy," says the lanky officer.

"Shit. Some insomniac detective rolls by to take a second look..."

"Why the hell they got us watching this place, anyway? Dude offed himself with a shotgun. Case closed. Another rich prick gets caught doing some dark shit—takes a one-way trip on the bullet train." My heartbeat slows as ice enters my veins.

"And what's he doing down here in this hood in first place? Probably banging some tranny hooker and getting tied down like a piñata."

"You don't tie down piñatas, idiot."

"Man, you got no idea what I do with piñatas!"

The two wet imbeciles die laughing—laughing at Elijah—mocking his death. *They don't deserve to breathe the same air that Elijah did.* Before I can stop myself, I'm already moving.

They reach for their weapons as I step out of the shadows. They see me and relax.

"Jesus, kid!" the portly officer barks. "You scared the shit outta us!"

"Damn, she's hot," lanky officer says, elbowing his partner. "Got like a young Beyoncé thing going on."

"Don't be an asshole. She's your daughter's age."

"And my daughter's friends are hot." He looks at me and grins. "How'd you get up here, beautiful? You live in the building?"

I walk toward them. I know I shouldn't, but I seem to have lost the ability to care.

The fat policeman takes a step back. "All right, J-Lo. Slow your roll."

But I keep coming at these pitiful men who talked about Elijah like he was something disgusting. *They* are disgusting.

The taller one steps forward. "Hey! The officer said stop! Whatchu think you're doing?"

"I'm going to hurt you," I say, keeping all emotion out of my words—allowing them to be mere observations, facts. The squat, piggish man's eyes go wide as he raises his gun…

CHAPTER 3

JUNIPER

Exiting the building, I know I have to move fast. Anyone outside would've heard the officers' two gunshots. I count again in my head. *Yes, two.* After several tries, it was best I could manage. Plus, I needed to save my strength for anything I might encounter afterward.

The rain washes the blood off my hands as I walk down the block. My knuckles are throbbing. I walk faster.

"Juniper!" a voice calls out. I know who it is before I even turn. They found me. He knew I'd come here. My body sags. Two black SUVs are stopped in the street just past the patrol car. One of the tinted windows of the first SUV is rolled down. My father stares out at me. "Are they dead?" he asks.

"They should be. But they're not." And now something burns in my mind, and I have to know the truth. *Did my father leave the note?* "Was it you? Did you want me to see this?"

He looks at me, confused and angry. "I don't know what you're talking about. What the hell were you thinking, coming here? This building has already been cleaned."

"It wasn't another Chapter. It was the *Faters*. They killed him."

My father stares at me. I can't read the expression on his face. *Did he know?* If so, why did he lie to me? I don't understand, and I *hate* not understanding.

"Juniper...I know he was your Teacher—"

"He was my friend! They tortured him. Why? They've never done that before."

He looks around, nervous. There's no telling who could be listening. I don't care.

"This is not the place for this. Get in the car."

"I prefer to walk." My voice sounds young and petulant. It disgusts me. *Why can't the way I feel on the inside ever match the way I
look on the outside? Just once!*

Then something strange happens. He doesn't get angry. His
expression grows oddly neutral, as if he's performing for someone.

"I'm afraid it's no longer up to you," he says. I couldn't be more
confused.

The doors to the second SUV open, and several men in black
suits step out. *Enforcers.* I take a step back. *Why would my father
bring Enforcers to retrieve me? Does he think that low of me? Is my
coming here being treated as some kind of a crime?*

"What is this?" I try to keep my tone even, but my words come
out shaky.

I see fear in his eyes. This is really happening. I'm being arrested
for wanting to know the truth. I will fight this with everything in
me. *Damn it, Elijah! You would never have let something like this happen!* But then I see something else in my father's eyes—something I
don't understand. It looks like...*pride?*

"You've been chosen, Juniper."

I just stare. Thunderstruck. He glances at the Enforcers. "We're
here to escort you back. Preparations for the ceremony are already
underway. It's terrible it happened like this. Still, Elijah would be
proud. You know he would be. The youngest ever."

There's nothing I can say. No words will come. *Chosen? Me?* I
feel nothing but the rain as it beats down on me.

"The vote was unanimous," he says.

This snaps me out of it. "We both know that's not possible," I say.

"Well...*almost* unanimous. Still, Trevor saw logic in the end."

Two of the four men in black suits pull out pistols with silencers
screwed on. They head toward the building. I look at my father.
"Where are they going?"

"To clean up after you. Those two didn't belong to us. No room
for sloppiness, my love."

I watch in dismay as the Enforcers disappear into the building.
I know that what's about to happen is my fault. I tell myself those
officers should've stayed downstairs, that they should've kept their

depraved mouths shut, that they deserve what's about to happen to them. But I don't believe it. One of the Enforcers holds the SUV door open for me. We look almost the same age. He has blond curly hair and a subtle arrogance to him. He offers me a reverent little bow of his head. Earlier today, he would've never lowered his head to me. If anything, he might have whispered to his friend, *Look at the prissy little dreamer standing out in the rain. Who let her out of the lab?* But everything has changed. I've just gotten everything I've ever wanted, and it makes me feel sick to my stomach. I get in the car.

CHAPTER 4

CHARLIE

The early morning sun begins to warm my clenched body. My back is not happy. I slept through the night, curled up on this hard-as-hell bench. The ache I can already feel is just the tip of the iceberg, I have no doubt. I'm cold and hungry, but there's something else—something feels different. My head feels clearer. Cleaner. I sit up, moaning the whole way, and notice that I'm still clenching the little orange bottle of pills. The bottle hasn't been opened. Every pill still accounted for. *I made it. Somehow.* I can already feel the clutching, clawing hands falling away from me, and with them the grey dullness. I have a headache, but I've had worse headaches.

At the edge of the bench, I see a wire trash barrel. I take a deep breath then toss the pill bottle inside. It rattles to the bottom. As I climb to my feet, my muscles roar with fatigue. I must have trembled through most of the night. I leave behind the wire barrel and my little bottle of escape hatches nestled at the bottom. But drugs were never going to help with this next part. Not the part I'm walking toward right now. Probably nothing will.

It takes me thirty minutes to walk from the bus stop to my old street. The neighborhood's gotten worse in the three years I've been gone. The sour, stale scent of trash cans and cheap marijuana drifts through the musty air. Loose asphalt and broken glass crunch under my feet as I step off the sidewalk onto the road, narrowly avoiding a busted sprinkler geysering in the opposite direction from the dying lawn it was built to protect.

A cluster of teens, with visible gang tattoos, posts up in front of a tricked-out lowrider. They eye me like wolves. My military haircut isn't doing me any favors right now. It would be insanely ironic if I got jumped for looking like a skinhead on this street, the day I return home, since nearly killing a skinhead on this street was what got me shipped away in the first place. I almost want it to happen—just for the brutal symmetry, if nothing else. *Come on, boys, make me a palindrome.*

"You lost, white boy?" the smallest of them calls out. He has 𝓔𝓝𝓙𝓐𝓝𝓞 tattooed above his left eyebrow. It's always the smallest ones that are the most dangerous—always fighting to justify their place in the group. I keep walking, eyes forward. A cursory glance at their size and posture tells me I could take even the biggest of them one on one, but that's not how these things go. Gangs fight together; that way, no one gets too much glory, and no one's allowed to be a coward.

They begin walking behind me. I can hear their menacing footsteps crunching on the asphalt. My breathing ramps up. A bottle is flung. It shatters on the ground to my right side. I flinch a little. Laughter erupts behind me. *They could've hit me if they wanted to.* They're enjoying messing with me. I keep moving, not looking back. Their footsteps grow closer. *Shit. I take it back. Fuck symmetry. This doesn't need to go down today.* I'm waiting for a kick from behind or a bottle to the head. *Five more seconds,* I think, *then I'll turn and run at them—hope that none of them are carrying a knife or a gun. If I can take the biggest one out quick, it might stun them long enough for me to try and escape.* My fists clench and unclench. Whether or not I'm ready, I'm ready. I start to count. *3, 2, 1...* But then my eyes land on something that might just save me.

Up ahead, on the opposite side of the street, a small pack of girls struts around the corner. Half the girls sport visible tattoos, and all of them walk with a decent amount of swagger. They're on their own turf. Behind me, I feel the thugs slow down, then break away. And just like that, I'm forgotten. I risk a glance back as I reach the end of the block, and I'm relieved to see the two groups smiling and flirting. The only stranger around is me, but they don't look over. Even when I walk through the waist-high chain-link gate in front of the last house on the block, they don't take any notice.

The metal gate clinks closed behind me as I cross the yard.

The tiny brown house, with its warped garage door and its weather-cracked driveway is one of the few with flowers in the yard and a freshly painted number by the door. I take the four creaky front steps in two strides, landing on the wide, wooden porch, where I freeze. I hold my breath as I step forward and knock on the door. Thick iron bars crisscross the front windows—a new decorative feature. Worry creeps into my heart. *Did something happen? Something I could have stopped…if I hadn't gotten myself thrown into a prison for boys halfway across the country?*

Suddenly, I want to bolt. I take a step back. *Why did I come back here?* What made me think I'd be welcomed back to a place where I caused so much pain? *Go, Charlie! Go!* I start to move, then I hear the distinct sound of a chain lock sliding free, and the release of a heavy deadbolt, and I know it's too late. The door opens and I turn into the awestruck face of Grams. Her mouth forms a shocked *O* of surprise and she slaps her leg with a crisp *smack*.

"My lord, Charlie Ryan, you walk into my arms this very instant!"

"Hi, Grams," I say, falling into her embrace. I stay there for a long time. Her arms are always warm, built for spectacular hugs. She steps back, smiling, still holding my hands in hers—taking me in piece by piece. Finally, she lands on my face.

"I was afraid I'd be sleeping in a pine box next time I saw you, child."

"Pretty sure if anyone's gonna live forever, it's you, Grams."

A tall, handsome young man in a shirt and tie, wearing glasses, and sporting thin, stylish dreadlocks appears behind her. Our eyes meet, and in spite of the guilt sloshing around inside me, I smile. "Hi, Ducky."

Part of me hopes he won't smile back. It's been three years without me around. Ample time for him to finally decide that if I hadn't yanked that steering wheel that night, his parents would still be alive. I wait for judgment, a bullfighter anticipating the charge. Only, I won't dodge. No sliding to the right at the last second for me. *You mess with the bull, you get the horns.*

But then a crooked smile spreads across Ducky's face, crushing all my well-made plans of martyrdom. "Welcome home, Rambo." His face says we're friends. Brothers. We were both ten when we came to live with Grams—two traumatized orphans with nothing left in the world but each other and an old woman with a heart so big, its edges can't be seen. Emotion swells inside me, threatening to tumble out. I force it back down.

"Is this your sexy professor look?" I ask.

"You know how I do. Gotta keep it real for all the females with high hopes of finding a man of honor. Don't you worry; I'll catch you up. You get the books I sent you?"

I nod. One of my favorite things about Ducky is we don't always have to talk. We've spent countless hours sitting side-by-side in Grams's "study," which is really just two torn-up armchairs by the living room window, next to her rickety bookshelf filled with a rotating collection of library books, birthday/Christmas presents (always books—sometimes graphic novels) as well as whatever gems we'd found at the used bookstore downtown. As kids, Ducky managed to power through novels while also balancing a vibrant social life, between sports and girls; but I've always gotten lost in books. They consume me. I want the worlds I feverishly ingest to be real so bad. I'd gladly shed this skin and emerge inside the constructions of Hemmingway, Salinger, Vonnegut, Twain, Tolkien, King, Gaiman, Le Guin, Fitzgerald...hell, I'd even take Orwell. Ducky's latest gift was Mary Shelley's *Frankenstein*. For hours, I soaked myself in the mind of Shelley's monster—the loneliness, the rage. I read it twice, back to back, lying on my bunk at Lazarus. Yes, I'd even trade places with Frankenstein's poor, brutalized monster, chasing its creator across that icy tundra. Anything but this. Anything but me.

I'm suddenly impaled by a thought: Ducky might have sent that book as an accusation. A thinly veiled indictment. Am I the monster in *his* life—the past that relentlessly stalks him?

Ducky sees my hesitancy and pulls me into a ruthless bear hug. Every part of it feels effortless for him. No delay, not an ounce of wavering, and just like that, my fear slides off my shoulders.

"Missed you, man," I say, my words muffled in his shoulder.

"I miss your old hair. This neo-Nazi look gots to go."

I laugh, pulling away and running a hand through my short hair. Ducky loops his arm around my neck as Grams ushers us both inside.

CHAPTER 5

JUNIPER

Only the steady clacking of the guards' steps behind me can be heard as I walk down the dim torchlit hallway. The black reflective marble floor spanning out beneath my feet makes it seem like I'm walking across a liquid surface. I glance up at the flickering torches. I can't help it; it all feels painfully archaic, as if someone came up with this ritual hundreds of years ago and no one has thought to update it since. Still, I'm on the top floor of Thessaly Tower. Just thinking about that takes my breath away. I've lived in Thessaly all my life, but I've never been up here. I've never been allowed. This floor is for the Council only. No one else is allowed up here without strict permission. The one exception is the ceremony.

Ahead of me, the hallway culminates in a round chamber. As I reach the threshold, I stop and look back. The guards stop as well. The reverent nod I received from the young Enforcer last night is not echoed here. These men are mostly veterans, and every molecule in their bodies is saying it shouldn't be me standing here. So, I focus on the only friendly face in the pack—a tall, broad-shouldered man with a thick grey mustache—my father's personal guard, Jeffrey.

"Through here?" I ask, trying to sound merely curious. The little smile at the corner of Jeffrey's mouth tells me he's not buying my nonchalance for a second.

"Yes, Miss Trask."

Jeffrey has been with my father for the last fifteen years. I've known him almost my entire life. In any other situation, he'd call me Juniper. The formality in his voice reminds me just how rare this moment is, and for the first time since my father told me I'd been chosen, I stop feeling confused and disbelieving, and I start to feel afraid.

"You're gonna be great, kid," Jeffrey says, his thick Brooklyn accent slipping through. I love his accent. It feels like he's actually from somewhere. I've lived in New York my whole life, but I don't sound like I'm from New York. I don't sound like I'm from anywhere. I love that Jeffrey does.

Someone clears their throat in the line of Enforcers, and I see Jeffrey stiffen. He is by far the lowest-ranked Enforcer standing in this hallway; he really shouldn't be here at all, but my father must've wanted him close to me. Maybe for moral support. Maybe just in case I decided to run.

I step into the round chamber. Darkness envelops me as I enter. The door slides closed, cutting me off from my escort. The shock I see on Jeffrey and the other guards' faces tells me they weren't expecting to be cut off from me either. This actually makes me feel better—at least I'm not the only one who has no idea what to expect today. The darkness doesn't frighten me. For the brief second it lasts, it feels like I'm inside a cocoon. Safe. Protected. Then a little light on the far wall illuminates a stylish white uniform hanging there. It's beautiful in its simplicity. I've only seen an outfit like this once before. Elijah and the rest of the Council wore something similar on the day I watched them hold a criminal trial for my brother. I can still see my father's clenched jaw and the thick bags under his eyes that day—the shame. I remember thinking how much his heavy, weathered look stood in stark contrast to the elegance of the uniform he wore. And now a similar garment waits for me in the muted little light.

It's clear I'm meant to put it on, so I do. I slip out of my clothes. The fabric feels silky smooth to the touch. The fit is perfect. I've never felt something so nice against my skin.

The second I finish dressing, the door blocking the guards slides open. The timing tells me one thing: someone just watched me get undressed. The idea makes my skin crawl. The guards all file inside. I look from face to face. *No one knows what to do next. They were told only to bring me here.* I recognize the youngest guard among them.

A ropy, pale kid, maybe three years older than me. He's avoiding eye contact. I wonder if he's thinking about the time he and several of his friends held me underwater during swim training. How I cried and coughed up water for ten minutes while the instructor berated me for being a weak swimmer. *I hope he is. I really hope he is.* Around me, the guards begin to fidget uncomfortably, waiting for something to happen. And then, finally, something does.

The entire wall, opposite where we entered, slides open and blinding light pours in on us. And with the light comes a booming voice: "Once, we were tribeless! Floundering about. Striking at the world around us in solitude." The voice is powerful, but there's also a distinct rasp to it, a scratchiness, the sound of a seasoned orator. "Our ancestors spent a millennium claiming their evolutionary right like sneak-thieves. And we would have remained that way, fragmented and crippled. The Code brought us together. Shaped us. And in return we give our service to the whole, striving boldly forward into our collective destiny. We are more than one. We are a Council. We are a Wing. We are a Chapter. We are the Leadership."

I've heard a version of this speech my entire life. The history lesson goes: Once, we were men, then we were more, then we were alone, then we fought against each other, trusting no one, then we agreed on the rules, then one became many and many became one. Every Chapter is taught this. The part they leave out is that today those Chapters barely trust one another—feuding and infighting— *just like the men we evolved from.* Life is an inescapable circle. We think we're better just because we say we are.

But these words do feel different today. Today, I feel as if I'm living within them. Somewhere between the letters themselves— between the pauses—surrounded by the dry, scratchy breathiness of that booming voice.

My eyes finally adjust, and I find myself staring into an immense hall where two hundred high-ranking members of our Chapter stand at attention, waiting. Waiting for me. They're sectioned into four quadrants—four Wings—with a cross shape of empty space separating them. One group wears all white, another wears grey, the third is in shades of blue and the last group wears black. We are not required to wear these colors at all times, and definitely not outside of Thessaly. I'm pretty sure the human world would take notice if they saw one of us only wearing one color every day, but this ceremony is a special occasion, so we represent our Wings.

At the center, several figures stand on a raised platform—four in black, four in grey and one in blue—none in white. They are nine. They should be ten. Each has a red cross-like insignia on their collar. These men and women are the Council of our Chapter of the Leadership. Every Chapter has a Council. This is ours. They are the chosen. I can't help but be a little awed by the spectacle. Then something strange happens. Big blots of color begin to fill my vision and the muscles in my thighs start to tremble, and all at once I feel like there's a very good chance I might just crumple to the ground. I don't understand what's happening, until suddenly my mouth springs open and I gulp in an enormous amount of oxygen. The cool air flows into me, pushing away the color blots and strengthening my legs. I didn't even realize I'd been holding my breath. The pure mortification of imagining myself fainting in front of all these people floods me with adrenaline. All eyes are on me now, and the only thing I can think to do is to start moving.

As I walk, I don't look at the rows of faces passing by on either side. I know I won't find any encouragement there, so I focus only on my destination. On the raised platform ahead, I see the man whose voice I've been hearing. Benjamin Acosta wears the sharp grey uniform of a Solicitor—those chosen to infiltrate the human world on a bureaucratic level. Solicitors become politicians, lawyers, judges, even carefully placed news anchors and TV personalities. Benjamin is the oldest member of the Council. He's also the oldest person I think I've ever seen in real life. He's in his eighties but honestly doesn't look a day under a hundred. His skin is so wrinkled it looks like he's wearing another person's body. He continues his diatribe:

"…Today, the Leadership is an international superpower, silently spanning the globe. And this Chapter—the American Chapter—is second to none." I'm not sure if there's anything worse than people bragging about themselves to themselves. "The Code decrees we must have a council of ten. Today, sadly, we are one short."

Once again, I can hear Jeffrey and the guards' footsteps behind me, only this time hearing their steps feels oddly comforting, as if I weren't alone in all this. But as I near the center, I hear Jeffrey whisper, "Good luck, Juniper," then the guards peel off and join the rows of black-clad Enforcers. Many Enforcers reside here in Thessaly, serving at the will of the Council, but on the outside, they become soldiers, police officers, FBI agents and even professional athletes. (Few things inspire the masses like sports and celebrity.)

I reach the center of the room, the center of the four Wings, where I stop and do everything I can to try and force the nervous flush out of my cheeks. Before me is a thin stone pedestal, on top of which sits an elegant ornate chalice filled with dark liquid. *Oh, God... Am I going to be forced to drink something disgusting?* I feel like I'm in the middle of some ancient Aztec ritual sacrifice. *Is this really how we raise up one of our own? We're the tip of the fucking spear, for God's sake.* I remind myself that both Elijah and my father went through this exact same ceremony. And suddenly I have to fight to keep from laughing, thinking about what Elijah must've been thinking when he was standing here. He despised any kind of pomp and circumstance. Elijah used to say events like this made him feel like "a poodle at a piranha party." Thinking about this takes the edge off my nerves a little. But then my mind flashes back to the dark events of last night...the blood...the chair...the Faters' horrible mantra painted on the wall: *May Fate Be Restored. Is this my fate?* If nothing else, this will get me closer to the vengeance I'm craving on an elemental level.

Benjamin Acosta's voice suddenly drops down low, and I feel the entire assembly lean in. And once again, my heart starts throbbing in my chest. *Who am I kidding? I can make fun of it all I want, but the truth is: this day has been at the center of my heart's desire for as long as I can remember. Just as I'm sure it was for Elijah.*

"As the eldest on the Council, I have the privilege of leading this ceremony," Benjamin says. "With the permission of our new Prime, of course..."

Everyone looks to the man standing next to Benjamin—our newly elected Prime—Elijah's replacement—my father.

Underlining our belief in the group above the individual, our

Prime has no more power than the rest of the Council. He or she can advise, but they cannot dictate. Our Prime also serves as our face to the outside world, acting as the CEO of ValCorp—the multinational corporation that our particular Chapter wears as a mask. The position does mean something to us, though. One still has to be elected—raised ever so slightly above the rest, if only in command of respect.

I examine my father's crisp, tailored, navy-blue suit. He looks handsome. Imposing. I'd say *inspiring* if I didn't know him. I see him rubbing his thumb and two fingers together. Nobody else would notice this detail, but I know all his little ticks and tells, and I've seen this one for over a decade. He's craving. Craving whatever his newest escape might be. He doesn't like people watching him. He likes attention, always has, but this is a different kind of attention. He knows today requires precision. He must have come here clean and sober. I bet he's regretting it right now.

My father is the only Council member wearing blue. Not because of his new status as Prime but because he is the only Provider on the Council. The Provider Wing is responsible for pulling in huge amounts of resources through corporate finance, banking, currency exchange, venture capital, to name a few. Cameron Trask—my father—is the single most successful Provider in the history of our Chapter. His technique for rapidly trading volatile high-risk currencies (as an example) has become the Leadership-wide standard throughout the world. He's a brilliant man. But his new position as Prime feels ill-fitting to me. It's not just his addictions, or even the irrevocable pessimism wound around his heart like a python. Truthfully, I can't really explain it. I just feel it. Perhaps I'm comparing him to Elijah. Not fair, I know, but I can't help it.

He gives Benjamin Acosta a nod to continue, then looks down at me. A tension saturates the air between us. We've been through a great deal together since my mother's death. I wish I could say it's brought us closer. The truth is: I don't think my father likes me very much. I think I remind him too much of her—of what he lost.

Benjamin Acosta aims his skullish, deep-set eyes at me. He

takes a long pause, and in the silence, I suddenly feel he's going to shake his head and say that a mistake has been made—that I should not be standing in this sacred hall after all. At least it would justify the harsh stares I've been feeling from all directions. They don't have to say it; it's radiating off them: *"She's too young." "She hasn't earned it." "Daddy must've pulled some strings." "She always was Elijah's little pet."* Finally, Benjamin breaks the silence…

"If the humans below were to look up here…at that window, right this moment…" He points at the wall of glass at one side of the hall. The Manhattan view is breathtaking. "…What would they see? A fortress? A hive of activity, as we systematically strip them of their power and predominance? Would they see *monsters* lurking above them?" I hear pops of laughter from the assembly. Benjamin looks around and the laughter cuts off. "No. They'd see a window—opaque and impenetrable—one of the thousands of muted eyes of Thessaly Tower gazing down at them. We are the dragon. Not the eyes, not the teeth, not the scales. A thing without parts. Nothing about today is about you, Juniper. So, breathe."

Hearing my name out loud in this place gives me a mini panic attack. *This all feels so huge, and it's happening so fast. They're right; I don't deserve it.* Their eyes feel like cannons aimed at me. But Benjamin Acosta said to breathe, so I do. I try to push down my fear, try to turn it into anger, into defiance.

"Do you accept our choice for *you*, Juniper Trask, to make our Council of ten whole once more?" I swallow. My throat is a desert.

"I do," I manage to say.

Benjamin takes another beat, staring into my very core. Then he turns to the rest of the Council. "Who will make the marks?" I have no idea what this means.

Three Council members step forward:

My father is one.

A thick, leathery Native American woman follows him down from the raised platform. Her name is Maya Steele. Her silver-streaked hair is tied back in a long braid, and her flowing grey dress almost gives the illusion that she's floating. She's a legendary Solicitor. My father once told me that few Solicitors leave Thessaly for any appointment without spending time training with Maya.

The third Council member who steps forward is Trevor De'Vant, a tall, intimidating man in his early sixties. His body speaks to decades of intense training, yet age and appetite have curved his edges some. He wears a black-on-black suit. I can feel his eyes on me, but I don't meet his. Not yet. Not him. I can't. I feel vulnerable enough as it is.

"Since Elijah was the only Seeker on the Council," Benjamin says, "Silvia Orimo will stand in for this ceremony."

An extremely thin woman, with a face like a sharpened tool, steps out from the group wearing all white. I know her well. She's the oldest living Seeker and also the head administrator of the labs where I spend most of my days. Everyone was pretty certain that Silvia would be the next Seeker chosen for the Council (if she lived long enough for a spot to open up). Silva believed this as well. She was wrong. Her expression as she faces me is nothing short of vicious.

Benjamin looks to the four standing before me. "We are four different Wings: Seekers, Providers, Solicitors and Enforcers. But the Code says it is imperative that this Council think as one." He turns to Silvia. "You may begin."

She steps up to the chalice sitting on the stone pedestal. I'm waiting for her to scoop it up and hand it to me for my first taste of whatever's inside, but instead, she dips two fingers into the dark liquid, crosses to me, then paints a thick, sticky line from the center of my hairline down to the bridge of my nose. The liquid is much colder than room temperature. It must've been refrigerated. *But why?* A putrid odor reaches my nostrils, and as Silvia pulls her hand away, I see the crimson stains left on her fingers. Goose bumps surge down both my arms. *It's blood. It's the twenty-first century, in the most powerful city in the world, and I have blood on my face like an Incan foot soldier.* No one would ever call me squeamish, but I can almost taste the stench of rust and rot gouging into my senses. I feel a fury building inside me, and then it gets so much worse.

"The blood of your predecessor wets your face," Benjamin says. "Let it remind you of who and what came before you."

Oh, God… It's his blood. Elijah's blood! The level of decay I can smell tells me two things: it must have been a while before they discovered his body, and it must've been even longer before someone thought to extract the ceremonial vial from his corpse. I try and keep my breathing steady, but it's impossible. I feel like a cornered animal. The entire assembly is watching me, laughing at my panic. I can feel it in their eyes.

Two brownish-red drops land on the white satin blouse covering Silva Orimo's sagging right breast. Now the nausea hits me, but I force it away. *No more, Juniper. You will not show them any more weakness.*

"The Seeker mark aims upwards…" Benjamin Acosta's voice feels far away, as if he were speaking from inside a deep cave. "…reaching for our great potential."

Hearing this brings me back. It means something to me. I am a Seeker. Elijah was a Seeker. Silvia Orimo is too. Science, technology, philosophy, psychology, literature—our corner of this silent empire is mostly invisible—matters of the mind. I know it has to be my work that a has brought me to this moment—despite the hurtful conspiracy theories endlessly whispered about me. My lab work has brought me here, my theories, especially now that tensions between Chapters have grown so high.

My particular focus as a Seeker has been experimentation into the specific vulnerabilities of our kind. For the last year, my attention has been concentrated mainly on *sound*—on our inherent connection to each other on a sonic level. Just recently, Elijah assured me that my work was not going unnoticed by the Council. Looking back, as much as I'd love to remember that moment with pride, I actually remember feeling surprised by his tone. It was odd, more like he was explaining a fact than congratulating me. It made me feel strange. He was always so supportive, yet I know some part of my work has always been seen as "searching for weapons," and that just wasn't Elijah's way. I never got to ask him about it, but I guess today proves just how right Elijah was. The Council was paying attention. *But they don't know just how close I've actually gotten to a significant breakthrough.*

"Congratulations, Juniper," Silvia says. "We're all so proud of you." Her eyes tell a very different story. Silvia returns to the cluster of Seekers. From childhood, we all hope to be chosen to join a Wing someday, honing our talents and skills. But the secret dream we all hold in our heart of hearts, and which very few openly share, or achieve, is to one day be chosen for the Council. Seekers have never been viewed as great candidates to become Leaders. Too heady, too impractical, too lost in intellectual ideas instead of actions. But the Code dictates that all four Wings must be represented on the Council. Elijah was the only Seeker, so a Seeker *must* replace him. My journey to this moment has been extremely narrow.

Maya Steele steps forward next. Seeing her pretty, glowing face somehow allows my mind to swim back into itself. I watch her delicate movements. She glides her hand through the chalice, then lightly drags her wet fingers across my right cheek to the ridge of my nose.

"The Solicitor mark aims in, enticing the world toward us," Benjamin says.

Maya smiles at me—all warmth and welcome. She leans close. "I'm looking forward to having another woman on the Council. It might be just what we need in these uncertain times. I'm excited to see what you're capable of, Juniper."

"...Thank you," I say, hating the meek little voice that comes out of me.

Maya gently touches my face with her non-bloody hand, then returns to the others. All I can think is: *Please don't let me let her down.*

And then it comes—the moment I've been dreading since I stepped into this hall, since the moment I found out I'd been chosen. Every part of me tenses as Trevor slowly approaches, leveling his pale eyes at me. My left cheek feels itchy and tingly just knowing his fingers will soon be there, touching my skin, tracing the Enforcer mark. I meet the gaze of the man I once called Teacher, bracing for the hatred I expect to see. But he simply stares at me. Hard. But there's something in that look—something so familiar. A memory wraps around me like an old coat. *Our favorite game from Enforcer training.*

PAP! My little, six-year-old fist smacked into the huge leathery palm of Trevor's hand, followed by a slew of punches, *PAP, PAP,*

PAP, PAP, PAP! Our movements so quick anyone would've thought we'd choreographed it. He blocked every hit. The winding rang in the air—a choir of little drones. Then one of my punches broke through, striking Trevor squarely in the mouth. He spat blood onto the mat he was kneeling on. Fear shot through me. But then, to my surprise, he laughed. And I felt embarrassed, because I knew why he was laughing.

"You let me hit you," I said.

"And reinforce bad habits? Not a chance. If you were ten years older, I might have a broken jaw right now. Did it feel good?"

I nodded. Trevor smiled. "Just wait till the world has to compete with you."

This prompted a question that had been building in me for some time. Normally, I might've kept it to myself, but his good humor gave me the courage. "...But the humans won't know how big of an advantage I have over them. Doesn't that seem...unfair?"

Trevor arched an eyebrow. "You've been walking in the park again, haven't you?" I didn't say anything, but I had no doubt my face betrayed me. He knew I had a strange fascination when it came to humans. There was so much I hadn't been told about them. Only one single change in our evolution separated us from them, and yet that change felt like a vast chasm. Trevor sighed. "I realize it can be confusing. We look the same, we often act the same, but we're *not* the same. Evolution isn't personal, nor is it kind. It simply moves in one direction, without emotion. Don't waste your heart on pointless sentiment. I've seen such empathy cripple the strong at the worst possible moments. Do you trust me, Juniper?"

"Yes. Of course."

"Your body says you're lying." He smiled at my confusion. "Your voice is telling me I should believe you, but your jaw is clenched. The body is a pane of glass, if you know where to look. You'll learn for yourself that I'm right about them. Hopefully, not the hard way."

Then Trevor got that conspiratorial look on his face that so often made me feel special, and wanted, and important, and with a low, serious voice, he said, "Now, focus." And with that, Trevor swung fast, his massive fist torpedoing toward my face, but at the last second, I dodged the blow. He swung again. I blocked. Trevor smiled wide. In that moment, I felt closer to Trevor than I had ever felt with my father.

But now, standing before Trevor, eleven years later, I see his cold eyes burrow into me. We haven't spoken in the six years since I left the Enforcer Wing.

"The Enforcer mark reaches forward," Benjamin says, "confronting all who would threaten us."

Trevor lowers his fingers into Elijah's blood, then gently runs his fingers *down* my nose, grazing my nostrils, making sure I get a good whiff. Then he slowly traces his wet, sticky fingers over my lips, one at a time, pausing on each one. He finishes the mark at my chin, then he waits there, watching, eyes gleaming.

The entire assembly takes in a collective breath of shock.

"Trevor..." I hear my father's voice. His words are barely over a whisper and I can tell he didn't mean to actually speak them out loud.

"You made the wrong mark," I say. I don't know this ceremony, but I know which Wing each leg of the cross-shaped Leadership symbol represents. I can feel my face burning red, but I don't let myself look away from him.

He smiles, impressed by my restraint. I have no doubt there'll be whispers about my botched ceremony for the rest of my life. Whenever I fail, my enemies will say, "Well, what do you expect with a start like that?" I beam hatred at Trevor. Then I see something else in his eyes—something strange—unexpected. For a second, I see a glimpse of...*pain*—an undeniable sadness. Then it's gone, replaced by an expression of fake concern.

"Did I?" Trevor looks at Benjamin, who simply stares, speechless. "It's been a while. Would you mind helping me out, Cameron?"

Trevor turns and walks past my father, who's already moving rapidly toward me. In one quick motion, my father dips his fingers, then finishes the last leg of the bloody cross symbol on my face, painting from my nose across my left cheek.

My father keeps his voice low, barely audible. "I'm sorry. It's fine. It's fine. ...Damn him." *It will be fine. I won't let it not be.*

Won't let them get to me. Won't let him get to me. They needed this stupid superstitious ritual, not me. I don't need anything.

Benjamin Acosta stumbles on, trying to move past the sacrilegious act. "...And the Provider mark...pulling resources down into the whole."

I lift my chin and pretend I don't hear the whispers emanating from all sides.

"Now turn and face your Chapter, Juniper Trask," Benjamin says.

I slowly turn, taking in all the faces. The symbol of the Leadership Council, thick and sticky on my skin, covers my freckles like war paint. Benjamin clears his ancient throat. Then his voice fills the space again: "Now repeat after me, Juniper Trask..."

CHAPTER 6

CHARLIE

"You got a crazy white brother? That's *so* weird," the girl says to Ducky as the first of the fleet of school buses begins to chug out of the high school parking lot behind me, making the conversation much harder to hear. I hate eavesdropping on people, I swear to God I do, but for some reason, this shit is always happening to me. Seems like people have been talking about me right before I enter a room for most of my life. I lean my back against the concrete wall of the building. One more step around the corner and Ducky would've seen me, and I wouldn't be standing here, waiting to hear what awful things he really thinks about me. I feel stupid. Ducky doesn't deserve this bullshit.

"He's not crazy," Ducky says.

"My cousin got sent to one of them boot camp juvies for six months, and that kid is bananas. Always trying to fight his dad and shit. BIC-ing his head down like a gangbanger, and he ain't even balding or nothing."

I rub my head, thankful that—despite Ducky's denials—my hair has finally left the skinhead look, ever so slightly, in the dust.

Okay, enough snooping. I walk around the corner and come face-to-face with Ducky and an extremely attractive girl. She has dark, wavy hair and long multi-colored fingernails with little shimmering jewels on each of them. One of her legs is draped over Ducky's, and she's lightly scratching her fingertips over his right knee. They sit on top of an outside lunch table as a sea of kids, clad in our school uniform (light blue polo shirt and navy, black or tan skirt or pants) hustle past them toward the buses, heading home for the day.

It's only been a week, but so far, I've kept my head down and tried to work as hard as possible. New Brunswick High School is big enough for me to disappear into the crowd, and the uniform has been a secret blessing, because I couldn't possibly feel more out of the loop when it comes to fashion or trends. Not that I've ever felt *in the loop* on that stuff. T-shirt and jeans has pretty much been my look since birth. Grams says it's classic. Ducky says I'm a lost cause.

Ducky spots me and says, "See for yourself."

The girl eyes me up and down, and I can't help but feel like a mouse meeting a cat for the first time.

"Damn, you didn't say your 'brother' was so hot, Ducky." She slides her leg further up on Ducky's lap, and I can just make out the edge of a tattoo on her upper thigh peeking out from under her hiked-up skirt. I'm trying not to look, but she's definitely not making it easy.

"Don't make me jealous, girl. Charlie, this is Gina. Gina, this is my little brother, Charlie."

"*Little* brother?" Gina looks confused.

"Delusions of grandeur. He's older by six days," I say.

Ducky grins. "In Korean culture, you'd be calling me 'big brother' for your whole life."

"Well, last time I checked, we're not Korean. Nice to meet you, Gina."

Gina turns to Ducky. "I gotta get to recital, baby." She kisses him deep but glances at me briefly during the kiss, which irks the hell out of me, even if it is kind of creepy-sexy. Gina struts away. We both watch her go.

"That girl is some serious trouble," I say. "The real kind. No joke."

"Yeah…I know. She's a dancer. I'm helpless. I think I'm in love, man."

"Oh, God. Don't say that."

"Why?" Ducky looks a little hurt.

"Never mind," I say. "You know better than me."

"Damn right. Follow my lead, young one."

I shake my head, noticing the newspaper folded next to him.

It makes me think of his dad. Every morning after sleepovers, I'd see Ducky's dad reading the paper. It used to make me wonder if my dad did that. Ducky used to say, "It's our duty as citizens to be informed." *I'm sure he came up with that one by himself.*

He notices me looking at the newspaper and yanks it up. "Yo, you seen this ridiculousness?" He shows me the front-page headline:

VALCORP CEO SUICIDE AFTER CYBER ATTACK REVEALS SCANDAL

"Sometimes, it feels like it's all one big conspiracy, man," Ducky says. "The biggest financial conglomerate in the US, manages over a trillion of other people's money, and they can't keep their shit straight. Dude went out the easy way, you ask me."

I stare at the photo below the headline. *Elijah Spencer, dies at 38,* the caption reads. The handsome face staring back at me from the newspaper wears a subtle, confident smile, but something in Elijah Spencer's eyes unsettles me somehow. *It's the contrast,* I think. Like he doesn't believe himself. There's also a kind of sadness…or fear…*fury?* Or maybe I'm just seeing what I want to see. *Why do I need everyone to be as messed up as me?* Though he did kill himself, so I can't be too far off the mark.

"And GO!" Ducky yells as he jumps up and takes off running.

"Where the hell are you going?" I call after him.

"Don't act like you don't know! *The safest place!*"

I grin and tear off after him. We dodge through other students, who shout curses at us.

It feels great to run. The pavement reaches up through my legs, feeding me, pushing me. Ahead, Ducky veers off the street we've been jamming down and disappears into the trees.

I barrel through the lightly wooded area. For a moment, I'm back at Camp Lazarus, huffing in the smell of pine and B.O. Everyone despised the running they forced on us. I acted like I did too, but secretly I welcomed anything that pushed away the poltergeists inside my head. Running had a special prolonged quality, but any kind of pain would generally do the job.

My first year there, I must have fought half the kids at Lazarus. Not anyone younger. *Never* anyone smaller. That's not how it works. Half the point is to get hit. Hard. The taste of blood was a constant in my mouth that first year. But the "Majors" eventually ironed out my violent streak. The threat of a dark, suffocating night down in "the boiler room"—a four-by-eight storage space stomached beneath the barracks, with nothing but cockroaches and my own merciless thoughts was enough to mold me into a model inmate—at least on the outside.

But I'm not there now. Lazarus is behind me. There's a break in the trees, and then Ducky and I are surrounded by light as an old, abandoned industrial plant brims up around us. This place is where tetanus goes to die.

Now we split up, weaving down different paths across the post-apocalyptic wreckage. We leap over fences, sprint across beams. Our balance and agility have always been nearly equal. One of the best things Grams ever did for us was getting us into martial arts soon after the accident. She marched us straight up to the instructor and said, "These two boys are gonna wanna hit something. Figure they better learn to do it proper." Besides the obvious physical advantages, without the kind of mental discipline martial arts had demanded, I think I would've ended up in an actual psych ward long before I was shipped off to Lazarus. I was far from an apt pupil—unlike Ducky, whose zen would rival a Tibetan monk—but I never quit, and having something that took even my worst days in stride definitely made a difference. And I did, eventually, get much better.

Ducky races up the stairs of a bombed-out-looking building. He's seriously fast, but I've been trapped inside a bad episode of *American Ninja* for the last three years. He blasts onto the second floor of the condemned structure—one of its walls is entirely missing. He raises his hands in the air, jumping up and down.

"Winner! You got nothing on me! They gotta train you soldiers better, because I am NOT impressed!"

I clear my throat, stifling a laugh, and Ducky whips around as I step out from behind the immense, rusted, refrigerator-sized safe.

"I've been examining this baby for a while now—while I was waiting for you," I say, dispassionately. "I don't remember it being this rusted. Did it rain a lot while I was gone or something?"

Ducky cannot believe his eyes. He's gasping for breath, winded as all hell. "First time you've ever beat me," he says. I'm already surveying the contents of the ancient safe. It's filled with all kinds of childhood treasures. *Our* treasures. This was our refuge. "The *safest* place," we used to call it as kids, loving our own oh-so-clever pun. I see old maps, baseball cards, toys, comic books...

"Remember this?" Ducky reaches in and holds up a disintegrating nudie magazine.

"How could I forget?" I say. "Those were the first boobs I ever saw." Ducky gives me a look. "What?" I ask.

"'*Boobs*'? What're you, eight years old?"

I sheepishly attempt... "Tits?"

Ducks snorts out a blast of laughter.

I try again: "Titties?" More laughter. "Ta-tas?"

"No more!" Ducky croaks, barely able to speak.

I spy something metallic twinkling toward the back. Using a thin copper wire fragment off the ground, I spear through the object and raise it up.

"Why the hell is your retainer in here, Ducky?!" A dust-embalmed, fleshy, pink dental retainer hangs from my copper wire. "This does not qualify as a secret treasure. This is disgusting. I vote for immediate expulsion from our vault of sacred memories."

"You won't try and expel nothing once you realize whose mouth that belongs to."

"*What?* Whose?"

"Alicia Peterson."

"Jesus, Ducky! Alicia Peterson who had the trampoline?"

"No, Alicia Peterson who had the best body in our seventh-grade class. *That* Alicia Peterson. Oh, man, did I crush on that girl."

"So, you stole the only hope she had of keeping those enormous teeth straight?"

"Yo, those teeth weren't the only thing of hers that was enormous. I bet her mama had to custom-make her jeans. That booty was just—"

"She was in seventh grade!"

"Yeah, so was I!"

We both bust up laughing. I try and press on: "Ducky, that girl—"

"That *body*," Ducky interjects, waggling his hips.

"That girl was *so* boring, man. Come on."

Ducky suddenly stops, looking at me so serious. "There was NOTHING…boring…about that body." And now we're both dying again. I have tears in my eyes, I'm laughing so hard. I make a show of catapulting the retainer back into the safe. It smashes into other items inside, causing something to fall out. Instinctively, I reach out and catch it in midair and freeze when I see what's in my hand…

A baseball.

I can't move. Ducky sees the ball in my hand and his laughter falls off a cliff. The sight of it goes through me like a polished bayonet: smooth, no friction, relentless. I'd forgotten it was here.

The coach from the other team had the ball. Apparently, he kept them as trophies from the games his team won. Ducky and I found out where he lived, went to his house and asked if we could have it. The heavy-eyed man, with his glistening, red stare didn't even speak as he led us out to his garage. He knew who we were. I imagine somebody had called him. Probably our old coach's wife, who gave us the address in the first place; she had him on her Christmas card list.

Once inside the dusty, wooden garage, which reeked of beer and old cigars, he opened an old plastic beer cooler where he kept all his "winners." It took him a moment or two, but he eventually pulled it out and handed it to us. He had written the date on the ball in blue ink:

04-05-06.

"Three numbers in a row," he said, because there was nothing else to say. I don't remember if we said anything in response. We both quit organized sports after that day.

"You ever wonder…" I begin. "If I'd hit that ball… If I hadn't struck out, and you had run home… Would things have been different? We would've left. Been celebrating somewhere else, instead of on that highway at that exact moment." I leave it there in the air, thick and ugly.

"No. I don't," Ducky says quickly, then takes a long beat. "Wouldn't have done nothing for your mom's cancer."

I stare at the faint blue date written on the ball, just below the stitching. The preciseness of the quiet lettering makes it strangely intoxicating to look at.

"In my mind, it changes everything," I say. And in the deepest part of me, I know I mean it. I look up at him, waiting for judgment, but what I see totally derails me. Ducky's staring at me with a big, lopsided grin.

"What's up?" I ask.

Ducky takes the ball from my hand and gently places it back in the safe.

"We can't do nothing about the past, man," he says. "As for the present…I just remembered something Gina told me. Don't say no yet…"

D eep, flexing hip hop pounds throughout the raging house party. A college party. We're high school kids on the Rutgers University campus, because A: we're lucky enough to live in a college town, B: we look older for our age, but mostly C: because Ducky's girlfriend knows the dude throwing the party.

I stand alone, at the edge of the packed room, watching Ducky and Gina grind into each other on the dance floor. I've never been a big dancer.

Five minutes later, I find myself in the kitchen, staring down my sixth shot of Jäger. Part of me feels like I might have permanent esophagus damage now, and that perhaps I'll only be able to taste black licorice for the rest of my life, but I'm already feeling a warmth permeating from my deepest core, expanding and consuming anything not fun-related.

And now I'm on the dance floor, and there's no move I can't do, no choreography (that probably took decades to perfect) that I haven't instantly mastered. A twiggy, blonde college girl, wearing a baggy sweatshirt and short shorts, places her hand on my waist and leans her hips into me as we start to move together on the dance floor. She's pretty damn gorgeous, as far as I can tell, and she smells like sweaty strawberries (which sounds awful in theory, but for some reason, it isn't in real life). She turns around, her back against me now, pressing herself into me, holding my hands on her hips. I'm lost, and turned on, and drunk, and lost, and she smells so good. I can't believe I'm keeping up with her rhythm. I know it won't last for long.

Across the room Ducky yells out at me, "My man! Taught that boy every move he knows!" I look over and he's smiling ear to ear. Gina stares at the girl I'm dancing with in disgust. I wonder if she knows her. Then she looks at me, and her expression changes into something hard to read. *Jealousy, maybe?* All I know is it makes me uncomfortable, so I grab my girl's hand and spin her into an odd step. She laughs, surprised and delighted by the unexpected move. I like her laugh. I want more. I adjust my dance routine into something not unlike the Funky Chicken.

Ducky bellows, "Not that one! I did *not* teach him that! I swear!" I laugh hard. The girl laughs with me. I can't remember the last time I felt this good. No time for sad, angry Charlie—that whiny little bitch. Cuz right now, I just gotta dance.

I'm halfway through what I assume is a flawless *Thriller* reenactment, when the world seems to tilt a good forty-five degrees on its axis. I stumble across the room and smash into a small group of people, who have somehow remained immune to the planetary shift.

One of the victims of my involuntary wrecking ball maneuver is a densely built dude, easily five years older than me, who's wearing one of those long T-shirts that go halfway down to his knees. His full beer cup blasts from his hand, drenching his legs. I quickly scoop up his empty beer cup off the ground and extend it back to him as an *obvious* peace gesture.

"Oh, man, so sorry about that... My moves have a mind of their own sometimes." I don't mention my tilting-planet theory because, truthfully, there isn't time. The burly goon swats the cup out of my hand.

"You got beer on my shoes, bitch! I just bought these!"

"It was an accident. Seriously, man, I'm really sorry." I want to elaborate, but my brain won't lock on to anything more profound to say. Even in my drunken state, I see his elbows move long before he's able to leverage his full weight into the massive chest-push.

Always watch the elbows. Before he can touch me, I deftly capture his wrist, twist, and pull his hulking upper body downward in pain as I swiftly bring my knee up into his face. The dull, meaty impact snaps his head back and he goes down hard—out for the count. It all happens so fast. My vision spins, taking in the frightened faces around me. The girl I was dancing with is long gone. And now Ducky is in front of me, holding me by the shoulders, looking about as serious as I've ever seen him. "Hey, hey…you okay?"

I wriggle out of his grip, backing away. "Give me a minute… I'm sorry, man."

"Charlie, tell me you're okay."

"I'm good, I just need a minute." I flash him my best smile, but he's not buying it.

"Charlie—"

I turn and push through the crowd. But as I get close to the front door, a fresh crop of partygoers starts pouring in. I dodge through them, but there's too many, and suddenly I feel like I'm drowning. I cut to the right, where I find a hallway, then a staircase. I head upstairs, where the population thins out drastically. I start down another hallway, but I only get a few meters before someone switches the filter on my vision to kaleidoscope and I almost throw up. And suddenly, I'm ten, and my mother is twisted up in her soiled bedsheets in front of me—thin and tortured-looking, reaching out to me in agony. The memory cuts me off at the knees. I plant my hand on the wall. But it's not the wall; it's a door. I fumble for the handle, then lurch into an empty bedroom, shutting the door behind me.

I swim across the dark room and come ashore on a twin bed. The stale air reeks of cheap incense. I sit, swaddling my head in my hands, attempting to clear my chaotic mind. *What the hell just happened? Shit! I could've just stopped him with the wristlock…I didn't need to hurt him. I ruined his new shoes. And maybe his face. Dancing sucks! I HATE dancing! No wonder so many religions forbid it. How can you keep civilization intact when everyone's dancing around, ruining people's shoes left and right?!*

The door cracks open. A sheath of light pours in, masking the silhouetted figure in the doorway.

"Sorry, I'm gonna leave…" I struggle to stand.

"I just wanted to make sure you're okay," a sultry voice says.

I focus and put the perfectly curved silhouette together with the voice. "Oh…hi, Gina. Yeah, I'm good. Tell Ducky I'm good, and I'll be right down."

"He's outside looking for you. But I saw you sneak upstairs." Gina is also very drunk. I can hear the bravery in her voice. She closes the door behind her. I sit back down on the bed, deciding I can't maneuver this situation *and* stand at the same time. "…So, I'm checking on you."

"I'm good. Go back down. I'm fine."

"What if I'd like to stay?" she says, moving toward me.

"Well…then…I don't know what." I'm flailing.

"Most girls would be scared of what you did. You don't scare me, Charlie." Gina is close now. I can hear her lips part, allowing her tongue to slice out and wet them. She presses her legs ever so slightly against my knees.

"Seriously, Gina…"

"What? You don't think I'm good for Ducky, anyway. I can tell. Who cares if I'm here, then? Better than with him, right?" She touches my face. Her hand smells sweet, like cocoa butter. I stay silent. Then guilt seeps out of me and I push her back away. She retaliates, grabbing my shirt and pulling herself in between my legs. She presses her full lips to mine. Her kiss rips a hole in me but then instantly fills it; this cycle repeats endlessly within a second, a vicious duel between betrayal and anesthesia. I should stand up. Right now. I should. But right now, I am wreckage, driftwood, a straw house before a wolf. And because I have spent the last eight years proving to myself that I deserve all this pain, and because I am lonely, and because she is right, I kiss Gina back. We grab at each other, graceless, sloppy, groping.

The bedroom door swings open, framing us in a door-shaped spotlight, but some roaches just aren't fast enough, and as I stare into the shattered face of my best friend, I wish this room was the mouth of some giant ravenous beast and that I would die screaming as its slathering jaws tear me apart.

Ducky looks like he's going to be sick. He staggers away. I push

Gina off me and race after him. "Ducky! No...wait! Stop, please!"

Ducky looks back at me as I struggle after him. *"WHAT'S WRONG WITH YOU?!"* His rage is big and brutal. If he wasn't so hurt, I know he would hit me. I can see it in his eyes and in his trembling body. He's always had my back, always been so loyal, even when I was in the wrong, even when no one else stood by me. Freshman year, I saw Derek King, a twisted fiend of a kid, punch his girlfriend in the face in front of all her friends in the school parking lot. I beat him so badly, I broke my hand, and I was seconds from slamming his head in an open car door, when Ducky seized me from behind. Later, I found out, when Ducky had heard there was a fight in the parking lot, he'd dropped his books and sprinted across campus. No one told him it was me; he just knew. It was always me. If he'd gotten there ten seconds later, Derek King might've been dead, and Camp Lazarus would've been a day spa compared to the places they send underage murderers. *And this is how I repay him.*

"Ducky...I... That wasn't... Let me just—"

"I just told you I might be in love with her, man—" Ducky's blurry red eyes go panicked as he slips on a discarded beer bottle. His legs shoot out from underneath him. I'm too far away. I can't reach him. He tumbles backward down the stairs. His body twists, and his face smashes against the thick wooden banister. A repulsive *crack* is audible as Ducky's neck cocks to the side at an inhuman angle. He lands, inverted, and a bubble of bloody snot blooms from one of his nostrils as his body begins to spasm.

A howling, belligerent, curdled cry escapes me as I watch Ducky's loose limbs waterfall down around his bent torso. And as desperate rage pisses out me like a severed artery...

THE WORLD AROUND ME BEGINS TO SHIFT.

DUCKY'S LEGS JERK BACK UP INTO SPACE, HIS NECK STRAIGHTENS, AND HE FLIPS IN REVERSE BACK UP THE STAIRS. AND NOW DUCKY AND I ARE RACING BACKWARD THROUGH THE HALL. I'M PULLED BACK INTO THE BEDROOM. BACK INTO GINA'S ARMS. OUR LIPS MEET AGAIN. DUCKY SEEMS TO CLOSE THE DOOR ON US, DRENCHING THE ROOM IN DARKNESS. GINA AND I JUMP AWAY FROM EACH OTHER JUST AS QUICK. SOME UNSEEABLE FORCE DRAGS GINA OUT OF THE

ROOM... THEN I AM ALONE AGAIN IN THE DARKNESS.

And then time starts moving forward once again.

I sit on the bed, a festering sore of panic. I can feel every stitch of clothing on my body—itchy, shrinking, collapsing in on me like a cage. *I'm crazy. Oh, God, I'm completely insane... "All work and no play makes Jack a dull boy" off my fucking rocker! Is this what being a schizophrenic feels like? Or... No! Don't say OR. There is no OR!* But I can't help it... My mind cracks open the lid to the Pandora's box I've held firmly in my grasp since that awful night on the highway: *Or could it all be true? Saving my mother, the accident, rewinding... How can these miraculous things be true? They can't. And what is that horrific ringing sound?*

The door opens. Gina stands silhouetted. I launch off the bed and push past her. Adrenaline burns through the alcohol-induced fog. I've never felt more sober in my life.

"Charlie!" Gina calls after me.

Halfway down the stairs, a harsh fatigue hits me like a dump truck. I fight to stay conscious as the world hurricanes around me. I reach the ground floor and slam into Ducky, who grabs me and holds me up, shocked by my state.

"Charlie! What's wrong? Did someone—" I wrap my arms around Ducky, collapsing into him.

"You're okay. You're okay..." I'm crying now—big, sloppy tears. I'm holding him so tight, terrified that if I let him go, I may lose him forever.

"Of course, I'm okay," he assures me. "You're scaring me, man. What the hell did—"

Then I yank away from him and rush out the front door, plowing my way through party guests, who re-converge angrily behind me, blocking Ducky's path. I see him trying to push through, then...

"Ducky!" Gina yells out the front door. She sounds angry and embarrassed.

Ducky looks back.

I do not.

By the time he faces the street again, I'm gone.

CHAPTER 7

JUNIPER

Mrs. Fernandez attempts to gain control as the border-line-feral eight-year-olds in the inner-city classroom treat her like some kind of incorporeal specter. "Buenos días, class," she says. "BUENOS DÍAS!" Not one child looks up. *Is it really a good morning?*

I hate the Gathering. I realize it's important—any powerful Chapter must maintain its population—but it's still annoying. I feel exposed and claustrophobic at the same time. Thankfully, this is the last time I'll ever have to do it. The Gathering falls to the Seeker Wing, but it's also seen as an unnecessary security risk for Leaders. I just have to get through the next hour. At least my task today isn't as terrible as Daniel's.

I look from child to child. Apathetic, overweight, hopeless kids, trying not to be noticed, sit like islands in the sea of talkers, screamers and pushers. A chinless, redheaded boy yanks the braid of a petite Hispanic girl sitting by the window, staring out. The girl bats his hand away, and as she does, a handsome, dark-skinned boy, with caterpillar-thick eyebrows, pulls her other braid, and her head with it. The little girl cries out in pain.

"Tyrese! Bobby! Leave Sofia alone!" Mrs. Fernandez is trying to sound stern in front of me. Her best effort is less than believable. No wonder these kids are horrors; they don't understand discipline. If any child at Thessaly acted like this, they'd be beaten with rods.

"I didn't touch her!" Tyrese yells back in a vicious tone. I think to myself, *If it ends up being him, I might come home empty-handed.*

Mrs. Fernandez sighs. "Sofia, tell them you don't appreciate that." *What a stupid thing to say to such a weak little child.* I almost laugh at the absurdity of it. Little Sofia, in her faded red flannel dress, simply faces forward, defiantly.

"Class, we have a guest here today. Miss Amelia Temple from the district office. Please give her your full, undivided attention." Mrs. Fernandez smiles at me. She thinks I'm older than I am. Most people do.

I think of her words: *full, undivided attention.* Eight-year-old brains buzz like a thousand trapped fruit flies. She might as well have asked them to juggle water. The only reason their oscillating hive mind is now laser-focused onto me is because I'm holding a stack of fresh, white papers, and they are collectively preparing for the worst.

"Hello. It's nice to meet all of you," I say. A child in the front row unabashedly picks his nose. *How did we ever evolve from this?* I set small stacks on each of the front-row students' desks. "Please take one and pass the rest back." *How many times have I said those exact words?* "Today, I'd like everyone to complete a little worksheet for me."

"Is it a test?" Tyrese asks. "Cuz I ain't doing no extra tests. Got enough already. Sorry, lady." A few of the children laugh at the insolence. Not the islands; they remain silent.

I smile. "It *is* a test. But it's the kind of test where absolutely *nothing* happens to you if you fail. Go on, give it a go."

Some students move through the questions quickly. Some blatantly copy off of others, and again I have to clench my jaw to keep from laughing—thinking of the utter uselessness of cheating on *this* test.

My phone buzzes in my back pocket. I casually pull it out. *Daniel is in position.* I answer the text, then wait.

BANG! BANG! BANG! Small explosions burst from outside the window. Every soul in the room drops low. Terror floods Mrs. Fernandez's face. The children all look to her for what to do and find a helpless woman cringing behind her desk. And then they see the first pop of color.

Now the entire class—even Mrs. Fernandez—rush to the

window to see *the show*. Outside, the school buildings rise up in a collective crescent shape around a grassy courtyard. All the classrooms have one set of windows that overlook the courtyard. We are on the fourth floor. I imagine someone looking up would find the sea of faces staring down a little eerie.

Below, there's a chase going on to take down the culprit behind the explosions: a homeless man, who's dodging several enraged security guards and tossing lit fireworks as he runs. The fireworks were Daniel's idea. The costume was mine—payback for him pushing to "have a little more fun this time." The kids are enthralled, looking out the window.

I focus my will and PULL BACK A FEW SECONDS. There's a *ringing* in the air—not loud, but it's there—distinct and sustained, a sound just slightly more pleasing than a microphone feeding back. My skin tingles with the slight effort. I've participated in enough Gatherings to know that the majority of our efforts will go unanswered. I'm not complaining. It's good that it's rare. *Exceptional* is the word I usually use, but recently I've grown to like *special*. It feels more personal somehow.

I surprise myself as I realize I'm hoping for one of the *islands* to turn around. I guess I'd love to turn the tables on some sad kid who's come to consider their young life as a death sentence. That state of mind can feel so crushing. So, I look for one of their faces. But, instead, I get something different—something unexpected.

As the *ringing* continues, little Sofia, in her muted, hand-me-down dress, looks up and around the classroom searching for the origin of the *strange noise*, like when you're sure you hear a mosquito but you can't quite see it. Her eyes fall on mine. Sofia sees recognition in my face, but she doesn't know what it means. I smile. *Hmm…maybe not so weak after all.*

CHAPTER 8

CHARLIE

I wake up drowning, clawing my way out of unconsciousness into a hell of multiple proportions. I try to breathe, find only water, and know that I don't have long to live. Then I'm on my feet and fighting to remain that way. My head is a playground for wrecking balls, and I'm pretty sure the bitter taste in my mouth is stale vomit. I huff in oxygen as my periscope eyes sweep my surroundings. The sludgy dumpster next to me reeks like a thousand dirty diapers. I know the exact spot where I slept last night, because there's an outline of my body where the water didn't touch.

Hearty laughter comes from behind me, and very close. I whip around. The sudden twisting of my body nearly ends me, but the strangeness of my view stiffens my spine and clears my eyes. The man standing in front of me, holding a big, clear, *empty* water bottle, and currently chuckling his ass off, looks like a survivor from a post-apocalyptic movie. Wild, oily, shoulder-length hair splays across his scruffy, beige face. His hands and neck are covered in tats, and he's wrapped in an old, mangy trench coat. His boots are the only outlier—alligator skin, and brand-new. All at once, my mind zeros in on the fact that this leather-clad freak is definitely responsible for my near-drowning, which leads me to a single animal-instinct response:

"What the hell, man?!"

"Rough night?" my waterboarding pal asks. His face is all smiles and innocence. I back away from him, wincing, as the dynamite picnic going on right behind my eyes pulses my stomach with nausea.

The creepy hobo slowly pursues me. "What was it? A fight? An accident? Some sad little break-up? Someone confuse heroin for cocaine and...oops?" He puts one hand to his temple like he's some kind of mystic or mind reader, watching my face for a response. "Close friend? Cousin? Niece? No..." He shakes his hands out, like he's cleaning his mental slate. "Okay— You walk in, your precious *Katlyn* is gettin' it from your best friend, NO, your DAD. Daddy's just banging the hell out of her, pigtails flyin' everywhere and then... ASSHOLE! BLAM! You blow them both away! Then you think, *Hmmm, homicide...maybe not the look.*" He sees my utter confusion, and his face flashes frustration. "COME ON! Give me a hint, kid! Careful..."

I stumble backward over a trashcan, almost go down, but manage to stay on my feet, never taking my eyes off him. Then I turn and scramble out of the alley like I'm being chased by wolves. I risk one last glance back. The lunatic gives me a little wave as I escape around the corner.

I run. And run. And then I run some more. Seriously, I don't consider myself someone who scares easily, but that was just too weird. Chatty, homeless psychopaths wearing ridiculously expensive boots...not my thing.

CHAPTER 9

JUNIPER

I exit Mrs. Fernandez's classroom into a large hallway. I'm carrying the stack of completed worksheets. Another classroom door opens about ten feet in front of me, and a thin, clean-cut man in his late thirties walks out, holding an identical stack of worksheets. His name is Joel and he's one of Silvia Orimo's close confidants. I'm glad he didn't see me. I don't think I could bear his clench-toothed smile as he tells me how *proud* everyone is of me and makes some painful attempt at small talk. I slow down, letting him get farther away. After a beat, I glance around, making sure nobody's watching, then I shove the worksheets into a garbage bin as I pass.

"What do you think you're doing?"

The aggressive whisper comes from right behind me. I've never encountered an enemy during the Gathering before. *Of course it would be on my last day.* I swing around, ready to do battle, but I find myself staring into the grinning face of Daniel, my lab tech, who I last saw dressed as a firework-tossing vagrant. Daniel fights to hold back his rolling laughter. He may be three years older than me, but his lack of maturity more than compensates for the age gap. I hate being startled. *Hate* it. "What exactly is so funny?" I ask.

"Mostly your face," he says, slipping his glasses back on. I want to stay angry at him, but it's no use; I feel myself smiling in spite of my annoyance.

"You shouldn't be so reckless," I say. "We're not exactly on safe ground here."

"Reckless like throwing those papers out on school property?" he says, not missing a beat. "Someone could find them and ask scary questions like: *Why are you so bad at your job?* or *Did you think that trash can was a mailbox?*"

I feel the flush on my cheeks. *Would it be wrong to fire my lab tech for being too charming?* His bad jokes are an overcompensation. He's trying to act like me being a Leader isn't all that strange. I appreciate the effort, regardless of how he actually feels. Others have been far less graceful. I've only been a Leader for a week and I'm already completely over the part where everyone treats me like I'm something extraordinary. I just want to go back to my lab. I have important work waiting for me. But my days have been filled with endless briefings on where we are as a Chapter on the world stage: politically, economically and strategically. They don't bother with *scientifically*. My first Council meeting is in two days. I'm scared and excited. *Please don't let me look stupid.*

Daniel is right about my carelessness with the papers, but I'm not about to give him the satisfaction of admitting it. "Don't you have security guards searching for you?" I ask. Daniel has shed his filthy costume, but he still has a little makeup (meant to look like dirt smudges) streaked across one of his cheek. It makes him look far more rugged than he is. But it is actually kind of cute.

"I won't lie. That was fun." He walks beside me. "Aren't you going to miss this just a little?"

"No," I say, without hesitation.

"Really? You may never encounter humans again, now that you're a Leader, unless you become Prime someday, which I wouldn't put past you." Dealing with human society is a part of everyday life for most Enforcers, Solicitors and Providers—operating inside the military, Congress, or the stock market, for example. Such powerful institutions must be intimately guided from within. But this hands-on monitoring and manipulation does not extend to Seekers. We have people placed in top scientific labs throughout the world in order to keep tabs on any breakthroughs, but for the most part, Seekers operate within Thessaly. Daniel knows I could limit my world entirely to the Council and the lab if I wanted.

A security guard steps into view at the end of the hall. Daniel uses my body as a shield. The pudgy guard takes a cursory glance in our direction, yanks up his belt, which has sagged from running, wipes his sweaty brow, then continues down another hallway.

Daniel steps out from behind me, his face filled with disappointment.

I roll my eyes. "Let me guess—you wanted him to chase you?"

"Why are security guards at schools so often overweight and stupid?" he asks. "They're supposed to be watching over the precious young of their community. It makes no sense. Just on a survival level alone. What if I *was* a threat?"

"Don't fool yourself; you *are* a threat to them."

Daniel acts like he hasn't heard me. "I should've been detained within seconds."

"You're lucky that wasn't the case."

"You know what I mean."

"My father would say, 'That's why they're a subspecies.'" Daniel gives me a sharp look. It says, *Stop pretending to be something you're not.* I don't like it. He quickly retracts the look when he sees my cold expression. He's overstepped. He may suspect that my true feelings align with his, that I see all the glaring hypocrisies myself. But I have fought my entire life to become what I am now: a Leader. And I'm not quite sure yet if that means taking the ugly parts in stride or not. Daniel and I have never shared our feelings on this matter—such a dialogue would border on treason—but certain facts are unavoidable: the more time one spends as a Seeker, the harder it is to claim superiority over the human race.

In our world, it is considered a given that we are the apex species—that we are demigods walking among normal humans. My father believes this. So do Trevor, Maya Steele, the entire Leadership Council, and nearly every single member of our Chapter. But here's the problem: for three of the four Wings, this goes without saying. An Enforcer versus a human, in a fight, would be a slaughter. A human trying to get the edge on a Provider in business will always be fighting a losing battle—for so much of business is about timing. Try to compete with a seasoned Solicitor in a debate, as a human, and you will swallow your own tongue, perplexed by the seemingly psychic level of anticipation coming at you. In these three capacities, we rise, we conquer; there is, in fact, no competition. But as a Seeker, nearly all of *my* heroes—almost all of the great minds throughout history—the philosophers, the scientists, the great writers, the inventors, the *geniuses*—they have all been human. There have been a few notable exceptions, but not many.

The rich history of human genius sits like a morbidly obese elephant at the center of the Seeker world. No one talks about it. Not even us. Mostly because the second rule of the Code forbids it. We are to accept our dominance, believing that empathy for our inferiors will make us doubtful, and "The road to extinction is paved in hesitancy." That's one of Trevor's famous axioms.

As a Seeker, my primary function is to study, understand and expand the limits of *our* species. Advance *us*—widen the gap between our kind and humans. And if, during my strivings, I make discoveries that gain us an advantage over other Chapters, all the better. But one cannot read the writings of Aristotle, Einstein, Marie Curie, Newton, Wollstonecraft, Darwin, Alice Walker and Hawking, and not be filled with awe at the endless capacity of the human mind. Mary Wollstonecraft once wrote, "No man chooses evil because it is evil; he only mistakes it for happiness, the good he seeks." Sometimes, I wonder if these words apply to our enemies or to us. The Leadership props up democracies around the world, for the most part, maintaining that happiness and contentment for all species comes from *believing* they are free—that there's an even playing field. But make no mistake, what we call "happiness" for our kind, the human world would call economic slavery. *If they knew about it.*

As a little girl, I once stood next to a human woman in the park. She was tall and beautiful, dressed in an expensive form-fitting pantsuit, tapping away at her Blackberry and sipping her coffee like the modern apotheosis of feminine power. And I just remember thinking how much further from the top this woman is than she thinks. And it made me feel sad and a little guilty. But then I remember wondering, *If she doesn't know it, does it even really matter?*

Humans don't know we exist; therefore, the huge amounts of wealth and control that we've achieved, *while playing by their own rules*, remain invisible. But the real reason it goes unnoticed is that in the modern human world, whoever has the gold makes the rules—modern civilization is built upon capitalism and perceived merit. True monarchies are extremely rare. *As long as you don't consider ExxonMobil a monarchy.* So, in reality, we're just doing to humans what they already do to themselves. We're just much, much better at it. One might call it cheating, since we have such an advantage, but I don't recall anyone telling Thomas Edison to dumb it down so the masses don't get jealous. Nobody said it was unfair for Usain Bolt to compete in the Olympics because of his natural superior physical gifts. And so, we work together, as a species, to rebuild the master's house, using his own tools.

We're just lucky humans can't perceive our powers. Sure, we beat them at their own games, but it would be a *very* different story if we were ever discovered, and suddenly we were pitted against the greatest minds the human race has at their disposal. If all the war machines of man were pointed in our direction…

So, Daniel is right: I'm not a blind believer in our evolutionary right. But he's also wrong in thinking that I believe our silent empire is a bad thing. It's not a bad thing. Humans would destroy themselves without us. History has already proven this, again and again. The world is a safer place with us in control.

Awkwardness hangs between Daniel and me. He doesn't know what to do about it.

The recess bell rings and kids explode out of the surrounding classrooms like a breaking dam. Daniel watches the children for a moment, a contemplative expression on his face. Finally, he says, "Hard to believe we were all this young and naïve once, isn't it?"

As I look at him, I remember that the Gathering means something very different to him than it does to me. Daniel was found in the Gathering. I was born in Thessaly. He spent the first part of his life believing he was human. I wonder what that must've felt like. *Of course, his sympathies are different from mine.* Those found in the Gathering usually come to have the fiercest disdain for humans—an overcompensation for what they perceive as a glaring weakness. Children born in Thessaly are seen as purer somehow. Untainted. It's ridiculous, and prejudiced, but it's there. But Daniel has never been like that. And I'm thankful. I want to say something to him, maybe even apologize for my harsh look, but he seems to have already recovered.

"Oh, I almost forgot to ask," he says. "Any luck today?"

L ittle Sofia sits alone in the sandy area by the swing set. It's recess time and she's building a crude sandcastle, using a jagged rock to dig and one of her rubber bracelets to smooth out the sides. Suddenly, two sneakered feet obliterate the sandcastle as redheaded Bobby lands on top of it. The glee on Bobby's face makes him look less like a mean little boy and more like a plump, ghoul-eyed hyena. Tyrese, with the caterpillar eyebrows, giggles hysterically. Sofia tries to ignore the two bullies; she gathers more sand. Tyrese extends his arm, pouring half of his Dr. Pepper over the ruins of her little castle, splattering sticky brown soda-sand all over Sofia's dress. Sofia jumps to her feet. "Leave me alone!"

Bobby smiles, showing off the pink, mushy gums surrounding his tiny teeth. "Uh-oh, the little *puta's* mad."

Tyrese pushes Sofia in the chest, almost knocking her down. "Don't tell us what to do, bitch! I'll beat your ugly little taco-eating face in!"

"That's not very nice, Tyrese." The two young ruffians spin around, shocked to see me. They've been caught red-handed and are both gauging what to do about it. I watch them decide that I'm probably a toothless tiger like Mrs. Fernandez.

"I didn't touch her!" Tyrese barks at me, using the same words and tone he used in the classroom. Bobby chirps in, "Yeah, we didn't touch the little turd, Mrs. Amelia!" *"Mrs."? When the hell did I get married?* The child is an imbecile. I look into their eyes. They don't look away. So confident—the kind of kids that will prey on people their whole lives, openly or not.

I lean down close to them, knowing that whispering would be wiser here. "I know you didn't touch her, boys. Because if you *had* touched her, I wouldn't be talking to you right now. I'd be dragging both of you across the playground by your hair, into the *girls'* restroom, where I'd drown you one at a time in the toilet and leave your blue-faced little corpses there for the girls to find. Did you two know that most people shit their pants when they die? Especially children. I promise you it's true."

The two puerile thugs look at me like my face just cracked open and a demon crawled out of its cavity. They lunge away, slipping on the sandy blacktop and scuttling across the playground like soft-shell crabs.

After a moment, I sit down next to Sofia. She doesn't look up. I can tell she's terrified of me, regardless of whether I just saved her from the two Cro-Magnon eight-year-olds.

"Can I tell you a secret, Sofia?"

Sofia nods ever so slightly.

"My name isn't really Miss Amelia."

Sofia takes in this strange statement from a *grown-up*. "…What's your name, then?"

"My name is Juniper. And I've come to tell you that you are a very *special* little girl." I go with *special*. It just feels right. "I'd like to talk to your mommy and daddy, if I may."

"Just got a mama. Don't have no daddy."

"I'd like to talk to your mommy, then." I stand and reach out my hand to her.

She looks confused. "Now?"

"Yes."

"What about school?"

I smile down at her. She looks so small in that dress. "You won't be going to this school anymore." After a moment of weighing what every child is told about going anywhere with strangers, Sofia glances over at the looming building that has been a place of daily torment and degradation, then she looks back at me; and in her eyes I see something new, a strength I didn't see before—a self-possession I don't expect. Her eyes burrow into me, and I'm half-convinced she can see my duplicity—that she's going to turn and run away or call out for help. Part of me almost wants her to. Thessaly can be a very hard place for someone so small and alone. And in that brief moment, I tell myself I won't go after her. But then she slips her miniature hand into mine and we walk off the playground, past the gate and out of the school.

I know what comes next. I've seen it many times. Sofia will

live somewhere she'll be embarrassed to take me. She'll look at my pristine clothing and hope her world won't rub off too easily on me, hope that the second I see just how dirty her life is, I won't change my mind about her being "special." She'll bring me to her mother. Her mother will be untrusting at first, afraid that I must be taking advantage of a poor, single mother with a poor, fatherless child. Gradually, she'll be won over by the promise of a better life for Sofia. Tears will come to her eyes when she thinks of the many opportunities her little girl will have that she never did. There is even, on occasion, the tinge of jealousy on the mother's face. But I'm going to guess that Sofia's mother is one of the secret believers, the women who hold, in their warm hidden centers, the possibility of happy endings. Even if she knows it makes her a fool. Even if she realizes it's not the safest of world views for her perilous environment. From Sofia's tiny courage, I guess that she has seen *big* courage in the form of a mother's hope.

I see the moment where Sofia says goodbye to this woman. This will make me think of my own mother, a memory I will push down and lock beneath my unwavering discipline. Then I'll take Sofia's little hand, once again, and lead her away. I picture the woman waving to Sofia, having no idea that this will be the last time she will ever see her daughter. What I don't picture is why these mothers never come looking for their kids. After weeks, months, years. It would seem, just statistically speaking, if nothing else, that *one* would've shown up, banging on our door, saying she's changed her mind, begging for her daughter back, proving they're not an emotionally stunted "subspecies" after all. That all those amazing books they write can't just all be words.

But they don't come.

They never have.

And I don't allow myself to imagine why. I just keep walking with Sofia's tiny hand held firmly in my own.

CHAPTER 10

CHARLIE

I keep looking back, making sure the creepy dude hasn't followed me. So far, so good. I have no idea where I am, though; nothing looks familiar. I've been jogging down a street parallel to some raised train tracks, and now I find what I've been searching for: stairs, leading up. A train station. Two steps at a time, I scale the stairs and feel relieved as I fade into a light crowd of people waiting for the train. My heartbeat finally normalizes, and I sit down on a bench. I pull out my phone and say a silent "thank you" that it still has a little juice left. The screen shows:

9 MISSED CALLS

I hit Callback and wait as it rings.

"Charlie?!" Ducky's voice brims with worry, and a wave of guilt washes over me. "Where the hell are you?"

"…I'm at a train station." I find the station sign. "The Metuchen stop."

"Metuchen? Dude… I'm so sorry about that crap last night. I don't even know who that guy was."

"What guy?" I ask. Last night feels like a million years ago.

"*What guy?* Jackass whose nose you nearly put through the back of his head."

"…Oh, yeah. I forgot about him. …Is he all right?"

"I feel like such an idiot, man. I shouldn't have let you drink. You just got back."

"It's not your fault…"

"Grams half-crucified me when I came home alone. She's been on the phone with the cops all morning. And you know how

Grams feels about the police."

"Listen, I'm fine. I'm headed home, okay. Tell Grams—" Blood drains from my face. "Ducky...I gotta go." I hang up the phone. The ancient wood beneath me creaks as I uncoil myself from the bench. Sweat itches all over my body as adrenaline dumps into me. Walking toward me, across the platform, through the sparse crowd, sporting a wide, shit-eating grin, is the lunatic from the alley.

I can feel the train approaching behind me as he gets closer and closer. As the train thunders into the station, the psycho casually grabs a random pedestrian and hurls him—briefcase and all—screaming, into the speeding train. The man is demolished before everyone's eyes—like an uncooked chicken tossed up and drilled with an aluminum baseball bat. A severed arm flops onto the platform, a pulpy mess. Chaos erupts as the few waiting passengers lose their fucking minds.

I stand there, stunned, as the murderer swiftly closes the gap between us. He gets within a few feet when my mind finally snaps to. I strike out fast and hard, but for all his homeless vagabond posturing, he effortlessly dodges my attacks, like he knows where each blow is coming from. A strange *ringing* permeates the air. The sound feels oddly familiar, almost nostalgic. Finally, he grabs my arm, puts a hand on the back of my neck, then looks me directly in the face. "Hello, Dorothy. My name's Aeman." He winks at me, like a mischievous uncle, and suddenly...

THE WORLD AROUND ME BEGINS TO SHIFT.

"AEMAN" CONTINUES TO SMILE AS HIS BODY IS RIPPED BACK-WARD. THE PEDESTRIAN'S SEVERED ARM SPIRALS THROUGH THE AIR AND, LIKE A FLESHY MAGNET, SNAPS BACK ONTO ITS OWNER AS THE MURDERED MAN BURSTS FROM THE FRONT OF THE TRAIN BACK ONTO THE PLATFORM, ALIVE AND WELL. AND AS THE TRAIN NOW HUR-TLES BACKWARD ALONG THE TRACKS, AEMAN SLITHERS ACROSS THE STATION PLATFORM, IN REVERSE, WEAVING THROUGH PEOPLE AS HE GOES, UNTIL WE'RE A GOOD THIRTY FEET AWAY FROM EACH OTHER.

And then everything begins moving forward again.

Frozen in place, I watch the previous events replay: Aeman strolls toward me as the train enters the station. He approaches the "pedestrian" he just murdered seconds ago. He reaches for the man, and...

"DON'T JUMP!" Aeman screams, grabbing the man by the shoulders and scaring the living hell out of him. Aeman chuckles as he keeps moving. The pedestrian looks at him with a hatred only bullies see. Aeman radiates glee as he stops in front of me, seeing that I'm having a quiet panic attack.

"I...I didn't do that..." I half-whisper as alarm throbs inside my head.

"Nope. I did," Aeman says.

"But...I saw it."

"Physical contact does that. Kinda like riding shotgun. Pretty cool, huh?"

I don't answer. I am a swirling gas planet. Groundless. Aeman looks me up and down. "I live above Goldstone's Pub. In the city. If you get curious enough about what you are, stop by."

"...Manhattan?" The idea of this diabolic creature living somewhere as simple as an apartment in NYC feels ridiculous.

"It's a big, wide world out there, kid. And you've got a lot to learn. I wouldn't bother telling anyone about this, either. They won't believe you, and you couldn't prove it to them, anyway. Only Winders can see or do it."

"Winders?"

"Stupid name, right? See ya soon, kid."

And with that, Aeman steps onto the train. After a beat, he pops his head back out. "Oh, and Charlie... You're standing on the wrong platform. Other side's headed to New Brunswick." He tosses something to me. I catch it. It's my wallet. He must have taken it while I was passed out. Aeman disappears back into the train, which slowly pulls away.

What I am, he said. If I get curious enough about *what I am*.

I am alone, standing on the shore, staring at a foreign sea, my world cracked open.

CHAPTER 11

JUNIPER

Sometimes, I wish I was a cell. I stare at the little universe through the microscope as it churns with a singular beauty. Tendrils of cilia, mitochondria tightroping across microtubules. I've spent almost six years in this lab staring at cells, watching their inherent discipline with awe—always adding up to one irrevocable contract: live, thrive, multiply, die—a perfect system. No one cell is unique. No one cell is supposed to do anything special. Each just dispassionately propels the whole. But somewhere along the way, that simplicity falls apart as trillions of cells add up to a thing—let's say a girl—let's say a young woman—with thoughts and feelings and desires and fears—a thing that no longer is supposed to be alone, *even if it is.*

I couldn't sleep last night. I've never been a good sleeper, but last night was particularly bad. As I blink my eyes, I can feel how red and scratchy they are. I'm sure I look as terrible as I feel, which is just great, because today is the day…my first Council Meeting. A day I've worked toward since I was a little girl. So, why do I keep wishing I was far away from here? There's only one person I feel like I could talk to about any of this, yet his absence is the reason I'm a Leader in the first place. But I want to feel close to him somehow. I need to. So, I'm here—in my lab—my refuge. The refuge that Elijah gave me.

I love the sterility of it. This place demands focus. Which means all other thoughts get shoved to the side. I retrieve cell group 284-B from the soundproof chamber at the center of the lab. The work I've done this morning has left me pretty exhausted. My hand trembles from fatigue as I attempt to carefully slide the sample into the computer. I sit back down and lean over the microscope, waiting for the multimillion-dollar machine to process and feed the results back into my view. My body tenses as I wait. I've been chasing a theory for months. A dangerous but potentially incredible theory. It has to do with sonic variance, in terms of the auditory side effect of our abilities and the potentially lethal vulnerability of our kind if such variance were to— "AAHHH!!" I shriek as something heavy lands on top of my lap. My arms fling out in defense, almost knocking over a row of precious cell samples. I catch hold of my attacker as my fingers disappear beneath a chaos of grey and orange fluff. My attacker lets out a proud *meow* and begins kneading his paws into my lap.

"Vic! You scared me!" I look down at the satisfied expression on the old cat's face, and despite my galloping heart, I can't help but laugh. It's been thirteen years since Elijah gave him to me, but other than some white around his whiskers, he's going as strong as ever. We've been through a lot together. More often than not, we've been each other's sole companions. "You're supposed to be taking dictation, old man. How will I get an accurate record of this without your help, huh?" I bury my face in his fur, kissing the skinny creature at the center and inhaling deeply; he always smells so good.

"I truly don't understand!" a voice rings out across the lab. I turn to find Daniel standing in the doorway. He holds a coffee in each hand and his face looks grim, but for a moment, I can't help but notice how handsome he is—in a gangly, glasses-and-white-lab-coat kind of way. "Can you please explain to me, with all our money and influence and tip-of-the-spear technology, why the hell we can't we get a decent espresso machine in this building?" Daniel is twenty-one, but sometimes he acts like he's sixty. But his curmudgeony layer is one of my favorite things about him. "Now that you're a Leader, I'd like to personally request that the Council make this their first priority."

Vic crawls off my lap and onto my desk. As Daniel tries to set down the coffee he brought for me, Vic stares up, unapologetically, blocking him. Daniel meets Vic's eyes. "What? Don't look at me like that. Are you trying to tell me you don't appreciate my attitude this morning? Well, then just say it. Don't dance around the subject, Vic. I expect nothing less than brutal honesty from you." Vic just stares up at him with as much ambivalence as his cat face can muster. Finally, Daniel's shoulders slump in surrender. "Fine! I apologize. You're right; your mistress has a lot on her mind today, and I'm not helping. There. Are you happy?"

I put an end to his little performance by reaching out and taking the coffee. "Thank you."

"You got it, boss." Daniel offers up his best Italian-mobster impression. I roll my eyes at being called *boss*, but inside, I've always enjoyed that Daniel gives me a certain amount of respect. Even if he does it playfully. Daniel may be three years older, but he only became a Seeker two years ago, so he works for me. It's my lab. He's my lab tech. So, I *am*, essentially, his boss. Which makes the way my heart sped up when our fingers touched, as I grabbed my coffee cup, more than a little awkward/inappropriate. I take a sip. The coffee warms my insides.

"Wow, I didn't realize how cold I was," I say.

"We could always turn the heat up in here. It's not like we're studying penguins."

"No, that's okay. The cold—"

"—is better for focus. I know, I know. Had to try."

I smile. But as quickly as I do, I feel it crumble. He notices. "How you holding up?"

I don't know how to answer this. There's a million different thoughts poltergeisting around inside my head. I say the only truth I feel like I can share at the moment: "I keep expecting Elijah to come around that corner. Maybe give us a surprise inspection. Ask me about my work."

"So you could watch the other labs drip with envy?"

"Oh, come on. All the other labs lived in mortal terror of his surprise inspections. Elijah despised clutter."

"The apple didn't fall far from the tree." He glances around at my spotless desk. I feel myself blush. There's literally not a paper clip out of place. I know he's just making a joke, but I can't seem to get out of my own head. A silence sits between us for a moment. When he speaks again, his voice is quieter. "You know, I keep thinking about the day Elijah found me," he says. Daniel has never spoken to me about his time before he came here. It means something that he's doing it now. "I was living in this terrible group home. At least, I thought it was terrible. We've seen a lot worse since then during the Gathering. I was about seven. I don't remember his face or anything he said. I just remember he was wearing the nicest pair of shoes I'd ever seen." Daniel laughs to himself. "I fake-tied my laces right next to him twice just to get a better look. …I never told him that." Daniel trails off, lost in the memory. "Anyway…what I was trying to say was…I've always taken pride that it was Elijah that found me."

I'm suddenly so annoyed with myself for acting like I'm the only one who cared about Elijah, or that I'm the only one who's been affected by his death. I should be listening, not feeling sorry for myself. That's what Elijah would say.

"He really cared about you," Daniel says. Then he quietly adds, "…We all do."

I force myself to meet his eyes. There's something deeper there—something unspoken. I'm devastatingly terrible when it comes to moments like this. Not that I've encountered many. It's not that I don't think about stuff like love or attraction; I'm not a block of wood. Just something about it makes me feel paper-thin. The only reason I can talk to Daniel, normally, is because I tell myself he's a colleague—an employee. But is there something more? More than just attraction? I don't know.

I lean back over the microscope, attempting to escape my own awkwardness—attempting to look at something that can't look back at me.

Daniel tries to shift gears. "…Care about *your work*, I mean. Your research is really important… It could mean…you know. And now that you're on the Council—"

"Oh, my God…" The words barely escape my mouth. My heartbeat doubles—then triples. I look up at Daniel, then back to the microscope, then back up at Daniel.

"What? What is it?" The sudden change in my behavior has thrown him.

I focus back on the cell sample. It's a horror film down there.

Shredded cilia. Murky, ravaged cytoplasm. Nuclear membrane cleaved apart. It's horrendous. My heart leaps.

"The cells are destroyed! Split and ruptured," I say, quickly. "Cell group 284-A remains healthy and clear, while 284-B is definitely damaged. The effects of the auditory attacks are undeniable." I didn't think Daniel's eyes could go wider, but they do.

"…You've proved it," he says.

"I've proved it," I say, wanting to *feel* it more than just know it. The goal of my work has always been discovery, and now I've made one—a huge one. No longer just one of my theories; it's now a fact: *The aftershock of our abilities is not benign; it has the potential to harm us.*

"Okay, whoa. What does this mean?" Daniel stumbles through his thoughts. "…I mean, I know what it means, but in a larger sense, you know… This could really change things."

This *will* change things, I think. I know it will. *But do I want it to?* All at once, I feel a strange hesitancy—like I'm holding on to a fish, knowing that if I loosen my grip at all, it will race away beyond my reach and I'll only be able to watch it disappear. I'm not sure I'm ready for that quite yet. *This discovery, in the wrong hands…*

"It could be used as a weapon," Daniel says, as if reading my mind. His expression is so intensely serious; it frightens me. Because it feels foreign—like I'm seeing part of him for the very first time—a part he keeps hidden behind his goofy antics. It makes me wonder what else I might've been missing with Daniel. I search his face, but I can't tell if he likes the idea of a weapon, or if what I'm seeing is his fear of its potential. And which way, exactly, am *I* leaning on that subject, while we're at it? "You know that, right?" he says, when I don't answer. I don't like this feeling. Do I trust Daniel? I think I do, but how well do I really know him? *How well do I really know anyone in my life?* I feel a hollowness at this thought, but then, all at once, thinking of Daniel in this new light, something occurs to me: *What if Daniel left the note?* In the last week, I've tried to piece together any possible clue or motive someone might've had in leading me to the truth about Elijah's death, and I've come up empty.

As I work through this train of thought, I pull the wrinkled note from my pocket—the note that sent me into the darkness a week ago—the note that cost two human lives. I watch his face as I hold the note in my hand, looking for any tiny glint of recognition, but he gives me nothing. My mind is racing, making connections. Honestly, I was shocked when Daniel applied to be my tech a year ago. Daniel was a rising star, and most thought he'd want to be a big fish in a small pond, or that he'd choose a lab with an older Seeker at the helm who would vacate that position sooner rather than later. I was accepted into the Seeker Wing at twelve years-old—the second-youngest ever, second only to Elijah himself. Choosing to be a tech under me was seen as a catastrophic career move by most. *Unless he had another reason. Unless he was placed here.*

I'm about to hand the note to him, but something stops me. I don't think I want to reveal this secret quite yet. *Unless it was him. Unless he already knows what's written on it. Could someone have sent Daniel to watch over me? Trevor? Could I ever be that blind?!* But if that was the case, then why lead me to the crime scene? What could my enemies hope to gain by sending me there—by revealing the truth to me? *…But what if it's not an enemy? What if it was an ally trying to show me something vital?* Would that make it even more likely that it's Daniel? He is kind of my only friend at this point. I hold up the note, still folded.

"I found this note in my chamber last week," I say. "Someone slid it under my door."

Daniel's expression goes from serious to dark. "…Oh, yeah? What's it say?" he asks. His clenched-jaw hesitation mixed with a flash of very real anger (that he quickly tries to hide) tells me two things: One—Daniel didn't write the note, and two—he's jealous of whoever did. He thinks it's some kind of love note from a secret admirer. I almost laugh. I feel stupid. *What was I thinking? If I can't even trust Daniel…*

I look away, shove the note into my pocket, truly embarrassed now. I'm trying to think of any intelligent thing to say when my eyes land on the clock. *Oh, God!* I spring to my feet.

"I have to go," I say. "I can't be late to my first Council meeting."

"Okay, calm down. You still have twenty minutes," he says.

"There's something I need to do first."

"What are you—"

"Don't tell *anyone* about my discovery," I say. "Nothing about the work."

He looks confused at the intensity he now sees on *my* face. "I don't understand. You've already sent reports to the Council about your theories."

"But they don't know it works. I want to keep it that way for a little longer. Send all the files to my drive, encrypted. Okay?"

"Okay," Daniel says, almost to himself. I can tell he's struggling to say something more. The last few minutes have been a brutal whiplash of emotions: Elijah, Daniel sharing his past, my discovery, the implication of it, the note, the amorphous feelings that may or may not exist between us. Too much. I don't give him a chance to speak. I turn and head for the door.

CHAPTER 12

JUNIPER

I have fifteen minutes to get to the Council Room. Fifteen minutes to get my rapid breathing under control. I push all thoughts of my discovery out of my mind. There are people all around me now as I walk down the wide corridor, and if any of them are ever going to accept me as a Leader, I can't walk around looking like a frightened little girl. This thought reminds me of my current side mission, and I pick up my pace. I know I could do this after the Council meeting, but my instincts are telling me that timing is key.

As soon as the elevator opens onto the training level, I'm assaulted by the familiar atonal symphony coming from all directions. The ringing is muffled, but it's everywhere. I've heard this sound so often in my life, I barely notice it—the sound of our abilities being used. I spent so many years making this same trek, but somehow, the distance from that time feels greater than I expected. I pass several rooms with clear glass walls. In one room, standing around a conference table, young men and women in tailored suits debate openly. Solicitors. The argument looks heated. Back when I was wingless, my Solicitor classes consisted of me watching other kids break a problem down until it eventually felt meaningless. Each side fervently defended their point of view. Then the Teacher would have us switch, and we'd have to argue just as hard for the opposite point of view. The other kids saw it as a game, but to me it felt like we were being taught that truth is relative. *Bureaucrats.* I could never be a Solicitor.

A pretty blonde with straight bangs—I think her name is Robin…or Rachel—pushes open the thick, glass, soundproof door as she exits the conference room, and the ringing gets louder. Then the door swishes closed behind her and the sound dips down again. As she passes, she gives me a little reverent nod. There's no irony to it. She's merely giving me respect. I'll admit, it feels good, and it instantly makes me like her—even though I can't remember her name. I keep moving.

Farther down the hall, an even larger room, also behind glass, reveals a fleet of lavish, cherrywood desks. Behind these wooden fortresses, watching multiple monitors and juggling various devices, sits an army of Providers. They look effortlessly stylish, which makes me feel anxious. Providers live at the cutting edge of social and financial movements—using micro-shifts in trends and markets to reap enormous profits. I could also never be a Provider. Aside from being completely hopeless when it comes to recognizing the "cool" in anything, the idea of stacking assets feels antithetical to my soul somehow. Accumulation inherently deals only in the finite. The very nature of something being limited is what gives that thing its value. Scarcity. I've always felt pulled toward the infinite. Infinite possibilities. The fact that the universe is as infinitely small as it is infinitely large gives me the chills just thinking about it. If you don't believe me that something can be infinitely small, just take the absolute smallest measurement that your mind can comprehend, then cut that in half. Now cut *that* in half. Now cut THAT in half. Infinity! It never stops. Some people think that's scary. I think it's beautiful.

All at once, a loud voice blares out from hidden speakers:

"ATTENTION, PLEASE. ONE MINUTE OF SILENCE WILL BE OBSERVED FOR OUR FALLEN PRIME. VICTOR MASON. THANK YOU."

Everyone around me stops. A tall, attractive woman, who I recognize as one of the Provider instructors from my youth, stands so close, I can hear her huff out a light breath of frustration. She looks at her watch. She's probably running late. Still, her eyes furtively glance over at me. I was once her student, and now I am her Leader. She doesn't smile—I get no reverent nod this time—she simply faces forward, waiting for the minute of silence to end. *I can't believe it's been a year.* I saw it on my calendar just this morning and still I forgot it was coming until right now. It has nothing to do with Elijah's death, regardless of the timing. Once a year, our entire Chapter observes a minute of silence to commemorate the day our first Prime, Victor Mason, was murdered by the Faters, nearly thirty years ago, prompting decades of bitter hostilities and covert bloodshed. And now the Faters have done it again.

I hope the Council's response to Elijah's assassination will be swift and mighty. My father's nature has never been particularly bellicose, but like I said, our Prime holds no more power than his own one vote—just like the rest of the Council—so we'll see.

I wait in silence. No such ritual will be observed for Elijah's death. Not that he would've ever wanted such a thing. The Leadership has grown far more partisan since Victor Mason's day, and though I think Elijah made a wonderful Prime, he was not universally adored. But my father always told me how much Elijah looked up to Victor Mason—who, as a young man, was one of the architects of the Leadership as well as the Code. I can still hear Elijah's laughter when I reintroduced him to my cat "Vic" all those years later. He thought it was a perfect name for him.

And all at once, I realize that this silent minute commemorating a murder feels oddly comforting—more comforting than almost anything else since Elijah's death. Because some part of me thinks Elijah would find it fitting that he followed in Victor Mason's footsteps in both life and death. That might sound insensitive, but I just know he'd have appreciated the symmetry. And deep inside of me, I feel a little piece of my heart begin to mend. So, I tear at the scab with all the rage and hatred I have in me. *I will not forget. I will not forgive. No, Elijah, I won't. They've taken two Primes from us, and they will never take another.*

People around me start to move again. In my fury, I charge toward the entrance to the private elevator that leads up to the Council Room, where I'm hoping some real power will help bring justice for my mentor. But then I remember where I was going before that frozen minute, and I force myself to redirect. *I still have time; I just have to move faster.* I use the anger in my belly to push my legs to make up the time I lost standing in place. I can't run—that would call too much attention to me. But I can definitely walk with purpose.

After snaking down several corridors, I finally arrive at my destination. My body instinctively slows as I enter the dim gymnasium. Far from the luxury of the training rooms used by actual Enforcers, the old wooden flooring squeaks beneath my feet as I glide behind the forty small bodies moving in formation.

An instructor leads the trainees, ages six to twelve, in martial arts training. They yell in unison as they collectively strike the air, wearing loose-fitting black gis. Many have bruises and open wounds on their faces and hands. This is Enforcer training. All of these children are wingless. You have to be chosen to join a Wing. It takes most many years. All wingless students receive training in all disciplines. I spent years in this space. The smell of dust, sweat and blood still emanates from the ragged red mats leaning against the wall. The other three Wings use the most up-to-date equipment, even during training, but pre-Wing Enforcer training forgoes almost all frills. Under Trevor's leadership, the wheat is ruthlessly separated from the chaff. Only the Oban—the Japanese Chapter's version of Enforcers—has a worse reputation for severity in their training. I do not miss this room, though sometimes I do find myself longing for the simplicity that exists here.

As I skim around the outside of the students, the instructor spots me and stands at attention, calling for the trainees to do so as well. It is strict protocol when a Leader passes. I remember doing the same as a child. Again, the formality fills me with a certain amount of prideful glee, which I do not let show on my face. But I did not come here to be admired. And I know that this next moment must be handled delicately, or I will do more harm than good.

I stroll up the center aisle, between the rows of trainees.

Little Sofia stands between two larger girls, making them look like giants. She's smaller than almost all the rest of the trainees, drowning in her ill-fitting gi. A yellowing bruise glows on her left cheekbone already. There's no slow welcome in Thessaly; it's fight or fall. The devotion to this severe culture begins and ends with Trevor himself. Sofia apes the other students, standing straight. When our eyes meet, she looks surprised that it's me that all the reverence is being aimed at. She gives a little wave, her hand barely rising above her chest. She looks frightened. And all at once, I realize how strange it is for me to be here. I've never visited a child I found in the Gathering before.

Three rows over from Sofia I see a thirteen-year-old boy—Joshua. I discovered him during the Gathering two years ago at a summer camp upstate. He was a sweet boy who talked about dinosaurs the entire ride back. Now I see a coldness in his stare as he focusses on me. It makes me feel sad and a bit angry. *It happens so fast.* You can lose your spirit in this room, so quickly, as discipline and violence get pounded into you.

I focus back on Sofia—her big eyes and little moon face. We didn't share any defining moment that I can remember. Truthfully, we've barely spoken to each other. *So, what is it? Why her?* Maybe it's because I've never had the power to do anything for any of the children I've brought to Thessaly until now. That's probably part of it. But I think it's because of the defiance I see in those little brown eyes—the same look I saw on the playground when she faced off against her two bullies—the way she won't let them break her. They'll try. She's at a serious disadvantage, not just because of her size but because so much is still new to her. That will eventually pass. She'll just have to survive until then. I hope this will help.

I look Sofia directly in the face and give her a little wink and nod, making sure all the kids around Sofia see. Her face breaks into a smile. Surrounding kids look at Sofia, wondering why she's been singled out by one of the Leaders. *Good. Word will spread. It always does. For better or for worse.* In the school Sofia came from, such a gesture by an authority figure would probably lead to teasing and cruelty, but here, no trainee would dare harm a child favored by the Council. Then, for a moment, I wonder if I've done her a disservice. *The deadliest knives are sharpened on the hardest stones.* I push away Trevor's voice in my head. No. Cruelty never really helps anything, I tell myself. I just hope that letting the crowd know that Sofia has friends in high places will give her more of a chance. Time will tell. I continue out of the gymnasium. I have three minutes to reach the Council Room five minutes early.

CHAPTER 13

CHARLIE

Ducky's pissed. Really pissed. I chuck clothes into my duffle while he paces behind me. Grams hovers in the doorway.

"This doesn't make sense, man! You're just gonna leave school? You just got back. You said you were gonna work hard, start over. Was that all bullshit?"

I want to tell him. I want to tell them both. But they wouldn't believe me. *How could they?* I guess I could show them. I could say, "Pick a number," then wait for them to get over their confusion and play along. Then I'd have to tell them to tell me the answer; then I'd need to figure out how to do something that I have only achieved under two life-and-death circumstances, and if I managed it, I would tell them the exact number they picked and watch them think it was a lucky guess. How many times would I have to do that to convince them I have some special power? If I did it enough times, maybe I could convince them I'm psychic, but convincing them that I am single-handedly winding back time? *God, it all sounds so ridiculous in my head.*

I have to keep moving. One piece of clothing at a time, until there are no more to pack. Then I can leave Grams and Ducky alone in their hurt and bewilderment. It sounds cruel, but the alternative feels worse. Saving Ducky was miraculous, but in my mind that miracle can't be separated from the fact that it was my actions that sent him spiraling down those stairs in the first place. If there's a way I can learn to control this, I have to try. I have to. "Only Winders can do it," Aeman said. *Winders.* Plural. There are others. Other people that can do what I can do. *But he killed that man. I watched him die, then snap back up like an inflatable, clown-faced punching bag, completely oblivious.*

I pull off my shirt, reaching for a thermal. The nights have gotten colder. Ducky and Grams's startled expressions make me realize they've just seen the armada of scars crisscrossing my back, tokens from the constant daily warfare inside Lazarus. I've kept them hidden until now. Grams puts a hand on her chest. I don't know what she's imagining, and I know I should put her fears at ease, but I can't find the words. So, I just pull the thermal on over my head. "Look, I'm not *moving* to New York, okay?"

"Charlie, man, I know last night was…" Ducky's anger feels more muted now. He thinks he's losing me. But I know that if I turn back now, if I don't plunge out that door immediately, I may never have the strength to go. And if I don't go, I'll never learn how to stop whatever strange madness has gripped my life for the last eight years.

"This has nothing to do with last night. I just need time to figure a few things out. I don't expect you to understand—"

"Understand what?!" Ducky's face burns bright again. "Understand you're losing it?! You need help, man. Grams, talk to this jackass!"

"Donald!" Grams hates to see us fight. Always has. One of my earliest memories of Grams was the day after Easter, when Ducky and I were seven; I was sitting in Ducky's room staring at the foot-tall, solid-chocolate Mickey Mouse that Ducky had found in his sizable Disney-themed Easter basket. Being raised by a single mother, with a single mother's income and a fierce prejudice against paying for cavities, made for fairly anorexic Easter baskets at my house. The giant chocolate mouse looked like the Holy Grail to me. So, in exchange for cleaning Ducky's room, I was supposed to receive an entire chocolate appendage. I was hoping for one of the two monstrous ears—the obvious choice for such a fantastic room-cleaning job—but to my dismay, Ducky used a butcher knife to lop off Mickey's minuscule choc-olate *ass*. I promptly refused the buttocks and demanded a fresh amputation. Ducky dug in his heels and soon we were shouting. At this point, Grams slipped into the room like a ninja Lady

Justice, scooped up the candy rodent (ass and all), leaned back on Ducky's bed, stacking both his Batman AND Robin pillows behind her, and proceeded to devour the entire rabbit *whole*. We were so shocked, and in a strange way fascinated, that we just sat there and watched Grams teach us her lesson about fighting over stupid shit one bite at a time, until there was nothing left but the sticky remnants on her fingertips, which she promptly sucked clean. Grams could be a real badass when she wanted to be.

So, I wait for her to rip into me about my sudden rash behavior, but it doesn't come.

"Where you gonna stay, Charlie?" Her tone tells me she senses how important it is to me, and that trying to dissuade me would be pointless. Plus, I'm eighteen, and I know Grams was shoved out of the house to fend for herself when she was only fifteen—not that she wants that for me. She's saying she trusts me, but I know she's just as worried as Ducky.

"With a friend...just off Union Square. I'll call as soon as I get there." I don't tell her the actual address. I don't know what I'll be walking into, and I sure as hell don't want either of them showing up if this whole thing ends up being a tragically bad idea.

I reach a fist out to Ducky. A peace offering. Hoping he'll give it a bump and wish me luck. I want to say, *I'm sorry, man. I love you. But I've hurt you in ways you can't even imagine, and I need to figure out how to protect you and Grams, and anyone else I ever hope to care about, from me and the horrible things I'm capable of.* But instead of saying any of that, I just stand there with my fist extended and some dopey-ass Charlie Brown expression on my face.

Ducky turns and walks out of the room. After all we've been through together, I'm giving him exactly zero justification for my sudden departure. But it can't be helped.

"That boy just loves you," Grams says, "and don't want nothing but good for you. Be careful, Charlie. You hear me? We just got you back. Can't lose you again."

I wrap my arms around her. I don't want to let go. I make a promise to myself to return as soon as I possibly can. Then I grab my bag and exit the house.

CHAPTER 14

JUNIPER

I'm here. At the table. One of the ten. A childhood dream come true. A moment of triumph. And yet, the cold, imperial chamber seems to underline just how little *real-world* experience I bring with me. I know this room wasn't designed to make *me* feel small, but even the vaulted, angular ceiling feels deliberately intimidating. The thick, wooden table we sit around looks like a relic from some ancient Viking war room. I do love the walls, though. Each of the four walls is made of steel and represents one of the four Wings. Rows of deeply carved lines engage and direct the eye—upward, downward, forward and inward—much like the blood ritual. The patterns are magnificent in their simplicity. *I wonder who made them?*

I straighten my spine, trying to project confidence, or at least competence. Despite our little animosities, I don't want to make my father look bad. Putting my name forward must have been hard for him, knowing that people might cry nepotism.

There was no friendly introduction to the Council. No going around the table and saying names and sharing stories. I'll admit: I'd even prepared a little thank-you-for-this-great-opportunity speech, if prompted. Now such pastel-colored expectations feel foolish.

My father sits two seats away from me. He is our Prime, but there is no head of this table; the table is round. There are seven men and three women. Four Solicitors, four Enforcers, my father is the sole Provider, and I am the only Seeker, and thus the only Leader wearing white. We all wear the cross-like Leader symbol on our collars.

The conflict erupted as soon as we sat down, as if someone had pushed pause on a previous argument and just now let it play. Maya Steele faces off against Trevor, her face pink with frustration. "It's a question of security, Trevor," she says.

The expression on Trevor's face makes me flush. I know that look. I hate that look. It's both calm and hostile at the same time—a difficult combination to pull off. He's telling her with his posture he couldn't find her less threatening, regardless of her passion. Trevor has not even glanced at me since I entered the room. I'm trying not to look at him either, and I'm completely failing. It's a round table, after all. Geometry is my enemy today. I fight to strip any emotion from my face. The least I can do is look totally bored if our eyes ever do meet.

"The perimeter will be secure," Trevor says. "Too strong a presence inside will only communicate weakness."

I'm trying to follow, but I honestly have no idea what they're talking about. There was no catch-up-Juniper-so-she-can-actually-contribute moment. *So, they want me to hit the ground running. I can do that.*

"The Carrion Ring has not been on American soil in over fifteen years," Maya says, "As Grand Enforcer you must—"

"If we hope to lead this brave new world of ours, Maya, we should at least make an *attempt* at looking confident."

"I will say..." My father leans back in his chair. "The amount of 'security' this year was more than a little ostentatious. The Russians spared no expense. But it *was* a little distracting."

I can't contain my surprise. *They're talking about the Carrion Ring.* I've only ever heard whispered rumors about it. The Carrion Ring is not mentioned in the Code. It precedes it. Only the most powerful and infamous of our kind are invited, and none but they know the secrets of the mysterious competition. My father is the current reigning champion of the Carrion Ring. (This definitely helped with his election.) He's never shared a single detail with me about it, but I do know that the winner's Chapter hosts the following year, and as a hosting Council member, I will get to attend next year.

I feel myself smiling, and then my eyes land on the squat, sweaty man sitting next to me. Gordon Tang. A Solicitor. He eyes me greedily, tracing the length of my body. His mouth is ravaged with cold sores, to which he has obviously applied makeup and done a poor job matching his skin tone. He gives me a little wink. I avoid further eye contact, looking for a friendlier face at the table. I notice a poreless shine to many of the faces around me. Most have had some form of plastic surgery. Nearly all sit back in their chairs, seemingly disengaged. A cold lethargy hangs on them. I'm finding it almost impossible to imagine Elijah calling Gordon Tang his peer. But I remind myself not to be fooled; their physical edges may be dulled, but our world is a sophisticated jungle, and right now I'm sitting with the lions.

Still, seeing all these famous faces so close has my mind churning. *Will this be me years from now? Is this the inevitable end to true power—plump and choked with boredom?* I'd be lying if I didn't admit I feel disappointed. I don't know what I was expecting. Grandeur, perhaps? Vibrancy? *Hope?* Not disillusionment. Not bad makeup and herpes.

Benjamin Acosta, the speaker at my ceremony, stands now, entering the argument.

"That's exactly why we must decide on a location now," he says. "Proper security needs time!"

"ENOUGH!" Trevor smashes his hand down on the table with a resounding *bang*. The room goes silent. "Listen to yourselves! You cry like billy goats about security for other Chapters. What about *our* security? Our Prime has been murdered." At last. Someone is talking about Elijah. I don't even care that it's Trevor. I want answers. Trevor looks from face to face. He seems disgusted by what he sees. He still doesn't look at me. "So, what are we going to do about it? While you were arguing over curtain colors, my men found the best of us gutted and tortured! We left a shotgun pressed to his—"

Trevor stops himself. All eyes drift to a gorgeous woman in her late fifties. She wears a tight, black, leather dress, her hair is platinum blonde and quite long, and she makes the rest of us in the room look like we're made out of lesser materials. Virginia Spencer—Elijah's mother. From everything I've heard of Virginia, I expect to see fury boiling on her skin, but what I see is a lost woman. She turns toward us, and she suddenly looks so much like Elijah, I feel my nostrils burn with sorrow. Virginia feels the attention on her and smiles, but the smile never reaches her eyes.

Trevor lowers his voice. "Forgive me, Virginia. I didn't mean to…" There's a sadness in Trevor's tone that I have never heard. A care.

"I used the shotgun as an ironic gesture," Virginia says in the light, musical twang of a born-and-bred Southern belle. "Little inside joke between me and Elijah. He used to hate going down to Alabama to visit family and hunt 'coons with his cousins. Wouldn't even touch a slingshot. He was always such a little bookworm. Besides…my boy wasn't in that broken scarecrow we found tied to that chair. His spirit had long departed." Her tone makes it feel like she's speaking to herself, as if the room were empty. "Those crime scenes are nothing but dioramas. So little boys dressed as policemen can write their stories. And they like their stories simple. But I pulled that trigger on a mound of dust and bone. Nothing more."

The lightness in her tone is chilling. Why would she have to be the one to make Elijah's death look like a suicide? Surely, someone else could've done such a dark job. Maybe she wanted to do it. Maybe she insisted. I don't know if that's better or worse. All I know is that it feels horrible to me. I can smell Virginia's perfume from here. At first, I thought it was pleasant, but now I'm not so sure. I don't know what the scent is, but I'm positive I would find it choking if I was much closer. Something about it feels intentionally invasive. Behind her back, people call Virginia Spencer "Queen Cottonmouth" and whisper all kinds of rumors—mostly dark, often sexual. My father told me she arrived at Thessaly as a young, single mother-to-be, and though she was only twenty, she had already trained with other Teachers. Her reputation as a merciless Enforcer is practically unrivaled. The room pulsates with tension. Nobody knows what to say. My father finally breaks the silence. "What are you suggesting, Trevor?"

"Extermination," Trevor says. "We've endured these barbaric hostilities long enough. Before we invite other Chapters to our fine city, we must sweep out the vermin. Why not make hunting down the 'Warriors of Fate' a new pastime? Perhaps we'll take scalps." Trevor turns ever so slightly toward Maya Steele, who glares back at Trevor. The other Enforcers on the Council nod at Trevor's proposal.

"Nobody wants a war," Gordon Tang says. The sweat blistering on his forehead says he's far from comfortable engaging with Trevor.

Virginia looks over at the toadish man. "Who's next then, Gordon? *You?* Those heathens'll gobble you up like peach pie, first chance they get."

Maya comes to Gordon's aid: "Elijah believed that open conflict would be a perilous business decision." And now I see the other Solicitors at the table nod in agreement.

"With all due respect, Elijah is no longer our Prime," Trevor says with a controlled voice.

All eyes shift to my father, who remains unreadable.

"Elijah wanted us safe," Trevor continues. "That young man cared about all of us far more than we deserved. And we owe him more than this sad apathy."

"We have a public face to consider!" Benjamin bellows out, trying to achieve the same gravity he held during the ceremony. "We threaten to compromise that by getting caught up in pointless scrimmages. Right now, they're a bunch of scattered thugs and saboteurs. Why give them a reason to unite? It's foolish, Trevor."

"*Coward!*" Trevor snaps at him. "You'd sit on your hands till they're clogged and purple while these savages piss on your bed without consequence. Are you sure you're in the correct room, Benjamin? I know the Code says we must have all *Wings* on this Council, but it never once mentions anything about spineless, geriatric weasels."

Trevor's tone is lethal. Benjamin hesitates, looking to his fellow Solicitors for support, but finds only fear. Humiliated, the older man sits back down.

If, ten minutes ago, someone had told me I would be sitting in this room, siding with Trevor and Queen Cottonmouth over Maya Steele, I would've laughed in their face. And yet here I am. I want blood as much as either of them—maybe more—and all Benjamin and Maya can say is that seeking revenge for Elijah's murder would be bad for business. I can't believe their callousness. It disgusts me. *Where's the loyalty? Where's the love? He was better than all of you put together! Trevor is right: at best, you're cowards; at worst, you're selfish…weasels.*

The murky silence goes on and on in the aftermath of Trevor's chastisement. The call for, or against, striking at the Faters seems to be deadlocked between the four Solicitors and the four Enforcers. My father's vote will break the tie. He's never been one to go against the grain, but at the moment, there is no grain. And suddenly, I realize this whole show has been for my father—all the shouting and jousting—each side attempting to pull him their way. *So, Father: vengeance or cowardice—which way will you go?*

"What's your opinion, Juniper?" Maya says.

My head snaps in her direction. I know it sounds stupid and completely naïve, but somehow, the thought that I have a vote here never even crossed my mind. Maya must see my surprise, because she adds, "Everyone has an equal voice here."

I take in all the faces staring at me. Most of the Leaders have barely made a peep the whole time. *So, why the hell am I being pulled into this fistfight?* I look into Maya's eyes, which seem to be telling me: *These are the moments you make yourself known, if you're strong enough to be counted. Better pick a side before it's picked for you.* She doesn't know that I've already picked my side, and she's not going to like what I have to say.

Gordon Tang clears his throat and says, "Since it's Miss Trask's first day at the table, I think it would be best if she recuse herself from—"

"Let her speak," Trevor says. The surprise at Trevor coming to my defense is palpable.

"I'm sorry," Gordon Tang continues, unabated, "but this is a matter of war, Trevor."

"She has a greater understanding of that word than you can ever hope to," Trevor says. He looks around the table at the other shocked faces. All but my father, whose expression is hard and focused. "It's no secret that Juniper did not have my support in her election," Trevor says. "But she has always had my respect." He stares deep into Gordon Tang's sweat-covered face. "You voted her into this room; now stand by your decision like a man." Then Trevor turns to me for the first time. "Go on, Juniper."

I could not be more astonished by Trevor's words—his *support*.

I feel my father watching me like a hawk, but I don't look at him. I can almost hear him saying, "*Take a pass on this one, Juniper. There will be other fights. Other opportunities.*"

My mind spins. *It's too early. I know it is. But they murdered you, Elijah.* In this moment, I get a glimpse of how this room can devour someone. A few swallowed words, and pretty soon you're ingesting whole sentences, then thoughts, and eventually ideals and principles. And somehow, I know if I look under this table right now, I'll see a pile of bones—remnants of those who thought they could stay out of the fight.

"…Elijah was a great man. A great Teacher." I try to keep emotion out of my voice, but I can feel a tremor and desperately hope it's not noticeable. "…As some of you, I'm sure, know, I went to the location where Elijah was found…" My mind skips a beat as a thought comes to me: *Is the author of the note in this room? Did someone here send me to that dark building on that horrible night?* Then I remember the timeline. *No. It's not anyone here.* The note was left under my door well before the Council voted for me to replace Elijah. No one here would have anything to gain by sharing such intel with someone *not* sitting at this table.

That dark, bloody room flashes in my mind. The chair. Those taunting words slashed across the wall. I dig in and press on, forcing resolve into my voice. "They tortured him… His killers deserve nothing less than destruction."

My eyes land on Trevor. His face looks relaxed as he listens. But then I notice his *hand*. Trevor's right hand is clenched, blood draining from his knuckles. I hear Trevor's own words coming back at me: "*The body is a pane of glass, if you know where to look.*"

He's lying.

His face doesn't match his fist.

But what could he be lying about?

Trevor sees me notice his fist and he lets go, but it's too late.

And then I know…

As the memory hits me, I can almost smell the slight sulfuric odor of the peanut-shaped koi pond and see my gaunt, haunted face reflected in the water.

At twelve years old, half a decade of intense Enforcer training had left only lean muscle wrapped around my bones. The indoor park on the forty-fifth floor of Thessaly was always deserted at training time. I knew, if I'd run to my room, my father would've found me. I couldn't face him. Not after what I'd done.

I bent to wash the sticky, drying blood off my hands. By the look of my knuckles, I thought my right hand might be broken. A beautiful speckled koi fish glided through the water below me, and I stopped, deciding not to contaminate its world with my sins. My body went rigid as I heard the footsteps…

"Juniper." Elijah's voice sounded kind but sad. I don't know how he found me. I felt anger swell in my chest. *After all these years, you choose this moment to talk to me? You said you were going to keep an eye on me! Then I never saw you again. Well, I don't need you now!* And then I realized he had most likely been sent to find and punish me. *Good,* I thought. *I deserve to be punished.* I wondered if the punishment would be death. I'd killed one of our own. A boy. Beaten him to death. *Death is what I deserve*, I remember thinking—resolved to face such a fate bravely. I would show them nothing. No weakness.

"The boy is alive," Elijah said. At his words, I felt a deep release in my chest. My head drooped forward, as if the string holding it up had been cut, and hot tears poured out of me.

"…I…I didn't want to… I swear I didn't—"

"I know," Elijah said. "I know you didn't." The only sound was the tiny bubbling of the pond's filter. After a long time, Elijah spoke again.

"Trevor thinks in violence, Juniper. And violence is a complicated subject with our kind. Some would argue that's how he keeps us safe—that such cruelty is a necessary evil. Now…I'm aware your Teacher finds the thoughts of humans repugnant, but in my opinion, they've already made a lot of the mistakes for us, so if we don't learn from them, we're just as foolish, right?" I only listened. I didn't make a sound. "Einstein lived through the worst war this planet has ever seen. And that war scared our kind. It brought us together as a species, paved the way for the Leadership to be born. But it also made us believe that humans needed to be controlled at all costs. Fear does that to folks. Makes it easy to hate. The humans believed the fear of mutual annihilation would keep such a war from repeating, so they made bigger and bigger guns. But Einstein, despite his fears, despite the horrors he saw, believed that building weapons will always lead to the use of them. He said, 'Striving for peace and preparing for war are incompatible with each other.'"

At that, I looked up at him. He seemed surprised by the anger on my face. "But that's stupid," I said. "If we don't prepare, the other side will. Don't we have to protect ourselves?"

"Of course. Defending yourself is a very important thing. But let me ask you, Juniper: was what you did today for your own protection?"

Trevor had made me fight a boy that he'd brought into the Enforcer Wing a year prior but who had not been showing the aptitude that Trevor had hoped. He seemed to lack the lethal instincts that Trevor praised his students for. Normally, such a student would simply fall to the back of the class and would eventually become a guard or be sent out of Thessaly to fulfill a thankless, but necessary, job in the human world. But, instead, Trevor had taken the boy's lack of talent as a personal insult. And as I pummeled the boy, though he was a year older than me, Trevor didn't stop the fight. Even when I tried to give mercy, Trevor demanded the fight go on. Even as I felt my fist break the boy's cheekbone, Trevor still pushed for the fight to continue.

Elijah put his hand on my shoulder. His palm felt warm against my chilled skin. "Trevor is a brilliant man," he said. "But he's also a collector of weapons. Do you know what he sees in you, Juniper? What he's always seen in you?"

I looked up at Elijah. This was something I'd always wondered. Something that I deeply wanted to know: why Trevor chose me. What intrinsic talent had Trevor seen in me that caused him to accept me into the Enforcer Wing two years earlier than any other student. I waited.

"Your rage," Elijah said.

Now, as I stare at Trevor across the table of the Leadership Council, I can feel the fight he's pushing me at—the weapon he's trying to make me into once again. Trevor's lie is that he knows

Elijah would never want this. That he would despise a war in his name. "*Wouldn't even touch a slingshot,*" Virginia said. *But I'm not you, Elijah. And like you said, I am filled with rage.*

I take a small, even breath, not knowing what I'm about to say, even as I begin to say it…

"Personally…" I feel the entire Council lean in. "Well, personally, I don't believe we can win a war against violent fanaticism. The Warriors of Fate are a terrorist cell and nothing more. They *want* a violent response from us. Why bend toward their barbarism? We prove our evolutionary status by our tolerance and discernment. I can completely understand Trevor's *knee-jerk* reaction, having spent a lifetime protecting us from our very worst instincts… But I think this time, his *old* tactics might prove to be, at their best, wasteful, and at their worst, counterproductive. War has always been the fruitless answer of humans. Let's not repeat their mistakes. I believe we can do better." I look at Trevor. "And so did Elijah."

Silence recaptures the room.

My heart throbs inside my ears. I want to swallow. I don't.

Then Maya smiles. It means nothing to me. She is no friend of Elijah's. Not really.

So does Benjamin. *Another bureaucrat.*

My father stares at me like he's not quite sure what he's seeing, that perhaps he missed something vital, and that he will not underestimate me again. But what gouges at me, in a way I can't quite articulate, or maybe don't want to, is the very real *fear* I see in my father's eyes. He's afraid for me.

I feel the call to war die in the chamber. For the time being, at least. Virginia Spencer's expression as she looks in my direction is that of someone who just smelled something vile.

I hope you're happy, Elijah. Not the best first day.

Trevor stares at me.

I meet his crocodile eyes.

I do not flinch.

CHAPTER 15

CHARLIE

I jerk awake, violently. My heart pummels the inside of my chest. The nightmare felt so real. I was in the car again. Only, in this version, my mother wasn't the vibrant, beautiful woman who died and was resurrected on that dark highway; in this version, when I looked over, the twisted skeleton my mother would soon become stared back at me—lost and disoriented, barely able to grip the steering wheel. And then the headlights came. It stopped there this time, and I feel grateful. But I can tell my body's still in motion, which makes me feel panicky. I look around. The world flashes by me on either side in a blur. It's the smell that brings me fully back. The seats. The smell of old fabric and dirty nylon. I'm on the train. I breathe out. My breath feels shaky. My groggy head still wounded from the multilayered abuse I put it through last night.

"YOU OKAY?" a voice calls out.

I look over at the seat across the aisle. What looks at first like a pile of loose sweatshirts slouched in a seat diagonal from me turns out to be a mousy-haired girl with a tiny, silver nose ring and too much baby blue eye shadow. She's chewing gum like she's attempting to return it to a subatomic level. Her question was oddly loud, which makes me glance around the car to check if anyone else might be staring at me. The closest other passenger is a mother fussing with a very squirmy toddler roughly six seats behind. The girl is still looking at me expectantly, waiting for me to answer.

"…Uh…yeah, fine," I say.

She pulls her hoody back and removes her headphones, which

explains her obnoxiously loud question. One of the headphones gets caught in her hair, which she yanks at clumsily, letting out a little "Aeeakgh" as she pulls it free. "What? Sorry, I couldn't hear you," she says. The girl seems a little all over the place.

"I said I'm fine."

She tucks a piece of hair behind her ear, exposing her chipped black fingernail polish, and I notice for the first time that the girl, despite her gangly demeanor, is really quite pretty. Her gently angled jawline frames her smooth, lightly flushed cheeks. "Okay, good," she says. "Seemed like you were having a pretty intense nightmare. It actually looked kind of dramatic with my music playing over it."

"Well…glad I could entertain you." My tone is not inviting.

"Yeah, me too," she says, taking my coldness in stride. *She's not getting that I'm not in the mood.* She smiles at my discomfort and seems to make some kind of decision. "I'm Tristen." She extends her hand across the aisle to me. I don't reach out. It feels like an aggressive action to not take her hand, but I can feel the twisted burden of my reality creeping back in, choking me with the unknown that lies at the end of this train ride.

A train conductor walks down the aisle between us, snatching the ticket stubs from above both our seats. This means the next stop must be Manhattan. *I'm almost there.* Tristen raises her arm, letting the conductor pass, then she brings it right back down into the same position, waiting. The look in her eye says she'll definitely hold it there for a while. No choice. The awkwardness is worse. I reluctantly reach out and take her hand.

"Charlie," I say. Her hand is warm.

"You live in the city?" she asks.

"Nope. You?"

"First year. I study film at NYU. My excuse for watching you. Research. You could be the subject of my next short film and you'd never know it."

"…Cool."

"I like to think so."

I can't help it; I'm totally disarmed by this strange girl's charming confidence. Our eyes linger. I feel a little flutter in my stomach, and I instantly start sweating a little. *So stupid. I don't have time for this kind of shit.* But like I said, I can't help it.

"So, you from New Jersey, then?" she asks.

"Yep. You too?"

"Hell, no," she says in a tone I don't appreciate. I'm not like a die-hard New Jerseyan or anything, but it is my home, and I don't need anyone trashing it. "I was out there tracking down a source," she says. "Sometimes, you gotta go to some dark places to get what you're looking for."

"Jersey is not that bad. Lots of cool people are from New Jersey."

"Name one. And your family doesn't count."

"Um, how about Allen Ginsberg, George R. R. Martin, Queen Latifah, Bruce Springsteen, Whitney Houston. Just to name a few."

She looks genuinely impressed. "Shit. Can't argue with that. Whitney's from Jersey?"

"Newark."

"Ugh, gross." She put her hands up in apology. "Sorry. Old habit. Still working on my newfound respect for your home state. Why you headed into the city? Got a date?" She wags her eyebrows at me, and I can't help but laugh. But what's my answer? I can't exactly say *I'm headed into the city to meet a creepy guy with super-powers, which I've just recently discovered I have as well. We should grab a slice after.*

"I'm meeting someone," I say. "Not a date," I add, quickly.

"Business or pleasure?"

"You ask a lot of questions."

"Yeah, I'm a documentary filmmaker. Kinda comes with the territory." She looks me over, then says. "Okay. So, that's it?" The question is confusing. *Am I supposed to say something? Am I missing some social flirting norm that I might have missed during all my extensive dating courses at Camp Lazarus?*

"…Uh… Guess so," I say.

Tristen pulls her headphones back on, and slouches back against her seat.

"NICE TO MEET YOU, CHARLIE!" she shouts, half-deaf once again from her music. I give her a little awkward wave, then I turn and face out the window. In my mind, I replay our gawky exchange as the last dregs of New Jersey landscape rushes by. I decide I didn't make too much of a fool out of myself, which makes me feel like maybe I'm not a complete lost cause. Next time, I'll do better. If there is a next time. The train dips under the Hudson River, plunging into the darkness.

CHAPTER 16

JUNIPER

I slam my fist into his face as he comes at me. His head snaps back and a spray of blood and spittle coats my gloved hand. He rolls with my punch and sends a vicious backhand toward the right side of my face, which I dodge under, pumping my other fist into his gut. He makes a sound like *Oommf* and then I dance backward into my corner of the ring before he can retaliate.

Hector is nearly a foot taller, with a much longer reach, but I'm quicker, so the hit-and-run guerilla warfare I'm putting him through has me at a controlled advantage. I like the look on his face. It says, *How did a little girl just do that to me?*

The Enforcer training room has always helped me escape my thoughts. When everything can be analyzed, everything *gets* analyzed, and at the end of it, it's just me and my carefully-arrived-at opinions and nothing more. Here it's just *hit* or *be hit*. My father says I push people away, that I'm more comfortable with ideas than with people. I think maybe Elijah believed this too but never said it. They're probably right. I've never exactly been a joiner. I think I'm seen as arrogant, maybe even elitist. Mostly because I give nothing—offer no targets. If you give people a way to hurt you, they will. Every time. Perhaps loneliness is an inevitable byproduct of a serious mind. But someone needs to be serious. *Right?*

I think of Daniel. Do I push *him* away? We're friends. At least, I think so. But does he want more? I feel like he might. ...*But do I?* What if I'm wrong about his feelings? That would be humiliating. Just thinking about it makes me shudder. The feeling doesn't last long, however, because Hector's fist suddenly cuts through my distracted guard, landing a punishing blow to my face. Stars blossom across my vision as I stumble backward. The ropes barely keep me from falling. I dodge his massive right hook by inches, which would have left me unconscious. He's not taking it easy on me, not pulling punches. *Good.* I'm thankful for his honest fighting. I need it. Need to feel something truthful right now. People are treating me different—smiling at me when they normally wouldn't, asking me how I am when I know they don't care. It's making me feel even more alone than normal, and that's a high bar. My chest heaves as I retreat to the opposite side of the ring.

I wipe blood from my nose with my glove and blink hard, trying to clear my tear-filled vision. He flies at me, quick, machine-gunning hooks and jabs, knowing he has to take advantage of my sudden weakness. I PULL HIS PUNCHES BACK AGAIN AND AGAIN, TIME SLIDING BACKWARD AROUND ME, AS I MEMORIZE HIS EVERY MOVE. But I don't take back my bloody nose. Trevor taught me that pain is the best way to remember mistakes. I release, then block Hector's fists as quickly as they come. No mistakes. Nothing gets through. *Just remember the pattern.* Hector, despite his powerful frame, is weaker in more fundamental areas. He hasn't figured out how to connect the mind and body as one instrument, one weapon. He fights with a brawny tenacity, but I only had to wind his moves back five times to memorize a winning pattern. *I wonder how he'd react if I gave him some pointers. Probably not well.*

This thought distracts me again, and one of his fists gets through, glancing off my ribcage and changing the algorithm I've memorized. Hector's arms are powerful, and the blow almost knocks the wind out of me, but I know I have to stay focused, because it's coming…

I hear the *whoosh* of the discharge. Without looking, I dodge Hector's uppercut, spin one hundred and eighty degrees and catch the thick, black, rubber sphere midair as it rockets toward my head—blasted out of one of the anticipation machines from ten yards away. It slaps against my palm and stings like hell, but my successful trapping of the ball makes up for the pain. Enforcers use the anticipation machines to add an extra layer of difficulty. The randomness of the machines reminds them to always keep their senses fully open while engaging an opponent. Tunnel focus can be lethal. The Faters very rarely fight man to man. They slink, relying on clandestine acts of terrorism. Explosives. Snipers. Even poisons. If they do ever use their hands, their victims are usually found stabbed from behind. *Cowards.* The thought of Elijah being ambushed by such vulgar methods sickens me.

Hector knifes out a leg sweep. I leap over it, twist in the air and level him with a spin kick to the side of the head. As he falls, I feel his mind instinctively reach out, trying to wind. The attempt is unfocused and surprisingly thin, and I easily brush it away. No wonder Hector agreed to spar with me; he must be struggling as an Enforcer. Perhaps he thought giving me a beating would boost his confidence, maybe give him some bragging rights. But despite his size, his ability feels anorexic and mostly impotent. He'll probably be sent into the police academy or be enlisted into the US military as a spy.

The gym goes silent except for the faint ringing and the light panting of Hector, who's lying on his back.

"Wow! Very impressive!" Two hands boom together in an enthusiastic clapping. I turn to see Trevor crossing the gym toward me, grinning. Hector's face goes white. He grabs his towel and disappears out of the ring, and then the training room, leaving me alone with Trevor. My senses could not have been more heightened, and yet I still didn't hear him enter the gym. Trevor's stealth, despite his bearish body, has always astounded me.

I don't really belong here. There's an unspoken rule that non-Enforcers shouldn't use the training rooms. But I've always thought that rule was absurd, and I'm not about to scuttle away like some frightened beetle, so I casually slide out of the ring. I equalize my breathing, doing my best to hide the dread I feel. My thin tank top clings to my sweat-soaked chest. I grab my towel and start patting my face and arms as he approaches. Trevor plucks a black rubber ball from the anticipation machine. He tosses it up and catches it, gives it a tight squeeze with his fist.

"If only *all* weapons were made of rubber, eh? The world would be a very different place. Wouldn't you say?" His tone is agreeable, but I know it's a lie. He's still seething from the Council meeting this morning. Trevor despises losing. But then, all at once, I see something strange; Trevor actually looks a little vulnerable as his gaze passes over me, his scaly eyes peppered (for a brief moment) with a kind of odd curiosity.

"I'm surprised to see you've kept up your training. You must be the only Seeker that ever comes in here." I search for the insult, but his voice sounds genuine. He sighs. "What an Enforcer you would've made. I'll be honest: I've always secretly hoped you'd have a *second* change of heart someday." He smiles and something twists inside of me. I feel drawn to his approval. Even now, after all these years. I'm disgusted with myself, but it's still true.

When I was six years old, just after my mother's death, my father seemed to disappear. He was there, but it was as if some vital part of him had been swallowed whole by grief. It was Trevor who filled the gap. He took me under his wing, and I trained with him for six years. He called me "powerful" and marveled at my quick mind and relentless work ethic. He said I would become a great Enforcer—someone to be respected and feared. He made me feel special and wanted at a time where I had never felt more lost. But in the end, it was all a lie. He never really saw me; he only saw what I could do.

Leaving Trevor was a slap in the face to him. Almost no one chosen for a Wing ever leaves on purpose. I know he's never forgiven me. Not that it matters, or that I want him to, or that I think he's even capable of thinking in such emotional terms.

I'm in danger. I know I am. My eyes flick to the exit.

"Be honest," Trevor says. "Do you not miss your Teacher's guiding hand from time to time? I will admit I've thought of you often."

He looks so sincere. *I have to think faster.* The awful truth is: I'd be lying if I didn't admit that I've felt the absence of him in my life—that sometimes, when I'm feeling most lost, there's a part of me that yearns for the simplicity of his world view. But I know that Trevor's sincerity is nothing more than him slowly wrapping his scaly coils around me. We haven't been this close and alone since the day I left. The fact that he thinks I might fall for his act is insulting. *I won't allow him to think that.*

"I'm exactly where I'm supposed to be," I say. "And if you

don't mind, I believe it's inappropriate for you to refer to yourself as my Teacher."

The smile in his eyes evaporates. Betrayal flashes, and suddenly I start to truly fear for my life. *No, he wouldn't dare.* Still, I feel trapped. Again, my eyes dart toward the exit. *Could he have one of his minions on guard outside the door? Maybe even his most lethal lieutenant, Gael Falcón?* Gael is spoken of with a certain hush in Thessaly. A powerful Winder with a reputation for being Trevor's favorite boogieman when more shadowy tactics are necessary. Few Enforcers have ever been more feared. And I wouldn't put it past Trevor for a second to have him waiting outside that door for me.

"My apologies, Juniper," he says, voice calm and collected. "Oh, and I quite agree: you're right where you're meant to be. From your performance today on the Council, it seems the fight has gone out of you."

"You know Elijah wouldn't want war."

"And look where he is now."

I feel heat rise inside me. I start to move past him, but Trevor puts a hand up.

"I don't mean that to disparage him. Elijah was a kind and brilliant man," he says. "I'd never wish for a tribe of men like me. We'd kill each other off in a week."

"You don't make it sound so bad," I say.

"Why such cruelty, Juniper?" Again, his hurt looks real, and it makes me want to scream.

"Whatever you're doing, Trevor, stop. I know you hate me. Don't play games."

"That's your fear talking. Truth be told, I *was* hurt when you left. Even cold-blooded creatures are capable of pain. But I don't hate you. On the contrary, I'd like you as an ally."

"You tried to block me from the Council."

"If I wanted to block you, you would not be sitting at that table."

Trevor sees my disbelief and chuckles. "Oh, Juniper, sometimes I forget how terribly sheltered you've been. Who do you think was responsible for your name being put forward in the first place? Dear ol' Dad?"

"That's ridiculous…" My voice sounds feebler than I'd like. "Your behavior at the ceremony—"

"I couldn't make it *too* obvious. I allowed someone else to endorse you, then I openly tried to strike down the idea, knowing full well that my enemies would fly to your aid. People are embarrassingly predictable, Juniper." His eyes pierce into mine, and all at once, the pride I had at feeling I'd earned my way onto the Council drains out of me. He sees the change on my face. "No, Juniper. I'm not saying I tricked the other Leaders into believing you have value. Your value is undeniable. You belong on the Council. But I know you. And you still have a lot to learn. You need guidance." And just like that, I know it's all true. My father would not have put my name forward. I don't know how I believed it was him. I feel stupid. But now I feel anger building as a realization forces its way to the surface of my mind:

"You left the note under my door."

Trevor smiles. "I thought you might want to know the truth."

"Bullshit," I say. *How could I have been so naïve? Did I really think I had some secret ally? An invisible friend? Pathetic.* Trevor has maneuvered me like a puppet. "You knew you had the votes to confirm me on the Council, and you wanted me foaming at the mouth with fury when I sat down at that table today—furious enough to help you start a war. But I let you down, didn't I?"

"You've seen the Council now. A bucket of spineless *bureaucrats*. Consumed with their empire-building. I wish you'd been there to see Elijah when we first found him in that chair. Those savages… He deserved better, Juniper. You and I may not agree on everything, but at least we can agree on that."

"You're not fooling me, Trevor. You used my pain over Elijah to try and push forward whatever dark agenda you'd like to see played out with the Faters. I won't help you. You say I need guidance, but I've been under your guidance before. Six years of unquestioned loyalty. And I still have nightmares from it. I don't miss you. If I could take back those years, I would. I was a sad little girl, and you tried to make me into a monster. I looked up to you so much. More than I ever should have. But you never really cared about me. So, stop pretending you do now."

Trevor searches my face. I try to remain unshakable.

"You really think I never cared," he says, his voice even. Then his expression becomes amused. "No, it's worse than that, isn't it? You actually think I *lack the ability* to care. Like I'm some kind of animal. That's not very open-minded of you, Juniper. What would Elijah say?"

"Don't say his name. You don't deserve to."

Trevor's face darkens. I know I'm being reckless; I can't help it. His tongue slowly slides across the bottom of his top teeth as he considers my righteous indignation.

"Did I ever tell you how I came to discover my ability, Juniper?"

I don't answer, so he continues. "My powers emerged in the winter of 1964, when I was nine years old, during a brutally long February that felt like a year, the winter I kept a box of dead baby rabbits under my bed. See, I spent the first nine glorious years of my life in a home for shipwrecked boys in the South Bronx. That's right, I'm a local boy. The woman who ran the home was a harsh, pitiless woman. These were desperate days in our little corner of the five boroughs, and truth be told, we were just as merciless to her.

"I stumbled upon the helpless little litter in the park. The mama rabbit was gone. Probably victim to a fox, or maybe even one of the growing hordes of emaciated stray dogs that haunted my neighborhood after the pound closed down due to budget cuts.

"I spent every waking hour curled up on my bunk, holding the shivering little creatures. I'd look down at their helpless faces and see how much they needed me, how lost they were in the world, how much they *loved* me. I'd never felt such a feeling of euphoria. Of *purpose*. I fed them torn-up pieces of lettuce and cheese and milk I'd managed to squirrel away at breakfast. And when I couldn't find any way to feed them the milk, I took tiny sips and acted the part of the mother bird, drooling the nutrients into their miniscule mouths.

"When the first rabbit died, I sobbed. Then I vomited. *So unfair,* I thought, shaking with anger. I sat in the corner all night, knees to my chest, staring at the cardboard box, listening to the tiny scratching sounds coming from within, until I felt I'd grown numb to it. And eventually the box fell silent.

"None of the kids living in the children's home ever said a word about my pets. I was smaller than most of them, but they feared me all the same. It was the stink that gave me away.

"The rotten bunny bodies were eventually found, and I was promptly shuttled off to a place that made our little group home look like a summer resort—a state-run facility touchingly referred to in social-work circles as the Zoo. It wasn't that every child that came there was bad, but the Zoo had a way of curing kids of kindness.

"I think I could've dealt with the violence and stress that seemed to almost seep out of the walls there, if it weren't for one person in particular: Ricky Betkis. My bunkmate. The kids called him Dicky Buttkiss. Isn't that mean? Turns out, Ricky didn't mind at all, however, because Ricky was retarded. And this simple-minded mongoloid made the mistake of announcing to every kid at the Zoo, on my first day, that Santa had answered his prayers and given him a brother. As you can imagine, my fellow animals at the Zoo turned on me like hyenas. I was chased, and hit, and spat at, and pissed on, all because I was the *brother of the retard*.

"You must be asking yourself: Did I go after my tormentors, slit their throats in the night, bash their brains in with a hammer while they slept? No, I did not. Because I've always had an innate sense of my place in the food chain. The predators didn't deserve to be punished. I've always respected fear, Juniper. No, not them. Never them.

"The funny thing is, if you'd asked me on that frozen February morning if I was planning to kill Ricky, I probably would've laughed and said, 'That sounds like a pretty damn good idea.' Because up until the very last moment, I honestly remained ignorant to my own intentions—as if part of me was afraid that if the thought was let into the light, I might not have the stones to go through with it.

"In my own mind, despite how far-fetched it sounds now, I believed I was doing the spastic imbecile a kindness when I invited Ricky to sail paper boats with me down at the icy, broken edge of the East River. And let me tell you, Juniper, Ricky was ecstatic. On that early winter morning, my cow-eyed, masturbating bunkmate was about as close to pure joy as I'd ever seen him.

"Confusion. Deep confusion was what I remember the most about Ricky's face as he felt the violent shove from his *brother*. There was also terror in his expression, but I think that he was mostly terrified that he was going to land on the paper boat he had just placed into the freezing water, and that all of his imaginary sailors were going to drown. I wish I could say he flailed around a lot—that I could remember the specific glugging sounds he made—but unfortunately, Ricky couldn't swim. So, he just sank like a stone.

"Then there was nothing. Darkness. Deadness. Ricky was gone. And I started to cry—a big cry—the ugly kind. And in my despair, I yanked with all my will at the injustice that you could only kill a kid like Ricky Betkis once. And to my terrified amazement, time slipped in reverse, and before I knew it, Ricky was standing on the shore next to me, grinning like a fool—dry paper boat in his hand.

"I was so stunned by the bizarre wish-fulfillment, I just stared at Ricky. I think I actually remember smiling. He went down just as fast the second time. And once again, I pulled with my mind, fully conscious of what I was asking of time. And when Ricky Betkis popped back out of the water like a well-trained porpoise, I knew I was addicted.

"That first day, I wound back Ricky's death so many times, I passed out on the ice and almost froze to death. And that was where Victor Mason found me. He said he'd heard my powers— that he was just like me. I told him I'd gotten lost and that I was desperately trying to retrace my steps when these strange abilities emerged. I remember feeling proud of my quick thinking. I was never blamed for Ricky's disappearance. Even after the body was discovered six weeks later. It was simply written off as a tragic accident, the hapless wandering of a mentally challenged orphan. I was also not blamed, because that was the last time anyone from the Zoo ever saw me."

Trevor smiles at me. "I haven't told that story to a single living soul until this moment. It actually felt good. Thank you, Juniper."

Sweat itches my scalp, pooling at my lower back. My stomach feels like a spinning dryer with a broken bottle tossed inside.

"…*Why would you tell me that?*" My words are barely audible.

"You were doubting my ability to care—to *feel*. I didn't want you to think of me like that. I loved those rabbits. And I hated Ricky. Love and hate are two sides of the same coin, are they not? But I'll always be grateful to Ricky. Without him, who knows where I'd be."

"You're sick," I say before I can stop myself.

"Why?"

"You're a murderer." My mouth is outpacing my mind. *I need to get control.*

"For a scientist, Juniper, you have an extremely small grasp on the concept of *species*. Do people call a hunter shooting ducks a murderer? Is a man who kills a cockroach thrown in prison? Is the woman who puts her poor old cat to sleep because she decides she can't afford its cancer treatment protested in the streets? No, my dear. Prizes. Pests. Pets. That's what a difference in species means." Trevor grows more agitated as he speaks. "Have you forgotten the second rule of the Code? Somehow, I doubt that. It does, however, seem you've forgotten that those beasts tortured and killed the man who held your hand and told you the world is a soft, beautiful place. The Faters slaughtered him, Juniper. As they've slaughtered so many of our kind. They'd kill us all, and you want to spare them? You little fool. If you sleep with rats and rats eat your eyes, do not cry out that you are blind, because you were blind before you laid down with vermin."

White foam has collected at the corners of his mouth. I have to get away from him. I don't care if his words are true; I don't care if we are the superior species. Right now, I feel dirty and revolted, and in desperate need of a shower. But I know the only way out is through. I am now, theoretically, his equal, at least as far as the Code is concerned. *I can use that.*

"Trevor, I'm aware that you and I, as members of the Council—"

"You are aware of nothing, girl. Let me ask you something: if the Code says it is right that I dominate normal men because they're weaker than me, what's to say that I don't have every right to do the same to the weak among us?"

"I am not weak," I say, fists clenched, daring him to disagree.

"No. You're not. But there are weak spots on the Council. Aren't there? And since you've decided to fill your chair so robustly, perhaps I need to find another vacancy." My breath catches in my throat. He's talking about my father. Very few know of my father's vices, but he and Trevor came up the ranks together and were actually once quite close. So, Trevor is well aware of my father's potential for self-destruction. He continues: "In two days, at the next Council meeting, I will call for a vote. If you fall on the wrong side of that vote, do not hold me responsible for the consequences."

"You just threatened a member of the Leadership Council."

Trevor stares at me evenly. "Do you remember our favorite game, Juniper? Now, focus…"

Trevor looks amused. Then he slaps me across the face. Hard. The vicious *crack* echoes through the high-ceilinged chamber. It happens so fast, it almost doesn't register as real to me, except for the dull, throbbing sting beginning to emanate from the left side of my face. I turn back to him, my eyes now filled with knee-jerk tears at the unexpected violence.

I flex my mind. He raises a hand in a hushing gesture. Rage pulsates on my face. I pull harder, but it's no use. *He's too strong.* I release and gasp a quick intake of breath. All traces of faux friend-liness have vanished from Trevor's face.

"This is not a game, little girl. You will not be coddled. Some advice from your old Teacher: there are wheels spinning in this grown-up world that are not for children's hands. Put your little fingers in the wrong place and you will lose them. Be warned."

He starts to leave, then he stops and turns back, smiling again.

"Oh…and feel free to run to Daddy. But as you open your spoiled little mouth, remember how few friends you really have left, and why your jaw *still* aches, and how powerless you were against the pain." He stares at me for another beat. "Have a wonderful evening, Juniper. Happy training." He turns and stalks out of the room.

CHAPTER 17

CHARLIE

Holy shit, it stinks. Even at night, without the heat of the day boiling the pavement, the swampy stench of leaky trash bags clouds the air outside Goldstone's Pub. On the left of the building, about six feet off the sidewalk, is a nondescript, numberless doorway. I check the grimy callbox and see that every floor's buzzer has been destroyed—except one. I inhale slowly, then, with my quick exhale I press the buzzer.

Nothing. No alert, no doorbell, or any kind of buzz. I go to press it again when I hear a tiny electronic *whrrrr* above my head. I look up and see a miniature, high-tech surveillance camera twisting to aim at me. From a hidden speaker, a garbled, high-pitched voice blurts out…

"Whooo are youuu?" The voice sounds like an old, creepy butler to a Chinese gangster in a kung fu movie. I picture him having eyebrows down to his knees.

"Um…Charlie."

"What do you want, little Charlie?"

"…Uh… I'm looking for a man…"

"Ooooh, you here for a little sucky sucky?"

"What? NO! Sorry…I must have the wrong place…" As I turn, *pealing laughter* erupts from the speaker. Someone's having the time of their life at my expense. The door buzzes and unlocks. *I don't like this.*

The hallways on each floor are sealed off with rotted boards and caution tape. Only the stairs are open. On the fourth floor, I see a door. It's been left ajar. I try my absolute hardest to feel the aura or vibes from whatever mortal danger lurks behind it. I push the door. I'm surprised by how heavy it is: thick iron, almost like the door to a safe.

As I cross the threshold, I switch my duffle to my left hand, clenching my right fist, preparing to fight my way out if need be. I make my way into a dark, cavernous loft apartment. The loft is like a physicalized Trent Reznor song. A humongous, purple velvet couch with a thick stainless-steel frame sits like a gaudy throne on the far side of the space. High-end electronics permeate the room. A massive TV has hardcore porn streaming off a filthy laptop, which sits on a cracked, green-glass coffee table cluttered with clothes and drug paraphernalia.

Above the door I just entered I see a monitor showing the entrance alcove downstairs on the street. To my left is a surveillance station made up of a desk, a rolling chair and three desktop computers with various screens showing downstairs, inside the loft, a garage, and several other anonymous rooms. I wave my hand and see myself on one of the screens. Above my head, a huge, gothic chandelier hangs from the ceiling. It feels so out of place and yet in some depraved, ostentatious way, it's the cherry on top.

"What the hell…" I say out loud, to myself.

I hear a distinct ringing sound, like feedback. I've heard this sound before.

"Never judge another man's batcave!" The voice comes from above me. I look up and see Aeman sitting with his legs dangling down from a four-foot-wide hole in the ceiling. He's grinning down at me. Grabbing the edge of the exposed wooden beam in the ceiling, he swings himself down through the hole, landing in front of me.

"…Kind of a fixer-upper, huh?" I try hard to sound nonchalant.

"Nah. I put that hole there. Easier than taking the stairs."

Aeman is staring at me, taking me in. *Can he tell that I'm slowly coming apart at the seams as I stand here?* "CHARLIE?!" Aeman yells in my face, clapping his hands together for emphasis and succeeding in scaring the living shit out of me.

"What?!"

"Just making sure you're with me. I'm Aeman. You're Charlie. Charlie and Aeman are going to be friends."

Aeman reaches out his hand. I awkwardly shake it. "…I'm Charlie."

"Totally already got that."

"Do you hear that ringing sound?" I ask.

"You can always hear if someone winds near you. It's kinda like an aftershock."

"*Winds*? So, you…"

"Yeah. I didn't like my entry line. I said something like *Welcome to the jungle*; you looked at me like I was retarded, so I tried again."

"I didn't feel any kind of—"

"You wouldn't. Your life is one linear event. I just hit rewind for a few seconds, then started again. If we're not touching, you're not gonna know. Except for the ringing."

I'm reeling. I can't seem to put my mind on straight. I watched this man kill someone. I came here looking for answers, but already I feel like I'm being pulled underwater by a thousand grey, faceless hands. I want to run.

"Man, you're totally freaking out right now. You need to calm down. Seriously. Everything's gonna be fine. Better than fine. Better than you can possibly imagine." Aeman heads for the door. "Drop your bag and bring a jacket," he says over his shoulder.

"…Why?" I say, barely able to get the words out.

Aeman stops at the doorway and looks back.

"Um…because it's cold outside." He shoots me a Cheshire grin, then walks out the heavy metal doorway

I'm not going anywhere with that guy.

No.

Nope.

Hell, no!

…Absolutely not, Charlie…

I drop my bag, unzip it, pull out my green fatigue jacket and follow him out the door.

CHAPTER 18

JUNIPER

I hear the moans before I see my father's face. Jeffrey was not on guard, and the front door was left unlocked, which means only one thing: it was left unlocked for *someone*. I walk into the living room of my father's dimly lit, elegant apartment to find him spread across his magenta chaise lounge while two half-naked women, barely older than myself, crawl on top of him. Bile catches in my throat. My father is still fully clothed, thank God. I avert my eyes. But this is beyond important, so I force myself to look back. The giggling coming from one of the girls might be the worst part.

"Father."

The giggling cuts off. My father and both girls look up at me. I see his momentary embarrassment, then I see him rally and decide he won't be made to feel like a fool.

"Yes, my love?" he says, looking directly at me. The overconfidence in his stare tells me he's actually quite intoxicated—probably not just by alcohol. One of the girls continues to stroke his chest, which boils my already-hot blood. She only knows that he is now Prime, and power only moves in one direction.

"I need to talk to you," I say, keeping my voice under control.

"I'm sure it can wait until tomorrow...don't you think?" He whispers something in the ear of one of the girls, who laughs in drunken glee, then reaches for a champagne bottle.

The sadness hits me harder than I expect. I turn and stride toward the front door. As I reach the doorway, I stop, yank open a drawer in the wooden sideboard next to the entrance and pull out my father's gun. The gun is nearly identical to the one I received upon becoming a Leader. At the ceremony we receive three gifts: a dress uniform, a watch and a gun. My gun is white with a pearl handle and is currently sitting inside my nightstand. My father's gun is silver with a sapphire-jeweled handle. He's always kept it here in this drawer. I don't think he's ever removed it. I stride back into the room and aim the weapon from one nymphet to the other. The girls sober instantly.

"Leave. Now." They quickly collect their discarded clothing and exit, avoiding eye contact the whole way. I watch them go. When I turn back, my father's eyes are closed. But I can tell he's not asleep, because the muscles in his jaw are clenching and unclenching, as if he were chewing his own tangled thoughts.

"Father—"

"Did you come here to humiliate me, Juniper?"

"No."

"Please go away. It's not a good night for a chat."

"I need to talk to you about Trevor. He came to see me tonight—"

"What in the hell were you thinking?! Do you think what you did in the Council room today was wise? Because it wasn't. It was very, very foolish."

"Maya Steele asked my opinion."

"Oh, please, you're smarter than that. She called on you because she thought it would help her cause. If you don't know the game, Juniper, then stay silent."

"I'm trying to earn my place!"

"AND I'M TRYING TO KEEP YOU SAFE!"

He has not raised his voice to me for as long as I can remember. It stuns me. It seems to shock him as well, because he turns away and walks back toward the couch. He fishes a little brown tube out of his pocket, unscrews the top, plugs the opening with his forefinger then turns it upside down. When he turns it back upright, the tip of his finger is coated in clear liquid. He quickly sucks his finger dry, then screws the cap on and shoves it back into his pocket.

"What was that?" I ask. I know it was a drug, but I can't believe he would take it right in front of me like that. He's never been that flagrant, but tonight seems to be a night for firsts.

"But maybe I'm the foolish one," he says. "Thinking I could ever protect you."

I hate self-pity. It's ugly and unproductive. And it's the opposite of him trying to protect me. It's him trying to numb himself to the wound before it happens. And it pisses me off. *How can such a powerful man be so weak?* "I don't have time for this right now. Listen to me. Trevor came to me tonight—" He suddenly spins around and grabs me hard. It scares me. I freeze. He tries to look me in the face, but his eyes are already beginning to roll back in his head. *What the hell did he take?* "...No...no, don't talk to him, Junebug. ...Just stay away...He can't hurt you... He won't..." His grip on my arms slackens, then he stumbles to the side and almost falls. I grasp onto him, holding him up. It's not easy; he's much heavier than me. I dig into his pocket and yank out the little brown tube. He doesn't try and stop me; he doesn't even notice. The label reads FENTANYL. *Oh, God. That's why it took effect so fast.* Liquid fentanyl. A brutally powerful opioid. I feel my entire face heat up with rage.

He pushes away from me and staggers across the chamber. "Just...don't look at her, Trevor... YOU'RE NOT ALLOWED!" The force in his words surprises me. He trips and his hand slaps against the door to his bedroom. It smashes open, crashing against the wall inside. I follow him in. He's far beyond me being able to talk to him tonight, but I need to make sure he falls asleep on his side. The last thing I need right now is to find my father dead in the morning, having choked to death on his own vomit.

But he doesn't aim toward his bed. Instead, he heads for the bathroom. I guess the vomiting is ahead of schedule. At least he might be more clear-headed afterwards. It'll be easier to get him into bed. He doesn't make it, though. He stumbles and falls face-first onto the tiled bathroom floor. I rush to him, slipping my arms under his heavy chest. An intense feeling of revulsion hits me. *How many times have you let us find you like this? You held us all in your hands and let us slip away one by one. I won't sympathize with your surrender. Not tonight. Not when I need you to be my father so badly.*

His body starts to shake, which frightens me. He hit his head;

he could be having a seizure. But as I turn him over onto my lap, I realize he's *laughing*. The skin above his right eye has split open and blood is leaking down his face. "Just like the bottle!" he cries. "My face broke like a bottle!" The blood makes his manic laughter look even more insane. But then his face twists up in fury. "It's not just a minute! It's forever!" he bellows, thick-tongued and frantic. *"It's forever, God damn you, Trevor!"*

My father looks up at me, and suddenly, all his fury seems to melt away. His eyes fill with tears as he reaches up and strokes my cheek. I can't help but relish the rare moment of affection. His voice is almost a whisper: "…I knew who he was…*what* he was…. I'm so sorry, Arabel." My skin goes cold. I feel sick. In his twisted, drug-induced state, he actually believes I'm his Arabel here holding him. His dead wife. My mother. *What the fuck does my mother have to do with Trevor?*

My father first met Trevor when they were in their twenties and both fervent disciples of Victor Mason. It was a more innocent time in our Chapter, a time when taking a human lover or spouse was not frowned upon—so long as the Code was not violated. Such relationships rarely ended well, however, and were eventually discouraged. You might end up with a human child that you could never be fully honest with—not to mention a marriage filled with lies and deception. But it was an exciting time nonetheless. The new global collective power of the Leadership meant an influx of unprecedented wealth and opportunity, and Trevor and my father were rising stars in one of the most powerful Chapters.

"He said you were beautiful…" My father's voice sounds haunted. My mother *was* beautiful. Young, with perfect skin, red hair and bright green eyes. But I find this part of my father's slurred confession hard to believe, because Trevor hates humans. Loathes them. On more than one occasion, I've heard him call love between humans and Winders *bestiality*. My father fights for his words. "…I shouldn't have… I was just so…*surprised*. He never came to the lower levels…" He trails off, slipping toward unconsciousness.

I shake him. "Wake up. What did Trevor do? Tell me."

His eyes reopen. I've never seen him look so sad. "Do you

hate me? …You *should*. …It was my fault… I LET HIM IN!" He smashes his fist against the hard tile.

"Why was Trevor there?"

"The treaty…" His eyes implore me to understand him, to empathize: "…with the Mexican Chapter. He was angry… *'Let those little brown bastards in the door, and they'll never leave,'* he said. His teeth were red… The *wine*…made him look like a fucking vampire…" Tears drown my father's eyes—two quivering pools. "No more," he says, and covers his face with his hands. But I can't stop. Not now. I *need* to know.

I lean in close and whisper, "We were drinking. What happened next? I can't remember." The act of impersonating my mother takes something from me. I feel a tiny sacred place inside me begin to burn to ash. *I hope it's worth it.*

"…We were drunk," he slurs. "You joined us for a nightcap… You looked so beautiful… I felt so lucky. But both bottles were dry, so I went for more…"

"Yes. I remember now. What happened then?"

"…You two were laughing when I left. And I remember thinking…perhaps I'd misjudged Trevor in some way—" He stops mid-sentence. His chest rises and falls several times. I think maybe he's fallen asleep, but then I see his lower lip quivering. It looks childish, pathetic. He speaks with his eyes closed—his voice is so quiet. "You were still laughing when I returned…*smiling*. But the bottle slipped from my hand…" My father's eyes go wide with terror. Adrenaline seems to momentarily focus his thoughts. "It was so loud. The *ringing!* A long wind—at least a *minute*. He'd done something. Something he didn't want me to see. Said he'd botched a joke…tried to get it right. But it wasn't multiples. It was *one* wind. God damn it, I know the difference. But I couldn't prove… You smiled at me as I cleaned up the broken bottle, and I pushed my hands into the glass. *Needed to hurt.* Because all the halls of hell could be filled with the horrors possible in just one minute of time. …I would have used one of those dripping shards of glass to cut my own throat, if it hadn't meant leaving you alone with him."

He finally goes quiet. I hold him until he loses consciousness.

My body trembles. *Trevor. How can one man need to devour another man so completely? What did you see in my father that made you so greedy? Happiness? You took everything from him.* Trevor says he'll make room on the Council if I don't fall in line. He said there are weak spots. And I agree: my father is weak. I want to hate him for it, but I can't. I feel too sorry for him. But I also don't believe that if I simply comply with Trevor's terms, my father will be safe. Cameron Trask holds the only place of power within Thessaly that Trevor has yet to claim for his own. Prime.

I need help.

CHAPTER 19

CHARLIE

A eman struts across the center of Union Square. Young people swarm the park: skaters daredeviling down steps, gutterpunks dividing up the day's swag, Asian kids performing some kind of in-sync dance practice, and girls, lots of girls, city girls—the kind that smoke and say they've been trying to quit for years. A twenty-first-century Norman Rockwell would have a field day as long as he avoided the two wackjobs burning their way across the sprawl, talking about being supernatural beings. Aeman speaks as fast as he moves. I grapple to keep up on all fronts.

"Have you ever wondered how some people are just winners? Luck is just seriously on their side? There's a reason a fat slob like Babe Ruth was able to point to the lights and send his ball smashing in that exact direction *every* time. Cuz he was able to do it over and over till he got it right! Bet he *wound* that shit thirty times, but the audience only saw it once, and the rest is history. No one knows where we began. But I guarantee you, there was some Winder caveman taking down woolly mammoths by the truckload with like a cave full of hot wives. We've always been part of the elite. Humans always wanna be ruled by the miraculous." Something about the way he says *humans* sends a chill up my spine, as if he and I don't belong to this category.

"I'm talkin' Caesar, Hannibal, Alexander the Great, fucking Lincoln! I'm talking David hitting Goliath with that sling, Napoleon knowing which way his enemies would attack from, Genghis Khan never losing in hand-to-hand combat. I heard JFK wound back like twenty-five times in his last debate against Nixon for the presidency. I can think of a better moment for him to repeat."

"What? Maybe not go with a convertible?" *I'm making jokes. Great.*

Aeman sniffs a laugh. "Yeah, that too. But I was thinking more like tapping ol' Marilyn. I would've given that more than a few goes."

"Wait. Wouldn't they have been touching, so…"

"Only Winders can do it. If it's not a Winder, doesn't matter who you're touching. Or *how* you're touching them," Aeman says with a sly smile. "Anyway, those are big uses of our powers, but below that are a thousand different amazing little indulgences that make life just a whole lotta fun." With that, Aeman shoves a middle-aged, spectacled man, wearing a massive Yankees scarf, backwards over a metal trashcan. The man tumbles ass over face, his glasses catapulting away from him as his scarf octopuses around his startled face. He lands with a terrific *thud*. He jumps up, screaming vitriol at Aeman, who grabs my arm, still laughing.

AND EVERYTHING WINDS BACK. THE MAN RUNS BACKWARD AWAY FROM US, THEN SEEMS TO DO A FRONT FLIP OVER THE TRASHCAN AS HIS GLASSES ARC THROUGH THE AIR, SNAPPING BACK ONTO HIS FACE JUST AS HE PLANTS HIS FLAWLESS GYMNASTIC MANEUVER. AND AEMAN AND I SKIP BACKWARD ABOUT TEN FEET IN OUR STRIDE.

Then the world moves forward again.

Without skipping a beat, Aeman says, "No impulse is off limits, cuz it's just like erasing a whiteboard. Not that I've ever erased a whiteboard. What the hell would I need a whiteboard for? And the best part is, you only have to deal with the consequences if you *want* to…"

As we re-approach the Yankees fan, Aeman shoves the guy *again*. And again he goes tumbling; glasses rocketing away, and like clockwork, the man rages back up at Aeman, his angry tirade identical to its predecessor. Aeman pulls me along. I look back, apologetically, and the furious man flips me off.

We plunge down the stairs into the subway station, walking swiftly toward the downtown 6 train platform.

"So…we can just *wind* back forever?" I ask.

"Nope. It's just a little burst. The longest wind we know of was a little under two minutes. A hundred and seventeen seconds, if you wanna get all nerd-precise on it. I like to wear a watch. Let's me know how much time has elapsed." Aeman flashes me his shitty Casio wristwatch.

"Cuz once too much time passes, then it's history. Set in stone. The stronger and more experienced you get, the further back you can wind. But it definitely takes a toll. Every time you wind, you get physically weaker. So, you gotta moderate how much energy you use. Early on, a big wind will just knock your ass out, but as you get stronger and learn more control, you actually have a greater chance of *winding out* with a crazy big wind."

"What happens if you 'wind out'?"

"Dead. But don't worry; it's close to impossible to do it by accident. And new Winders are like baby rattlesnakes. You use almost all your power up at once, then pass the hell out. That's how I found you. Went off like a goddam lighthouse. Coulda heard you ringing for miles. First time I was ever happy I was in Jersey. Crap! Come on!"

Aeman takes off running. Up ahead, the subway has arrived. I hear the *ding* indicating the doors are closing. I race after him, but just as we reach the platform, the train pulls away.

"Dammit!" Aeman turns back to me. "A'right. Bring it back."

"What?"

"Wind it back. We're getting on that train."

"But…I don't really know how."

"It's easy. It's like jumping. It kinda feels the same. A quick build and release. Find that part of your mind. It's really just another muscle. Gotta build that muscle memory. Up until now, you've probably only wound when you got all blubbery and emotional. That kind of winding is like when the doctor smacks your knee. Reflex. This'll be different. Go ahead and try."

"But I really don't—"

"Better hurry. Ain't got much time before we're gonna be stuck waiting for the next train. And that's not how we roll. Give it a go."

I search my mind, trying to remember how it felt when I did it at the party. It's so hard to remember anything from yesterday night. God, I can't believe it's only been a day. It feels like a million years have passed since—Crap, time's ticking by. I've got to at least try. *Why did I drink so much last night? If I hadn't...* I push into my mind, thinking about the train moving backward. Willing it to return to the station. Nothing. As I try again, Aeman puts his hand on my arm. He laughs.

"You look like you're gonna poop your pants. You're going the wrong way. It's not a pushing. It's more the opposite."

The second the concept hits my brain, I feel it. I get an image in my head of stepping up to an infinitely tall wall, and on the wall are two handles. I wrap my hands around the handles, and when I pull at the monolith, the edgeless wall *moves.* It doesn't make sense, but it moves. There's a tingling in my body, a drawing-in, as if, for a brief second, there's no real difference between me and the wall. I give it a yank, and suddenly...

TIME STARTS TO SPIN BACKWARD RAPIDLY. AS WE'RE PULLED IN REVERSE, I SEE THE TRAIN ENTER THE STATION AND THEN WE DISAPPEAR AROUND THE CORNER. I TURN AND GLANCE AT AEMAN AND HE WINKS AT ME. AND I RELEASE US!

Time moves forward and I bend over, feeling like I just got off a bad, spinny carnival ride. I barely have a second to breathe before Aeman is tugging me toward the train. We barely make it inside and flop down onto the bench. "Attaboy," Aeman says. "Used too much energy, but hell of a first go. I thought for sure we were gonna be shipwrecked on that platform. I'm actually pretty... I mean that was impressive."

"You didn't think I was gonna be able to do it?"

"Hell no. Most Winders take weeks, sometimes months, to do what you just did in a few seconds. Who were your parents?"

"So, we could just walk into a casino right now and do really well, huh?" Not the most graceful changing of the subject, but my reality is fractured enough without going *there.*

"In theory, yeah. But most casinos at this point are owned and operated by Winders, so we would be not-so-gently removed at breakneck speed."

"How many Winders are there?"

"Hard to tell. But not as hard as it used to be. Rogue Winders aren't really allowed anymore. It's against the Code."

"What's the Code?"

"A set of laws created by the Leadership."

"What's the Leadershi—"

"Can you spot the Winder on this train?"

My eyes dart around. All other thoughts vanish. The idea of seeing another Winder thrills me, but it also strangely terrifies me. As if seeing another Winder would cause this crazy carnival world to ossify around me, and all thought of escape would crumble away. But I see nothing. Everyone looks normal. As normal as any random group of people riding the subway can be. A mishmash of age and status. Aeman sees my skepticism. He smiles and gives a little nod.

"Oh, there's one, all right."

I look again. Old. Young. Fat. Skinny. I truly have no idea.

"Probably not this guy," I say, indicating the drunk, homeless man passed out next to me. A long line of drool falls, connecting his mouth to his jacket.

"No chance," Aeman says.

I subtly point to a man in a nice suit, sitting across from us. Aeman touches my arm…

HE WINDS BACK ABOUT TWENTY SECONDS. THE DROOL SLIPS BACK INTO THE HOMELESS MAN'S MOUTH.

Then time moves forward. There is a distinct *ringing* in the air.

Diagonally from us, a very stylish, Asian-American woman in a grey skirt suit, wearing fancy gold jewelry, looks up from the novel she's reading. Aeman gives her a little wave. She stares at him, then she glances over at me. I give her a little awkward *What's up?* nod. She returns to her book. An electricity surges through my body from the acknowledgement from this total stranger. *I need to know everything.*

"What if two Winders wind at the same time? Like one here and one in China?"

"I asked that same exact question once. Great minds, kiddo. Turns out it's nearly impossible for two winds to spontaneously happen at the exact same time. This shit happens on like an atomic level, and there's not that many Winders on the planet."

"How many?"

"Thousands, maybe tens of thousands—maybe even a hundred thousand, for all I know. Though for sure some backwards-ass smaller Chapter is pumpin' out babies, overtime, to get their Winder population up, right? I don't focus on shit like that. My point is: the odds are insanely low. And as far as China goes, if a dude spilled his won ton soup in Beijing and tried to wind it back just as you were setting a new record for amount of times you could beat off in under a minute, whichever one of you was a fraction of a second ahead of the other would go first, then the other would follow, and neither of you would have any idea the other was even alive. You won't know if anyone's winding unless you're close enough to hear it. Or feel it."

"What do you mean feel—"

"Baby steps, my young friend," Aeman says. "All in good time. First, we have some fun."

The high-end, exclusive loft party we walk into feels a million years away from the college party from the night before. Aeman leads me through people talking and laughing on all sides. Above everyone, perched in cages, are nude women and men painted in shards of sparkling, mirrored silver. *This party's version of disco balls, I guess.* I try not to look but find it nearly impossible. People dance in all directions. There's a thin, limo-sized bar cutting through the main area. It looks more like a UFO than an opulent watering hole. The party lighting is low and the vibe is dangerous and erotic. I pass by a young woman, maybe a year older than me, standing on a ceramic block, dressed in shredded vinyl, leaving very little of her incredible body to the imagination. She dances in place, tasseled boots and eyes like dead lamps. I look away, feeling grossly complicit. The light swells of ringing emanate from all directions.

"There are other Winders here," I say.

Aeman smiles wide. "Yes, there are. A playground for the fortunate masters."

"Everyone?"

"Nope. Can't be a master without things to play with, right?"

I look around. So many attractive people... But not all. For every ten of the beauty pageant people, there might be one *normal*—one heavy or ill-shaped man or woman who is staring wolf-like at the rest. And all at once I realize that it's the Winders who are the "normals." It's not the beautiful people. The Winders have surrounded themselves with pretty things. I guess it's just like any other party for the rich and powerful, but something about it definitely feels more sinister. Because here, the *playthings* have no idea what they're up against.

Aeman moves to an ornate table filled with every kind of eye-popping dessert imaginable. Without even taking a moment to differentiate good from great, he begins gorging himself on delicate milk chocolates, still-steaming tarts, fancy French donuts, éclairs, multicolored macarons and meringues, little cups of cobbler, and some kind of fudgy burnt flan. With his mouth grotesquely full, he offers me a slice of whiskey-soaked angel food cake. I decline, feeling like I've somehow stumbled onto Pinocchio's Pleasure Island and that any second, everyone around me will start sprouting fur and tails as they mutate into braying donkeys. Aeman shrugs, then pushes the whole piece of cake into his mouth, chewing heartily. He swallows, puts a hand on my shoulder, leaning on me for support. Then a broad grin swells on his face. *What's so funny?*

TIME RIPS BACKWARD. THE MYRIAD OF DESSERTS COME POURING OUT OF AEMAN'S MOUTH IN A FLOOD. CHOCOLATES, DONUTS, MACARONS SEEMINGLY VOMIT INTO HIS HANDS. THEN THEY GET GENTLY PLACED BACK ONTO THE DISPLAY TABLE AS AEMAN'S GLUTTONY IS ERASED PIECE BY PIECE, UNTIL...

Time moves forward again.

I cannot hide my profound disgust. Aeman sees my repulsed face and dies laughing.

"What was the point of that?"

"I'm watching my delicate figure. But I still got to taste it all." Then Aeman spots someone in the crowd. I follow his gaze to see a stunning older woman with dyed white-blonde hair and the curvy, staggering body of an old-timey supermodel as she glides through the crowd. Aeman lights up when he sees her, but just before his showy delight fully unfolds on his face, I see a split second of something else. If I hadn't been looking directly at him, I would've missed it, but it was his reaction that threw my attention to the woman, and in that briefest of moments, I saw fear on Aeman's face.

"Virginia, my God, I don't think you could possibly look better."

"I suppose I get to choose how to take that, Aeman," Virginia says in a gentle, cooing Southern drawl. "And if I choose poorly, you will not enjoy the rest of the night. Regardless of who your daddy is."

Aeman fights to not look intimidated, while the woman, "Virginia," seems to be restraining herself from going further. I don't understand the hidden dynamics being played out here, but I assume I'll get an earful the second she's gone.

"Who's this handsome young ruffian? An offering?" She eyes me greedily.

"Only if you're a good girl," Aeman says, then laughs at his own joke.

I'm trying hard not to look appalled at being called an offering. And all at once, I feel like I might have to fight my way out of here, as if I've mistakenly traipsed into a den of vampires without realizing I'm covered in blood. But then Virginia's gaze leaves me and never returns.

"I need a meeting with him." Aeman tries to sound confident, but for whatever reason, his statement comes out stilted and smacking of desperation.

"That's obviously not happening," she says, her syrupy tone heavy with power.

"It will, if you ask."

"Probably. But I have no intention of doing such a thing. Hmm. Too bad."

Aeman stares at her unwavering, fake smile.

"Enjoy the rest of the party, Aeman." She moves to walk past him, but when they're almost eye to eye, she stops. "I heard the truth about how you looked after my boy. And if it was up to me…" Virginia leans in close to Aeman's ear and whispers something I can't hear. Aeman's jaw clenches and his left eye gives an involuntary twitch. He swallows hard. His face is smiling, but his eyes are not. Then she walks past him, disappearing into the throbbing horde.

Aeman turns back to me, his previous playfulness diminished. He waves at the rest of the enigmatic party. "Explore! Mingle!" Then he gets very serious. "But no winding. Not here. Do you understand?" I confirm with a nod. I have no idea why I shouldn't, or why he's worried, or why he imagines I would even think of winding in this place. I'm already ready for this night to be over. The last thing I'm going to do is try and prolong it even a second longer. I want an explanation for Aeman's opaque conversation with Virginia, but he's already following after her. No one is looking at me, yet I feel like I'm standing on a stage under a spotlight. I head for the bar, order a beer, and when I try and pay, the bartender looks at me awkwardly. *Idiot. Who pays for a beer at a party? Jesus!* The bartender, with his chiseled jawline and his perfectly combed Clark Kent hair, smiles at me. He doesn't understand the power in this room, but he senses it, and he doesn't know where I lie in the food chain. I take my beer and move away quickly.

I keep hearing tiny ringing surges all around me. It's happening so frequently that I find it impossible to even try and guess who's a Winder and who's not. I find my way to the edge of the party. My eyes drift compass-like toward a dark hallway lit only by rows of tiny lanterns, making the dim corridor look like a landing strip. I wander down the runway, pausing at an old wooden credenza. A perfectly preserved Revolutionary War musket sits atop it. Above it, a jewel-handled samurai sword hangs on the wall in the shape of an ancient smile. My eyes drift down to a small crystal box refracting candlelight onto the wall with a kaleidoscope effect. My curiosity gets the better of me. I lift the crystal lid. My eyes go wide. I've heard of stuff like this, but I suppose in my head it was always ghoulish little men with mustaches keeping them hidden next to their kiddie porn collections… (But I really have no idea whose loft this actually is. And I didn't check the crowd for mustaches.) But somehow seeing a Nazi command pin displayed like a cherished treasure in *this* world creeps me the hell out. *How is any of this helping me learn to control my powers?* I find myself longing to be back with Grams and Ducky.

A quiet moan comes from further down the hallway, barely audible over the music. My need to investigate feels almost involuntary.

The door where the moaning's coming from is slightly ajar. I know I shouldn't, but I risk a glance. Through the door, I see a tangle of male and female bodies, all with masks on, undulating in some kind of seriously messed-up orgy. One of the masked figures turns in my direction and I jump out of the way, desperately hoping the scaly, fish-faced mask is as hard to see out of as it is to see in.

I move stiff-legged back toward the party. The candle runway flashes by on both sides, then I hear the scream of a young woman coming from another room—a room with its door closed. I freeze, anger flooding me. Anger at myself. *Why the hell am I here? You shouldn't be here, Charlie. Whatever's happening inside that room (or any of these rooms) has nothing to do with you.* I hear breaking glass inside. *Just turn and go!* I stare at the dark frame of the door. I'm so far out of my depth here. *What if I misjudge something?* Aeman was very serious about not winding here. There could be danger. The girl screams again. This time, her words are clear: "Help me… Please, help me!" I'm already moving before I realize it.

I yank open the door. Standing with his back to me, and his pants around his ankles, a startled, ferret-faced young man (only a year or two older than me) twists around to see who's interrupted his depraved progress. He's holding a pretty red-headed girl, in only her bra and underwear, face down on a bed. Around her throat he holds a polka-dot piece of fabric. She turns back to me. The pleading look on her face fills me with shame for my hesitation. The obvious look of horror on my face delivers a clear message to Ferret-Face: *I do not belong at this party. I am not one of the "fortunate masters."*

"Get the hell outta here, pervert! I ain't into sharing!" he squeals at me and slams the door in my face. I no longer have to worry about winding, because I'm just going to kick the living shit out of this guy. My knuckles tingle as I rip the door back open. Ferret-Face almost seems to snarl as he wheels around on me. I don't wait; I blast my fist toward the side of his face. I'm trying to end the fight quick, so I hook toward his temple. I've seen the effects of this blow many times, and it usually does the job to anyone around my size. But Ferret-Face ducks my blow with such ease that I completely lose my balance. I topple onto my enemy, but just as quickly, I'm doubled over by a massive blow to the stomach. I swing again at his head, and again, I watch him effortlessly move beyond my reach—as if I had announced out loud exactly where I was going to try and hit him before I swung.

Then, before I can move, my half-naked assailant smashes his knee up between my legs, crushing my balls. I drop to the floor, completely ruined. Fact: a half-naked man is seriously kicking my ass right now. The man laughs, and behind his thin, ugly laugh I can hear the girl quietly sobbing on the bed. I dive and lock my arms around the asshole's legs. He claws at my face, drawing blood, which runs down my cheeks, but I still manage to pull him to the ground, where I'm hoping he'll be less dangerous. I get an arm around his throat, and then all at once…

OUR BRUTAL WRESTLING MATCH BEGINS TO SPIN IN REVERSE. BLOW BY HORRENDOUS BLOW, THE FIGHT GALLOPS BACKWARD, PULLING FERRET-FACE AND ME AGAINST EACH OTHER AND AWAY IN A DIZZYING FLURRY OF MOVEMENT. *I'm not doing this. This isn't me. I'm not winding. It's him; he's doing this.* THEN I'M RIPPED OUT OF THE DOOR, DRAGGED DOWN THE HALLWAY, PAST THE ORGY ROOM, BACK TO THE EDGE OF THE PARTY. I SCREAM IN FRUSTRATION AS I'M PULLED ALONG AGAINST MY WILL. THE SOUND OF MY CRIES IS MASKED BY THE POUNDING MUSIC CHURNING BACKWARD.

Then everything moves forward again, and I stand tottering in place, swallowed by the horrors this new world is capable of. It all feels so frightening and unfair. Again, I think about Ducky and Grams. There are things in the night that the people I love need to be afraid of. Dangerous, powerful, unstoppable things. *Including me,* I think. *Including me.*

My head is chaos. I know I should be exhausted from the fight, but I'm not. My testicles should be screaming in agony, but they aren't. I reach for my face and feel nothing but smooth skin—no injury anywhere—no bloody oozing claw marks—nothing. Like Aeman's desserts, my wounds have rocketed off me. Then I remember: *the girl.*

I sprint back to the room. Aeman told me not to wind, but I'm not sure I can keep that promise. He must've been winding me back the whole time I was fighting him. *That's* how he knew every move I made before I made it. I didn't know, because we weren't touching, and there was so much ringing already in the air, I didn't notice. Now that I know what I'm walking into, I realize I'm at such a disadvantage. If I could barely coax this power out in the subway, how can I hope to utilize it in the split-second chaos of a fight? *Guess I'll have to learn the hard way.*

I reach the door, and I tear it open. I'm shocked at what I see. Ferret-Face stands next to the young woman. She's fully clothed now, wearing a little polka-dot dress, which was formerly wrapped around her neck. They both turn to face me. Ferret is now also fully dressed.

"Enjoying the party?" he asks me, a twinkle in his eye. My shocked expression tells him I'm a Winder. And the strangest thing is he doesn't seem to be upset in the slightest. He gives me a wink, like we're both in on some monumental joke. I feel nauseous.

I look to the girl. "Are you all right? Come on, I'll get you out of here," I say. I'm on the balls of my feet, ready to wrench the frightened girl to safety.

But the girl's face curls into a red fist. "Who the hell are you? Don't you understand privacy? Get the hell out of here, weirdo!"

I cannot believe my ears. "No, you don't understand—"

"GET OUT!" she screeches at me.

The man with a face like a ferret beams at me, looking like he's trying hard to hold his laughter in. I have no choice. I slosh backward out of the room, my heroic tail between my legs. The door is slammed shut—this time by the girl.

Feeling sick and disoriented, I stalk back toward the party. The second I hit the crowd, someone smacks into me, hard. I turn—excited to have something to take my anger out on—but I find myself staring into a strangely familiar face. It's the mousey-haired girl from the train, now in dark fitted jeans and a leather jacket. She looks good. She also looks pissed at being slammed into so hard. Then her eyes go wide when she sees who it is.

"Oh, wow. Charlie, right?" I stand there like a gaping idiot. *Is she one of them? One of…us?* She continues on full steam: "…It's Tristen. From the train. Remember? Cute director girl—watched you have a sleeping seizure…"

"What are you doing here?" I ask, not disguising my distrust.

"Um…it's a party, so hmmm…" She smiles, but there's something else in her expression. She's trying to figure out why I'm being such a dick.

"You shouldn't be here," I say. I know I must look and sound kind of manic, but at the moment, it's the only thing I have to hold on to. Tristen's face darkens at my words.

"Whoa. Why?" Then it's her turn to look panicked. "…Oh, no, is this like your birthday party or something? Am I crashing it? I swear, this random guy at a bar invited me. I didn't even—"

"What guy?"

"The guy by the pool table eye-lasering a hole in your head for talking to me."

I turn and find the pool table, and sure enough, a roguish-looking guy with a dirty blond ponytail, wearing a perfectly tailored black suit, is staring daggers at me.

"I don't usually go for long-haired dudes, but *Interview with the Vampire was* my favorite film as a kid, so occasionally I make an exception—"

"Come on!" I grab her arm and pull her toward the exit.

"Hey! Where are we going?" I can feel the fury through her wrist as I tug her along, but I don't care.

Back out on the heavily populated city streets, I beeline toward an approaching cab, wave it down and physically force Tristen into the vehicle.

"Really?! You're just gonna shove me in a cab without any explanation?"

I close the cab door and face off against the firestorm staring back at me.

"Tristen, listen…stuff is going on that I can't really explain… and even if I could…I don't think it would make *this* particular situation any better. It's not… Please, just trust me. You don't want to be at that party."

"Then why are *you* at that party?"

"That is a perfectly valid question, and the answer is, I'm leaving right now. I came with a friend and I really wish I hadn't."

Tristen searches my face. She seems to be looking for something. It's a penetrating moment. Finally, she turns to the cabby in the front seat.

"320 East 10th Street. Drive."

I lean toward the window. "I'm sorry—"

Tristen rolls her window up, flipping me off as she does. The cab lurches away. I sigh in relief but barely get half the air out before I'm no longer alone on the sidewalk.

"Jesus. Thought you got gobbled up, kid. What're you doing out here?" Aeman says as he emerges from the nondescript doorway leading up to the party.

My face burns through a spectrum of colors as I fight for what I should say first…

"What is this?! I don't get…*anything!* What are the rules of the Code? *Are* there rules?! Cuz it really doesn't seem like—"

"Let's take a walk."

"I don't want to take a walk!"

"Well, do it anyway."

Aeman starts walking down the street, away from me. *Shit! What are you doing, Charlie?*

I walk quickly to keep up.

CHAPTER 20

JUNIPER

"I need to get into Trevor's private files. Right now," I say.

Daniel stares at me like I just shouted in a foreign language at the top of my lungs. He stands frozen in the doorframe of his chamber. His disheveled hair and half-buttoned shirt resemble an album cover to one of the obscure bands he's always playing in the lab. His chest is slightly exposed, and I might find such a thing quite appealing if my heart weren't slamming in my chest, and if I couldn't still smell the stench of sweat and despair from my father's chamber.

Daniel was chosen to be a Seeker due to his skill level with a computer. He probably could have become a Provider, but I suspect he might lack the competitive edge necessary for their mercantile jungle. In even the tiniest of transactions, there is always a winner and a loser, and when the odds are always stacked in your favor, you have to be okay with the feeling of domination. I've always gotten the sense that Daniel finds such injustice vulgar. I just find it boring. The reason I came here tonight is because, aside from being my lab tech, Daniel is also on the team involved in implementing all of Thessaly's IT security. He scans my face for the joke he hopes to find there, and when his search comes up empty, he takes a deep, measured breath.

"No," he says, with more than a little finality.

"What do you mean, 'No'? I'm a Leader; you have to obey me."

"Trevor's a Leader too. And he also happens to be the most dangerous man in Thessaly."

"Yeah, but I'm standing in front of you right now. And I am

also dangerous." I know how ridiculous I must sound. Daniel's expression looks more concerned than angry, but I can see the scale starting to tip.

"Why do you want to see Trevor's files?"

"That isn't any of your business."

"*Exactly.*"

I can feel my temperature rise, but I know anger won't help me in this situation; still, he's making it very difficult. "…However, right now, it *is my* business, so—"

"Nope."

"*Stop telling me no!*" The words flare out of me. I have enough enemies and not enough friends at the moment. He yanks me into his chamber and closes the door. For a moment, our bodies are so close that I can smell his scent. It scatters my thoughts, so I pull my arm out of his grip. He barrels past me into his chamber, his hands laced behind his head in frustration.

I can't help but look around. He has about a third as much space as my chamber, which I've had since I was fourteen; yet he has floor-to-ceiling bookshelves, interesting art on the walls, a glass-topped desk by his window. He even has a plant—a droopy philodendron, which I'm sure he's probably named. The personality packed into this small space makes me feel incredibly insecure about my own spartan, white-on-off-white dwelling.

"What is this, Juniper? What's going on? You can tell me."

I look into his eyes and there's honesty there. An honesty I think I might be able to trust. But telling him the dark theories rattling around inside my mind would also mean involving him. *But I've already involved him just by coming here. And won't whatever Trevor's doing undoubtedly affect Daniel as well?*

"Trevor wants me to vote for war."

"War with who?"

"The Faters."

"Why?"

"He says to avenge Elijah's murder." *How the hell did I get on the opposite side of that mission?* I *want* revenge for Elijah's death. I'd like to do it myself. But… "But I know that isn't Trevor's actual motive. He doesn't really care about Elijah."

"Ok. So, what is it, then? What does he gain from a war with the Faters?"

"Maybe it's a distraction for something else."

"For what?"

"I don't know! That's the whole reason I'm here, Daniel!"

"And what do you even think you're gonna find in Trevor's files? A Bad-things-to-do list?" I do not appreciate his sarcasm. Not one iota.

"I have to do something," I say. "Trevor thinks he can do anything he wants. I have to show him he can't."

"Juniper, this is crazy."

I can't stop it, no matter how hard I try. I can feel the sting of oncoming tears. I want to rip my eyes out! I fight it back with everything in me. It's not sadness. It's not. It's rage. Just like Elijah said all those years ago. *Pure, unadulterated rage.* I'm losing control. Daniel sees my struggle and concern floods his face again.

"There's something else, Juniper. I can tell. Please, you don't have to be alone in this."

I want to tell him the truth—the truth about Trevor's threat. But what is that truth? I can't tell him about the physical violence, because I don't want him to feel like he has to stand up for me when I know he can't. And the last thing I want to see is the look in his eyes when he realizes that *I* know he can't. It has nothing to do with his courage. It's a simple reality: Trevor and his Enforcers are trained killers, while Daniel is a skinny, witty young man who's sat behind a screen for most of his life.

I watch Daniel decide that I'm not going to trust him, and something in him deflates.

"There *isn't* a way into Trevor's computer," he says. "Each member of the Council's private systems is off-grid. I'm actually scheduled to take your systems off-grid this week. The inner workings of the Leadership are meant to be sovereign and anonymous."

"If you're the one who removes them, you're telling me you don't have a secret back entrance of some kind?"

"You think I want some Enforcer hack discovering an Easter egg in my coding and interpreting it as sabotage? Do you know what the punishment would be for that?"

"I think Trevor's going to try and kill my father, Daniel." The words come out before I can stop them. And then, in their wake, thick emotion blossoms up into my throat, and tears spill from my eyes.

Daniel opens his mouth, but no sound comes out. No doubt, the raw emotion brimming out of me is shocking to him. I'm not exactly a crier. He's probably disgusted by my weakness. I hate this feeling—hate it so much. I should've just gone back to my room after leaving my father's chamber. Somehow, his sloppy desperation has hooked into me like a parasite.

"Juniper…" My name sounds gruesome coming out of Daniel's mouth. He sounds so confused and worried. "Juniper…I care about you. I'm sure it's obvious." I want to feel the thrill that these words should deliver, but I know he's not done talking. "I don't want you to do something stupid. This is the Leadership Council we're talking about, not some third-world human dictatorship. Trevor's been at this a long time. Don't underestimate him."

"I'm not," I say. Out of all the foolish things I've done tonight, underestimating Trevor, and the horrors he's capable of, is not one of them.

"If you go against him, he'll find a way to turn it back on you. Treason to the Leadership is punishable by *death*. Don't go down this track. Please. If you think he's capable of killing your father, what's to stop him from killing *you*…or anyone that helps you?"

I stop. I have no good answers for this, just terrible ones. Daniel is scared. He thinks I'm going to get him killed. Of course he thinks that. Anybody would. Did I really think Daniel could help me? No, I don't think I did. Maybe I just wanted to feel like someone *wanted* to help me. (Even if they couldn't.) And now I see the guilt pouring out of Daniel. He's been a little too honest. He wants no part of this, of me, and he wishes I hadn't asked him. That's how he feels, no matter what he tries to say at this point. I know that's the truth.

"Juniper…I didn't mean to make it sound like…"

I glance at my elegant new watch. Just like I did the second before Daniel opened the door. Just like I do before entering almost any room. Just like Trevor taught me.

Ninety-one seconds have elapsed since Daniel opened the door.

I see the change on Daniel's face as he feels me gather my will. He doesn't try and stop me. Some part of me wishes he would.

THE SECONDS SLIDE BACKWARD AROUND ME AS I'M PULLED BACK INTO DANIEL'S GRASP. AS TIME REVERSES, IT ACTUALLY SEEMS AS IF DANIEL GRABS ME INSIDE HIS APARTMENT AND PUTS ME OUT- SIDE LIKE A DISOBEDIENT PET. THE DOOR CLOSES ON ME. THEN I'M PULLED BACKWARD DOWN THE HALLWAY. I WANT MORE DISTANCE. THAT WAY, IF ANYONE EVER LOOKS AT SECURITY FOOTAGE, THEY'LL NEVER KNOW I EVER WENT TO VISIT DANIEL BEFORE I DECIDED TO DO WHATEVER IT IS THAT I'M GOING TO DO. I CAN FEEL TIME CRUSHING DOWN ON MY MIND LIKE A MASSIVE VICE. I FIGHT TO PULL BACK JUST A FEW MORE STEPS IN REVERSE, JUST A FEW MORE, then I release.

The fatigue hits me so hard, I almost crumble, but I do every-thing in my power to stay on my feet and act normal. I look down at my watch. *I've wound back a hundred and three seconds.* By far the longest wind I've ever attempted, and I'm feeling every second of it. I see the elevator at the very end of the hallway. It seems a hundred miles away.

I keep walking. Sweat bubbles and drips down my spine. My eyes start to roll back in my head, my heavy chin dips involuntari-ly...*sinking* ...*I'm not going to make it...* I imagine Trevor rolling back the surveillance footage to this moment, again and again, watching me flop down onto the hard marble floor, gasping like an asphyxiating trout. I see his gloating face, grinning at the preco-cious child who thought she could sneak around behind his back. Burning red dots clog my vision as unconsciousness gets its hooks in me. I close my eyes and fight for a few more steps, but it all feels so pointless now. So much easier just to surrender...

I stagger, losing my balance. I reach out, falling, and my hand finds the elevator door. I slam the button and wait. My knees are locked, holding me up like stilts. I fight to slow my breathing.

Finally, the *ding* of the arriving elevator. The door retracts, and I step inside. As the doors slide closed, I pray to whoever's listening that I don't faint on the ride down.

CHAPTER 21

CHARLIE

"I'm telling you he was raping her, Aeman!"

"But he didn't rape her."

"YES, HE…" I feel beyond frustrated as Aeman and I hike across the giant bridge, its massive iron cables looming above us. "He was in the goddamn process, okay?! I stopped him. That's what I'm trying to tell you."

"Do you think that girl thinks she was assaulted?"

"That's not the point."

"No, that's exactly the point." Aeman stops, turning to face me. "Can you call something a murder if no one dies? Have you ever had the thought, *God, I could kill that prick!?*" I jab a *don't you dare patronize me right now* look at him.

"Should you have gone to prison for thinking that?" I don't know how to argue this. My head is swimming. "What if, while you were thinking about this unnamed asshole, you actually got to beat him to a bloody pulp? Only, no one really got hurt. How would that be bad? Other than maybe jerkoff never learns his lesson?"

"…I don't know," I confess. And I don't. I really don't.

"Of course you don't know! It's your first day! You're a baby. So, stop asking so many goddamn questions and start learning certain inalienable truths: absolute power corrupts absolutely, and there are a lot of people in your new world with a shit-ton of power and therefore are fucked in the head beyond belief. That's *man*. Period. Always has been; always will be. You fight that war, you. Will. Lose. And believe me, there's a super slippery slope between hating what we're capable of and trying to destroy it. You think *we're* crazy? There's actually a psycho cult who hunts and kills Winders. They believe our powers are a 'sin' and they fight to try and make us extinct. They won't win that war. Cuz you *can't* win that war. It just ain't in the cards."

"But how can they even—"

"They're Winders."

And the waters just keep getting darker.

"They call themselves 'The Warriors of Fate'. Such a stupid-ass name—makes them sound like knights of the crusade or some shit, and we know how righteous *those* assholes were. Look, the Leadership and the Code ain't perfect. But chaos ain't a world for guys like us. A world like that doesn't have a sense of humor. It makes us beasts. *Lord of the Flies* and shit. And I don't know about you, but I'm looking for a lot more out of this life than just survival. Hell, I'm only like a quarter the way through my bucket list." His crooked smile is asking me to take this absurd night in stride, but I feel like I'm drowning. I came here to learn how to control this ticking time bomb inside of me, not learn how to rape and pillage without consequence—or join some civil war between supernatural beings. If I'm ever going to be able to safely have Ducky and Grams in my life, I need to get a handle on this shit, and fast.

Aeman must see my struggle, because he takes a beat. "Too much?" he asks.

"…Too much," I say.

"Okay. I wanna show you something."

"I think I've seen enough for one day."

"Yeah, but this is the best thing."

With that, Aeman climbs up the bridge railing, above the safety gate. He waves me up.

"What? Are you crazy? I'm not climbing up there. No way."

"Come on! Gotta trust someone."

I stare up at him so long I imagine I look like a statue, a sculpture of an eighteen-year-old kid, with a little, white title card next to me on the wall that reads:

Charlie Ryan
INDECISION, *2014*
Skin, bone, blood, hair, cotton fabric, canvas, leather, rubber, fear, doubt, rage.

I wrap my hand around the rusty rung and start climbing. My ascent is far from graceful, but after considerable effort, I stand next to Aeman on the narrow cable facing out toward the New York City skyline. *Wow.* It sparkles in its glory.

"See that? Breathe it in." The wind whips Aeman's shaggy hair around his face as he stares out at the looming metropolis. My knees shake, but I take a deep breath. The air feels cold and crisp. Aeman looks over at me. And for a beat the awful night melts away, and I'm sharing my first completely truthful moment with Aeman—a world of infinite possibilities before us. And then he clutches my arm and pulls me over the edge.

We're both screaming, grasping at each other, as the freezing wind rushes up at us. Hitting the water at this velocity will be like hitting concrete. I brace for impact, when...

WE BEGIN TO SLOW DOWN. WE GET INCHES FROM THE WATER, COME ALMOST TO A FULL STOP, SURROUNDED BY FOG, BEFORE OUR BODIES GET SUCKED BACK UP THROUGH SPACE AND TIME, BACK ONTO THE RAILING.

Time moves forward.

"Nneeeeyyaa!" I gasp for breath, wrapping my arms around the thick metal cable. Aeman looks fatigued. This winding has been more depleting to him than I've seen. He steadies himself, while I white-knuckle the cable.

"Are you insane?!"

Aeman finally turns toward me with the same adrenaline-fueled clarity that I realize is pumping through me as well, fighting against the paralyzing fear camped out in my belly.

"The first rule of the Code is silence," Aeman says. "You can't tell anyone about us. Not that they would believe you, anyway. The second rule is accepting that you are a more evolved animal and that some rules that apply to simple humans no longer apply to you, just like a dog can't blame you for knowing math. Third rule basically says treason to the Leadership is punishable by death. I personally like to find the shades of grey in everything. We'll start with those three. The rules are there to tell you what you can't do. I'm here to show you there's a lot less limits to your life than you thought yesterday. You willing to trust me?"

I say nothing. Below I see a tiny tugboat quietly passing under the bridge. It makes me think about my mother. She once told me that her father, my grandpa (I never met him; he died before I was born) had worked on a tugboat when he was young. I remember that she seemed really proud of it, and I also remember thinking, *What the hell is so cool about a midget ship being linked to our bloodline? They don't even get to sail out into the ocean. No adventure. They're used to pull ships in and out of port.* But as I watch the tiny vessel glide beneath me, some part of me suddenly thinks that maybe I misjudged tugboats. The ships they pull are powerless at the two most important moments in their voyage: coming home and embarking on a new adventure. And that's where the tugboat comes in. Fierce little harbingers of destiny. So, maybe that's Aeman. And maybe this part of the journey is simply beyond me. Maybe I really do need the help. I look at Aeman, the only friend I have in this brave new world.

"Okay," I say.

"Great," he says, "Now *you* jump."

"*What?*"

"Go on. It's the easiest wind you'll ever do. Self-preservation is almost a reflex action. Just don't go nuts. You'll wake up the whole city."

I look over the edge. My breath shallows. *This is impossible. I know I just did this, but it wasn't me...it was a seasoned Winder with confidence for days.* My muscles start shaking, uncontrollably. I attempt to clench them to stop my quaking body, but it feels like trying to grasp a slimy eel; it just won't be held. Finally, with no moves left, no secret plan up my sleeve to keep the paralysis at bay, I simply surrender to the fear and panic, and let it wash over me. But just before it reaches the innermost *me* of my mind, I steel my wavering willpower, take a deep, icy breath of faith...and leap.

CHAPTER 22

JUNIPER

Vic purrs in my arms. I can't stop shaking. It's been almost an hour, but my body still feels weak from the humongous wind. Daniel won't remember any of it. Which I know is for the best. But I can't seem to escape the sadness. I've never felt more alone. It feels suffocating.

I tried to stay in my room, but it felt like the walls were collapsing in on me, so I came here, to the park. It's changed a lot since I was twelve, bent over that koi pond, my hands sticky with blood. Elijah will not show up this time to save me. Vic affectionately grinds the side of his face into the bottom of my chin. I hold him tighter, kissing the top of his head, leaving my lips pressed against the soft smooth fur between his ears. Then I set him on the ground and watch him dart off into the lush foliage. It's not Vic's first time exploring the park. From time to time, when I get too guilty about him being stuck in my chamber or the lab, I bring him here. Usually at night. No one is ever in the park at this late hour.

Tall trees surround me on all sides. This park was Elijah's greatest contribution to Thessaly Tower, in my opinion. He took a simple flat lunch destination and turned it into an oasis. A work of art. Influenced by the indoor gardens of Cloud Forest and Flower Dome, which Elijah saw when visiting the Singapore Chapter, the park has a wilderness-under-the-dome quality. There's even a waterfall pouring down through the center of the park. I walk between the trees, through the long grass, feeling the cool mist on my skin. My hand gently slides along the bark of each tree as I pass. The veiny, rough surfaces ripple under my fingers, scratching my fingertips, my palms. It feels good. It's nice to feel the presence of life that is completely indifferent to our self-important struggles. The trees seem to be hiding me in their shadows. And then I see a figure walking toward me.

She looks frightened. Lost. She seems so small amidst these dark giants rising up all around her. I reach out my hand toward her. She does the same. Two sets of fingers trembling ever so slightly from exhaustion. And then they touch. The glass feels cold against my hand. The web of windows rising up fifty feet above me feels like the end of the world. Then I step all the way up to the glass— so close, I can no longer see my reflection.

Steam from my breath fogs my vision slightly. The world outside looks cold. And dark. Pockmarked with lights with no connection to each other. I've always liked the height from these windows. The distance. Being closer to things, in my experience, has never ended well. A world at arm's length has always been a safer world. But not tonight. Tonight, my isolation feels hostile, maybe deadly. For a moment, I imagine the glass disappearing and me stepping out and lifting off; soaring higher and higher, tossed by the night wind. A discarded balloon in the darkness. *Who would miss me?*

Trevor was my North Star.

Elijah was my North Star.

Now I'm marooned, and the sky is black.

Snap. A twig breaks under someone's foot very close to me. Goosebumps knuckle up across my shoulder blades as my senses hone to a fine point. I slide behind the trunk of a thick oak just as I hear the whispers. The voice is male. Extremely close. I can't make out what he's saying, but if he's whispering, it means he's not alone.

Squatting down, I wrap my fist around a heavy stone. I yank it free from the ground. The bottom half feels damp against my palm. The weight of it is comforting. At close range, it will do a decent amount of damage. *We'll see who's weak, Trevor.*

Now a second voice. Female. They're almost on top of me. I tense my muscles, ready to spring, when I feel them pass by. I think about striking first—leaping out and sending a message to the Enforcer community as a whole—when I hear the laughter. I'm completely thrown by the joy I hear in their voices. Hidden in the shadow of the tree, I peer around the corner and see two kids, maybe fourteen or fifteen, holding hands. She turns back toward him, and he presses her back against the giant window. She yelps out in fright as she hits the cold glass at the edge of the abyss, then she covers her own mouth, knowing she has to be quiet. She laughs silently in frightened glee as she wraps her arms around him.

I want to turn away, to get out of there as fast as I can, but I can't move. Their lips graze each other's, and they smile. They look so happy. Fearless. I recognize her. Her name is Nicole. She was chosen for the Provider Wing at seven years old. A prodigy. I've heard my father talk about her. The boy she's with is wing-less, even at his age. He's as close to human as you get in our world. He'll probably end up being a maintenance worker or a groundskeeper—perhaps he'll work in this very park. I imagine his life is extremely hard. Thessaly is not kind to underachiev-ers—or those associated with them. She's risking so much by being with him. No wonder they have to meet in secret. And yet I see no fear in their faces. None at all. No hesitation. Just a kind of bliss I have never known. And all at once, I want them to stay this way forever. I want to keep them happy. And safe. And allowed to love however they desire. *Just like my father did.* And that means men like Trevor have to be stopped.

Something rubs against my side and I almost scream. I look down and find Vic staring up at me. I scoop him up, turn and move through the trees rapidly, careful not to make a sound as I go. My mind flies… *What do I know?* Trevor thinks only in brutality—crush or be crushed—and right now, that blunt instrument is aimed at his own people as much as it's aimed at the Faters or the humans that he hates. And that kind of thinking will eat us from the inside. He cannot be allowed to undermine a system that took great minds like Victor Mason so long to achieve—a system Victor Mason and Elijah both died for. A system I believe in. We're not wrong for being what we are. We have an advantage because the world is a merit-based game and we're simply more equipped to excel at it than humans. But this superiority does not extend to our emotions or our dreams or our loves. Such a belief would make monsters of us. It already has with Trevor.

But I don't think I can stop him on my own.

Elijah can't help me.

My father can't.

Daniel can't.

I could go to the Council. But why would they ever believe me over Trevor? *Believe what? I don't even know what he's doing! And I definitely can't prove anything.* Still, I know Trevor. He'd swallow the whole world if he could—shove each and every one of us into that frozen lake, again and again, if he were given free rein. The next Council meeting is the morning after next. I have so little time. The world I knew just days ago has tilted at a precarious angle, and I can feel myself sliding toward the edge. And I know I only have one last handhold to grasp. But every part of me dreads reaching for it.

CHAPTER 23

CHARLIE

It strikes my face with the unexpected brutality of a comet wiping out the dinosaurs. I rage to my feet, dizzy and sleep-clogged but ready to take on any— The second pillow cranks into my forehead like a corduroy cannonball, knocking me off my feet. Aeman belly-laughs above me.

"Training time!" he declares, legs dangling from the hole in his ceiling. He holds another small, square pillow in his grasp. "The bridge was easy. This'll be harder. Most things you'll do will require little bursts. Use too much energy at once, and you might be weak at the wrong time. Sometimes ya need the club and sometimes ya need the toothpick."

Shaking off my wooziness, I climb to my feet, determined to not look as stupid as I feel. I get in the loose stance my fight training has drilled into me as the most fluid position to face any attack. I take a breath. "Okay," I say. "I'm ready."

Aeman whips the pillow at Mach speed. As I attempt to wind it back, the little leather couch cushion smashes into my nose, snapping my head back and obliterating my sight, my sense of smell as well as every last drop of dignity left in my body. But it gets worse. My gathered power does not go to waste, because half a second later...

THE PILLOW HURTLES BACKWARD THROUGH TIME AND SPACE, DIGGING ONCE AGAIN INTO MY ALREADY-RUNNING NOSE, ON ITS WAY BACK UP TO AEMAN...AND THEN, JUST BEFORE IT GETS TO HIM... MY FOCUS VAPORIZES, AND (FALLING IN LINE WITH THE BEAUTIFUL MORNING I'M HAVING) time moves forward again, and the pillow reverses back on its original course and decimates my nose for a third time. I stumble back, legs noodling, and plant on my ass with a dull thump.

"Jesus!" I wipe my tear-filled eyes and the leaky snot from my nostrils with the first cloth item my hand finds.

"What? They're called *throw pillows.*" The glee in Aeman's voice is beyond annoying. "Ready for another?"

My hand shoots up, blocking my pillow-ravaged face. "Just… just hold on a second!"

"I can hear you ringing," he says. "I only saw it hit you once, but I'm guessing you got the freshman three. Huh?"

"…Like a stuffed boomerang."

"It didn't really hit you the second time; you just passed through the moment where it did, so it felt like you got hit again. That shit can spook a newbie—make you lose focus. It helps to make a gesture. Don't know why, but it does. Mind-body connection thing or something. You're lucky. I got taught with rocks."

"These pillows might as well be rocks."

"Just so you know, that's a four-hundred-dollar shirt you're wiping your nose on."

"Would you like me to wind my mucus off it?" It comes out more sarcastic than I intended, but it doesn't seem to faze Aeman in the slightest.

"Nah. You can keep it as a souvenir of our first training session. So far, you're scoring a hard F. Least I can do is give you a T-shirt for your efforts. Not that I should be rewarding such a piss-poor-performance. More of a pity prize, I guess."

"Okay, so, where does all this, you know…I mean…" *What do I mean?* I grit my teeth, trying to crank my sloggy brain into a higher function. "Where do Winders come from?" I feel like I just asked Aeman about the birds and the bees.

"Who knows? Where does anything come from? Evolution, my man. Or maybe some bored god decided to shake things up a bit—toss in some badass outliers."

"But if no one knows where it comes from, then how can we ever control it?"

"Oh, Charlie, Charlie, Charlie. Don't look for control in this world. It ain't there. Trust me. And what we got… This shit can make you powerful, it can make you rich, but it ain't never made anyone happier. The big questions don't change. They remain unanswered. But, hey, give yourself a nice pat on the back. You seem like a decent kid. You're not an asshole." He smiles wide. "Like me."

"You don't know anything about me," I say.

Aeman takes in the edge in my voice. I see him stifle a little smile, then he nods, looking off. "You're right. We don't know nothing about each other. But I'll tell you what… If I have a super-power—you know, like Batman?"

"Batman didn't have superpowers. He was just really smart."

"Shut up. I was right in the middle of saying something extremely intelligent. You know, like Batman."

"Sorry."

"I see bad guys. Always have. Liars. Thieves. Murderers. Dark souls. Conscience cut off at the knees. Black blood pumping through corroded arteries." He pauses for a brief second—the shadow of some memory plays across his face. Then he looks me dead in the eyes. "I seen a guy extinguish innocent lives like he was blowing out a candle." He gently blows air through his lips. "Don't play bad, kid. I don't know much, but maybe I know that. Bad is sticky. It don't like to let go."

His words are dark, but I can tell he's genuinely looking out for me. It's been a while since anyone has. Ducky and Grams, but they don't know the worst thing about me. Maybe I could tell Aeman. I toss the snotty shirt on the ground, climb to my feet and slide into my stance once again. "Okay," I say, "ready for number three."

"You sure?"

I nod and, without hesitation, Aeman chucks the upholstery missile with hideous velocity. I raise my hand, gathering my wind into the gesture itself, as I pull with my mind, and…

THE SAW BLADE OF A PILLOW BEGINS TO SPIN SLOWER AND SLOWER AS IT CLOSES IN ON ITS TARGET (MY FACE). I GIVE IT AN EXTRA MENTAL TUG, AND FINALLY IT SPUTTERS TO A STOP INCHES FROM MY FACE. THE PILLOW TREMBLES IN THE AIR, THE KINETIC ENERGY LOCKED INSIDE IT PRACTICALLY BURSTING AT THE SEAMS.

The feeling is strange. There's a waning deep within me, as if I'm leaking, but I couldn't tell you where from. It's almost like it's from everywhere at once. I can sense that holding this object suspended in time and space is a *very* short-lived event, like holding your breath under water. But there's something oddly beautiful to this everyday object hovering before me. And I can't help feeling that the magic lies in the pillow instead of in me. As fatigue creeps into my muscles, both mentally and physically, I reach out and grab the frozen pillow. Then I release my hold on time, and clutch the pillow hard as it bucks once, ferociously, the momentum living inside it completing its course.

"Hey, Randy Moss, I told you to wind it, not catch it," Aeman says from above.

"I did."

"What do you mean, you did?"

"I just stopped it first, then grabbed it instead of sending it back."

Something changes on an elemental level in Aeman. For the first time since I met him, his kneejerk wit and wisecracking ambivalence disintegrate. His eyebrows arch like two competing parabolas. I don't understand what it means. He seems so serious.

"What's up?" I ask. "Did I do something wrong?"

"Nope," he says, "In fact, you're actually in luck."

"Yeah? Why's that?"

"Because you've earned the privilege of buying me breakfast."

"You want…"

"Breakfast. I'm your Yoda, and right now, Yoda wants food. Head downstairs. I'll meet you in a sec."

Before I can say anything else, he pulls his legs up and disappears. Apparently, training time is over. I don't know if I did something good or bad, or if maybe it was a look of *I'm not sure if this kid is teachable*. It wasn't exactly a pleased look. An old defensiveness swells in me, tingling like pre-sweat. He wouldn't be the first mentor to decide I wasn't worth the effort.

The day I was sent to Camp Lazarus—the day I was catapulted into a pit meant to chew up violent teens and spit them out as docile animals—I waited in that courtroom for forty-five excruciating minutes, sitting next to my cheese-brained public defender, with his peeled-potato face and his ludicrous excuse for a hairpiece, until it was clear that Mr. Kipling wasn't going to show up to testify on my behalf. Mr. Kipling, my freshman English teacher, and my friend, left me to be buried alive for three years in a place where so many kids cried themselves to sleep every night that their sobs often blended together into a single hopeless howl—all because he was terrified the world would find out about our *after-school work sessions*. Turned out Mr. Kipling was on the sexual predators watch list and had moved between several states and changed his name, and was looking to keep a low profile. And testifying to having an intimate knowledge of a fifteen-year-old boy's character was not part of his plan, apparently.

In the eight months I knew him, he never laid a hand on me. He recommended me books to read and old movies to watch, and listened to me when I told him a group of neo-Nazi skinhead kids at my school had told me on multiple occasions that they planned to burn Grams's house down, with Grams and Ducky inside it. And the day I saw that particular group of white power assholes walk onto our block was the day I sent two of them to the hospital—one with a permanent traumatic brain injury. I hadn't told Grams about the Nazi kids, because I didn't want her to worry. And I didn't tell Ducky, because I didn't want him to get hurt. But I *did* tell Mr. Kipling. And he did nothing about it. Because I had told him while we were at his place listening to Steely Dan and Rolling Stones records.

Mr. Kipling swallowed two handfuls of sleeping pills shortly after I arrived at Lazarus. And I know it sounds stupid, and I feel like a complete fucking moron for feeling this way…but I still miss him sometimes. Sometimes kindness is kindness. Sometimes it's not. But sometimes it is. The feeling that Aeman could be having second thoughts about being my guide into this absurd new world of superpowers, time travel and Illuminati-like secret societies sits in my stomach like a tangle of thorns. I think about calling up to him, telling him that if he just gives me a little more time, I can get better—I know I can (at least, I think I can)—I can redouble my efforts, make him proud. But I don't call out. I don't make a peep. Because no one likes desperation. I just head for the door.

CHAPTER 24

JUNIPER

The second I step out of my chamber, I know he's there. Daniel has always used the same hair product and its scent is distinct. Not unpleasant. Just him. I'm not ready to have this conversation. Not ready to pretend things are totally normal with Daniel, when that couldn't be further from the truth. He won't remember a thing from last night, and I'm not in the mood to put on a show. *But why is he here?* Because I didn't come into the lab today. Of course. He's checking on me. Is my mind really that frazzled? I need to get my head on straight before I do something stupid. I head for the hallway, where he's no doubt waiting around the corner.

"Juniper." The sound comes from behind, which surprises me, because it means he was hiding in the alcove on the other side of my door. *Why would he hide?* A cold feeling in the pit of my stomach tells me something is wrong. I turn around. Daniel's face looks grim.

"What's wrong?" I ask. "Has something happened?"

"I don't know," Daniel says. The tone of his voice feels cryptic. I don't have time for this.

"Sorry I didn't tell you I was coming into the lab late. Go on ahead. I'll meet you there in a little bit."

"Will you?" he asks.

My eyes narrow. I've had enough. "If you have something to say, Daniel, say it. Stop this…*whatever* you're doing. I don't really have time for guessing games this morning." My tone is cold, which I know is not fair to Daniel. He doesn't remember last night, but I do, and I can't help but still feel the sting of his refusal to help me.

"I think I failed you," he says. I can feel my eyes go wide, and I try my best to cover.

"Don't be ridiculous," I say. "Failed me how? Don't tell me you've spoken about my discovery to someone in less than twenty-four hours from when I told you not to."

"That's the thing… I don't know how I failed you. I was lying in bed last night when I heard the sound of an enormous wind. It was so close." I fight with everything in me not to let the surprise show on my face. Of course he heard the wind; but he doesn't know anything more than that. He can't. "I went out into the hallway to investigate," he continues. "Lots of people did. Everyone looked confused, so I checked the surveillance footage this morning, and it showed you walking down a nearby corridor at that exact time. Did you come to my chamber?"

"Don't flatter yourself," I say, attempting to look scandalized. "My being on that level had nothing to do with you. And I heard that wind as well. I have no idea who produced it or what they were doing. It could've been anyone on that floor."

"I know it was you," he says, carefully but without hesitation. When I don't respond, he goes on. "It was in your walk. I've been watching your walk for a year, and I could tell you were struggling slightly. It was a big wind and you were trying not to show your fatigue in case anyone looked at the surveillance footage. But what gave you away was when the wind happened, you didn't look around. You didn't stop. You didn't acknowledge it at all. Anyone else would have. What were you doing down on my level? It's not like you know anyone else down there." His presumptiveness gets under my skin. What he's really saying is I have no friends. It doesn't matter that he's right.

"Maybe I do," I say. "Maybe I have a lover. I showed you the note. Maybe I found the author." His face goes pale. He's either already thought of this and he had chalked it up as his worst-case scenario, or it hadn't crossed his mind at all, and now the realization is landing hard.

"I don't think so," he says, but he doesn't look all that confident; in fact, he looks pretty miserable. Still, he pushes on. "I think maybe you came to me...for *something*. I don't know what. But you didn't want me to remember how it turned out. So, you erased it. Now, why would you do that?" Right now, I desperately wish Daniel was half as intelligent as he is.

"Why don't you tell me, since you've got everything figured out."

"Juniper, I want to help you," he says, his face filled with sincerity. *No, you don't, Daniel. Trust me; you don't. Not really.*

"Okay. I needed your help," I say, watching what he'll do with this information.

He relaxes ever so slightly. He was trying to project confidence, but I think there was still a generous amount of him that wondered if the secret-lover theory could have credibility. "What did you need help with?" he asks. I don't answer. He studies me, pondering the problem. "I said no. Didn't I?" His face looks tortured. He knows he let me down in some way.

"Actually, you said I was insane. And you were right."

"I don't understand."

"I've been thinking about destroying my research. Destroying all evidence of the success of my discovery." Daniel looks shocked, and I know my quick lie has done what I needed it to do. "You were right. It could be used as a weapon. If Trevor was allowed to wield it... I'm not sure I can allow that."

"If the Council discovers you hid such a thing from them, it could be seen as—"

"Treason. I know. Which is why I needed time to think about it. And why I decided not to burden you with the decision until I've made it."

Daniel watches me, closely, trying to discern if I'm holding anything back. I feel terrible for lying to him, but it's for his own protection. He doesn't need to be a part of anything I'm about to do. If I can't keep myself or my father safe, at the very least I can keep Daniel out of harm's way. Daniel lets out a deep sigh, and I know he's chosen to accept my explanation.

"You have to be careful, Juniper."

"I just need some time to think."

"I get that. It's a big responsibility." The care in his face fills me with guilt.

"I'll see you in the lab in a little bit. Okay?"

"Okay." Then his expression gets serious again. "But today… coffee's on me."

I smile. We, of course, don't have to pay for coffee at the lab. He smiles back. It feels nice to not have any tension between us. Even if it's a lie. He's always been kind to me. It was selfish of me to try and involve him. Daniel turns and goes.

I wait there for a long time, trying to wrap my mind around my next move, trying to get up the nerve to begin, knowing that once I start down this path, I may never be able to go back. But I know there is no choice. I start walking, hoping desperately that Daniel won't do something rash when I don't show up at the lab today. I could've told him I was taking the day off, but I don't think he would've left so easily, and it probably would've led to more questions and therefore more lies. The fact that he thinks he's going to see me at the lab soon allowed him to save any other questions for later. I shove Daniel to the back of my mind. I have a much tougher confrontation ahead of me.

CHAPTER 25

CHARLIE

We're back in Union Square Park, and Aeman seems to be searching for something. I'm staying silent, letting him roam around. I keep up, but I have no idea what he's looking for. I'm about to say something when he turns around, facing me and walking backward.

"Okay, so in the world of us fancy high-and-mighty Winders, we're kinda split into four groups. They have other names, but for the purposes of this lesson, let's call them thieves, hustlers, scrappers and smarty-pants pricks who just sit around, doing experiments and observing shit all day."

"Okay."

"So, you already got the fourth category down, cuz you're not blind, deaf or dumb and this whole thing we're doing right now is an experiment, so congrats."

"Thanks," I say. *Hey, when in Crazytown…*

"So, test number one: thieves." Aeman pulls out a wad of cash and hands it to me.

"Can't exactly call me a thief if you're giving me the money. How much is this?"

"A thousand bucks. Don't get too comfortable with it. You're gonna give it back to me in exactly five minutes. I'm starting my stopwatch. I want you to double that shit. And go!" He hits a button on his watch and stops walking.

"What am I supposed to do?"

"Your rodeo, chief. But I would suggest you stop talking to me and get to thieving."

"You want me to steal from people?"

"I don't care what you do. Just get me that paper, son."

I'm not going to just steal someone's money. That's not how this is going to go. But maybe I can perform for my supper. I scan the crowd till I see a guy in a nice suit. He takes a step back as I approach, but I hold up my hands. "Don't worry. I come in peace." I pull a hundred-dollar bill out and hold it up. "I happen to be…the famous…Union Square Park Magician. And I'll bet you a hundred dollars that I can guess whatever number you're thinking, between one and a hundred."

The guy looks dubious as hell. I smile. He seems to lighten up a little.

"I give you a hundred bucks if you can guess the number I'm thinking of?" he says.

"Yep."

"And I get that hundred if you can't guess it?"

"That's right."

He pulls out his wallet, holds up a hundred to match mine. "All right, you're on."

I make a show of thinking hard, then I say the first number that comes: "Five."

"Sorry, kid, I was thinking of twenty-one."

"Damn," I say, then hand over the hundred. He smiles. I give time a little tug. TIME WINDS BACK. THE MAN HANDS THE HUNDRED BACK TO ME AND…I release.

The man pulls out the hundred again and says, "All right, you're on."

I act like I'm giving it some real consideration—already feeling guilty—then finally, I say, "Twenty-one."

I feel bad. Now I see why Aeman calls it thieving. No way around the truth.

"Nope. Sorry, kid, I was thinking of fifteen." He grabs the hundred, but I hold onto it.

"No, you weren't," I say. I can't believe he's lying. What a dick! "You were thinking of twenty-one."

He lets go of the hundred. "I knew you were a scammer. Kiss my ass." He shakes his head and walks past me. *What a lying asshole!*

I don't know why I'm so pissed. I just tried to trick the dude out of a hundred bucks, but still: I may be a cheater, but he's a cheater *and* a liar. I hear Aeman laugh behind me. Now I feel determined. That was a stupid idea. I see that now. Okay… This time, I pick a guy that doesn't look super wealthy, just kind of normal.

"Excuse me, sir. I have a wager for you." The man looks up from his phone.

"I'm not buying your CD, kid. I don't care how good of a rapper you think you are."

I hold out the whole grand. "Here's the bet: I bet these thousand dollars that I can guess the exact amount of money you have in your wallet, down to the very dollar."

The guy looks skeptical as hell. "And if you guess it, what do *you* get?" he asks.

"Whatever cash is in your wallet."

"Even if it's just a dollar?" I nod. "And if you get it wrong?" he asks.

"Then you get this thousand bucks. You can even hold it." The guy takes the grand, then he holds one of the hundreds up to the light.

"You okay, man?" He looks a little concerned for me, like I might have just been released from the local psych ward. "This is a pretty shitty bet for you. Because I literally have no idea how much money's in my wallet, but it ain't even close to a thousand."

"I like the odds. But I have to warn you: I'm kinda psychic."

"And I'm a skeptic, so we're even. Besides, being psychic only works if *I* know the number, and like I said, I don't. Okay, I'll take the bet. Do your worst."

It's annoying, because he actually seems like a pretty decent guy. I go through the same process as before, making a show of thinking hard. I pick a random number: "You've got sixty bucks in your wallet." He opens his wallet, counts the cash, and looks sorry when he sees I'm off by almost fifty bucks. He's about to say something when I WIND IT BACK.

"You've got one hundred and eight dollars in your wallet," I say this time. He pulls out his wallet, counts the bills, and I watch his face go from curiosity to horror to fascination. He looks at me, knowing I've tricked him somehow, but he has no idea how.

"Psychic, huh?"

I just smile, trying to hide my discomfort. He sighs. "Well. A bet's a bet. That's what I get for being fucking greedy." He hands over the money. I hand him back forty, just to see if it lightens his mood. It doesn't. He pockets the forty and walks away. I watch him go, my conscience stabbing at me.

"All right, kid, forget doubling it. You're off the clock." Aeman puts his arm around my shoulder and walks me across the park. I didn't even hear him walk up. "I can't look at your sad little puppy-dog eyes. You're gonna make me cry. PS, that guy would've *gladly* taken your grand. Remember that when you're crying yourself to sleep tonight. Okay, next lesson." He starts walking quickly across the park.

"What now?" I ask, following. "Are there any babies in this park? Maybe we can take turns smacking the lollipops out of their mouths."

"Not a bad idea. I hate babies. But that telepathy you were bragging about must be really working, because you got part of it right. We're gonna do two lessons for the price of one this time. Get ready for the Hustler and Scrapper Extravaganza."

"Great. I'm sure this'll be painless."

"Definitely not."

"Awesome." It's not lost on me that I can obviously just walk away from this at any time. But if I'm being honest, like *completely* honest, this is actually pretty damn fun. And having somebody take an interest in me enough to teach me some stuff, even if he's kind of a scoundrel, and what he's teaching me is kind of amoral… hell, Han Solo was a scoundrel. Sure, he shot Greedo in the face, but he also got Luke and Obi-Wan to the Alderaan system in one piece. And if I thought losing that money would've really hurt that dude, I don't think I would've taken it. But he didn't even know how much he had in his wallet, so he couldn't be counting his nickels too much. When you don't have shit for money, you know *exactly* how much is in your wallet.

Aeman suddenly stops and turns to me. "Now, I'll be right here, supporting you, but it's not my place to interfere with your training, so you gotta talk your way out of this shit and not get killed."

"What do you mean, 'not get killed'? What's happening?"

"Two rules: you can't run, and you can't blame me."

"Blame you for wha—" And with that, I discover what Aeman was searching for in the park. Next to us is a titan of a man, easily six foot five and built like a lineman. Aeman rears back and slaps the man-monster so hard on the ass, it seems to echo throughout the park. Then he jumps behind me, making sure to keep physical contact.

"WHAT THE SHIT?!" The thing, which I will touchingly refer to as the Kraken, slowly turns, and in his eyes I see Dresden on a bad day.

I'm frozen. This is what a deer feels like. He is the headlights. He is the car. *Am I going to run? Aeman said I couldn't. But am I going to run anyway?*

"Dude..." I say. "I *totally* thought you were somebody else. I—" The Kraken swings a wild fist, which I duck under, but then I feel him grab my T-shirt with his other giant hand. He yanks me up and smashes his head toward my face. I turn at the last second, and his caveman forehead pulverizes my left ear! The pain is excruciating. I PULL BACK TIME. HE LETS GO OF ME, THE PAIN DISAPPEARS AND HE SPINS BACK AROUND. I release, and...

The Kraken's ass gets body-gloved for the second time. Aeman jumps behind me. I have so little time to think of anything. *Miyagi never did this kind of shit to Daniel-san.* The Kraken makes eye contact with me, and I put on my best super surprised face and point to a skinny beanpole of a guy standing to my right, laughing with his even skinnier pals. The Kraken seizes the dude by the throat. "You think that shit's funny?!" The look of terror on the guy's thin, bulging face makes me feel awful. Who's the bully here? The Kraken just got a blistering slap on the ass, and Skinny Bones Jones is just trying to have a fun night with his emaciated friends. *I'm the bully.* I'm the cowardly prick pushing a stranger into a tiger trap. *Well, I tried. Not my jam.*

"Hey, big guy! It wasn't him." The Kraken looks over. "It was me." He puts Skinny down, and he and his pals take off running.

He steps in front of me, and I feel the temperature drop as I'm encased in his shadow. "Listen," I say. "I didn't know what to say before. I'm usually a lot more up-front about this stuff. But you just seem like a really interesting guy. I know you're this huge jacked dude with a big beard and anger in your eyes, but I just bet there's a lot more to you than that. I bet that's all people see when they look at you, and I think that's bullshit. And I was just wondering if you're lonely. Because sometimes, I get lonely, and why be lonely alone, you know?"

The next second, I'm flying through the air, having been shoved so hard and fast, I barely know what's happened. I topple over Aeman. We crumble into a sloppy two-man pile-up on the ground. Then my hand explodes with pain. It feels like a horse is standing on my knuckles. I look up into the red face of the Kraken, who has all his weight crushing my right hand with his heavy black boots.

I cry out in pain just as I see his other boot flying toward my face. I flex my mind and watch as the anvil-sized boot closes in on me like a missile. I PULL HARDER, AND IT SLOWS...UNTIL THE BOOT STOPS, FROZEN, HOVERING AN INCH FROM MY FACE. I roll away from the deadly kick, but I don't release time. I feel the pressure around me start to build. I take several breaths—fascinated by the frozen world I'm momentarily existing in. Here in this impossible vacuum, all my fears float away. A thought strikes me: *Fear.* I focus my will and use the rest of my strength to pull time further back-ward. *This better work.* THE BOOTED FOOT MOVES BACK THROUGH TIME. AEMAN AND I SPRING BACK UP TO OUR FEET, AND I MANAGE TO WIND IT BACK TO JUST AFTER THE SLAP, BEFORE... I have to let go. I'm out of gas. Or energy. Or whatever the hell this freakish magic runs on.

Time moves forward, and I can still hear the aftermath of the slap just slightly ring in the air. This time, as the Kraken turns, I smack him again, this time on his side. He looks shocked as he looks at me. I hit him again. Hard. This time on the back of his jacket.

"WHAT THE HELL ARE YOU DOING?!" he yells.

"Dude! Take your jacket off! Now!" He pushes me away, but I come at him again, swinging hard into his back. I point to the bush next to him. "Yo, a big-ass spider just crawled out of that bush and onto your pants! It went up your shirt!" At the word *spider*, the Kraken absolutely loses his shit. He rips his jacket off and throws it on the ground. I kick his jacket, then worry I've gone too far. But the Kraken doesn't even notice. He's wriggling around in terror, desperately trying to reach his back.

"GET IT OFF! GET IT OFF ME!!!" I smack him again, several times. Finally, I grab him, trying to send authority into my hands.

"Okay, man. I think you're clean." I look him all over. "Yeah, it's gone. Jesus, that was crazy. That thing was huge."

The Kraken grabs my hand in his fierce grip. *He's seen through my trick.*

"Thanks so much, bro," he says. "I felt it. God, I hate spiders! Seriously, good looking out, little man."

"No problem. Have a good one." I start walking. Aeman catches up. His expression is strange.

"I know I didn't sweet-talk him or hustle him or whatever. But I really don't think he was hearing any sweet talk. I'm lucky I escaped with my life."

"You did good," Aeman says. There's nothing sarcastic or smarmy about the way he says it. It's a real compliment. It feels good. It feels really good. I don't quite know how to respond. Before I can, he says, "Hey, we were touching when you stopped time. That was a pretty good trick."

"Yeah. That boot was like two inches from my face. I could smell it. Not pleasant."

"You know, not every Winder can pull that trick off, actually. We call that kind of Winder a Thane. It's not uncommon or anything, but still a cool little arrow to have in your quiver."

"Can you do it?"

"Me? Nah. But don't go getting a big head. I got plenty of tricks up my sleeve, don't you worry," he says, some of his devil-may-care charm returning.

"A Thane? All these crazy names. I'm gonna need a vocab test after today."

"I told you, kid, a whole new world. Anyway, I gotta go check on something. I'll meet you back at the place in a little bit. You can get back all right, yeah?"

"Where are you going?"

"Don't forget to get me breakfast. I'm starving," he says, as he peels away.

"Why don't you just get something while you're out?" I call after him.

He answers without turning around. "Cuz I don't want to hurt your feelings. I know you had something really great planned. See you in a bit." Then he disappears around the block, leaving me alone.

I can't shake the feeling that I've been put aside again. Wherever Aeman went, he didn't want me with him. What do I actually know about him? Nothing. I look around. So many people. So many strangers. Being surrounded by others has always made me feel more alone. I have to get out of here.

CHAPTER 26

CHARLIE

I glide down the sidewalk like a specter. No one looks at me, and I look at no one. God, my mind's a mess. I can't seem to come to terms with the idea that this new reality is permanent—that I'm not going to wake up tomorrow back at Grams's place hoping that maybe some state university will be willing to look past my dismal juvenile record and less-than-stellar grades. Ducky got early acceptance to both Columbia and Brown and will be heading to one of those in the fall. Maybe I'll just be a shepherd. Settle down with a nice little flock somewhere. Don't need a four-year degree for that, right?

Grams and Ducky have always wanted something more for me. I wonder if what I'm doing now would fall under the category of *something more*.

The NYC grid system helps me not to feel like I'm on the moon. Upper Manhattan can be a jumble, not to mention the craziness you get below Houston Street, but in the middle, if you know an address, you can picture right where it is for the most part. *Streets* run east and west and *Avenues* run north and south. Houston Street is considered zero street, and the streets go up numerically from there: 1st Street, 2nd Street, 3rd Street, 4th Street, etc. Fifth Avenue is considered the dividing line between east and west, and each block is a hundred. So, if the address is 320 East 10th Street—just for an example—you know that it's ten streets above Houston and a little over three blocks east of Fifth Ave.

I tell myself I'm just testing out my grid knowledge, but as I stare across Tompkins Square Park at 320 East 10th Street—the address I heard a very cute, pissed-off Tristen growl at her cab driver last night—I wonder how much of a stalker this makes me.

The smell of kebabs and sweet roasted nuts saturates the air. I wander south on Avenue A. There's a rowdy basketball game going on to my left. They're playing two-on-two, and there's a decent crowd watching them. The chaos of guys shouting at each other on the court isn't exactly helping my already-frayed nerves, but this is the East Village, and I have to admit there's an energy to this part of the city that excites me. *No wonder Tristen lives down here.* Something catches my eyes and I stop in front of a newsstand. I see a headline from a local paper, its edges buried behind the two major publications adjacent to it on either side. The smaller paper's headline reads:

WOMAN'S BODY FOUND IN NYC SEWER.

The photo below this headline chills me. The happiness in the woman's face so contrasts the horror that's befallen her. Like she thought the world was fair, and just, and worth believing in, and then fucking *blammo*; the answer is D: none of the above. And without fail, I see a flash of my mother, smiling and laughing, driving her son home from his little league game, and then… There are so many jackals in this world. Some of them are drunk drivers not caring whose lives they endanger getting behind the wheel; some are angry boys talking racist shit about burning down houses, thinking no one's going to stop them; and some are just monsters preying upon the weak and vulnerable—wherever they may roam. And you simply can't kill them all. My stomach burbles with a sudden emptiness. A feeling not of hunger but of fear: fear of my own capacity for violence. I don't know that woman in the newspaper, have no connection to her, and yet the idea that creatures capable of stuffing her into a sewer pipe walk on the same Earth as the people I love leaves me wanting blood. But then my eyes fall on a different headline on the front page of one of the big national newspapers:

CHINESE PITCHER JU-LONG LO BREAKS ALL-TIME STRIKEOUT RECORD!

Below the headline, a dark-eyed, angular man in his late

twenties, smiles enigmatically into the camera. I contemplate this
record-breaking athlete. *Could he be a Winder?* Everything feels different. Is the concept of an equal playing field extinct? Did it ever
exist in the first place? Then my trepidation is suddenly swallowed
by a very fun thought. I feel myself smile. *Why not? Practice makes
perfect, right?*

S weat slops onto my cheek as the chubby Dominican dude bash-
es his shoulder into me, and my face presses against his wet,
hairy sweat-soaked body. His partner, a tall white kid with a tattoo on his back of a ferocious monkey with wings, dribbles by me
effortlessly. The Dominican dude's pick worked perfectly. No way
I can get around him in time. My gangly redheaded partner seems
more concerned with adjusting his oversized headband than covering his man. Monkey Wings makes an easy layup, giving them
a 5-0 lead. We're clearly outmatched, and we're getting clobbered.
I've never been very good at basketball; but playing with Ducky
for so many years has given me enough skill that it might just give
the illusion that what I'm about to do isn't impossible. Can't be too
obvious—first rule of *the Code* and all that. So, let me see if I can
even up the playing field a little.

I give time a tug.

MONKEY WINGS'S LAYUP REVERSES AND HE DRIBBLES BACK-
WARD PAST ME, then I let go, and this time, as the Dominican goes
for the pick, I dodge around him and grab the ball out of Monkey
Wings's hands, whose shocked expression fills me with delight. I
turn in triumph and shoot. The ball flies through the air, making
a perfect arc, then bricks against the rim with an anticlimactic
clang, rendering my maneuver pointless (literally). But that's not
how that's gonna go. I focus and PULL THE MOMENT BACK, TILL
THE BALL'S BACK IN MY PALMS. Then I shoot again. This time, it
smacks the backboard and sinks into the net. My partner whoops
in victory. Our first point on the board! The big Dominican gives
me a little head nod, letting me know that he was impressed by
the lucky move, but his expression is telling me he won't let it
happen again. No one who knows basketball and is watching me

play would ever think anything but that I just caught a lucky break. I know it didn't look smooth or remotely repeatable, but it did the trick. *So, let's do it again.*

We're playing winners outs, so I take the ball back to half-court and toss it to my Dominican friend, who tosses it back to me. The ball is checked. He gives me plenty of room, having seen what a mediocre shooter I am, but he's about to regret that. I toss the ball up from the three-point line, completely miss the backboard, WIND IT BACK, toss it again, *brick*, WIND IT BACK, then…*swish*. Nothing but net this time. I repeat this process several times until we're up 7-5, and the big dude covering me is apoplectic with frustration and confusion as to why I've suddenly become Larry Bird right before his eyes. My partner doesn't seem particularly excited either, despite the fact that we're winning. He's barely gotten to touch the ball, and that's no fun.

I decide it's his turn to score and I try for a showoff pass between the Dominican dude's legs, but Monkey Wings easily intercepts it. I WIND IT BACK and try again, going for an alley-oop pass right next to the basket, but my partner fumbles it badly, catching the pass but stepping out of bounds before he can get control over it. I WIND IT BACK. The next pass works like a beauty. He runs up the side, I pass him the ball, he pushes up the court; I set up a pick, and the big Dominican plows into me like a freight train, sending me flying (definitely a foul, but there's no refs). My partner makes it through, however, and sinks an easy layup, jumping in triumph.

As I slowly climb back onto my feet, I feel utterly exhausted and shaky—like I haven't eaten. But it also feels deeper than that. My core strength feels depleted. And not just from the game. My stamina should be pretty elite, being fresh out of Lazarus. It's the winding. It's really taken its toll. It's a fascinating feeling. My body feels so heavy, but I also feel exhilarated—like a bird stretching its wings for the very first time. And something about that irks me, deeply. It doesn't feel fair. That's the plain truth. These guys should be trouncing us. They *were*, before I used my abilities. It just doesn't feel right. I should not be able to beat these guys in basketball. They're probably out here practicing all the time, and here I step in, like an imposter, and rob them of what they've worked hard for. Somehow, that feels kind of gross to me. It feels like cheating. I already know I'm going to win this game if I can hold my strength a little longer. And knowing that completely takes the fun out of it. Takes away all the suspense. Why play a game if you already know the outcome? I can't imagine anything more boring or selfish.

To my partner's dismay, we quickly lose the next six points and the game is over. The loss doesn't feel good, especially when the Dominican dude laughs at me and blows me a kiss as he stalks away after sinking the game-winning basket right in my face. The loss feels shitty, like all losses do, but it feels more *just* somehow.

I leave the court and gulp down half a gallon of water at the drinking fountain. The cool liquid feels amazing going down. I lean over, fill my palms and wash my face. When I stand straight up again, I find myself staring across the park, directly at…Tristen.

She turns at the corner of 8th Street and starts heading west, toward Astor Place. The breeze flutters her hair, which looks almost auburn in the bright sunlight. I had hoped to see her, of course, had assumed I wouldn't, though my positioning was pretty strategic, given her address and the direct route to the NYU campus. But now I don't know what to do. *Last night was weird. Shit.* But before I even make up my mind, I find myself following her.

I stay behind her for several blocks, until she gets to Astor Place, then I can't take it anymore. Picking up my pace, I cross the street, get ahead of her, then cross back onto her side of the street and intentionally stand right in her path. She's wearing headphones. She doesn't notice me. I wave. She stops, surprised. Her face is unreadable.

"Hey," I say, deciding to take the nonchalant approach. She just stares at me. *I'm so bad at this.* "So…last night was a little crazy."

"Ya think?" Her annoyance is thick and grim and I'm out of ideas. *Last night was a little crazy* was all I had. I'm about to open my mouth and just divulge my entire last twenty-four hours, when I get an idea—an obvious idea—sitting in front of me like a game of T-ball…I give time a little yank—

AND THE SCENE WINDS BACK TO BEFORE I WAVED TO TRISTEN. And release. Not too bad this time, energy-conservation-wise. I'm getting a little better at this, but I still feel it.

I walk by her again, and this time, as she passes, I turn…

"…Tristen?" I try and make my surprise sound as natural as possible. I'm almost impressed with my acting skills, but she keeps walking. *Crap! Forgot she's wearing headphones.* I WIND THE SCENE BACK AGAIN. WE BRUSH BY EACH OTHER BACKWARD, AND I CAN ALMOST SMELL THE SCENT OF WHATEVER SHAMPOO SHE USES ON HER HAIR. (I SAID ALMOST. I'M NOT A STALKER.) And release.

This time, as I walk past her, I try to gently have our arms brush each other, which will cause her to look over, obviously. Unfortunately, in my nervousness, I misjudge the timing and smash my shoulder into her. She stumbles and almost falls.

"DICK!" she yells, not even recognizing me yet.

I RIP THE UNIVERSE INTO REVERSE AGAIN.

I walk straight toward her, pretending I'm looking at my phone. We're heading straight at each other on a collision course, but I'm watching out of the corner of my eye. She looks up first and stops. I look up and stop. She seems shocked to see me. I smile.

"Oh, wow," I say. "Hey…" So far, my performance is spot on.

"You come to tell me I'm not allowed in Astor Place?" she says, stone-faced.

"Yep. From Third Avenue to Broadway. Exiled."

Tristen does not like this joke at all. *Dammit.*

I WIND IT BACK SLIGHTLY. The fatigue is getting too much. I won't be able to do this much longer. Beads of sweat trickle all over my body. I say a silent prayer that I don't smell.

"You come to tell me I'm not allowed in Astor Place?" she unknowingly repeats.

I take a breath. "Look…I'm really sorry about last night. There was a whole bunch of creepy people at that party, and I don't know why…but suddenly I felt protective over you. Dumb, I know. But true."

Tristen takes this in. It doesn't seem to displease her.

"Go on," she says.

"I overreacted."

"Like *seriously* overreacted."

"…Totally overreacted."

"Because I'm a big girl, Charlie. I can take care of myself."

"I have no doubt."

A silent beat passes between us. The jury is still out…and then…

"Apology accepted," she says. Relief washes over me. And more sweat.

"Thank you." *Okay, Charlie, new topic.* "How are your classes going?"

"On my way to my first one."

"Right… Can I walk you to class? Maybe hold your books… quietly?" I aim as charming a smile as I can muster at her. It falls flat. She just stares at me with an odd, hostile intensity. I'm about to wind when, all at once, she laughs. She was messing with me. She has a great laugh.

She starts walking away, then turns back. "You coming?"

I heave after her, and my muscles moan at the sudden movement. Now I'm doing everything in my power to temper my stride into a casual canter rather than the fumbling chase it began as. We walk for a while in silence.

"So, what are you doing in the city, anyway?" she asks. "Besides attending creepster parties and shuttling beautiful young women off into the dark?"

"Oh…nothing much. Being stupid. Trying to become more evolved."

"How's that working out for you?"

"So far, so good. Made more progress than I thought I would, actually."

"Really? In less than twenty-four hours? That's impressive."

"Yeah, well, don't give me too much credit yet. I still feel pretty unimpressive."

"Where are you staying?"

I hesitate. *What is Aeman to me? Teacher, mentor, provocateur?* "With a friend," I say.

Tristen stops and turns to me. "Well, we're here." I look up at the NYU building's main entrance, wishing we'd been so much farther away, but my legs are also very thankful we're not walking anymore.

"That was quick," I say.

"So…that's it?"

"This feels familiar." From her confused expression, she's obviously forgotten the moment on the train. No turning back; I barrel on. "Can I see you again?"

"Maybe."

"Wow. Gonna make me work for it, huh?"

"Everything worthwhile takes effort, Charlie."

"I can handle that," I say. She likes my boldness; I can tell. Her eyes linger on mine. Then she gets that searching look again, the same look she had last night in the cab. It feels like she's looking for something specific. A lie, maybe. Or the sharp, icy point of the iceberg of whatever *issues* I'm pretending I don't have. *She has no idea.* But truthfully, I don't know her either. She could be a serial killer, for all I know, or an escaped mental patient from a high-security facility, and she's looking at me so intensely right now because she's planning out which parts of my skin she's going to make into a bathrobe. I meet her gaze, trying to communicate telepathically: *I'll show you mine if you show me yours, and that way we can both walk away from each other right now, unscathed.*

"Nathan?! Stop running right now! NATHAN!"

I turn as a frantic woman darts by me, chasing after a two-year-old toddler (Nathan, I assume), who sprint-waddles away from her—laughing hysterically—*directly toward traffic.*

Ahead of Nathan, a garbage truck is going to reach the boy before his mother. The driver is totally unaware, watching a group of girls on the opposite side of the street. Nathan leaves the sidewalk, sees the looming truck and freezes in shock. Mom howls, stumbling as she tries to force her narrow arms across a gap of space impossible for her to cross in the infinitesimal window of time she has left to reach her son.

The immediacy of the moment floods me with blade-like focus. I'm so fucking tired, I'm terrified that nothing will happen, or I'll pass out before I can help, but still, I *flex* my mind…

THE TRUCK, MERE INCHES FROM OBLITERATING LITTLE NATHAN, CREEPS BACKWARD, THE DRIVER STILL GAWKING AT THE GIRLS. IT HURTS. I FEEL LIKE SOMETHING INSIDE OF ME IS UNRAVELING, BUT I

CAN'T STOP. MOM SLOWLY LURCHES BACKWARD PAST ME, FOLLOWED BY NATHAN, LOOKING LIKE AN ANIMATRONIC AMUSEMENT-PARK CHASE SCENE BEING RESET TO THE BEGINNING. PEOPLE AND CARS RETREAT IN ALL DIRECTIONS AS WELL. Finally, I can't hold it any longer, and I release my hold on time…take a gulp of breath, and just as Nathan walks by, not running yet, I reach down and scoop the miniature hooligan up into my arms.

"Where ya think you're going, kiddo?" I say, playfully, sweat souping down my face.

I turn to Nathan's mother, sheepishly; I've never been comfortable with extreme gratitude or praise, but a big part of me is thrilled that it's going to happen in front of Tristen. But the look of horror I see on Nathan's mother's face freezes me in place.

"…Put him down…right now!" she says.

I'm so shocked by her response that I don't move a muscle. Random people look over. I glance at Tristen and see surprise and confusion on her face as well—it's awful. Then Nathan takes his mother's tone as a clear signal that he should be terrified, and he lets out a screech that nearly deafens me.

"…I'm sorry…he was going to…there was a garbage truck… and girls—"

"PUT HIM DOWN!" she shouts.

I plant the sobbing child on the ground. Mom dashes in, rips Nathan off the sidewalk with all the subtlety of an alien abduction and rushes away, never looking back. I stare after them, refusing to take in the disapproving glances I can feel poking at me from all directions. To my complete bafflement, little Nathan waves to me over his mother's shoulder. I can't look at Tristen. *"Ten seconds later and you're a hero,"* I whisper to myself. *"Great timing, Charlie."* Then my knees go wobbly, and I stumble—my strength gone— and I know I'm going down hard, and it's going to hurt really bad. *Please don't let me break any teeth.*

Tristen reacts quickly. Grabbing one of my arms, she loops it around her neck and steadies me, aiming for a bench at a bus stop a few yards away. We plop down onto the bench, and I almost throw up on her, which would've truly been the end, I have no doubt, but I manage to hold that particular humiliation at bay. (At least for the time being.) I take several deep breaths, then look up at Tristen, fully aware she just saw me get accused of accosting a little boy. But instead of judgement, I see an odd smile appear on her face. "You okay?"

"Just got dizzy. Listen…there was a garbage truck."

"I saw it. Dude wasn't even looking where he was going." Relief hits me so hard that she actually saw what was going on that I almost feel tears coming. I think my exhaustion is making me more emotional. "You grabbed that kid kinda quick, though. Seemed like the truck would've already passed through the intersection by the time he got there."

"He was gonna start running."

"Really? What makes you say that?"

I have no idea what to say. Everything will sound stupid. Or creepy. Or insane. But I have to say something. "…He just looked like he was ready to run. That's what kids do…. They're crazy."

Tristen stares at me. She seems unsure, but I just stare back, attempting to beam my sincere intentions at her. Finally, she says, "So, you were rescuing him."

"Yeah. I just wanted to do it in the most awkward way possible. Obviously."

Tristen's mouth breaks into a smile at this. "Nailed it," she says. I smile back, thankful for the lightness. Then she holds out her hand. "Let me see your phone."

Grateful for the change in topic, I pull out my cell phone and hand it to her. She types something into my phone. While she does, I watch her. She has light freckles on her cheeks, and her nose is kind of perfect on her face. She catches me staring. "Turn around. I need my privacy."

I turn around on the bench, facing away from her. A strong breeze wafts by, and now I do smell the kind of shampoo Tristen uses. It's citrusy and fresh, maybe even a little tropical.

"Is it some kind of secret?" I ask, my back still turned.

"Maybe. Okay, you can turn around now."

I turn back, and she hands me my phone. I see she's entered

her contact info into it, under the name (I read it out loud): *Tristen the Wicked Smart Super Sexy Girl I Met While Crying in My Sleep on the Train.*

I look up at her. "Wow. That's a really long name."

Tristen shrugs. "Blame my parents." Then she stands up, walks across the sidewalk and disappears inside the NYU building. I can feel the heat shining on my face. *Amazing.*

CHAPTER 27

CHARLIE

I enter Aeman's loft, breakfast burrito in hand, and chuck the burrito ahead of me through the door. THEN I GIVE TIME A QUICK YANK, CAUSING IT TO SNAP BACK INTO MY HAND; THE HEAT FROM THE FOIL WRAPPER WARMS MY PALM. I release and hear the little aftershock ringing in the air. It feels good. I have to say I'm getting the hang of this—the focus needed for smaller more precise winds.

I stop dead in my tracks.

Sitting on Aeman's massive, food-encrusted couch—looking like a pearl inside the grey, gushy belly of an oyster—is a girl. Our eyes meet as I enter. She's dressed all in white, hair pulled back in a loose ponytail with a lock escaping, falling slightly in front of her right eye. I can't help but instantly compare her to Tristen. I know that's not fair at all—this girl's not asking to be judged by some random guy she doesn't know—but I'm still basking in the exchange I just came from and feeling pretty good about myself, and I'm not quite ready to let go of that just yet. It's interesting, though; where Tristen wields a wild confidence and seems pretty damn aware of her own allure, this girl feels different. She's pretty, for sure, but I don't think that's the first thing anyone would ever notice about her. It's hard to explain, but there's a kind of gritty elegance to the girl sitting on Aeman's soiled couch, a sharp, thick intelligence, perceivable even at just a glance.

Her eyes narrow at me, and I'm suddenly painfully aware of how grimy and strung-out I must look. *Why did I pick this day to play a heated, sweaty game of basketball?* I suppose this is what

I get for trying to show off. I couldn't wind away my bedraggled appearance in front of Tristen, and now I'm getting a double dose of medicine.

She rises to her feet and I give her my best nice-to-meet-you smile. She doesn't smile back. In fact, I would call her expression unfriendly. "...Can I help you?" I ask.

"Who are you?" the girl demands.

"Um...Charlie."

Her face races through a bouquet of emotions: confusion, frustration and even fear, which leaves me totally lost. *What's this girl's deal?* She's acting like I just caught her doing something questionable.

"Are you wingless?" she asks.

I can't help but smile at the bizarre question. "Oh, no, I just keep my wings tucked away in the back. Helps with the whole walking-through-doorways thing." I laugh at my own joke. Sometimes, I can find myself extremely funny—especially when I'm feeling nervous, which this strange girl is making me, for some reason. *Maybe she's high. Could Aeman also be a drug dealer, in addition to everything else, and this odd girl is one of his "clients," here for a fix?* It feels more than likely, the more I think about it.

But the girl's face curls into an expression of disdain. "Do you mock me?" she asks, and aside from sounding strangely formal, her tone is more than a little nasty.

"Hey, you're the one asking weird-ass questions. I'm just trying to deliver burritos."

"Where's Aeman?!" she shouts.

"Why are you yelling at me?!" I shout back, refusing to be bullied by a drug addict.

"I asked you a question," she says, her voice filled with venom.

"So did I."

"You need to leave. Now!"

What the hell is this girl's problem? "Did I harm you in some way I'm not aware of?"

"I SAID LEAVE! Do you not recognize my authority?!"

I'd laugh if I weren't so thrown off by her belligerent dickishness.

"Listen, Looney Tunes—"

The girl snatches a ceramic egg off Aeman's table and launches it at my face.

First rule of the Code or not, I raise my hand and…

THE EDGES OF THE WORLD BLUR AS MY WIND BEGINS, but then just as suddenly those same edges slacken, and I feel my wind get ripped away. The egg passes by my outstretched hand and smashes into my forehead, shattering. I pitch backward over a small end table, crushing the unlucky piece of furniture beneath me.

The girl stands above me now, and for the briefest of moments, I see concern on her face—which really confuses me—but then it slips away, leaving only a sour, twisted expression in its wake. "You thought you'd raise your mind to me, Winder?! A member of the Council? Are you an idiot?"

Fresh blood leaks from my wounded head, and now I'm fucking angry. *This bitch just Fabergéed my forehead!* I leap to my feet, ready to do battle, until laughter breaks out behind me. I spin around to see Aeman drop down into the battleground we've made of his apartment.

"Sis! I see you've met my guest," Aeman says. "Juniper, this is Charlie. Charlie, this is my baby sister, the *honorable* Juniper Trask."

"You're *related* to this harpy?!" I wail, and Aeman's sister reaches for another object to strike me with.

"Easy. Forgive him his trespasses, baby sister. Everything's a little new to him." Aeman is finding everything way too amusing, and it's annoying the hell out of me.

"Why wasn't I able to wind?" I ask.

"Why doesn't he recognize me?" she squawks. "My election's been in every Leadership communication. Even to the wingless."

That word again, *wingless.*

Aeman smiles sheepishly at his younger sister. "Well…that question has a complicated answer." She gasps and looks back at me, taking a step away, like I might have an infectious disease.

"You haven't registered him with the Leadership, have you?" Her eyes look suddenly frightened. "I could feel technique in his wind. You've been teaching him. Are you insane, Aeman?! It's a Death Rule. If anyone finds out—"

"They won't. Not unless you rat on me. Which I know you won't. Just like I know you wouldn't be standing here, getting your pretty white clothes dirty if there wasn't something dire on your mind. So, out with it." She looks deeply conflicted. "*Of course* I'm gonna bring him to the Leadership," Aeman says. "I'm not a fool. We were just having a little fun. Now, what's up?"

The shrew glances at me out of the corner of her eye. "We need to talk," she half-whispers to Aeman. "Alone."

"What do you mean, *bring me to the Leadership?*" I demand, but Aeman doesn't answer. He's trying to gauge his sister's purpose. There doesn't seem to be a whole lot of trust or closeness between these two. Aeman turns to me.

"Charlie, will you give us a minute?"

I want to tell them both to go to hell. I want to turn around, walk out that door and never return. Instead, I do the next best thing. I stomp across the room like a petulant child, giving "Juniper" a go-fuck-yourself stare the whole way, which she returns evenly. Then I whip open the sliding glass door and exit onto the balcony.

Once again, I know nothing.

There is truly only one thing I do know at this moment: I hate that girl.

CHAPTER 28

JUNIPER

Aeman isn't taking me seriously. He never has. And I feel so distracted. The moronic *time bomb* now standing on Aeman's balcony has me reeling. *What is Aeman doing with an unregistered Winder? And how long has he had him?* Judging by how small his wind sounded as he entered—intricate winds being nearly impossible for beginning Winders—I'd say he's been working with Aeman for some time. Training a Winder without the Leadership's knowledge is seen as an act of sedition, of army-building, and is punishable by death. Just being here and not instantly reporting Aeman makes me complicit. I didn't think it was possible that things could get worse so quickly. Leave it to Aeman to defy the odds. *Why the hell did I come here?*

To make matters worse, his "trainee" is a complete fool and can't be trusted. I'm not blind; he's obviously *handsome.* That means nothing. Trevor always said, "The strongest poisons come in the sweetest forms." *Why am I quoting Trevor? It's ironic, and horrid, and I want to pry his voice from my brain!* But I can't deny that his teachings might be the only preparation I've had for my new reality. Not a lot of surviving mortal peril being taught in the labs.

I need to calm down, get control. My anger got the best of me with Aeman's new pet. He probably knows nothing of our world. *Was I too hard on him?* Aeman's the last person I'd ever want as a Teacher. I can't imagine what he's told him. My reaction was aggressive, I suppose, but the fool was being rude. …At least, I believed he was being rude at the time. I was simply ignorant to *his* ignorance. But *then* he *did* become rude, so…regardless of the brief moment, when his dark, lake blue eyes made me forget why I was standing in Aeman's apartment in the first place—*regardless of that*—he is adding an unneeded complication to my life right now, and therefore, I wish I'd thrown that egg a lot harder. I push the scruffy outlaw, who just called me a *harpy* and who is hopefully freezing to death at this very moment, out of my mind.

"Do you think I'd be here if I wasn't certain, Aeman? Or if I had anywhere else to go?"

"I've missed you too, sis." Aeman flops down onto his massive couch, grinning at me with the same smug look he's torn down my confidence with hundreds of times before. My face flushes with old fury. He chuckles. He looks so much like Mother when he laughs, it physically hurts me. Aeman has her pale, Scottish skin, her long neck and gaunt cheeks, with the slightest hint of rosacea. But those same elegant features, which etched a lean, beautiful shape on my mother, somehow add an element of menace to my brother's face. This is harder than I thought it would be. But I need his help, and I don't have time to be haunted by ghosts.

"I'm telling you, Aeman, Trevor's threat was real." Again, I don't mention being struck by Trevor. Even though it might help speed this debilitating process along. Trevor's slap feels private somehow. Personal. Like if I told someone about it, they might feel the necessity to *do* something about it. Not that I think that would be Aeman's reaction, having been Trevor's lieutenant for years and his number-one Enforcer. It used to be Aeman and Gael Falcón always on either side of Trevor, with Aeman's wild disposition giving him a slight advantage in Trevor's eyes, but now only one man remains beside Trevor, and it's not my brother. If all were as it was, I wouldn't want to find out whose side Aeman would choose between me and his Teacher. But things have changed. And since Aeman's exile, he could be feeling a bit bitter, and I'm not giving anyone a reason to steal my revenge from me. But I know I can't do this on my own. And I've run out of options. Aeman has access to a vast underground network as well as, I'm assuming, a certain amount of old Enforcer contacts. I press further. "If he's coming at *me*, that means he already knows where everyone else on the Council stands."

"I think a war against the Faters sounds nice." His voice is atrociously nonchalant.

"Stop it! This isn't a joke. You know Trevor as well as I do. He doesn't start fights he can't win. And there'll never be a clear victory against a terrorist cell. You can beat them into submission, but they'll never admit defeat, and they'll just grow back. Does that sound like something Trevor would waste his time on?"

"Trevor's always hated the Faters. Why does it have to be more than that?"

"I just know it does. Okay? Have you heard anything from the other Enforcers?"

"Not a ton of chatting since the whole excommunication thing, believe it or not."

He tries to sound dispassionate, but I see him grinding his teeth—a childhood tic—a sign that, despite his lackadaisical posture, his mind is moving rapidly. Then his eyes grow hard. It's only in these moments that I see our father in Aeman—the father who turned his back on his only son as Aeman was torn from the bosom of the Leadership like a malignant tumor.

"Does dear ol' Dad know you're here?"

"Of course not."

A little smile creeps into his eyes. "Did I ever tell you I almost killed him the night before I left? Held a knife to his throat. He never even knew I was there. Drank himself unconscious. One flick and his jugular would've simply dumped out all his misery, along with his life. Probably would've done him a favor. Haven't you ever wondered if he's as cold on the inside as he is on the surface?"

"Why didn't you do it?" I do not let my face reveal even a drop of emotion. That's what he wants. He's baiting me.

"I decided the only person who hates our asshole prick father more than me is our asshole prick father. Guess I didn't mind leaving him in that kind of company."

"Letting yourself off the hook there quite a bit, aren't you? He's not the one who caused you to be thrown out, after all."

He remains smiling, but his eyes lose all the wicked glee he was just enjoying. Aeman was caught stealing. Not just stealing: embezzling. Not just embezzling: using my father's own private coding to siphon millions from the secure Provider revenue banks to a private account in Kyoto, Japan. Aeman never revealed what he intended to use the money for. He seemed to treat the entire ordeal like some kind of joke when he was brought before the Council on trial. Some thought Aeman was making a deal with the Japanese Chapter, but I never did. I think Aeman just loves to make chaos—especially for our father.

He was not found guilty of having treasonous intent toward our Chapter, and therefore, his verdict was not a death sentence. But permanent banishment from the only home he'd ever known was enough to turn the dark shade of Aeman's nature several tints darker. I shouldn't feel bad; he brought it upon himself. But he's still my big brother—the only person who stood by me after my mother's death. When I wouldn't get out of bed—when I was sure, somehow, it was all my fault. Aeman stayed by my side. And now I need him again. I just don't know how much of him is left at this point.

"No, no. I take full responsibility for my actions, of course," he says. "But if you think he couldn't have weighed in when it came to the consequences, you're fooling yourself. He certainly placed his hand on the scale when it came time to choose a new member of the Council."

"Father did nothing. Trevor put my name forward."

This seems to really throw Aeman. He wasn't expecting that. For a brief second, he actually looks worried. He knows that such a move by Trevor makes little sense, given our history. And he knows it smacks of something larger on Trevor's horizon. But then he quickly slides whatever worry I saw behind a smug look of boredom. "What do you want from me, baby sis? Do you need a hug?"

"Find out what's going on." I can't bring myself to kowtow to him, like I know he wants me to. "I know you can." Then I clench my jaw and say, "...Please." The sincerity in my voice surprises me. I can't tell him Trevor threatened to kill Father, because I don't want him to look me in the eye and tell me he doesn't care. I couldn't take that right now—especially if it's true.

Aeman's stare pierces into me, hostility palpable. He's about to tell me to go ask my "new *pals* on the Council" for help; I feel it coming a mile away, vibrating the tracks like a far-off freight train. But then it never arrives.

Aeman suddenly gets a contemplative look. I try to imagine what he's thinking, but he's always been better at this part than me—the part where he hides his true feelings. His malice seems to flit away and he refocuses on me.

"Okay," he says.

"Okay? What do you mean, 'Okay'?"

"I'll see what I can find out. But that means you need to keep an eye on the kid for me."

I almost laugh. "That is *never* going to happen," I say. "Seriously, Aeman, no chance."

His Cheshire grin beams at me as he jumps to his feet. I can already feel the red-hot fury boiling relentlessly upward from my toes, swallowing me whole.

"Aeman…no!"

CHAPTER 29

CHARLIE

Below the balcony, taxis and buses brawl for dominion; digital lights and screens blink and belch out coded messages, while an aimless army of anonymous forms slips soundlessly down gum-speckled sidewalks—their footfalls just far enough away so that no matter how hard I strain my ears, I can't make out a single step. And because I can't hear them, I can't feel them. And because I can't feel them, I suddenly imagine every street and avenue filling up with water until I am the last soul on Earth. Things would be so much easier if I only had to think about me.

These last twenty-four hours, as insane as they've been, have been a welcomed distraction. But out here on this wrought-iron island, a fierce loneliness collapses in on me again, and I remember why I came to the city in the first place—to figure out how to get this curse under control. And it is a curse. As much as I've enjoyed ruling at basketball or serial flirting with a beautiful girl, I can't forget that every choice I make, every time I wind something back, I'm killing another future that could have been. A world where I don't get the girl's number, but also a world where Ducky's parents are still alive. It feels like such an unbearable burden of responsibility. I can't let anyone else get hurt because of me. And then I remember the promise I made. *Shit!*

The sun bakes the top of my head. I run a hand through my hair, feeling the short, heated, bristly strands. *This is going to suck.*

I pull my cell phone from my pocket and dial. I picture the clunky, yellow monstrosity pealing at the top of its lungs in Grams's kitchen. The ring on my side of the call feels so benign. As I'm thinking of that phone, a memory hits me. That early morning when Ducky and I were ripped out of bed by the woeful, gurgling moan of a dying beast. Inside the little kitchen, the pea-green rotary wall phone, with its crusty, gnarled, endless cord, breathed one last horrendous shriek, then never made another sound again. Grams slept through the entire thing. Later that day, after a ceremonial unscrewing and plopping into the trashcan, Ducky, me and Grams went to Mendosa's Hardware, where Grams picked out the second-ugliest phone I have ever seen.

"Who else is gonna give it a home?" Grams said to Ducky and me as our eyes greedily ogled the cordless Nokia hanging far too confidently next to the lemon-yellow relic Grams was smiling at. Ducky and I were still two years away from getting cell phones. We yearned for the new, digital phone, but neither of us said a word, because it was that same big-hearted attitude and sympathetic spirit that had been a life raft to two traumatized orphans only a few years prior.

What if I just had the courage to confess my sins? I think. She picks up.

"Hello?"

"…Hi, Grams." *I killed your daughter.*

"Charlie! You had us worried, not calling last night. Everything okay?"

"…Yep." *I killed your handsome son-in-law who used to call you Mom, even though you both knew it wasn't true.*

"You coming home soon?"

"I've still got some stuff I gotta figure out here for a minute." I don't want her to pick apart my vagueness, so I push forward. "Is Ducky there?"

She hesitates, which tells me one hundred percent that he *is* there. Probably sitting at the kitchen table, listening and signaling to Grams that he's *not home.* It seems almost impossible to me that just two days ago, we were standing in the Safest Place and laughing together about Alicia Peterson's retainer.

"Not sure where he's at, Charlie," she says with an accusing sigh. She hates lying. "Hoping he gets his mind right. You boys are family."

Heartache gags me for a moment. *I don't deserve these people. They don't deserve me.*

"…Charlie?"

"Grams… What if you you'd done something…something horrible…but you didn't realize you were doing it when you did it? But the pain you caused…it *is* your fault. I just—"

"Charlie Ryan, you listen good," she cuts me off. "You're a beautiful boy. I've known you your whole life, and you're the good kind. That inextinguishable good. And if you done something that's hurting you, I'm willing to bet you didn't have a choice in the matter."

She sees me. She always has. And for a moment, I allow myself to be seen through her eyes. Is it possible, on some magical, psychic level, that Grams knows exactly why I'm hurting and is imploring me to confess it, to allow the burn, and then let it go? Could anybody be that forgiving? All at once, I inhale so completely, you'd think I was a pearl diver. I hadn't noticed my lungs had grown cold and empty. Now they're full, filled with reckless potential, and I feel myself stepping off the cliff, when—

"Them skinhead boys was filled with hate. Don't you take none of that on your heart, Charlie." My hope evaporates. I close my eyes. *Fuck.* She has no idea how personal my actual confession would be to her.

"…I gotta go," I say. "I'll call again soon."

"All right, Charlie, but don't you disappear on us. There's people here that are always gonna love you."

I hang up and hate myself for it. *Why didn't you tell her you love her, too? Why didn't you demand to talk to Ducky? You know you could've got him on the phone if you really tried.* My brain feels belligerent—loudmouthed and drunk on remorse—thoughts as joyless as a swarm of hornets. Silent strangers glide along on the streets below. I want to scream down at them, *I CAN'T HEAR YOU!! NOBODY CAN!*

I sink down, my back scraping the jagged brick wall until I'm torn and sitting. I try and feel nothing. I can hear Aeman and that horrid girl arguing inside, but I can't make out anything being said.

I look at my cell phone lying limp in my hand. I scroll. I dial. I wait. After a few rings, she answers.

"I know what you're thinking," I say into the phone. "He's calling way too soon."

"*Way* too soon," Tristen repeats. "I just got out of class."

"I really can't think of anything clever to say, so I'm just gonna be awkwardly truthful. I'm dealing with something, and I could really use someone to talk to right now. Think you can handle that?"

Two seconds of silence bake and die upon my shore like jellyfish.

"Guess we'll find out," she says.

CHAPTER 30

JUNIPER

Charlie slides open the balcony door and reenters Aeman's disgusting chamber. Our eyes meet for a brief moment. *Those eyes.*

Aeman's request is ludicrous. "I don't have time for babysitting," I say. "And I'm not going to be found with him. I just joined the Council. Can you imagine how that would look?"

"They won't let me anywhere near Thessaly; you know that." Aeman says. "You want him registered? *You* bring him in."

"And where would I say I found him, Aeman? The fucking zoo?!"

"Language, little sister." I could strangle him.

Then the time bomb takes a step toward us. "Bring who in?" he asks. *"Me?"*

"You're the genius," Aeman says to me, not even acknowledging Charlie. "You think of something."

There is absolutely nothing about being called a genius in front of Aeman's mangy apprentice that I don't enjoy, but still I know Aeman's playing me. If he took this kid under his wing, it was definitely for a reason. He knows I won't betray him by bringing in an unregistered Winder who could, under various forms of Enforcer persuasion, reveal how he was found. They would think I was complicit. How could I prove I'm not? He knows exactly how much is at stake for me, and he's using it against me. *Why did I think Aeman would help me? I shouldn't be here!*

"I will not be left alone with him, Aeman! How dare you ask that."

"How about this?" Charlie interjects. "You two can mysteriously talk about someone else. Goodbye!" The imbecile heads for the door.

"You're not leaving!" I blast at him.

Charlie simply raises his middle finger at me and keeps moving.

I look to Aeman for help, but he's already hoisting himself up through the hole in his ceiling.

"Aeman...stop him!" I try for a commanding tone, but it comes out as an ugly whine.

"Sorry, sis. Got detective work to do." And then he's gone. I stare up at his absence in disbelief. Then I hear the front door slam. *This is not happening.*

CHAPTER 31

JUNIPER

Charlie's pace is brisk and I have to half-jog to catch up as the fool careens down the sidewalk as if lives didn't hang in the balance.

"Hey…" I call to him. No response. "Hey!" He keeps walking. "STOP WALKING RIGHT NOW!"

He stops, abruptly, and turns back.

"Hey, psycho"—his voice is a raging whisper—"how about we don't announce to the whole world that we're a couple of freaks. Sound good?"

He starts walking again. I look around, embarrassed. *What is it about this stupid boy that's making me act so reckless?* I'll give it some serious thought once I'm not dancing on the edge of utter disaster. The hairs on the back of my neck suddenly tingle, and I whip my attention to the rooftops. *Are we being watched? I thought I saw… Or was it a sound? Did I hear something? I'm not sure. Paranoia, maybe.* I glance at a middle-aged couple walking by. *Do they look familiar? Did Trevor send someone to follow me? This feels so exposed.*

"Where are you going?" I keep my voice down, but my agitation is clear.

"How were you able to stop me from winding?" he asks. "I felt you stop me."

We're walking single file. It looks odd. I speed up till we're almost side-by-side. I don't know what to say. Answering his questions is the *last* thing I should ever be doing. The more he learns from me, the more I put myself in danger, but I just can't help myself.

"A more powerful Winder can always block the wind of a weaker one," I answer.

"Wow. You don't hold back, huh?" I don't understand his meaning, but his tone is sarcastic. He's mocking me again. "Always?" he asks. "There's nothing you can do?"

"Until the more powerful Winder loses enough strength or focus, no."

"How'd you know I was going to wind?"

"An object was hurtling toward your face; I made an educated guess."

His irritated expression brings me joy, but I've never been asked this question, so against my better judgment… "Plus, there's a tiny collapse felt as a wind is about to occur. A transmogrifying of energy. It'd take too long to explain it to you. You've probably felt it but didn't understand it."

He stops and stares at me. His eyes are penetrating. I lift my chin as if it were some kind of shield.

"Are you like a mathematician or a scientist of some kind?"

His question catches me off guard. So, he's not a *complete* moron. Oddly, it makes me feel proud that even a dopey, ignorant stranger can sense such a thing. I actually feel myself smile, ever so slightly. "Well, actually—"

"Because you have so little personality when you explain stuff, I'm just assuming you're probably used to talking to mice or computers or something."

My smile disintegrates. No smile has ever died faster. The cruel half-wit turns and starts off again. I yank him back by the shoulder. He pushes my hands off. I grab and twist his wrist, but he spins with it, pulling *my* wrist into some kind of arm lock. His physical dexterity surprises me—it speaks of years of intense training—but he's no match for the dexterity of my mind. I focus and…

ALL OF OUR MOVEMENTS SPEED IN REVERSE UNTIL I STAND BEHIND HIM AGAIN AS HE TURNS TO WALK AWAY. I release.

We were touching when I wound, so he'll know what's coming, but I'm curious how fine-tuned his post-wind perceptions are, so I reach for his shoulder again in exactly the same way as before. He's ready and goes to block my grasp with a swipe of his arm. But this is what I was expecting, and I easily dodge under his attack, then sling-blade a kick into the back of his now-unbalanced legs, ripping them out from underneath him. He flies horizontally into the air and is about to crack onto the ground when I feel a—

" . . . I'm just assuming you're probably used to talking to mice or computers or something." The cruel half-wit turns and starts off again. I reach out to yank him back by the shoulder, but before my hand reaches him, he jumps away and turns, floating on the balls of his feet in the neutral stance of an experienced fighter. A wave of fatigue punches into me, stealing my breath. He's panting as well, veins nearly erupting from his neck. He looks even more spontaneously exhausted than I am. A clear and undeniable ringing trumpets through the air. What the hell just happened? Panic and confusion engulf me. I look at him, stunned.

"…You knew I'd reach for you," I say. "And I can hear your wind, which means you were able to wind while I was blocking you. How did you do that?" The question pours out of me without malice. I'm too baffled for anger.

"Guess I'm not the weaker one after all." His crooked smile gouges at my ego. His innate power might possibly trump mine, but I remind myself that he has no real idea what he's doing.

"You seem pretty out of breath to me," I say. "Use a little too much energy?" I rocket my fist at his face. He dodges, then ATTEMPTS TO WIND. THE EDGES BLUR. I RAISE MY HAND, FOCUS-ING ALL MY MIND'S MIGHT INTO THE GESTURE, AND RIP DOWN HIS WIND. The edges crumble. He seems momentarily dumbfounded by my defensive move, and in the moment of advantage, I savagely kick the handsome young man in his handsome face. He staggers back, loses his legs and falls hard onto his ass. The fight is over before it's barely begun. I'm almost disappointed he wasn't able to put up more of a fight. But what else could I have expected? I've been trained by Trevor himself—trained as a Winder and an Enforcer—while this young man was undoubtedly taught by some middling human instructor. Still, I have to say, his technique was surprisingly strong, despite its lack of effectiveness.

People around us look over in shock as Charlie sits on the ground. I step forward, looming over him. "That's what happens when you try and steal a lady's purse!"

Blood trickles from his nose. I'm proud of my quick cover story. Sometimes, I even surprise myself. An old woman gives Charlie a petrified look and scuttles away.

"She's not even wearing a purse!" he howls from the ground.

I allow myself a teensy chuckle at his expense. "No, you're definitely weaker. You're just stupid, too. Horrible combination."

"I'm pretty sure I hate you," he says.

"Darn. And I put my best foot forward."

Charlie gets to his feet, wiping blood from his nose. I expect another vicious retort, but his wrath is suddenly laced with a strange kind of sadness that I'm not expecting, which makes me feel immediately guilty.

His eyes stab at me. "Listen…the person I'm on my way to meet right now is very nice and very beautiful and many other things you couldn't possibly identify with. So, why don't you do me a favor and go flirt with someone else."

My face is molten lava. *Flirt?!* He stands and strides away.

"You're not going anywhere!"

"Watch me, bitch," he says over his shoulder, not looking back at me.

Never have I felt such fury.

"Fine!" My voice sounds far too shrill. "Let the Enforcers find you!" I cleave my way in the opposite direction, past the confused, idiotic human faces who've stopped to watch our altercation. I look at no one. And even when my neck tingles again with the sensation of foreign eyes upon me, I continue to plunge down the street, putting as much distance between me and the primitive fool as possible.

CHAPTER 32

THE THANE

Aeman stands before his former Teacher, drenched in sweat and nostalgia. The office, perfumed in old wood and polished iron, once felt like the safest place on Earth to Aeman. Now he knows it surrounds him like a tomb.

Trevor De'Vant's eyes bore into Aeman's, who attempts to wield as much bravado as will fit edgewise into his crooked smile.

"Have you missed me?" Aeman asks, and watches Trevor's eyes flash at the insolence.

Trevor leans back in his baronial chair. The creak of the ancient wood reminds Aeman of some old-world clipper ship, cannons poised and ready. His Teacher's voice is low and controlled. "Virginia says that you've promised a miracle weapon or your life would be forfeit. She was very adamant about the second part. There was a kind of glee in her that I've seldom seen. Not a deal I would've struck with a grieving mother. A miracle is a very high bar, old friend." Aeman stares back at Trevor, knowing the price of failure at this point. He's walking a razor-thin line, and one misstep will be disastrous. "I have to say, I'm at a loss," Trevor continues. "You know your sentence decreed that if you entered Thessaly again, it would mean your death; therefore, whatever you came here to share better be revealed in seconds. The guillotine waits for no man."

Aeman juts out his chin defiantly. "You speak to me of execution? I have handed you more lives than all of your Enforcers put together!" Aeman spits out. "You hold the power you do because of *me*! Don't you ever forget that!"

Trevor's eyes shift ever so slightly, and from a shadowed pocket near the doorway, a young Enforcer, cloaked in black, appears and points a pistol (with silencer) at the back of Aeman's head. Aeman tilts his head to the left at the last second and the bullet obliterates a priceless, ornate vase almost directly behind Trevor. Then Aeman ducks behind his attacker's defenses, and in one fluid movement, he twists the younger man's arm up, forcing the assassin to fire through the side of his own temple. Blood sprays. Trevor jumps up, furious.

Aeman turns to Trevor, his smile wide. "Thought that might spring whatever little test you had in store for me. I didn't want us to be disturbed. Sorry for the mess. If you have a mop, I could just—"

A metal ring cinches around Aeman's throat. With great effort, he twists to look into the hate-filled face of Gael Falcón, who's cutting off his windpipe with a weapon Aeman has always laughed at and called *Gael's little tin lasso*. It looks like a tool used by a dog catcher—a long staff with a metal loop at one end. From the other end of the staff, Gael slowly slides out the long, razor-sharp blade embedded within. Gael leans in close and whispers, "This has been a long time coming, mijo. Let's remember every moment."

The thought of being killed by such an *unimaginative lapdog*—a man who had rejoiced at Aeman's fall (even if he had very good reason to)—forces Aeman to push down the panic threatening to consume him.

"You were such a talented Enforcer, Aeman," Trevor says, his icy expression bordering on a yawn. "Sad that your death will be as anticlimactic as your life turned out to be."

Gael places the point of the razor sword directly behind Aeman's heart. Aeman yanks at time with all his might, but he's no match for Trevor, who easily blocks his former lieutenant from winding. Aeman feels the scalpel tip of the blade pop through the first few layers of skin without the slightest pressure being applied. He squirms for his life. A barely audible sentence crawls out of his mouth...

"...I've...found a Thane..."

Trevor impassively raises a hand up, pausing Gael.

Aeman chokes and gags, his strength fading.

"What was that?" Trevor asks.

"...A Thane... I've found a Thane..." His words filter through his gargled agony.

"You've 'found a *Thane*'?" Trevor chuckles as he repeats the words. "That's what you came here to say—what you've traded your life for?"

Aeman nods, furiously, on the verge of unconsciousness.

"Impossible. There hasn't been a Thane since—"

"Saw him…"

Aeman's legs give way. Gael catches him by the hair as he goes down, holding him aloft like a crumpled marionette. Gael looks to Trevor, waiting for the kill order. Trevor pulls his teeth over his lower lip, mind racing. He notes quickly, almost unconsciously, that only Gael has heard Aeman's words. Then he waves his hand down with an annoyed little jerk. Gael Falcón retracts the metal loop, which slurps back into the steel staff. Aeman flops to the ground, gasping for breath and drooling all over himself.

"Convince me quickly. Where?"

Aeman forces himself onto his knees. "…I found him in New Jersey."

"Now I know you're lying. Kill him."

In a flash, Gael thrusts forward. Aeman feels him coming and tries to dodge, but in his weakened state, he's not fast enough. With the resistance of cooked butter, Gael's blade slides through Aeman's back. Aeman cries out as the bloody tip of the sword plunges out the front of his chest, soaked in blood. Aeman was able to escape a killing blow, but the razor has pierced all the way through, popping out the front, just below his right lung. He feels close to passing out, but he does everything in his power to get his next sentence out…

"He achieved stillness," Aeman croaks.

Gael rips the blade out of Aeman's body and prepares to swing for his throat, but Trevor raises his hand, staying the execution once again.

"And you can prove this?"

"He's lying," Gael says.

Aeman doesn't even glance at Gael. He keeps his eyes focused only on Trevor, pushing the pain away, knowing that every word is a life raft. "…He stopped time…and manipulated an object within it. Imagine what you could do with such a weapon."

Gael waits, impatiently. Trevor stews in silence, but Aeman

knows he has him. *I know you, Trevor,* he thinks. *If there's even a fraction of a possibility…*

"Where would I find this person?" Trevor asks.

Aeman laughs, causing a bubble of snot and blood to bloom out of his left nostril and rupture on his moustache. "You really think I'm gonna tell you the location of the only thing that's keeping me alive?"

Gael kicks Aeman so hard in the stomach, he vomits on the ground. Trevor waves away the violence like it's an annoying gnat buzzing about him. Gael takes a step back, but Aeman can feel resentment resonating off his old rival.

"What do you want?" Trevor asks. "Not that you'll get it, or that I even believe you, but you obviously believe yourself, so my interest is piqued."

Aeman's words slowly emerge, wet and sincere. "I want forgiveness."

"That's never going to happen."

Aeman spits dark, thick blood onto the ground, momentarily clearing his throat. "Who has brought you more heads of your enemies, Trevor? The Warriors of Fate cringe in the shadows because of the terror I have inflicted on their fractured rebellion!"

Gael steps forward. "I have taken just as many—"

"You have suckled on Trevor's breast while I have done this Chapter's dirty work!" Aeman growls, risking a glance in Gael's direction, knowing he wouldn't dare murder him without Trevor's permission. Aeman turns back to Trevor. "You taught me how to hurt and destroy, Trevor. You never said I had to do it with beauty."

"I gave you your chance at redemption, Aeman. Elijah—"

"Was a traitor. You told me to expose him."

"Yet he was not exposed."

"His constitution was weaker than I imagined. His body crumbled in my hands. Blame his maker, not me."

Trevor darkens. For a moment, it looks as if he might grant Gael his vengeance. Aeman can sense Gael leaning his weight onto the balls of his feet. Given the slightest signal, he will probably decapitate him, leaving no more room for discussion.

Aeman thinks about the man poised behind him. Trevor fed the rivalry between Aeman and Gael from the start, fighting for their

Teacher's love—two starving wolves grappling over the same discard-ed bones. When the moment came to strike a wound at the Mexi-can Chapter of the Leadership, Trevor had sent *Aeman* to kill Gael's father—the Mexican Prime—the man who had been Gael's daily tormentor for his entire life prior to coming to Thessaly. Gael was given to Trevor like a gift—a show of good faith for their continued alliance. Aeman knew that he was stealing the only kill that had ever truly mattered to Gael, but he did what he was told. He did it for his Teacher—for Trevor. Everything for him.

Aeman wonders if his death will actually fill the ugly hole left at the center of Gael. He doubts it. It's never worked for him.

"I have an idea that suits me," Trevor says. "This *Thane* is not registered with the Leadership, I'm assuming?"

Aeman shakes his head ever so slightly, not sure where Trevor is going with this but feeling uneasy all the same. He knows Trevor too well not to understand that this next moment will be painful somehow.

"Arrange to have your sister found harboring this Winder, and if what you say is true, you shall have a home here once again."

Both Aeman and Gael Falcón stare slack-jawed at Trevor.

"What? …Juniper?" Aeman stammers.

"You can't be serious!" Gael snaps.

Trevor shoots Gael a silencing look.

Aeman hesitates, burning with shame for even contemplating such a proposal. *Is there no line I won't cross?* he wonders.

Trevor lets out an amused little laugh. "Come, now. With-holding an unregistered Winder is not a death sentence. So long as she has not made herself his Teacher, mercy lives on her side. I can even promise you she'll be saved from banishment as well. God only knows the pampered little princess would be eaten alive on the streets in less than five minutes. I'd simply have her removed from the Council. I have plans in motion—"

"What plans?"

"The kind you will benefit immensely from once you stand beside me again. There has been a great deal of movement toward our larger goals as of late. But change always comes with a price. You'd be a good big brother to keep her out of harm's way."

Aeman is doing everything he can to intuit Trevor's true intentions. Indecision undulates on his face. He's starting to feel lightheaded from blood loss.

Trevor stands and walks toward Aeman. "Oh, please. I have no reason to harm your precocious sibling," Trevor says. "Deny this one-time offer, however, and my position might change. I kept you from the fire once, Aeman. The flames are never thwarted twice."

Aeman feels his resistance slowly dissolve. He doesn't trust Trevor in the slightest, but he's been alone out in the wilderness for so long. The sigh that escapes him gurgles out from his very core. His knees begin to give out. Trevor catches Aeman and holds him up. He smiles, warmly. "Good. Now, let's see what your Teacher can do about fixing that little wound of yours. You don't seem in any shape to do it yourself."

Behind him, Aeman can practically hear Gael's seething thoughts: *Even in disgrace, you manage to outshine me.* But then, all of a sudden, Aeman senses Gael's body relax—hears his breathing steady. He knows this is a horrible sign, because it means Gael has settled on a plan of action. Then he feels Gael, ever so gently, lean his knee into Aeman's back. *He wants to remember whatever decision he just made*, Aeman thinks. *Why else would Gael secretly make physical contact right before Trevor winds us back? He doesn't want to forget. But forget what?*

Aeman reassures himself that outside of Thessaly, away from Trevor, Gael is no match for him. And whatever machinations he thinks he's cooking up will only give Aeman a chance to finally put an end to their bitter rivalry—as he should have done a long time ago.

Aeman's thoughts are still racing as he feels the pull of Trevor's powerful mind.

A eman bursts out of the art deco entryway onto the sidewalk. He's on his phone, trying to mask his panic.

"What do you mean, 'He's gone'?!" Aeman yells.

"I told you, I'm not your babysitter!" Juniper's voice stabs back at him.

Aeman looks around, thinking as fast as he can. "*This* is the thanks I get for siphoning out information for you?"

"What did you find out?" Juniper asks.

Aeman paces on the sidewalk, trying to feel some kind of final decision. Can he really aim these vipers at his sister? Then his eyes fall on Thessaly Tower, looming above him like some great monastic sanctuary, and he feels the last dregs of honor leak out of him.

"…Meet me at my place," Aeman says. "Two hours. Don't be late."

He hangs up, stands still, steeped in self-loathing. Then, all at once, he lets out a barbaric wail and kicks a suited pedestrian into oncoming traffic. Tires screech as a chorus of gasps nearly drown out the sound of sinew and bone exploding against the city bus's front window.

CHAPTER 33

CHARLIE

I'm drunk. Confession alert number one: I'm a serious lightweight. I've only had three drinks and the world already feels fishbowly. But not necessarily in a *bad* way. Like maybe I'm a really badass fish who's like the life of the party or at least a decent conversationalist, and who really *loves* his bowl, and is super proud of what he's done with the space, like maybe he blew the glass himself…and also, I'm drunk.

Tristen isn't a lightweight. Tristen can hang. Her three drinks have barely seemed to faze her, even though she probably weighs a third less than me. I'm holding a napkin filled with ice against my goose-egged forehead.

The bartender asks us if we want a fourth drink. He has an accent from some Nordic country, maybe Sweden or Holland; I'm terrible with accents. Might have something to do with the fact that I've never been *anywhere*. Ducky and I used to talk about taking one of those post–high school backpacking trips around Europe, or Asia, or maybe South America. You know, like in those soul-searching indie films about identity and finding yourself, or in films like *Hostel* or *An American Werewolf in London*, where everyone has sex, then ends up dead. Guess there's a decent spectrum of backpacker films. But somehow, any thoughts of the future that existed prior to two days ago feel like someone else's life.

Tristen gives the bartender a nod, and I marvel at how cosmopolitan she seems. Savvy. A city girl. But I don't even know if she *is* a city girl. She just feels that way. I mean, how else is she getting underage drinks at some random bar in the East Village?

Tristen looks amused by my sloppiness, and I hit her back with a big dumb grin, but the movement makes me remember that I have tissue stuffed up my nostril, damming the blood from getting face-kicked by a vicious, feral girling. I yank the tissue out and spear it over the bar into a trash can. But my bloody nose isn't ready to leave the party yet, and fresh fluid starts to flow. Before I can plug it, Tristen is dabbing at my nose with a handful of cocktail napkins.

"Who gets mugged in Manhattan? That's so nineties of you," Tristen says. "Lean your head back."

I sniff the carnage back up before it can drop onto the bar, and lean my head back as she plugs my nose with her fingers. She grabs my hand and guides it onto my nose, forcing me to take over nostril-pinching duty. That familiar taste coats my throat.

"I can't remember the last time I got drunk in the middle of the day." My voice squeaks out high-pitched and cartoonish—an unfortunate side effect of nose-plugging.

"Really? What were you doing all of high school?"

"…I was a soldier."

"What? ROTC or something?" she asks, since we're not in Africa and child soldiers are kind of a no-go in these here parts.

"More like a small island in the middle of the country where wayward, violent freaks go to either get better or get meaner." *There it is. Feel free to run, madam.*

She swishes my words around in the mouth of her mind. "Which one are you?" Off my confused look, she says, "Better or meaner?"

I don't answer. I release my nose and sniff. Only air pours through this time, and I know the damage has clotted. I reach for my fourth drink as my Danish friend sets it down. I take a sip. The bartender and Tristen exchange the smallest of glances. *What? Am I that drunk?* Probably. *Is he trying to ask her if she's okay?* That would be so shitty. *Or maybe he's an old boyfriend. How awesome would that be?* Then Mr. Norway walks away.

"How did you end up there?" she asks.

"Yeah. You don't want to know."

She's trying to figure me out. Her soft brown eyes, clutched in their no-nonsense shell, do not waver. "Surprise me," she challenges.

"Nah. I'm good."

"What do you want, Charlie?"

I laugh at this. I laugh hard at this. I fucking guffaw at this. "That's a good question. I'm supposed to say like *true love* or *become a lawyer* or *I want to help people,* right?"

"*Do* you want to help people?"

"That's not the point!" I spit out, irritably. *She's not getting it.* This conversation feels disastrous at best for me right now. I'd be much more into a game of Who Can Spill A Glass of Liquid First… or Pin the Country on the Viking Bartender. But she's still there. Waiting. Patiently. And then the membrane between my thoughts and my words disintegrates. "It's not that I *hate* people. I don't. It's just…I was an angry kid. My mom—" *No, not there. Never there. Not even for this beautiful, inquisitive girl. Sorry, Tristen. Some things aren't meant for the light…or even a dark bar.* "Anyway, that's what they said…I was an '*angry kid.*' I hurt people that hurt people. Like maybe it was a way for all my anger to be, I don't know…*useful.* Maybe make up for…" I don't continue. The silence that follows is ugly and feels endless. I've lost her. *How do I fix this? How do I turn this pity-party bus back around?*

"Make up for what?" she asks.

"For being so damn handsome."

She ignores this. "Why all the anger?"

"Why does *anyone* get mad? Saw too many bad things happen to good people—like life wasn't just unfair, that it was literally stacked against the good ones."

"Still feel that way?"

"More than ever, actually." This is the truest thing I've said all day. "I used to think I could throw myself in front of it somehow, but now it feels so much…bigger."

I set my glass down. The urge to throw up hits me hard. Not because I *need* to throw up but just as a statement of some kind, a symbolic cherry on top of the sad little sundae I've dished out to this lovely, far-too-curious-for-her-own-good girl. Tristen watches me wrestle with my dessert plans.

"Sacrifice is a brave thing, Charlie. Not many are up for it."

I don't know what this means, but it makes me want to cry. "…Have you ever done something…something wrong?" Tristen's left eyebrow spikes at the stupid question. I try to focus and continue. "I mean something *really* wrong? Something where you know a day won't go by without you thinking about it for the rest of your life?"

"Is this what you got sent away for?"

"Not this one. Unfortunately."

She thinks. Then: "Did you do it on purpose?"

I've been honest so far… "No. I did it protecting someone I loved. And I didn't realize I was doing it when I did it. That's the truth."

Tristen seems to be contemplating me on a deeper level than I'm comfortable with. Her eyes pry into me like I'm one of those hologram pictures where, if you stare at the bizarre, patterned image long enough, another picture reveals itself within the pixels.

Finally, she says, "I've done a lot of bad things in my life. But I don't have the luxury of knowing they weren't on purpose. Count yourself lucky, Charlie."

Her words feel deeply personal and therefore deeply intimate.

"Should I be scared of you?"

Her eyes narrow. "Definitely." I laugh hard. She smirks a sexy little smirk at me. Then the sadness returns, yanking me down like a lead balloon. She continues: "Sometimes, things that should scar us don't end up leaving as big a mark as we deserve. And that ends up hurting more. But then we go on."

"Wow," I say. "Pretty wise. …Not necessarily in that order."

She smiles at my little joke. *Jesus, she has a great smile.* A moment passes between us. It makes me swallow. Then Tristen leans in and kisses me. A *real* kiss. I feel it everywhere. A buried engine deep inside me roars to life. And no. Sound. Is. Heard.

Our lips finally pull apart. Our eyes bore into each other, pulling each other apart nerve by nerve, until all that's left is the dense, palpable heat emanating from our steaming bones.

Tristen slams me against a wall in the alleyway. Jagged concrete stabs my back, but I feel nothing. Our mouths are intertwined; there is a velocity inside me moving without bounds. We pull apart, every millimeter of distance multiplying our fervor.

"Where can we go?" Tristen asks.

"Your place?" I try to make the offer sound casual.

"Can't. I'm at my friend's till the first of the month." She kisses me again. "Can we go to your place?"

"It's not *my* place…" I start, but I'm close to completely losing control of all bodily functions as Tristen's hot, sensual body leans into me. "But if we go right now, we should be good," I say.

CHAPTER 34

JUNIPER

How can anyone with a serious mind waste time thinking about the opposite sex? Daniel is weak. Charlie is vulgar. I've never encountered anything so pointless. Of course, I have these feelings. All mammals do. Desire is built into us. And yes, Charlie is obviously attractive in a slow, primitive way. But it's acting on these primal urges that makes us look ridiculous. What did love and desire ever bring my family? My father's confession slams into me. "...I knew who he was...*what* he was..." But the truth is, no one can hurt you if you don't give yourself vulnerabilities. My father was more aware of Trevor's tendencies than anyone, and he still let him in the door. *Did Trevor hurt my mother?* I've kept this question at bay since I left my father's chamber, but it's been banging at the door ever since. So, I ask myself the question that occupies the moral center of my species: *If my mother didn't know something happened to her, then did it happen at all? And therefore, does it matter?*

It's a horrible question but a fair one. The collective answer of my kind is no. Our entire world is based off the idea that the more dominant species may do anything they want to those less powerful. *Does this apply?* The thought of Trevor with my lovely mother, whether or not she was aware, makes me want to kill. My father married a human because he fell in love. And that love ruined him in the end. I think about Trevor—that lost little boy, sitting in the dark, sobbing over that dead baby rabbit. He will never fill the gaping hole inside him, no matter how many of us he throws down into it. All of it for love—in all its grotesque forms. *Not me. Never.*

My phone rings. It's Daniel. I hesitate, but then I get a feeling that not answering might do more harm somehow.

"Juniper…" His voice sounds anxious. "…Where are you?"

"What do you want, Daniel?" I try and sound authoritative. I don't need this right now, and I'm a Leader, for God's sake. I can come, or not come, into the lab whenever I choose.

"I'm sorry. I wasn't going to call," he says. "I know you said you need time to think. But since you found her, I thought, I don't know, maybe you'd like to know…"

"What are you talking about? Found who? I'm in the middle of something."

"Sofia. The little girl you found in the Gathering. I saw it in on a field alert. Not that I regularly monitor the Enforcer communications. That would obviously be—"

"What about Sofia?"

"She's missing from Thessaly. It seems she slipped out in the early morning. Didn't report to training. At first, they thought she might be ill, but then they realized she was gone. They've sent a team to retrieve her."

"I can't deal with this right now," I say. His silence feels heavy with disappointment. Do I care if Daniel thinks I'm cold? I don't know. Why does he expect me to be worried about Sofia? They'll just bring her back. She may be punished for her disobedience, but I can't imagine that anything worse will happen to her. *But what if she tells her mother about us?* She'd be breaking the first rule of the Code. I can't imagine little Sofia knows how serious that would be taken. *I don't need this right now!*

"How long ago did the team leave?" I ask.

"Just now," Daniel says. I can't help but feel resentful. Just last night I asked Daniel for help, and here he is, pushing me toward danger. If Sofia has told her mother our secrets, I don't know if I'll be able to stop what follows. I'm a Leader now, but that also comes with a responsibility. I am one of the keepers of our rules. And it's not as if I can ask Trevor for leniency.

"Daniel, do not tell anyone you spoke to me today."

"What? Why?"

"If any of the Enforcers speak to you, you called me but I

didn't answer. Understand? Especially not Trevor. Promise me. It's important." I know I shouldn't be revealing this much, but if Trevor comes looking for me again, Daniel's best chance is ignorance.

"Trevor? Juniper…what's going on?"

Hearing the concern in his voice is nice. It makes me feel a little less alone. I feel myself forgive him for his reaction last night. What would anybody else have done? None of it is his problem, anyway; it's mine.

I hang up the phone.

I'm currently about halfway between Thessaly and Sofia's home. If the Enforcers just left, I could still easily beat them there. Or I can just let things proceed as they will, without my interference. No question, the latter is the smarter choice.

I follow the cracked and crumbling cement pathway leading to the tall tenement building. The trampled grass bordering the dirty brick-front entrance looks like someone was trying to grow tobacco and barley crops using old cigarette butts and beer bottles as seeds.

This is not smart, Juniper. A few hours ago, you were taking pride in being called a genius, and now look at you. Aeman said to be at his place in two hours. He must've discovered something. *I knew it.* And timing must be important, because I've never heard Aeman say *Don't be late* in my entire life. Coming here will be cutting it close, but I should be fine. If I'm honest, I've also come here to scratch a mental itch. Since I joined the Gathering, I have sat across from many parents—most of them forgettable, most so predictable I could almost plot out their responses by rote. Sofia's mother had been different. There was sadness, of course, but the overwhelming emotion she emanated was *gratitude*. It was an emotion so pure, it sent an unexpected shockwave of guilt through me. I promised I would report to her that Sofia was safe and doing well. I say this to every parent, but I never mean it. It isn't my job. I suppose, partly, I'm here to see what keeping my word to one of these parents feels like.

If Sofia is there and has already revealed things to her mother, the situation is out of my hands. Rules are rules. If she hasn't told her mother, I'll have to do my best to get her out of there before the Enforcer team arrives. If Sofia isn't there, I'll tell her mother how great she's doing, then I'll wait for the Enforcers to arrive and tell them to collect Sofia if she tries to enter. I calculate that if any of these three situations occur, I will still be able to make it back to Aeman's apartment in time.

As a tall, tattooed man in his early thirties exits Sofia's building, I slide in through the entrance behind him. I feel his angry eyes look me up and down, but he says nothing. I keep moving.

The light from outside barely makes a dent in the murky interior. I approach the elevator and hear the rusty squealing grind of the ancient machine slowly ascending away from me. This building must be fifteen stories tall. One glacial elevator servicing the whole building. *How can humans treat their own so callously?* As I climb the stairs, I pass an elderly couple. The husband huffs and wheezes. These people are wasting away. But are humans entirely to blame? Can we really say that anymore? If we have our hands in everything—politics, corporations, the police force, the FDA—then how responsible are we ourselves for such strife? When Providers work their magic and the money pours in, and Solicitors protect our growing assets with favorable policies, and Enforcers keep the credulous masses at bay, have we not made ourselves secret kings, beholden to none? But there is no castle for the serfs to storm, no way for the exploited to fight back. They do not even know we're there, because we're under the skin.

I prep for Sofia's mother: *Your daughter's doing excellent. Everyone loves her; she's making so many friends. I'm actually jealous of her social life.* Scratch that last part. She knows her daughter better than I ever will. Sofia is shy and watchful and miles away from a social butterfly. I'll tell her *Sofia's teachers think she has a great deal of potential, and that she seems to have made one close friend. A girl. Both girls are a little shy by nature,* I'll say, *but I think she's a good influence for Sofia, since this girl is a big fan of deductive reasoning (not restrained to Aristotelian syllogism), and while she's partial to empirical reasoning, visualizing qualitative and quantitative data through the implementation of physics, chemistry, cellular biology, et cetera, she also dabbles in the "left brain" realm as well (for what are*

*we if not explorers)—but this girl does admit that she's honestly much
better when dealing with the visible, observable universe.* Yep, that's
what I'll go with. What parent wouldn't want to hear that?

I reach Sofia's floor, step up to the door and knock. No answer.
I knock again, a little louder this time. Nothing. I knew there was
a chance Sofia's mother might not be home, but now that I'm faced
with it, I suddenly feel lost. Perhaps it's a sign that I should never
have come here at all. I check the door. It's locked.

"She ain't there," a clogged, raspy voice declares behind me.
I spin around. An old woman with thick dreadlocks stares at me
from her apartment. She's hunched in a wheelchair and wedged
halfway out of her doorway.

"Excuse me?" My measured tone fights the anxiety I feel at
being exposed.

"They came at night. They think no one seen 'em. But I see
everything happens in this building." The old woman casually
taps a hole drilled in her door right at eye level for someone in a
wheelchair.

"Who came—"

"Two of 'em. Man an' a woman. All dressed in black, like damn
ninjas. They had guns and they come with a big black bag, and
when they left, that bag was full." I can't speak. My heartbeat pulses
in my ears, low and dull. "She was a good woman. Loved that lil
girl so hard. I didn't tell the po-lice *you* had her. Her mama was
shinin' like Christmas mornin' the day you came. They found her
yesterday. Shot in the face. Monsters stuffed her in the sewer like
she was shit."

"...I'm sorry." The words escape in a quiet croak.

"There's boogiemen out there, girl. And they look just like us.
You be careful. Keep that lil girl safe. She ain't got no one else in
the world now." The woman stares at me, her thin, sagging face
ravaged by decades of poverty and pain. Her sunken eyes pierce
through me, making me feel more like a child then I've felt in a
long time.

"I will," I say. Then I hear a little click as the door opens behind
me. I turn and see Sofia standing in the doorway to her apartment. She heard my voice. She thinks I'm a friend. The woman in

the wheelchair shuts her door. I look at Sofia's tiny face. She's all alone now. A terrible revelation builds within me. The door it hides behind is now paper-thin and made of shame, and though I know it will hurt, I push it open.

They kill them. They kill the parents. And the grandparents. And the neighbors. Any witnesses. A silent culling. And I have been the first wave of this attack. Separate our kind from the pack, then exterminate all liabilities. And without a doubt in my mind, I know that such a savage system could only stem from one ruthless mind. *Trevor. Does my father know? Does Maya Steele? Does everyone? Did Elijah? Of course he knew. They all know. And they're fine with it.* I can almost hear Trevor's slithering justifications: "The tiger no more pities the lamb than the flood pities the village it consumes." I'm supposed to agree. The simple science of it tugs at me, but the horror feels suffocating. For some unexplainable reason, I think of Charlie. I called him ignorant. Took delight in my superiority. What would he think of this new little fact? He already called me "cold." Would this make me some kind of ghoul in his eyes? *Why should I care what he thinks? I don't. Even if he's right.*

I reach out my hand, fighting to keep my voice calm. "Sofia, come here. We have to go." Sofia doesn't move.

"Sofia, please. We don't have much time."

"Where's my mama?"

What can I possibly tell her? What will hurt the least? She's a smart girl. She sneaked out of Thessaly without being detected. I have no doubt that my little show in the training gym with Sofia and her peers led to the other children's silence while Sofia made her escape. None of them would've wanted to incur my wrath if Sofia said she was acting with my permission. At least, that's how I would have done it. And she made it all the way back to her building. She's smart and resourceful. And she'll be able to see through any obvious lie I tell her about her mother. But if we don't leave here right now, it'll be too late. If she makes a scene, this is going to end badly. So, I have only one choice: I have to make it hurt. She'll believe it if it's painful. I speak to her in Spanish, the language of her mother. I say, *"Your mama is gone. She left. She heard you were doing well, so she went to start a new life. She told us she only came here for you to have an education, and now that you're getting one, her job is done. She said you don't need a mama anymore."*

Sofia's eyes glisten. She speaks back in Spanish. *"Where did she go?"*
"I don't know. She didn't tell us. I'm sorry."

Tears spill down her tiny cheeks. I hold out my hand again, and Sofia slowly walks toward me, head down. I bend down low, coming to eye level with her. As I'm about to say something, Sofia wraps her arms around my neck. She holds me so tight. *"The other kids are so mean. A different kind of mean. Like they have no feelings. They said I'll never see my mama again."* Sofia's sorrow stings with familiarity. *Why are we so bloodless?* The children of the Gathering always have a coldness to them, as if something besides their mundane origins has been ripped out by the roots. I never asked why the parental amputation was necessary. We're not supposed to ask. But it's not our system that's flawed; it's Trevor's influence—his deranged point of view regarding normal humans. But doesn't that mean that it *is* the system, regardless of where it came from? *I can't think about that now.*

We descend the stairs quickly. As we near the lower levels, I start to move a few yards ahead of Sofia, watching and listening for Enforcers. The second I land on the third floor, I know I'm not alone. It's the odd silence upon silence. I'm not sure what I'm afraid of, exactly. Any Enforcer will know who I am. It's explaining why I'm here in the first place, and not letting them take Sofia from me, that will be the challenge.

I must project authority. Power is the only thing Enforcers understand. I throw back my shoulders, straightening my spine. And that's when I'm seized from behind.

CHAPTER 35

JUNIPER

The hand around my throat feels large and extremely strong. Trevor's men must have followed me and been given orders to attack. They would never hurt me without permission. As I'm dragged back into the darkness, I catch a glimpse of Sofia's terrified face peeking out from further up the stairs. *Please stay hidden.* Light trickles through the one filthy window in the corridor, making silhouettes out of two *new* assailants emerging from a hidden alcove and coming at me from the front. They resemble the number *10* in shape. The one on the left is tall and wiry, while the other is an obese giant.

"Damn, Cyrus, you weren't kidding. This bitch is more than fine," the giant says. His lanky counterpart leans toward me. It's the tattooed man I passed as I entered the building.

Skinny Cyrus runs a finger down my face: "Seems crazy, right? Ain't even my birthday." On his arm, a tattoo of a demonic clown carrying a hatchet stares back at me.

"Where we gonna do this?" the invisible predator behind me with the vice grip on my throat asks. His breath reeks of alcohol and stale marijuana. My attackers are a trio. Two in front. One behind. The odds are not good. *For them.* Through the chokehold, I whisper, "You have three seconds to release me, or I'm going to hurt you very badly."

Cyrus laughs in my face. His breath is no better. "She got spirit," he says to the Giant, who giggles menacingly.

"Sounds like this pony needs to get broke," says Vice Grip behind me, then he licks the side of my face, and I see red.

I flex my mind, AND THE ATTACK WINDS BACKWARDS, RIPPING

ME AWAY FROM THEM. I release, and this time, as Vice Grip reaches for me, I dodge under his grasp and stab a hard kick back, shattering his left knee. He goes down howling in pain.

A massive fist smashes into the side of my face, and I feel my jaw dislodge. My legs ragdoll to the ground, but the Giant catches me by the arm. Blood pours from my mouth and nose. My vision blurs. *Don't black out, Juniper! Focus! You cannot lose consciousness. These creatures have their hands on you... Think about Sofia!*

I spit blood onto the ground, clearing the gore from my mouth.

"What the hell?! This bitch thinks she's some kinda kung fu—"

I WRENCH TIME IN REVERSE AGAIN. BLOODY SPIT TORPEDOES BACK INTO MY MOUTH. My mind retches, and I have to remind myself that no sludge from the nasty cement floor gets to ride back through time. MY JAW SNAPS BACK INTO PLACE. MY MIND CLEARS AND MY SENSES SPIKE.

I let go of time and spin away from the Giant's crushing blow, dodging the knuckled club by centimeters, feeling the gravitational pull of his fist as it crackles past me. His momentum carries him stumbling into the dilapidated wall. I turn and kick him as hard as I can between the legs. He moans and crumples.

Cyrus comes at me with a wild punch, but I catch his arm and pull him toward me as I bring my knee up into his stomach, causing a loud "GAUUHH!" to burst from him. I whip a roundhouse kick into the Giant's face as he attempts to stand. He drops onto his back and I crane my heel down onto his chest so hard, I hear multiple ribs crack.

Only Cyrus is standing. He throws a blitzkrieg of punches. I WIND THEM BACK OVER AND OVER AGAIN, UNTIL I'VE MEMORIZED EVERY MOVE. Then I release. His face goes from astonishment to panic, to horror, as I effortlessly dodge fifteen strikes in a row, each growing more desperate than the last. At the end of his fruitless barrage, Cyrus heaves for breath. I'm winded as well, after so much consecutive winding, but my fury keeps me focused.

"...You a goddam ghost?"

My answer is a vicious front-snap kick into the bottom of his chin. I hear *plink plink plink* as teeth sprinkle the ground. Cyrus topples face-first, like a rotten tree, onto the wrought-iron railing, doing irreparable damage to his appearance.

Only Vice Grip is still conscious, twisting and moaning at his destroyed knee, bent twenty degrees in the wrong direction. I bend down to the terrified man. He flinches back, positive I intend to do more damage, but I just stare.

"I take it from your actions that you believe that a stronger creature has the right to do whatever it chooses to a weaker creature. Would you say that's right?"

"…Please… I'm sorry, man…"

"What are you sorry for?"

The wounds may no longer exist on my body, but I can still feel them—like a phantom limb. The feeling will pass, but for now it's a reminder that not everything Trevor taught me was wrong. These men would have hurt me. Maybe even killed me. But then my mind flashes to Sofia's mother and the hope on her face. *Dead in a sewer. We murder them; they murder us. We kill our own; they kill theirs. This world was built by butchers.* Tears cloud my eyes. I feel so overwhelmed and confused. "It's all shit…isn't it?" I say. "…All of it." He doesn't answer.

"Miss Juniper?" I look up and see Sofia on the stairs, staring at the carnage. My body is wracked with fatigue, but I take her hand and we descend the rest of the stairs as fast as possible until we burst outside. I try and keep our pace inconspicuous.

As we reach the sidewalk, a black SUV screeches to a stop in front of us. *They've found us. We're not going to get away.*

As the four Enforcers exit the vehicle, their surprised looks give me hope. They weren't expecting to encounter a Leader, and they don't know what to think. I'll help them.

"Miss Trask," the Enforcer in charge says. "You've found the girl. Did someone notify you?"

"I don't understand," I say.

The Enforcers all look just as confused as I'm pretending to be. "The girl ran off—"

I smile. "That's funny. Did you think a tiny girl could get out of Thessaly on her own?"

"Miss Trask, security shows her—"

"I told her where to go and when. I said to meet me in the park.

I promised we'd visit her home one last time—see if her mother left any of her toys before she moved away."

The look I give the Enforcers says, *We all know where her mother really went, but that's not something anyone needs to know right now.* The Enforcers look from me down to Sofia, who thankfully reveals nothing.

"This is highly irregular," the Enforcer says.

"I'm sorry. I guess I've always felt it was a little sad that those of us found in the Gathering are never allowed one last peek. Maybe I'm wrong. I lost my mother very young. Perhaps I'm being too sentimental." Out of the four Enforcers, three react to my words in a way that tells me they were also found in the Gathering. Hopefully, they're thinking about their own mothers.

"Our orders are to bring her back."

"Of course. Time to go, Sofia," I say. I look down, doing my best to send a telepathic signal saying to go quietly with these men. If I hadn't used all my strength fighting in that stairwell, I might've been able to wind Sofia and me back into the building and try to find another way out, but now it's no use; I'm totally depleted.

Thankfully, Sofia walks over to them, freely. She's escorted into the SUV. She looks back as she sits in her seat. She's scared, but I give her a little reassuring smile before the door closes. I look the leader of the Enforcers fully in the face. "I'd be very upset if I found out that girl was treated poorly. I know I shouldn't have favorites, but I feel that she's going to be something quite special. Am I understood?"

"Yes, Miss Trask." With that, they enter the vehicle and set off back to Thessaly. As soon as the SUV pulls away, I feel my body deflate. I grasp the gate next to me for support and hope that Sofia will be all right. I check my watch. I have a little under an hour to get back to Aeman's. A slow walk sounds good.

CHAPTER 36

THE LOVERS

Cameron Trask walks into the lab, already feeling uneasy. He awoke this morning filled with a deep regret. This was not an unfamiliar feeling to him; in fact, truthfully, he can barely remember a morning he's opened his eyes without some form of piercing regret. But today he can't stop thinking about Juniper. And he's not sure why. Was it something she said? Or was he supposed to do something and has forgotten? Perhaps it was the way Trevor was staring at her at the Council meeting. Those beast-like eyes. But he simply can't remember.

Last night had swallowed him whole, like so many nights before; he'd reached *the moment* early in the evening, the moment of black, of nothingness, which he has come to rely on so completely. But all day today, there's been an alarm in his mind telling him *something is wrong.* So, he came here—to her lab—a place he's only visited once since it became hers. *More regret.* He shakes it off, knowing he needs to be sharp. She'll see through any self-indulgent blubbering.

A beanpole of a young man leaps to his feet the second the door opens. Cameron notices his slightly frantic demeanor. He scans the lab but doesn't see Juniper anywhere.

"Where's my daughter?"

"She's not here, sir."

"I can see that. Where is she?"

"…I don't know, sir. …Miss Trask didn't come in today."

Cameron takes a breath. He doesn't know what this means, but somehow it feels as if he's been wandering aimlessly, only to look

6 Ryan O'Nan

down and realize he's standing in the middle of a vast frozen lake and the ice has begun to crack. He gets a sudden glimpse—a flash in his mind's eye—of Juniper standing in his chamber, her eyes hot with disgust, and then the nothingness swallows the image again. *Why do I feel so much dread?* he thinks. *Because you're a stupid, selfish old man and you deserve whatever you get.*

Cameron levels his eyes at the young Seeker, who looks simply wet with anxiety, and decides his anxiousness is not because of him.

"What's your name, young man?" Cameron's voice takes on a gentle quality, trying to put the kid at ease. He's always been good at this.

"Daniel."

"Do you know Juniper well?"

"...I'm her lab tech."

"That's not what I asked."

"Does anybody?" Daniel allows a little smile. *Something in that smile*, Cameron thinks. Almost all of Cameron's great achievements in his life have been based on his talent for making snap judgments faster than anyone else around him. And he makes one now.

"Do you care about her?" The question seems to take Daniel by surprise. His jaw tightens. Cameron sees this and knows his instincts were correct. And now he smiles at Daniel, warm and inviting. He's telling the younger man not to be afraid—that he's a friend.

Daniel, finally, takes a deep breath and says, "A great deal, sir. More than she knows."

Cameron takes in Daniel's confession. After a moment, he nods.

"I once worked with a girl who seemed untouchable. When I was not much older than you. I was in my final semester at Stanford, and I had an internship at JP Morgan. We were still doing things the old way then. I was dazzling my bosses—as we always do. But I was not the favorite. *She* was. She was so far beyond me that I could barely look her in the eye. Beautiful. But so serious. She seemed to fill up a room in a way I could never hope to. I tried a few juvenile maneuvers to get her attention—things that had worked on other girls. Sillier girls. But no matter how many times I tried, she never seemed to give me a second thought. It was hopeless."

"So, what did you do?"

"The only thing I could do. I dedicated my life to her. Everything. All that I was I gave to her." Cameron looks off. "And if I'm being honest…she still has it."

"This was Juniper's mother?" Daniel's tone is quiet; he knows how this story ends.

"In some ways, they're so alike it's impossible sometimes. Head-strong, proud…*intimidating.*"

The two men share a light laugh. But for both of them, something gets in the way, and their laughter falls short. Cameron aims his golden-brown eyes at Daniel, who is already trembling. "Is she in some kind of trouble, Daniel?"

Daniel looks tortured by this question. He stares down for a brief moment, then meets Cameron's gaze. "I act like I'm brave around her," Daniel says. "I always have. Like I could make it real if *she* believed it. But that's not the truth. The truth is I've always been afraid…of everything. Of *her*…" Daniel can't go on; he looks away, his face filled with self-hatred. "Is it possible to love someone and be a coward at the same time?"

Cameron suddenly feels so cold. "Yes," he says, sympathetic to Daniel's familiar agony. "Unfortunately for the people *we* love…yes."

Daniel takes another long deep breath, then he says, "I don't know what it was… She wouldn't tell me. She pretended she was stressed about her research, but I could tell she was lying. She was afraid. I've never seen her scared before."

And suddenly, another fragment of a memory hits Cameron. Something he desperately doesn't want to see. His daughter's face, trying to be strong, but hurting at the same time. She said, *"I need to talk to you about Trevor. He came to see me tonight—"* and in some dark cavernous swamp within his mind he hears himself say, *"Please go away. It's not a good night for a chat."* He closes his eyes against the pain—against the sheer mountain of his own ineptitude and shame. Because once again, he opened the door. *Fiend* is the word he feels but cannot say. Hungry, loathsome *fiend. Trevor.*

You said you'd leave her out of it. You've made a marionette out of me; how could I not have seen that you'd never be satisfied with me alone? After all, you consumed me years ago, didn't you? Cameron feels heavy. So unbearably heavy.

"Sir?" he hears Daniel say. The young man's voice sounds concerned, but Cameron is no longer listening. It's all just a little too much. He slowly turns and walks out of the lab.

CHAPTER 37

CHARLIE

Tristen's legs wrap around me as I hold her body tight against mine, wavering on my feet. We're standing. I mean, *I'm* standing. Some genius part of me thought it would be sexy or romantic to pick her up as soon as we got through the doorway to Aeman's apartment, and now half of my mind is focused on her as our lips and mouths continue to assault each other, while the other half is desperately searching for a place to land that won't make me look like an uncoordinated amateur. I have a strong feeling that tripping and rocketing Tristen's body into the ground would be the perfect way to obliterate this amazing moment. Finally, I fall backward onto Aeman's immense purple designer sofa. I'm shocked when our landing is soft. The entire couch is made of steel aside from the bulbous leather cushions. We laugh at the lumpy landing, alcohol still lubricating our courage. Tristen is straddling me. I feel her everywhere.

"What's with the giant hole in the ceiling?" she breathes out between kisses.

"Long story…"

Tristen crosses her arms low in front of her and slowly pulls her shirt off over her head. She's wearing a tight sports bra under her shirt—the kind I imagine long-distance runners use. Tristen's body is pretty damn astounding. Tight, lean muscles swell along the surface. I'm actually surprised by how cut she is. She has the physique of a competitive athlete. I bet she could easily outrun any security guard threatening to take her camera away on whatever unauthorized film location I'm now picturing her on.

The idea of a young, smart, subversive documentary filmmaker sounds crazy sexy to me.

My hands grip her lower back. Her skin is so smooth. *Will she be shocked by my scars? Will it ruin the mood? God, I hope not.* Tristen leans back on my lap, looking me deep in the eyes, and all at once I see a vulnerability that's been absent from all our other exchanges. For one thing, she seems far more sober than me, but it's more than that. She seems to be asking me a question, a question she's been asking ever since we met, and in this moment, every part of me wants to provide whatever answer will satisfy her. We hold each other's gaze. I smile, more with my eyes than anything else, and some kind of tension seems to fall away from her. Another few heartbeats, then she returns the smile, but hers now has a crooked mischief swirling in it. She reaches for the edge of her sports bra and my entire body contracts in anticipation—her fingers hook under the firm spandex—

"I have to say I'm proud!"

Tristen and I snap our heads in the direction of the joyful voice floating down to us from where Aeman sits, legs dangling down from the ceiling. "I was looking for you, and you were here all along—and with *company*. I should've guessed." I can almost hear the corners of his mouth crackle as his Cheshire grin reaches full capacity. "One night with me and already you're a total wolf!" Tristen scrambles off me, wrestling her shirt back on, as I shoot up next to her, reverberating with catastrophic embarrassment. "Don't mind me," Aeman coos. "I was enjoying myself. Just pretend I'm not here."

"Jesus, man!" I blurt out.

Aeman hops down, landing ten feet in front of us with an impressively soft *thud*. "Oh, jeez, did I ruin your attempt to deflower this gorgeous young thing in my apartment, Charlie. I'm so sorry."

I look at Tristen; words cannot begin to describe how miserable I feel. I look back to Aeman. "...I'm not... We... No...We were just—" I'm too drunk to get my head firmly around my thoughts. They keep slipping in and out of my grasp.

"I'm kidding!" Aeman's joy is merciless, like the older brother I didn't realize I never wanted. "However, I'm gonna have to ask you to say goodbye to your pretty little pal. We're gonna need a bit of privacy for our next exercise."

Tristen takes a couple hesitant steps toward Aeman. "I'm really sorry…sir. We didn't mean to… I mean, we *did* mean to… obviously…but not like *in* your place. Not that there's anything *wrong* with your place, it's quite nice, actually. Aside from the weird ceiling hole. But other than that, seriously great… I'm sorry, I ramble a bit when I'm nervous."

Aeman slinks closer to her, a greedy look in his eyes that disgusts me. "Well, pretty girl, you should know, Charlie and I are like brothers, and we do like to share *everything*."

Tristen's eyes go wide, and Aeman breaks up laughing. I didn't think it could get worse. I was wrong.

"Don't be stupid, girl," Aeman says, taking another suggestive step toward her. "You have nothing to be nervous about."

I want to speak, but nothing is coming out.

Then Tristen takes a much bigger step *toward* Aeman, smiling slightly, which confuses the shit out of me. "But that's where you're wrong, Aeman." The staccato, nervous fumbling in her voice suddenly evaporates, and I realize I haven't ever spoken Aeman's name out loud to her. In a flash, Tristen pulls a razor-sharp knife from a hidden place on her body and buries it in Aeman's heart. The confusion on Aeman's face is sickening. Tristen's expression festers into a sneer. "Your actions against my people have been nothing less than a genocide. I've waited for this moment for a long time. I'm still trembling."

Aeman's eyes go wide with pain and realization.

I am a block of granite—frozen and beyond gobsmacked.

Tristen pulls the bloody knife from Aeman's heart. "May fate be restored," she says, then slashes Aeman's throat. Blood explodes from the gaping wound. Aeman drops to his knees. I watch helplessly as the puckish confidence and thug-prince virility leak out of him. No more than a meaty husk, Aeman's body crumbles sideways onto the floor. A pool of blood spreads in all directions at once. Tristen hits a button on her watch, and something unhinges inside of me.

"NO!" I scream, my face white with desperation. I focus hard and THE EDGES OF TIME BEGIN TO BLUR—

Tristen reaches out, clenches her fist in the air, then yanks down, and I feel my wind violently torn away. She's blocked me. *Tristen is a Winder.*

I yank at the fabric of time, but once again, she forces my efforts down. I feel fatigue burn into my body after this second attempt. I go again, harder! TIME MOVES EVER SO SLIGHTLY, THEN I FEEL HER SLIDE IN BETWEEN ME AND MY POWERS SOMEHOW, and all my momentum fractures and slips through my grasping mind like sand. Her ability to deconstruct my winding feels almost unsurpassable. I don't understand it. I'm too inexperienced. I gather strength to try again.

"Charlie, stop!" Tristen says. "You don't know who he is. He's done unspeakable things."

"Bring him back! NOW!"

"I can't. All Warriors of Fate take a vow of abnegation. I couldn't bring him back even if I wanted to."

Juniper said that the only way to overpower a Winder is to make them lose either strength or focus, and I only know one way to accomplish that. I rush at her. Tristen swings her knife, but I manage to kick her wrist hard, and the knife goes flying. I grab her by the shoulders, but she falls backward and uses our momentum to kick-launch me back over her head. My world is turned upside down as I fly inverted through the air and crash into the wall. Tristen jumps up and looks at her watch. I'm dazed, but luckily, I have a very thick head. The real wound is the level of betrayal I'm experiencing. I opened myself up to this sociopath, and all that time, she was reeling me in, using me like some pathetic hunting lure.

"Charlie, listen to me—"

"Don't ever talk to me again! Everything you said to me was lies, wasn't it?"

"It was necessary to get to Aeman. He's a monster, Charlie." The coldness in her voice gives me hives.

"You manipulated me to murder my friend. Who's the monster?"

I climb back onto my feet and come at her again. She swings. I catch her arm and pull it behind her back. She cries out in pain.

"Stop blocking me!" I hiss into her ear as I yank her arm up higher.

"Time can't be in the hands of men, Charlie. We can't be trusted."

Tristen thrusts her head back, smashing it into my face, and I feel my nose break. I stagger back, eyes blurry. Tristen vaults into the air, wraps her legs around my shoulders, then, using her entire weight and torque, she knifes her body backward in a kind of back handspring, using the physics of her body like a slingshot, and once again I am airborne. My body smashes into Aeman's glass table. Glass explodes around me and one of my flailing arms strikes the table's iron crossbar. I feel the smaller bone in my forearm snap. The impact knocks the wind out of me. I'm getting my ass seriously kicked. I gulp for breath.

Tristen picks up her knife. "I know you're not one of them, Charlie. I know this is all new to you." Apprehension trumps my anger. *How does she know so much about me? Does she know where my family is? How careless have I been in this strange new world?* "I was tracking Aeman when he found you. I followed you on the train. In the city. I bugged your phone in the park. I've heard everything you and Aeman have said since then. He was using you, Charlie. I don't know what for, but I know he was. The Leadership treats regular humans like cattle. I need you to trust me. There are greater things in motion here than you understand. But I can show you. Come with me, Charlie. Please."

"I'm not going anywhere with you!" We stare each other down. I want her to see the hate on my face. She does.

"I don't want to kill you, Charlie. But I can't let you become one of them."

I look over at Aeman, who stares lifelessly at the ceiling. He looks like he's floating on the surface of a crimson pond. Aeman was far from perfect, definitely a scoundrel, but he was also as close to a friend as I've had in a while—at least, one that wasn't drenched in my own shame.

I struggle to my feet, pain from my arm stabbing through me. I see Tristen come to terms with the fact that there is zero chance I'm coming with her, and I see her steel herself, rearranging the knife in her grasp. She believes she can't leave me here alive. With my broken arm and nose, my ability to fight her is going to be fairly pathetic, but I won't go down easily. Tristen's muscles flex and I know the attack is coming. I shift my stance and put my good arm forward. She compensates for my change in position, lowers her center of gravity. Then I brace as I see her start to move.

"Hey!" A voice suddenly rings out behind Tristen.

Tristen is barely able to turn before Juniper levels her with a savage right hook. She drops the knife and crumples to her knees, stunned by the intense blow. Tristen attempts to stand, but Juniper kicks her hard in the face, and she slams into me with a force that spills us both into a heap on the ground. Juniper kicks the fallen knife far across the room, then runs to Aeman.

"Aeman… No, oh, no…" Juniper looks distraught as she kneels in front of her dead brother's body. A ringing ekes into the air, barely audible but definitely there. Juniper must have tried to wind. She turns to me. "She's blocking me! Wind it back, Charlie! Now!"

Tristen twists on top of me and holds her watch up in front of my face. The rolling numbers on her stopwatch read: *2:09… One hundred and twenty-nine seconds.* "Too late," she says. She's not gloating. It's simply a fact. The window for correcting history is gone. Too much time has passed. The shore has disappeared into a sea of seconds, and Aeman is a victim of the numbers. But I've always hated math. All my fury boils to the surface, spilling out *my* brutal truth: Another soul I've allowed myself to get close to has been destroyed due to their proximity to me. I let the wolf in the door. I welcomed Aeman's killer in with a kiss. I can still taste Tristen on my lips and it makes me sick to my stomach. I look Aeman's murderer in the face…

"Not yet," I whisper as I tear into the fabric of time like a rat clawing its way out of a burning box. I feel her mind reach out to stop me, and then I feel myself break free of her grasp.

Tristen is thrown back toward Juniper. Face and foot reengage, then disentangle once again as Juniper's throttling of Tristen slams backward.

Juniper is forced from the room, and now my battle with Tristen cranks in reverse. I'm thrown upside down. I

PITCH THROUGH THE AIR BACK INTO TRISTEN'S ACROBATIC TOSS. THEN I RISE UP AND DO THE SAME PATTERN AGAIN.

THIS TIME, AS I FLY INVERTED THROUGH THE AIR, I TURN MY HEAD AND SEE THE ENORMOUS POOL OF BLOOD FROM AEMAN'S THROAT BEGIN POURING BACK INTO HIS BODY. FINALLY, AEMAN IS THRUST BACK ONTO HIS FEET AND PULLED AWAY FROM TRISTEN.

TRISTEN TEARS HER SHIRT OFF AS SHE FLUMPS BACK ONTO THE COUCH, STRADDLING ME ONCE AGAIN. And then my hold on time disintegrates.

Tristen stares down at me. We were touching, so we wound together. Her face is frozen in a mask of horror and amazement.

"...Impossible." She blinks. I stare at her with disgust. I want to throw her off me, but I feel it coming...

"I have to say I'm proud!" I hear Aeman's voice déjà-vu down from the ceiling, but I can't look. "I was looking for you, and you were here all along—and with *company*. I should've guessed."

The pain overwhelms my senses, and I feel my body start to thunder with convulsions. Tristen rolls off me, turning to face Aeman, who leaps down, already on guard.

"Charlie? What the hell is this?!" I hear Aeman's voice, but it's faint.

Tristen jumps back, pulling the knife from a slit in her pant leg. I flop onto the ground.

"Do you hear that, Aeman?" Tristen says.

Aeman pulls an even larger knife from inside his jacket, but the expression on his face says he does indeed hear the *roaring feedback of an impossibly long wind.*

"Charlie just brought us back from a time, not far from now, when I watched mountains of blood escape your thoroughly lifeless body."

Aeman goes ashen. Tristen smiles, viciously. "Your debt to fate, as well as to my family, has been paid."

Then Tristen sprints and leaps through one of the large loft windows, presumably to her death. Glass bursts out with her, bathing the loft in a dusky puke-colored light.

Aeman rushes to the window. Incredibly, Tristen managed to land on the fire escape; I can hear her footsteps pounding down the side of the building. Or maybe it isn't incredible at all. Perhaps Tristen had that escape route mapped out the entire time. She'd been watching us, planning. The betrayal burns and burns. I think Aeman is going to go after her, but instead, he charges back to me, violently grabbing my semiconscious form, his face frantic—

"Did I die?! Did you see me die?!" he screams at me. His bittersweet alcohol breath stings my nostrils.

I can barely put words together. "…I…brought you back."

Aeman suddenly looks completely defeated. I can feel his hands on me tremble. A red light flashes above the doorway—a light that was missed the first time it happened. Aeman looks up at the camera monitor and sees Juniper standing at the front entrance below. She enters the code, opens the door and slips inside.

"Aeman…?" I can't finish the sentence. He lets my body drop. Pain explodes behind my eyes and nausea pinches me into a ball. He hustles across the room, then stops. His head hangs. He looks back at me one last time; his face seems almost corpselike.

"Keep her safe, Charlie. Tell her I'm sorry." Aeman leaps up onto the iron frame of his once-shattered table. "…Tell her you're just like Victor Mason."

Then Aeman disappears up through the jagged hole in his ceiling.

And I know I am on my own again. Alone.

CHAPTER 38

JUNIPER

I shake Charlie again. Still no response. The moment I entered Aeman's apartment, I knew something was off. It wasn't just the ringing, though the pitch and body of the sonic feedback felt disturbingly massive. It was the breeze. I'm used to the noxious stench of Aeman's den overwhelming my senses as I enter. I saw the shattered window a half-second before I saw Charlie's body on the ground.

I'm thankful he's not dead; I need to find out what happened. I check his body for bullet wounds, thinking it might have been a sniper. It would explain the shattered window, but there's almost no glass inside the apartment, which means something big went *out* through the frame, taking the glass with it.

I start to move to the window when Charlie grasps my arm, startling me. His words are incomprehensible, but the anguish in his voice is clear. Then his body arches and he calls out, "Mom! Watch out!" He cries, "No!" over and over again, and I'm forced to acknowledge that I know absolutely nothing about this strange young man or what traumas he may have endured.

I shake him harder. "Charlie! Wake up!" His eyes pop open, red and tear-filled. He looks at me so intensely.

"You…" he says. Then he starts to fade again. I give him a strong but not blood-vessel-breaking slap. His eyes open again.

"Charlie! Where's Aeman?" He tries to move but he's too weak. "Charlie, focus. Where is Aeman?"

"…Gone."

"Gone where? What happened?"

"…He said to tell you…he was sorry."

"Sorry?" He's not making any sense. "What is he sorry for?"

A red light flashes at the corner of my eye, and I whip my head up to the monitor. I see three individuals—two men and a woman, all dressed in black—standing at the downstairs entrance—each holding a Glock with a silencer screwed onto the end. *Enforcers. Three of them.* I feel a lump in my throat as I recognize the female Enforcer, a pinched-faced girl who I remember from my Enforcer training. And if I remember correctly, not my biggest fan.

The taller of the two men punches in the door code and all three enter. My mind sprints. *How could this be happening?* The truth slips out through my lips, ugly and crushing, "Aeman, what did you do?" Facts: *Aeman told me to arrive here now. Aeman is gone. Charlie, an unregistered Winder, has been incapacitated on the ground like a smoking gun. The loft is thick with the sound of winding, pointing to a treasonous act, punishable by death. Three Enforcers have been sent here at this exact moment. They possess Aeman's personal security code. Their guns are already drawn before they've even reached this disastrous scene. A tiger trap has been set for me, and I have walked directly up to the hanging meat.*

Charlie moans. I look down at him. *Was he betrayed too? Where did he come from? Why did Aeman have him?* I felt a surprising amount of power in Charlie, but what could Aeman have hoped to gain from him? This ambush couldn't have been it; he didn't know I would come here seeking his help. *Was Charlie complicit?* No. I don't think so. He might be annoying, but I don't believe he had any idea what Aeman had in store for him. *So, how does he fit into all this?!*

With tremendous effort, I force a lid onto the broken fire hydrant of my thoughts. Enforcers are going to come through that door any second. I have very few options. I could wind back and get myself out of this deathtrap, but it would take a lot of energy, and if they were following me before I got here, instead of being told when to show up, I won't be able to put up much of a fight. But I don't think this is the case. My instincts are telling me I wasn't followed—that winding is the best move—the only move. But that would mean leaving Charlie here for the Enforcers. I don't owe Charlie anything. In fact, he might deserve it after what he—

I hear footsteps outside the door.

Whatever I'm going to do, I have to do it now.

CHAPTER 39

CHARLIE

I'm in a hospital, on a gurney, hurtling so fast down a whiskey-brown hallway that I feel I might actually be in the large intestine of some food-poisoned giant. Another gurney catches up to me, pushed by an invisible force. On the gurney is Ducky's dad, his big, muscular body held down by straps, which cut into his ebony skin, drawing blood. He turns toward me and now the restrained figure is Ducky's mom, her face broken and bleeding, fixed in a silent scream—so angry—her eyes pierce into me, accusing me of stealing everything from her. Then her face spasms, the bones crack and contort, mutating into...*Juniper.* She looks terrified, gasping in agony: "*Charlie...you have to help me...please...*"

I clamp my eyes shut in horror. Then, all at once, the rushing force around me vanishes, replaced by a stillness found only in deep space. When I open my eyes, the gurney has stopped. Nothing moves. No sound. And there lying on the gurney next to mine is *my mother.*

She looks as gorgeous as she did on that Little League field all those years ago. She smiles at me. I can't help myself; I smile back—knowing full well this image is nothing more than a phantasm. Tears soak the side of my face plastered against the gurney.

(*I miss you, Charlie,*) she says without speaking. I *feel* her words inside me, as if the definition between sound and touch has been severed, and her words are also a caress.

I miss you too, Mom. I miss you so much. The words twinkle inside my head like wind chimes. She smiles wider, eyes glassy.

(*We can't seem to get rid of each other, huh?*) She laughs through her own tears.

I feel so lost, Mom.

(*She needs your help, Charlie.*)

Who does?

And then my mother begins to deconstruct before my eyes. I try to reach out, but my hands are crucified to my sides. I feel her leave my mind as her perfect skin falls away like a husk, then the exposed muscles and tendons sag off her face in globs of gelatin, until only a skeletal form remains. I scream, lurching away from the monstrous image. The stretcher tips and I plummet toward the greasy linoleum floor. I brace for impact—

Gunshots rip me awake. My mind is telling me I'm still falling, but I'm not. I'm back in Aeman's loft, but I *am* moving. I'm being dragged. Sharp debris pelts my face as bullets annihilate the shattered, glass-topped remnants of the iron table in front of me.

"Charlie! I need your help here!" I hear Juniper's strained voice cry out. *Just like in the dream.* But I'm not in a dream. Juniper is dragging me. Through my marbleized vision, I can make out three people, dressed in black, standing by the doorway. My eyes focus further, landing on two men and a sour-faced young woman who aims her silencer-clad pistol directly at me. Juniper yanks me to the side, barely saving me from a headshot. I kick out with my feet, trying to help push. She hulks me around behind Aeman's giant steel-backed designer couch as bullets smash through furniture all around us. Juniper leans her back against the sofa, exhausted—sweat pours down her face. I shake the confusion from my head and try to knuckle down and concentrate. My body feels like it's been used as a punching bag. *Ringing* clots the air.

"…We're lucky they're terrible shots." I manage to say.

"They're *not* terrible shots," Juniper says. "I was hit twice; you took three shots, one in the leg and two in the chest; one severed your femoral artery."

I look down at my body. Nothing. "How…"

Ignoring me she moves to the edge of the couch and yells to

our attackers, "I am a member of the Leadership Council! How dare you attack me! You will be tried and executed!"

Bullets strike all around her. She dives back ungracefully.

"Why does nobody get what a big deal you are?" I say.

Juniper levels a scathing look at me. "I should've left you out there."

A gaudy porcelain statue explodes above our heads, showering jagged white fragments down on us. My mind swims again, weakness threatening to pull me back into the darkness. My eyelids start to flutter. Juniper slaps me. Hard.

"Charlie! Wake up!"

My eyes burst back open. She slaps me again.

"Will you please stop hitting me in the face?!" I turn on her and notice how worn-down she looks. The veins around her neck bulge; she huffs short breaths. Something about her reminds me of my mother. The ways she's trying to project more confidence than her body allows her to wear.

"I need your help," she half-whispers. "I've been shifting my mind between the three of them, blocking their winding, but I'm too fatigued. They're free."

I feel utterly wrecked, but the fear and vulnerability in her expression force me to rally. I know she wouldn't be asking me for help if she had any other choice. "What can I do?"

"They're going to come at us again with their minds. I've weakened them. Thank God Trevor didn't send stronger Enforcers."

"Who's Trevor?"

"They're going to try to wind us back, pull us back out into the open. If they do, we're going to die. You have to block them."

"I don't know how." I can't mask how terrified I feel.

"Concentrate. You'll feel it. I would help you, but I need to regain my strength or we're never going to get through this." Juniper looks at her wristwatch *(I need to get one of those)*. It's number count runs rapidly upwards. It reads *:45*. Juniper fights to steady her breath. "None of them are powerful enough to break a minute. They only have a few more seconds until they won't be able to pull us out from behind here."

And just like that, I feel them. They come in quick succession.

I feel their minds like hands, pulling at the fabric of time. It's as if my mind's eye is suddenly tethered to my hearing as well, because my sense of their hands on time is shaped by the sound vibrations they're causing. Maybe it's a bit like how our sense of smell shapes the way things taste.

Only two of the three Enforcers have any real strength at this point. The first attempt feels weak and flailing. I flex my mind and easily push it away. It does feel like pushing, but not entirely. It's also like a tearing, a breaking-up of the delicate mental fibers they're attempting to connect to time like grappling hooks. And time feels…I don't know… somehow, it feels like the most basic thing you can imagine, like gravity or air, but also it feels unexplainable—a bendable, infinite…*thing*.

The other two attempts to pull me and Juniper back through time—into their grasp—come right after the first. But they feel more tactical and coordinated, as if the first, weaker attempt was meant to fool my expectations. It feels crazy insurmountable, the amount that every other Winders knows. *I'll never catch up.* The edges start to blur and I force the first mind away in a blunt blow that takes an enormous amount of effort.

In my depleted state, I bash into the third Winder's mind. As I push, I feel the Enforcer's mind bend with me. It's the sour-faced young woman. I don't know how I know this, but I can feel a sliver of her essence as our minds shove against each other. I can't grasp anything, can't find any edges. I feel myself, and the world around me, sucking toward the Enforcer's will as time begins to obey her command. *It would be so easy to just let go*, I think. I want to. I'm so tired. I've waddled into a world so far beyond me that it's only a matter of time (no pun intended) before some form of this moment ends poorly for me anyway. Somewhere, I feel that part of me—the part that secretly seeks self-destruction—rear its ugly head.

But then I remember that it's not just my life at stake. Juniper is relying on me, and as irritating as she might be, she's been fighting to save my ass while I've been sleeping like a damn baby. And it's this last thought that swells my mental muscles enough to shove Sour Face's grip away. I hear her gasp from across the room. I wait for another attack, but nothing comes.

"Well done," Juniper says. She has an odd expression on her face, like I'm a math equation she can't quite figure out.

"How could you tell that I—"

"Because we're not dead," she says. She holds up her watch. It reads: *1:03*. "We're good. Now I just have to come up with a plan."

"Why aren't they charging us?"

"Because they think I have a gun."

"*Do* you have a gun?"

"Every member of the Leadership Council carries a weapon."

My eyes light up. "Great. Where's yours?" But Juniper hesitates.

"…In the drawer of my nightstand," Juniper says with a dismissive tone, somehow managing to make me feel like I asked a stupid question.

"They're gonna figure that out pretty quick," I say.

"We need to distract them. Split their focus."

"Okay…" I may not know a way out of this, but I can definitely create a distraction. I move to lunge out from behind the couch. *Maybe I can get to the kitchen, find a knife, or —*

"What are you doing? Stop!" Juniper grabs me. "Do you hear that?" I listen. The gunmen are silent. "They wound us back," she says. "I must've been distracted when you moved to rush out." I focus. The ringing from Juniper and my previous mental battles with the Enforcers still permeates the air, but I realize that I can tell the difference between those winds and this new one. Somehow, I instinctively feel the distinction in the size of a wind as well as how much time has elapsed since it occurred. It definitely doesn't feel like an exact science—more like looking at the ripples in a lake after several stones have been flung into the water at different intervals.

"They know you're about to come from there, and they're waiting. You won't make it a foot," Juniper says.

I kick a cheetah-print footstool toward where I was about to lunge. Bullets instantly shred it. I nod a thank-you to Juniper and sit back against the sofa foxhole. I've never fought like this. I'm so out of my depth here. I have no idea what to do next.

Juniper suddenly gets down low, her eyes searching frantically for something.

"What are you doing?"

"Aeman's kept a weapon taped under his table since he was fifteen… *There.*" I follow her gaze and see a sawed-off shotgun duct-taped under Aeman's dining table directly behind us. Without hesitation, I grab a handful of porcelain shards from the shattered statue and start lobbing them toward our three assailants. It's a pitiful attempt at distraction, and I'm sure our enemies will think the same, but they'll have to take the time to think it's pitiful. Juniper sees what I'm doing and takes the opportunity to shimmy on her chest the ten feet to the table. The immense couch shields her movement from the Enforcers. A new flurry of gunshots masks the sound of Juniper ripping the gun free from the tape. She crawls back. Once safely behind the couch, she checks the chamber. One shell. *Shit!*

"We only get one shot at this," she says.

"One shot at what?"

"I think I have enough strength to do it if they're *all* distracted."

"Do what? What are you going to do?"

"They'll all be clustered together. They'll have to be in contact to effectively capitalize on winding us back."

That makes sense. In order for the three Enforcers to use the winding to their advantage as a team, they'd all have to know what's going on, and that means they'd have to wind together, and to do that they all need to be touching.

Juniper raises the shotgun toward the ceiling, and I see she's aiming at Aeman's giant gothic chandelier hanging above the heads of the three Enforcers. It's a big chandelier, but even if it hits them all perfectly, there's only so much damage it could do. This isn't a cartoon—they won't be knocked out or pinned helplessly under it. I decide to risk a glance over the sofa, but as I attempt to peek at our enemies' location, I hear a shot and the intricately beveled crown of the sofa bursts in a cloud of shrapnel and stuffing. Steel fragments cut into my face in tiny sprinkles of shattered metal. I hit the deck, landing on my back. I feel my face. Nothing serious, but it hurts like hell. Juniper looks down at me with a worried expression and I give her a little thumbs-up to tell her I'm okay. She shakes her head at my stupid move, leaving me feeling foolish and angry.

Juniper focuses back up at the enormous ceiling ornament, and I'm about to protest this ridiculous use of our only bullet when she yells, "Hey, Gretchen! I remember you from training. Never really thought you'd make it to be an Enforcer after you pissed yourself in class when I kicked you in the stomach. Well done!"

The acidic voice that comes back is almost gagging with vitriol: "You self-righteous slag! We're going to—"

Juniper fires. The support for the chandelier is blown apart and it comes crashing down like one of the claws in those clear boxy toy-grabber machines. I stick my head out the side of the sofa. I know it's a completely reckless move, but I need to be prepared for where to go once her plan utterly fails. The three Enforcers dive out of the way of the chandelier. She was right; they were all standing together. The impact sounds like a car crash. I'm about to shoot a reluctant compliment at her when Juniper suddenly leaps on me, slamming me back down to the ground. I land on my back, stunned.

Juniper is lying on top of me, her body pressed against mine. Blood leaks from a cut on her face, and I can feel her sweat-soaked skin through her clothes, which reminds me just how much effort she was having to put into keeping us safe. Juniper seems fiercely embarrassed to be in such intimate contact with me, and I am at a complete loss as to why she's chosen this moment for a wrestling match; but then, all at once, something in her expression—her fear, or maybe her burning anger—feels like a mirror, and for a second, I believe she feels it too. A strange, unexpected intimacy flashes between us. Then she does something truly odd: she places her hands over my ears, pressing down extremely hard. "This is going to hurt!" she yells, but I can barely make out her words.

"Wha—"

And then I see the blood vessels in her face nearly rupture with effort as...

THE EDGES OF TIME BLUR IN A RAPID, ALMOST STROBE-LIKE EFFECT, OVER AND OVER AND OVER, PULSING BACK AND FORTH BETWEEN WINDING AND UNWINDING. THE GALLOPING OSCILLATION BUILDS TO A FEVERED PITCH, THEN, JUST AS QUICKLY, EVERYTHING

SLAMS BACK TO NORMAL AGAIN as Juniper releases.

A microsecond of silence. Then a shrieking, cacophonous roar reverberates from everywhere at once. Like the howl of some demented phantom lion / percussion grenade. My body arches in agony. The pain is beyond excruciating. My head feels like it's going to implode. And once again, the world goes dark.

CHAPTER 40

CHARLIE

I open my eyes and pain sloshes around inside my skull like rancid water. I'm still lying behind Aeman's sofa. Juniper's gone. I sit up, but my head weighs a thousand pounds. My core feels stronger now (an upside to being forced to nap), but my head feels divorced from my body, like I've been decapitated. My chin drops and I stare down at my own feet with an open-mouthed slackness. Clambering onto my hands and knees, I start to crawl. As my hands clap the ground, I realize my hearing is far from solid. I snap my fingers next to my ear, but there's definitely a clogginess. I wiggle my fingers inside my ears, and when I pull them out, they both have dried blood on them. *Hmm. Gonna worry about that later.* I force myself to my feet. The three Enforcers lie splayed out on the ground. Trails of blood leak from their ears and noses. *Guess I didn't get the worst of whatever the hell that was.* I know Juniper caused it somehow, but that's where my knowledge ends.

A rapid tapping sound gets my attention, and then I see Juniper, across the room, machine-gunning code into Aeman's surveillance console.

"What happened to them?" I ask. "Are they dead?" Juniper doesn't answer. She pushes away from the console, whizzing around the room like an electron. She yanks a shredded grey leather jacket off the bathroom doorknob and pulls it on, along with a Yankees cap. Wearing beacon white isn't the best attire for dodging assassins. I guess this is her idea of incognito. She looks kind of thug-cute in the getup—not that I'm about to tell her that.

She scoops up two of the Enforcers' guns and hands me one with as much nonchalance as if she were handing me a sandwich. I've never held a real gun before. Even with the silencer, the gun's lighter than I imagined, and something about that gives me the creeps. *So easy. Too* easy. Like the less weight the weapon has, the less weight goes into the decision to use it.

"We have to go right now," Juniper says. "I wiped all memory of you from Aeman's surveillance system. Whatever Trevor is after—" Juniper's legs go to jelly on her, and she stumbles, nearly passing out. I catch her as she falls. Her body is trembling horribly.

"Easy," I say. The fact that I'm holding her in my arms is not lost on either of us.

"Let go of me…" She attempts to protest my support, but she doesn't even have enough energy for that. I get my arm firmly around her waist and prop her up. The smell of her body goes right through me. I wouldn't even say it's a super great smell. After all, she's been moving and sweating like crazy. But somehow, that makes it even more *her*. Too bad I despise all women right now, or I might actually enjoy this a little. There's also the fact that we're in imminent danger.

She fights to hold herself up, but it's no good, whatever freak winding she pulled off back there; her tank is now below empty. "Look, just consider us even for dragging me behind the couch like a cavewoman. Or kick my ass later if you want to, but right now, I need to get you out of here before someone starts asking where their three goth pals went. So, where can we go?"

I watch her surrender to the idea of me helping her. "…We need to get out of the city," she says. "Somewhere safe… I need to contact my father." She fights to stay standing, and I can tell she's hanging on by a thread. Suddenly, her eyes fill up with tears. "…I felt her die," she says "…I *felt* it. I…I didn't mean to…" Juniper glances toward the fallen Enforcers. She looks so damn vulnerable. Whatever mental anguish she's going through, however, I know the longer we wait here, the greater chance we have of someone else busting through that door.

"Does Aeman have a car?" I ask.

"...Parking garage." Juniper holds up a set of car keys she's snagged. She seems grateful that I'm not prying into her strange confession. I slip her arm over my shoulder and together we shuffle for the door. As we lurch out of the loft, I hear a low buzzing sound—*a cell phone.* They're going to find out what happened here pretty damn quick.

Outside, I'm shocked to see the world has turned to night. Shadows everywhere. Couples, drunks and hipsters mob the streets on all sides, taking no notice of the wobbly duo running for their lives from a powerful shadow organization bent on killing both of them—you know, normal New York City bullshit.

We make our way around the block until Juniper points out an anonymous garden-level side door cloaked beneath a set of stairs. It's an elevator entrance.

Juniper and I ride the clunky, antique elevator three flights down into the belly of a parking garage. Inside the slow-crawling elevator car, I hold Juniper tight against me. She's given up arguing and now freely holds on to my body, trying to stay conscious. I try not to focus on how close our faces are to each other.

"Who is Trevor?" I ask. "And why does he want to kill you?"

Juniper's breathing sounds labored. "I'm not sure it's me he's after. It's something larger…"

"I don't understand."

"Trevor controls the Enforcers. He's extremely dangerous. Once we're clear, I'll contact my father. I need him to find out which Leaders are loyal to Trevor and which ones we can trust. Trevor wouldn't have done this without support."

"What did you mean when you said—"

"Can we please talk about this once we're over the bridge?"

"Okay," I say. But I don't feel okay. Not in the slightest. *What have I gotten myself into? How do I hit the eject button on this shit?*

It's only three flights, but it's just enough time for the harsh loneliness of my current situation to ooze into me. I can't reach out to Ducky or Grams about any of this; I've brought enough darkness into their lives already. The only friend I had in this insane world left me for dead, and now I'm on the run with a girl who loathes me and who I don't think I like very much either (regardless of how good she smells). So, basically, everything is awesome.

The elevator dings, then opens into the dim parking garage.

A black convertible Pontiac GTO sits in the nearest parking spot. I know it's Aeman's without even having to ask. I wonder if this is a good time to tell Juniper I don't actually have a driver's license?

CHAPTER 41

THE INTEROGATION

Daniel sits cuffed to a chair shaking, terrified. Trevor stands behind Juniper's lab tech, drinking in the younger man's fear like syrup. He stoops down close to the young Seeker's ear.

"Have you had contact with her?"

"*No…*" Daniel hates the sound of his own voice, quivering and weak, and though he knows he's lying, he also knows that when he's really nervous, he also *sounds* like he's lying. He thinks about how many times his voice, and his moppy, wet brow, and his gangly tongue have been his enemies when it really counted—when what he truly wanted was standing so close by, and all he had to do was be anyone else but himself.

"…I haven't," Daniel half-whispers. "I haven't talked to her."

"That's strange," Trevor says. "We found you in her chamber, and your phone shows a call placed to her a little over three hours ago. Where is she, Daniel?"

Daniel cringes inwardly at his own carelessness. If he had only purged his call log like he planned to…but he simply hadn't appreciated the level of danger he might be in. Even with Juniper's fear so apparent, he couldn't imagine it, and now that lack of imagination is unraveling his life before his eyes. "She…she didn't come into the lab today… I was worried." Daniel's words dribble out, soft and clumpy, like mouthfuls of wet sand. "So, I called…but she didn't answer. I left a message. I swear that's the truth."

"And you just happen to know the code to her chamber?"

"She's a Leader now. I was set to pull her private systems off-grid."

Trevor stands up straight, clucking his tongue. "I wish I could believe you, Daniel. I really do. You seem so sweet. So undeserving of this harsh treatment." Trevor yanks Daniel's head back by the hair. Daniel gasps at the sudden pain and makes inverted eye contact with Trevor. He sees the brutal joy in the big man's face, and a squirt of urine soils his pants. He shuts his eyes to the shame of it. *Please don't let him notice I've pissed myself,* he thinks. *Please…*

Trevor reaches with the hand not entwined in Daniel's hair to a nearby cabinet and pulls open one of the upper panels. Daniel hears a sinister *clicking* sound as its clasp disengages, and Trevor withdraws a small vial. He holds the translucent vial out like a peace offering.

"Any guesses?" he asks as Daniel stares at it with dread. "Sulfuric acid," Trevor says with a balmy deadness. "I'm going to pour a little bit in your eyes."

Daniel cannot stop himself. He begins to cry. He knows it's already too late. That there's nothing he can do. Even if he knew Juniper's exact location, it wouldn't save him now. *A snake never shows its fangs without biting,* he thinks. Juniper said that once. He's just thankful Trevor isn't asking about her discovery—their lab work. He's too bent on knowing the answer to a question Daniel will never have the answer to. But he also knows that, given enough time, Trevor will eventually get around to it. Daniel thinks, *Perhaps I am capable of one small moment of bravery.* And so, because he knows it's expected, and because he knows it will tunnel-focus Trevor, he begs for his life: *"No, please! I swear! I haven't spoken to her. Please don't hurt me! Please!"*

"Within seconds, you will be blind," Trevor instructs. "At that point I'm going to ask you again. And if I don't get the answer I want, I'm going to use the entire vial. Minutes from now, it will have dissolved most of your brain. An email will be composed, explaining how lonely and sad you've been, and how this world was just too much for you. It will be sent from your computer to your friends, and colleagues, and Juniper Trask, and the rest of your contacts. And you will be destroyed. Left unrecognizable. All because of a spoiled little girl who isn't worthy of your friendship or your loyalty."

Daniel doesn't have to fake his suffering; he can barely get a word out. *"Please…"*

"WHERE IS JUNIPER TRASK?!"

Daniel kneels somewhere deep inside himself, praying he can get through this next part. A brief memory invades his mind—his first day at the lab. Instead of a speech explaining the rules of the lab and what her expectations were, Juniper had handed him a piece of paper, then stood watching him. Daniel could tell the paper was old by the look of it. It had not been folded, but the edges were curling ever so slightly. On the paper was a passage of text. Daniel has the passage memorized now, *carved into the very fabric of his being*, he thinks, but he remembers being shocked by it then. It read:

```
I seem to have been only like a boy playing on the
sea-shore, and diverting myself in now and then
finding a smoother pebble or a prettier shell than
ordinary, whilst the great ocean of truth lay all
undiscovered before me. — Sir Isaac Newton
```

It was the writing of a human. Daniel thought for a moment that she might be testing him, probing his sensitivities toward the weaker species of man. But the look in her eyes told him another story. She wanted honesty. *But would honesty get me flung from this place after working so hard to get here?* he'd thought. He decided that if this wasn't going to be a place of truth, perhaps he'd come to the wrong place. So, he screwed up his courage, took a small breath, then spoke honestly. "It's beautiful," he said.

There was a terrible silence that seemed to go on and on, and then all at once, something in the guarded, intelligent, green-eyed girl seemed to relax ever so slightly.

"It is," she said. "I want our work to be like this."

He would later learn that she'd been handed the passage by Elijah Spencer on her first day in the lab. Elijah had used it to tell her that she was in a safe place, and she had wanted Daniel to feel the same. Daniel had never felt safe in his entire life.

"That sounds great to me," he said.

"Good" was her only reply. Then she turned and walked back to her desk. Daniel watched her all the way, and somewhere between him and her workstation—maybe fifteen steps—he fell in love with her. *And now*, Daniel thinks, *if I can just be as strong as I was then…* He thinks of that vast ocean of truth spreading out endlessly before him, his feet and ankles washed in the cool tide.

Above him, Trevor sighs, then leans in and begins applying the acid.

CHAPTER 42

THE CAUSE OF DEATH

The door to Trevor's chamber swings open, and Gael Falcón enters. Trevor turns on him, his face twitching with rage. "You send three Enforcers to bring in a Leader and a possible Thane?! Are you begging for disembowelment, Gael?!"

"They were only kids, my Teacher," Gael says, bowing his head. "...I was attempting to remain inconspicuous. It was a miscalculation." Gael's words speak to his failure, but Trevor watches his lieutenant's face as he glances at Juniper Trask's lab tech writhing in agony. Trevor sees an acceptance on Gael's face that he doesn't like. It doesn't feel fresh; it feels like it's been thought through and arrived at before this failed capture. *I should have gone myself,* Trevor thinks. Gael's choice to send that girl—an Enforcer who has openly despised Juniper Trask for years—feels more than sloppy; it feels deliberate. *Someone who wouldn't question orders, even if those orders were to kill a newly minted Leader.* Trevor sees the simplicity of Gael's maneuvering. *With Juniper dead, I'd have no reason to accept Aeman back into the fold. Did you really need to destroy Aeman that badly, Gael? That you would risk your own destruction to keep him from my good graces?* Trevor contemplates that perhaps his little gladiator match between Aeman and Gael, all his careful manipulations, have finally come back to bite him at the worst possible moment. *Fucking children!*

Daniel lets out a nightmarish cry as the acid digs farther.

Trevor pulls out a silver gun with an onyx-jeweled handle and shoots the wailing Seeker in the head. Gael jumps back, spitting the slaughtered kid's brains from his mouth. He blazes with anger but quickly calms himself in the face of his Teacher's fury. Trevor tosses the gun onto his desk, trying to focus his turbulent thoughts. "Where is Aeman?"

"Fled. Like a pinche coward," Gael says.

"And you have no idea where Juniper Trask took this unknown Winder?"

"Security footage from the adjacent building shows them heading east...but I'm afraid that's all we have at the moment." A heavy silence presses in on Gael, who attempts to double down on his misstep. "I cannot imagine that a newborn Winder, regardless of his potential, can possibly pose you a genuine threat, my Teacher."

"Then what happened to your men, Gael?! Did they commit suicide?!"

Gael's careful tone says he knows just how close to the flame he is: "...Cause of death is...undetermined."

"What the hell do you mean, *undetermined*?"

"Dozens of rounds were unloaded. They were definitely firing at something, yet evidence shows that no direct fire was returned. All three Enforcers have suffered some kind of internal hemorrhage caused by an unknown force."

Trevor's thoughts suddenly burn inward. *Did he miss something? Something he should have seen?* He glances over at Daniel's body. His eyes narrow with suspicion, his mind churning.

Gael's phone rings and he answers. "What?" After a moment, he stops and his face drops. Trevor notices the change, and he begins to dread what it could mean. Gael hangs up. "My Teacher..."

Trevor clenches his teeth in irritation. His instincts are telling him to wind back Juniper's lab tech to get more information out of him regarding their research, before too much time passes, which it almost has, but the wind would take an enormous amount of energy at this point, and it might not leave him with enough stamina for whatever Gael is about to tell him. He hesitates, but finally, he lets time move on unaltered. "What is it?"

"You're needed in the Prime's Chamber, immediately. There's... been an accident."

Trevor feels a damp, cruel ache creep into his stomach. He

decides Gael's insubordination can be dealt with at a later time. He speaks quickly: "I want all contents of Juniper Trask's lab stripped and analyzed. Now. Do it quietly."

"Yes, my Teacher. We also found this in Aeman's apartment." Gael withdraws a grey cell phone from his pocket and sets it on Trevor's desk. "The phone is registered to a New Jersey address—"

"Why are you still here?! Go do what I just told you!" Trevor snaps. "And pray you do not mishandle this task the way you did the last, or it will be *you* gurgling and writhing in that chair, Gael." Trevor strides past his lieutenant, his face clenched with rage. The thought of this day getting any worse feels catastrophically unfair to Trevor.

CHAPTER 43

JUNIPER

The filthy motel room smells of mold and disinfectant; I don't want to touch anything. We're roughly ten miles outside of the city. My credit cards would all be easily traceable, and I didn't have any cash, so Charlie had to pay for this room. And now we've been stuck inside this disgusting box, which makes Aeman's loft look like a palace, for most of the night; and I'm beginning to doubt that any kind of rescue is possible. My father hasn't answered his phone. I tried him repeatedly over several hours, calling from a prepaid phone that Charlie also had to purchase. I don't like feeling indebted to anyone, especially a complete stranger, but I keep telling myself it's only temporary—not to mention vitally necessary. It would be so easy to triangulate our location from my phone, so I jotted down two numbers before we crossed the bridge, then I powered it down for good. We could've used Charlie's phone, but he lost it during all the fighting and dragging at Aeman's. It's hard to not feel like fate is against us. My father not answering means he's most likely passed out again or too high to notice my calls. My body pumps with fury, thinking of either of those possibilities.

In my desperation, I try the other number. I have no idea what I'll say to Daniel, if he answers. Some part of me just needs to hear a friendly voice. Maybe he can get a message to my father. Getting Daniel involved is the last thing I want, but I'm out of options. But the call only goes to voicemail. My stomach fills with dread. *No one left.* Last night was such a horror show: Trevor's threats, my father's intoxicated confession, Daniel's refusal to help, I barely got an hour of sleep, and now my mind churns like a hurricane. It's humiliating how unprepared I am for my current circumstances. What was I thinking, racing off to seek help from Aeman without imagining that there was a chance I might end up fighting for my life? *It's Aeman. When has he not rained down chaos on everyone around him?*

I push away all thoughts of my brother and how he clearly betrayed me. My mind needs to be clear. Anger will not help me right now.

Charlie sits on the bed. The way the motel manager winked at Charlie as he informed him that he only had rooms with a single bed available, made me want to stick a knife through his eye. I wanted to yell, *We're not planning on sleeping!* But then I realized how *that* might be interpreted and held my tongue. I watch Charlie now. He looks so lost. We've barely spoken a word to each other since we left Aeman's, and I can't imagine what he might be thinking, how he's processing his new reality. He must be so confused and frightened. We both needed time to recover, but there's something else that's been caus-ing the silence. We're strangers. I know nothing about him, and he knows nothing about me. But we've survived together—at least so far—and that does feel like it means something. I don't want to tell him my fears. Instead, I say, "We're going to be fine." The words sound thick and stupid coming out of my mouth, and I instantly wish I hadn't spoken. Who am I trying to convince with this false promise: him or myself?

Suddenly, Charlie stands, bends down, and lifts up the side of the bed, tilting it all the way up until the whole bed leans against the wall. An outline of filth marks the edges of where the bed just was, while an army of dust bunnies lie clumped and exposed within its borders.

I couldn't feel more confused. "What are you doing?"

Charlie faces me. "I want you to teach me how to fight. Not how to fight, I mean…I know how to fight. I mean, how to fight like a Winder."

"We don't have time for this."

"Please. I'm sure we're going to eventually face off against someone worse than what we've already encountered, and from what I can tell, I'd probably get my ass handed to me from anyone that's been trained like you. Just give me some pointers. The basics. Whatever. Please."

I look at him and realize he's right. Without some basic technique, he's going to find fighting against anyone from Thessaly nearly impossible. Not that that's my problem; if he'd been brought to Thessaly in the first place, we wouldn't even be in this situation. But somehow, I'm not sure that's true. There's something greater happening here, and I can't help but feel that Charlie is a part of it. Aeman doesn't just take in strays. That's not his way. Plus, on top of all that, if we are found by more of Trevor's Enforcers, or worse, maybe this time Trevor sends Gael Falcón. The thought makes me shudder. We wouldn't stand a chance. Other than Aeman, Gael is the deadliest assassin Trevor has ever trained. Charlie will be my only backup, regardless, and then his ignorance *will* be my problem.

Reluctantly, I square off against him. Maybe it'll take my mind off of how frustrated and alone I feel. Besides, I've already sparred with Charlie, and his fighting skills were not entirely unimpressive. His speed and agility may help make up for some of his obvious shortcomings. Not to mention the sheer power I've sensed in him as a Winder. How quickly he learned to block those Enforcers as they tried to pull us out from behind the couch was fairly astounding. Maybe his natural gifts will help compensate to an extent.

The displaced bed has given us much more room to work with, but instead of using the extra space, I step forward until I'm inches away from him and watch his eyes go wide. "You need to stay close," I say. "Close enough to make contact whenever possible." I reach out and place a hand on his chest. The intimacy of feeling his well-built body under my palm sends a little thrill through me, which feels ridiculous. I've sparred with countless partners before. It must be the heightened sense of danger that we're in. My brain is scattered and it's taking my emotions with it. I steady my breathing. "Now try and hit me." His eyebrows raise. "Don't worry; you won't be able to." And now I see the look I hoped for. Competition. "You're free to wind, but I will not. Now hit me."

"Um, okay…" Charlie halfheartedly attempts to push me away, but I roll around his arm, keeping my fingers tracing along his midsection. HE WINDS US BACK, BUT SINCE WE'RE IN CONTACT, I'M JUST AS AWARE AS HE IS ABOUT HIS COMING PUSH. This time, he doesn't try to push me. Instead, he swings with his left arm, but I duck under, again, making sure to keep my hand touching his hip. I use his momentum to pull myself around his torso until I'm standing behind him. I give him a kidney punch, and HE RIPS TIME IN REVERSE, BUT I'VE GOT MY HAND AGAINST HIS BACK, SO I SEE IT ALL. We're facing each other again as he releases, and this time, instead of dodging, I simply give him a tight, quick slap across the face. He freezes. I take a step back. He touches the side of his face. I'm expecting him to complain, but to my surprise, he laughs.

"Wow. That was pretty amazing. Embarrassing for me but cool to see. Even if it cost me a nice slap." I like that he's a good sport. It makes me think about my sparring session with Hector yesterday, and his hostility at having someone both smaller and a girl besting him in spite of his size. Charlie doesn't have any of that arrogance. He seems to have enough self-confidence that he doesn't have to. I have to admit it's refreshing.

"You let your guard down because you got frustrated," I say.

"Okay. Stay close. Got it."

"If you think you can win the fight one-on-one, then the more contact the better, because it will render your opponent's winding meaningless, regardless of their strength, because you'll both be aware at all times. This will particularly help *you*, because, despite your ignorance, you have power and speed."

"Really trying to just take in the compliment part of that."

"I'm not trying to compliment you. Pay attention." I can tell he wants to say more, but he stops himself. *Maybe not such an idiot after all.* "Whoever can wind first without making contact will always have the advantage, because they'll get to see what their opponent does before they do it. And that advantage will almost always go to the Winder with the most strength. That doesn't necessarily mean you should wind back the very first strike, though. You're looking for weaknesses. You're looking for a mistake you can exploit. Sometimes, that will come at the very beginning, and sometimes it will come five moves in. So, if you happen to be the stronger Winder, your best move is to block your opponent's winding until you find the right moment: they turn their head too much, or they're off-balance, or they swing too hard. Then you wind it back and exploit the mistake. But always be aware that your opponent is trying to do the same thing to you, and each time you block your opponent's wind, you'll lose energy. So, as soon as you see an opening, you need to strike fast and hard and try to make contact as you do. Because, if your plan doesn't work out, you need to know what they did to stop you. If they wind you back without you having contact, then the advantage will now be theirs."

Charlie looks like his mind is swimming. I just threw a lot at him, but these *are* the basics, and if he can't even get a handle on these...

"So, how can a less-powerful Winder ever hope to win a fight?" he asks.

"Energy isn't just about winding and blocking. Getting hit makes you tired. Swinging and missing gets you tired. Just like in a normal fight. No matter how powerful a Winder is, once they lose enough energy, anyone can take them."

"Or if they lose focus."

"Exactly," I say. "I've seen a more powerful Winder get distracted in a fight and lose very badly. Focus and energy. Stay on top of both and you will always have the advantage."

"And if they're still stronger?"

"Then you'll probably lose. But I once had a Teacher who said, 'If you find your back against the wall, your only chance is to let everything else go in order to truly find your strength. All your rage. All your sorrow. All your pain and hate. These are the things that sharpen the blade, but they are not the blade.'"

"That teacher sounds intense."

I almost laugh. "You have no idea." Then I feel the bitterness sink right back in.

"What about if you just freeze time?"

"You can't freeze time. It's impossible."

Charlie looks puzzled. I don't know what it means. "Really?" he asks. "Never? Aeman said Winders that can stop time are called Thanes."

I can't help but laugh. *My God, Aeman, you were really having fun with your little apprentice, weren't you?* It feels cruel at this point. "He was lying," I say. "Nothing more than legends. There's never been an ounce of proof that a Thane has ever existed. I shudder to think what other nonsense Aeman has been telling you." I feel the darkness welling up in me again, thinking about my lying brother. I look at Charlie, deciding to burn a little of this heat up inside me. "Now I'm going to try and hit you, Charlie."

CHAPTER 44

CHARLIE

Juniper stares at me with an intensity I find fascinating. Her guard is up; she's ready to fight, but there's also a calmness to her movements—an elegance. Against my better judgement, I feel drawn to her. Perhaps it's because we're running for our lives together—the way the hero and heroine in thriller movies always seem to have these momentary infatuations, fueled by the danger around them. Or maybe it's because I've truly never met anyone quite like her. She's arrogant, for sure, but then there was the vulnerability I saw in her when she talked about feeling that Enforcer girl die. She's tough. Self-reliant. She strikes me as someone who's had to take care of herself, and I can definitely identify with that. She speaks her mind, unapologetically, which makes me feel like I can trust her. So, why didn't I tell her about the few times I've actually managed to stop time?

Am I a *Thane*? Aeman talked about it like it was no big deal, but Juniper is treating the idea of a Thane like it's a magical dragon. One of them is lying, and I'm sure it's Aeman. But what if it's something he knows about that she just doesn't? She does put off the vibe that she doesn't get out a whole lot. The inconsistency makes me not trust any of it. So, I decided to keep it to myself. At least for now.

I take a step toward her, reach out and place a hand gently on her waist. She lets me. It makes me feel like we're about to dance. I guess we are, in a way. We hold each other's gaze, and this time, her eyes no longer have the rage I've seen there. She stares back at me with her own odd fascination. And then I feel her move.

—

We both heave for breath, dripping with sweat. I'm no match for Juniper as a fighter. She's been trained in a way I can't hope to compete with, but I do feel that I have a certain natural knack for blocking—for tearing down a wind before it even gets started. Each wind feels like a tiny puzzle in my head. Finding the quickest way to unravel a wind and pull it apart feels almost intrinsic. Admittedly, I'm stealing a certain amount of technique from Tristen. Her ability to get in between me and my ability to wind while we were fighting in Aeman's loft felt more advanced than how Juniper's blocking. Juniper is strong, for sure, but I get a sense that her badass fighting skills have allowed her to rely less on blocking, whereas Tristen—since she's not allowed to wind in her fucked-up cult—has made blocking her bread and butter.

There's also something that I experienced briefly with the Enforcers but that I am encountering in a much more concentrated way here with Juniper. As I block each wind, somehow I touch some essential part of her, a part that is not tied to her personality or life experience—it feels more like the part of her that makes her eyes blink and keeps her lungs moving or her heart beating. It feels like a core part of her inner-self—a part she can't mask or change—and it's beautiful.

The lesson is over. We're both seriously depleted. And now I'm starving. "I have a little money left over. I saw a twenty-four-hour diner a block over. You wanna grab a burger? My treat." I try to give her a little smile, but it feels like a serious effort even to do that. "It'll eat up some of the time until someone calls you back."

Juniper's eyes flicker away from me.

"What?"

"I don't think anyone will be calling me back tonight. I think we're on our own." The fear I see on her face makes me angry. Not at her, but at whoever's made her feel that way.

"Then we're on our own," I say. "We'll figure it out." I grab my jacket off the bed and slip it on. "But empty stomachs aren't gonna help us think."

"Okay," she says. And she looks relieved, as if she thought I was going to get pissed because she'd run out of answers. What would that help? And I'm pretty sure she's already beating herself up about it enough. I don't know anyone she's been calling, anyway. Meeting new Winders doesn't sound great right now. Part of me is curious about where Juniper lives, and this place she and Aeman referred to as "Thessaly," but I've had about enough I can handle for one day. We need food and we need sleep. I'll give her the bed, and I'll take the floor. Won't be that different from what I had to sleep on at Lazarus. But first, I think I need to see Juniper eat a cheeseburger. The entire idea sounds bizarre to me somehow. I smile to myself as I pull open the flimsy red door.

Tristen stands outside.

Before I can even breathe a sound, she raises a gun and fires into my chest. I smash backward into Juniper. *Oh, my God, I've been shot!* Juniper and I are touching, so I can intimately feel Juniper gather her will. Then I feel Juniper's wind get eviscerated. It's there, and then it's gone, but I can tell it wasn't only Tristen who blocked her. Her wind was pummeled between multiple forces, like a sheet of paper caught in a swirling wind devil.

Focus, Charlie! You're not going to…get out of this…if you…don't… My mind is a pool of muddy water, getting filthier by the second. I can no longer stay standing. I drop down onto my ass. Then Tristen re-aims her gun and shoots Juniper in the throat. Juniper's body crumbles down on top of me. Raging tears burn my eyes as I look at Juniper: the second person today I've seen destroyed by the malicious succubus standing above me. Then I notice something.

Protruding from Juniper's neck is a tiny dart. I want to reach for it, but I can't move my arms. I look up at Tristen as she steps through the doorway and squats down, bringing herself to eye level to me. Behind her, two large men fill the doorway. One is the generous Nordic bartender from the bar Tristen brought me to. The other I don't recognize. The trio looms over us, and just as I black out for the third time today, I think I hear Tristen's blurry face say, "It's going to be all right, Charlie."

CHAPTER 45

THE PRIME

Trevor stares down at Cameron's vacant eyes and has to resist a deep urge to smash his fist into his old friend's face until his head caves in. *Goddammit!* The slimy pale color to Cameron Trask's skin and the greyish-green trail of bile leaking from the side of his gaping dead mouth feel like a death sentence to Trevor. He sees the clear tube on the ground next to Cameron's curled fingers. He picks it up. The tube reads FENTANYL, and it is empty. *That amount of fentanyl would've killed a small pack of elephants*, he thinks.

Trevor seethes. He let himself get too distracted, interrogating Juniper's lab tech. He should've contained all information of Gael's failed assassination attempt on Juniper. Of course, Cameron would think Trevor had ordered it and that he'd reneged on their little deal. Trevor's plans concerning Cameron had been carefully crafted over an entire year, and now those plans were as dead as their newest Prime. *All that fucking work…* Trevor thinks.

Arranging for Cameron to win the Carrion Ring had been no small feat, but it had led to Cameron being named Prime, and even more importantly; it meant that the Carrion Ring would be hosted by their Chapter next year. This was the task Trevor had been given, and Trevor had lied, cheated and murdered his way to that goal. Cameron's only stipulation for being moved about like a puppet was that Juniper be left unharmed. Trevor knew that Cameron had always been one to sense how the winds were blowing, and that he had aided in Trevor's machinations because he knew who the winner would be. If Juniper had been brought back to Thessaly in disgrace, like he'd *ordered*, he would've had even more leverage over Cameron. But somehow, Cameron must've gotten word of the attempt on Juniper's life before he could control it.

The fucking coward! Careful plans ripped to shreds. He needed Cameron for so much more. Grooming someone else for Prime and getting them elected feels near impossible under the current time constraints.

This sloppiness will not be understood, he thinks. *They will punish me for my failure. Let them try. I will not lose all that I have been promised! Damn you, Cameron! You visionless fool! You spineless fucking parasite!* Trevor wants to scream, to hit something, anything, but he refuses to show this kind of vulnerability in front of the two young Enforcers standing behind him. "Go check the bedroom for his cell phone." The two Enforcers move into the adjacent room.

Trevor kneels down close to Cameron's face and whispers, "I plan to torture your little girl, Cameron. I hope you hear it all the way down in whatever hell you're currently boiling in. She will feel every ounce of pain you wriggled away from, and she will receive no mercy."

Then Trevor reaches into Cameron's pocket and withdraws his cell phone.

"Never mind; it's here," Trevor calls to the Enforcers. They reenter the room and Trevor hands it to the older of the two. "Have all recent calls traced," he says, knowing full well that Juniper is far too clever to call her father from her own phone when she knows she's being pursued.

And all at once, something clicks in Trevor's mind. Something he heard. Recently. *From Gael,* he thinks. They found a phone in Aeman's apartment registered to a New Jersey address. *Aeman said he found his mysterious Thane in New Jersey.* Most of Trevor had assumed Aeman was a desperate liar, working some plan of his own. His own scheme with Juniper had been a stroke of genius, Trevor had thought. And now that plan has withered and died. *But could Aeman's desperate claim possibly be true?* It's too much to hope for. Trevor allows himself to think of the possibilities. Having a Thane under his control could make him unstoppable. Such a weapon could bring even the ones he's learned to call his masters to their knees. It could be all for him. *Everything.*

—

Trevor lunges back into his office, strides over to his desk, and there it is—the little grey cell phone. The device stares up at him like a death row prison key. He picks up the phone, handling it delicately. He opens it.

On the home screen he sees *Missed voicemail from Ducky*. He hits Listen. A young man's voice plays:

"*...Charlie, man...what can I say? I'm sorry I freaked on you. Think maybe if things were reversed, you probably would've been better about it than me. I just... Shit was scary the other night. Probably scarier for you though, right? ...Anyway. Look...I know you're going through something. Something you don't think you can tell me, but I want you to know...whatever you gotta do in New York...Jersey is always here if you need us. Love you, bro.*"

The message ends.

Trevor checks the previous incoming calls on the phone. Nearly all read *Grams's landline* or *Ducky's Cell Phone*.

He finds Charlie's last received text message. It's also from "Ducky."

Ducky's text reads: *Charlie!! Where are u?? Me and Grams are freaking out!! I'm so sorry about the party last night man. Please let us know you're ok. Come home bro!*

Trevor types a return text: *Hey man, I really need your help.*

Trevor waits. After a moment, a text comes back: *What's up?*

Trevor types, *I'll explain when I see you. I wanna tell you and Grams together. Where are you?*

Ducky: *At home. Where are u? You're scaring me man.*

Trevor: *Are u and Grams together?*

Ducky: *Yeah. WHAT'S UP???*

Trevor: *I'm coming there now. Please, don't leave.*

Trevor pockets Charlie's phone.

CHAPTER 46

JUNIPER

I'm dreaming of our old apartment on the lower levels. The lower chambers within the belly of Thessaly are where normal humans are allowed to reside, making Thessaly Tower *seem* like any other skyscraper in New York City—giving the avatar of ValCorp its flesh. Inside Thessaly, the powerful and power*less* are collected at each end, with everyone else falling or fighting in either direction. I see our old kitchen, its mint-colored walls, and her hands firmly planted on the sink. Gripping. *Always gripping. And then the squeal—that old teakettle—and the smell of burning meat—*

Light floods my corneas and I realize I've opened my eyes without noticing. The dream slips through my conscious mind like a sieve. I'm awake. But *where* am I awake? My last thoughts: *I've been shot... I can't breathe... I'm dying... Charlie, we're... Father!* The dank smell of must hangs in the air. I'm in a place where people don't come often. And then the feeling hits me again. *I felt her die.* Nausea curls me into a ball. The others two Enforcers were there as well, but the girl's mind—Gretchen's mind—felt so prominent, as if I'd hacked her to pieces with my bare hands. I didn't mean to kill her. I believe that. But she's still dead. She tried to kill me; she *would've* killed me. Still, I don't think I can ever use my discovery again, and I certainly can't let it fall into the hands of Trevor.

Panic sets in as I snap back to the reality of where I am. I sit up on the canvas cot I've been sleeping on, to see I'm surrounded by the concrete, windowless walls of a holding cell.

A sharp moan comes from close by, and I turn to see Charlie on a matching cot, writhing in agony. I move toward him. My muscles feel atrophied. I almost fall. Charlie cries out again as I reach him. *Have they poisoned him? Has he been wounded?* Then I realize he's still unconscious. He's having a nightmare, like before.

"Charlie…" He grabs me and yanks me down close as he cries out, *"Mom! NO!"* And then his eyes are open. I can tell he thinks he's seeing someone else at first, because for a second, his dark blue eyes swell with tears. Then I watch the walls of his awareness close in tight around him. He sags in my arms. All at once, he looks so weak and sad that I find it impossible to imagine that this is the same young man I joyfully kicked in the face on the street mere hours ago. At least, I think it was hours ago. I have no idea how long we've been unconscious.

Charlie pulls himself to a sitting position. I want to ask him what happened to his mother. I want to know what could have made him look so afraid. So tortured. But instead, I simply say, "You screamed for your mother." *No wonder you have so many friends, Juniper.*

"…I'm sorry," Charlie says. There's shame in his voice. He doesn't elaborate. We sit in silence. "Where are we?" he finally asks.

"I don't know." I force myself to my feet and slog over to the steel door barring our exit. Tiny cameras point at us from all four upper corners of the room. I bang on the door, less because I think it will help and more because it's what's expected, and until I can think of an alternative plan, I might as well seem predictable to whoever is watching. And then I remember something— "That girl…" I turn to Charlie. "The one who shot us. She knew you. Who is she?"

Charlie darkens. "Your guess is as good as mine," he says. *I bet my guess would be better.* "She used me to get to Aeman."

Hearing Aeman's name right now feels like poking an already-festering wound. All of this, *all of it*, is because of him. But there's something else. The edge in Charlie's voice makes me think that the "using" she did was somehow more personal than I care to think about. My rambling thoughts on the matter flush my cheeks slightly, which annoys me to no end. *Why should I care what he does with some disgusting—* I pound the door. Harder. I want it to hurt.

Focus me. There are certain palpable truths right now, and I need to find their root. There's always a root.

"Aeman meant for us to be found together by those Enforcers," I say.

Charlie looks shocked, and I believe his ignorance. And something about that makes me hurt for him. How many times have I been there, hoping like an idiot, wanting to believe, against my better judgment? *Welcome to the minefield that is my brother, Charlie.*

"Why would he do that?" Charlie demands.

"For greed, or personal gain. Some people are just bad, Charlie. I'm sorry if you thought he was your friend. I don't think Aeman's ever had a real friend in his entire life." *Not that I have.* "We're all just chaff to him."

I watch this information soak into Charlie. But instead of the ache I expect to see, I watch him sop up the bitter truth, then swallow it whole, like it's a predictable pattern he knows all too well.

The fact that my feckless older brother handed us over to Trevor for God knows what deal he made feels like it wants to be a lethal wound, but it's not. I don't have the mental energy for anything but survival right now. I have a good idea who has us, and the thought of it dries my throat.

"Who is Victor Mason?" Charlie suddenly asks.

His question takes me by surprise. It seems bizarre to me that Aeman would've been teaching Charlie even the basic histories of the Leadership. Doesn't really seem like his style.

"Why are you asking me that?" I try to keep my voice even.

"The last thing Aeman said to me before he disappeared was to tell you that I'm just like someone named Victor Mason."

My eyes narrow. I don't know what this means, and I don't like that feeling.

"What would make Aeman say that?" I ask.

Charlie shrugs. "Who is he?"

"He was our first Prime—one of the founding members of the Leadership."

"So, basically, he was a super evil dude with a ton of power."

"Do you want to hear this or not?"

Charlie shuts up, so I continue. "For most of Winder history, what we now call Chapters were once various shadowed factions existing in countries all around the world. Every country had them, usually several. But there were also hundreds, perhaps thousands of lone Winders working in the fringes as well as at the highest levels of business and government. As technology grew, so did communication between different factions in different countries. With this came allies and enemies. Victor Mason, along with several other prominent Leaders around the world, created the Leadership as well as a global treaty among all Chapters."

"The Code," Charlie says.

I nod, taking in his inappropriate knowledge. Then again, every word I'm telling him is inappropriate. But we're locked in a cell, with little chance of survival, so…

"Several countries held out, usually those who had more than one powerful faction within its borders—like us. Powerful countries with dictatorial governments had long since weeded out internal enemies and consolidated power: Russia, China, Saudi Arabia, Cuba… But those with ongoing civil wars used the treaty to strike down rival groups. The faction who embraced their place in the Leadership became that country's ruling 'Chapter,' and the full force of the Leadership worked with them to wipe out any opposition. The world fell like dominos, and soon there was a unified world of Winders living in peace, operating as one multi-armed organism."

I realize how dry my telling of this information was. It's something every Winder is taught at a very young age. I don't have the energy to make it sound more interesting right now. *I'm not here to entertain anyone.* Still, I brace myself for his attack.

"So, Aeman was telling you I have the makings of a great community organizer? That sounds strange."

Charlie's right. That can't be it. My resentment toward Aeman spikes anew. Then something floats into my mind. A memory. Something Elijah said once. I look at Charlie. "I heard someone say once that Victor Mason was supposed to be the genesis of a new evolution of Winders."

"What do you mean, 'supposed to be'?"

"He was assassinated thirty years ago by the Warriors of Fate."

This dead end seems to cover Charlie in a dark cloud.

"What does any of that have to do with me?" he asks.

"Probably nothing," I say. "I think it's pretty obvious that it's foolish to trust a single word that comes out of Aeman's mouth." My anger feels more transparent than I'm comfortable with. Charlie takes in my raw state and doesn't comment on it, which I'm grateful for.

"Thank you…for helping me," he says, his voice quiet. "I didn't say it before. You're the only reason I'm still alive." His stare locks on to me, and for a moment, I feel helpless. It's so strange. I do feel drawn to Charlie—to the loneliness I sense in him, but also to his reckless courage. I allow myself to wonder what our meeting would've been like in a simpler time. But I suppose that kind of thinking is pointless.

"We haven't found out why we're still alive yet," I say. "We're here for a reason."

Charlie stays quiet. The dungeon quality of our surroundings bears down on us.

"She died," Charlie says. I don't understand his reference. "My mother, I mean." Charlie doesn't look at me when he speaks, allowing me to take in every detail of his face as he works through his thoughts. "Cancer," he says. "I don't know if you people get diseases like that…but you're lucky if you don't."

"We do," I say, attempting to contribute, but instantly wishing I hadn't said a word.

Charlie nods slightly. "Oh. …Well, just hope you don't get her kind. It's a bad one. Rare, they said. Doctors didn't even have a name for it." He looks up at me. "My mom would've liked you, I think." Charlie's mouth takes on the smallest of smiles. "She liked smart girls." Then Charlie exhales, blowing away whatever memory is playing inside his head. "Anyway…thanks."

As he leaves his sad, vulnerable gaze aimed at me, something tenses inside my body. The back of my neck feels hot. I can't tell if I like this feeling or not. I know I should say something back, but I'm at a loss. I open my mouth to speak, not knowing quite what's going to come out—

Clank. Our attention slams toward the door. A large locking mechanism rattles. Charlie jumps to his feet as the heavy door slides open.

The girl who shot me in the throat walks in, flanked by two powerfully built men. One man has long, wavy blond hair down to his shoulders, a beard and the physique of a professional boxer. The second is even more immense than the first. His skin is dark and his face is quite beautiful.

"Fate be with you, Juniper Trask," the girl says.

"You'll get nothing from us," my voice spits acid. I glance toward Charlie. "He doesn't know a thing, and I'd sooner die than betray the Leadership."

The girl obviously holds a higher rank than the two men, because they both look to her for how she'll respond. Her focus lands on Charlie, who stares back with loathing. *What's their connection? How does Charlie have history with the Faters? Could he be one of them?*

"Such strong words, Juniper," she says, "and yet you don't even know why you're here." She's baiting me. Trying to get me to talk. I remain silent.

"Why the hell have you brought us here, Tristen?" Charlie demands. A quick but noticeable sadness passes over her at his tone.

"I know all I need to know," I say, steamrolling over their little *moment*.

Tristen looks at me. "That's funny. From all I've learned about you, that couldn't seem further from the truth."

"You know nothing about me, assassin." I know I should hide my disdain, but my longing to bash this girl's overconfident face in overwhelms my reason. These people murdered Elijah.

"Maybe not," Tristen says. "But I do know the truth. And you do not. That doesn't seem fair, does it?" Tristen and I hold a death stare. "How about a tour?"

Charlie and I are led into an elevator, our hands bound in front of us with plastic zip ties. The same ties used on Elijah. I think of those little grooves in the armrests—the torture he must've endured. *They will pay. I just have to wait for the right moment.*

The sides of the elevator are made out of thick glass, but they might as well be made of steel, because everything outside the transparent walls looks like the dark sheathing of a subway tunnel. The doors close and the elevator begins to rise.

"We should've known you'd hide underground like rats," I say.

"Not quite," Tristen says.

Light floods the elevator. We're entering some kind of torture chamber. Adrenaline floods my body, leaving me shaky and bird-eyed. But then I realize the light pouring in isn't artificial; it's from the outside world. We must be gliding up the side of a massive skyscraper on the north side of Midtown, somewhere just south of the park, because to my utter amazement and horror, looming up before us, so close it almost feels sarcastic, is Thessaly Tower. I'm racing through city layouts in my mind, trying to imagine what building we might be coasting up the side of, but I can't place it. They've been so close for so long. Watching us. Laughing at us. I simply can't believe my eyes.

Behind me, the elevator doors open into a normal-looking office space. We walk between rows of cubicles. People on all sides wear suits and ties, hold coffee cups, watch things on each other's computer monitors. No one seems to take any notice of the two bound prisoners being led along by armed escorts. Charlie suddenly jerks away from the huge, dark-haired man who's been holding him.

"*Hey!*" Charlie hollers. "We need help! These people have kidnapped us! Someone call the police!!"

The entire workforce looks over. Then, like they've seen nothing that could possibly interest them, they all turn back to their work. The bearded Fater laughs. "Not the response you were hoping for?" he says in a Swiss accent. He grabs Charlie and yanks him forward. *They're all Faters. Every last one. It's too much, too fast.*

"How is this possible?" I say. "You've been here all this time?"

"Hidden in plain view," Tristen says. "Sometimes, the best camouflage is none."

We approach an opaque glass door. Tristen enters a code and the door hisses open. The room is much bigger than it appears from the outside. One entire wall is covered with screens. Advanced surveillance equipment fills the room in all directions. It doesn't look as state-of-the-art as what the Leadership possesses. Everything inside the upper levels of Thessaly is the very best money can buy. The Faters are making do with less, and yet this room is impressive. My innate curiosity tugs at me. I want to probe the consoles, test their limitations. I force these thoughts away. I have to be ready, find the moment to strike.

"There's no way the Leadership wouldn't have noticed an operation this big." The words fall out of me, but it feels more like I'm trying to make them true.

"This is the old CDC building and it still operates as the Centers for Disease Control," Tristen says. "Nothing's changed. Except we've added one more plague that threatens humanity to the pile."

My temper flares. These insurgents have killed countless of my people throughout the years. Mostly Enforcers but not all. I keep the image of Elijah's bloody chair at the center of my mind's eye. "Listen to me, terrorist. We're not the plague. You slink in the shadows like rodents. You cowards murdered someone that meant a great deal to me, and I will see that you answer for your crimes. Every last one of you."

Tristen stops and turns to me, a fury in her eyes I'm not quite prepared for.

"It's taking everything in me right now not to simply put a bullet through your face to destroy any resemblance to the man who exterminated my entire family. So, will you kindly shut your goddamn mouth?"

"I don't know what the hell you're—"

"Your brother, and others like him, have slaughtered men, women and children in nothing less than a systematic genocide, because the Leadership saw our peaceful way of life as a threat to their power and greed. Don't speak to me about terrorism, you pampered little princess. Your very way of life is a terrorist act as far as I'm concerned."

"You're a liar," I say.

"I'm afraid she isn't," a soft, deep voice says from behind us.

All turn to see an old man, in possibly his late eighties, slowly approaching from across the room. I didn't see or hear him enter. Perhaps he was already in the room when we came in. He smiles at me despite the thick hostility on my face.

"We were not always called *Warriors* of Fate," he says. "We had to become what we are in order to protect ourselves from extinction."

"Who the hell are you?" Charlie says.

"I am something of a relic these days, Charlie. I come from a day when a group of Winders, having grown tired and sick to our stomachs from flaunting our power over time, and having bathed in decadence and fame, swore an oath to leave all fate to God and just be men once again. Our community grew exponentially as Winders from all around the world sought out a place of peace, a place that believed in the future and left the past to its own devices. Our numbers doubled each year until the size of our community grew too large to be ignored. The Leadership began to fear our strength, and when their wrath finally came, it came quick. Those who had been Leaders were the first targeted. Entire bloodlines were wiped out. A vicious, well-planned holocaust."

All at once, every screen in the room lights up with images from surveillance footage. My eyes flick from one screen to the next. Each shows an Enforcer entering a home or apartment and ends with a murder.

The old man points to a large screen at the far end of the room. "Pay attention to this screen here, Miss Trask."

I turn to see *Aeman* on one of the larger screens. I watch him shoot a crying man begging for his life, then he turns and shoots the man's wife at point-blank range; and then, to my disbelief, he coldly assassinates their young daughter, who can't be any more than ten years old. The three bodies fall in a lump on the ground.

Charlie stares agape at Aeman's horrific deeds.

Yesterday I would have laughed off these images as obviously counterfeit, but Sofia's mother drifts into my head—smiling—so hopeful—*stuffed into a sewer pipe*. And the other parents of the children I've found in the Gathering. *They've killed them all.* But this…this has to be a manipulation.

"…I don't believe you." I stammer, my voice fighting for

purchase. "You've created this as some sort of a trick."

The old man contemplates me for a moment. "No, Juniper. Let me ask you this: Your father is the current champion of the Carrion Ring. How much respect for life does that disgusting game take into consideration?"

I decide not to reveal my ignorance regarding this subject. But hearing the old man mention the Carrion Ring causes a memory to float back to me. Shortly after the Carrion Ring last year, which took place in Moscow, Trevor's Russian counterpart, Dmitri Golovin, visited our Chapter. During the reception, I remember my father complimenting him on his "choice of weapon." The Russian Enforcer smiled and said, "Yes. I was worried perhaps it would move things along too quickly, but in the end, everyone seemed quite pleased." I remember wondering what weapons they were talking about and who they were using them against. But then, over my father's shoulder, the thick, bald man, with his veiny neck and sunken Slavic cheeks, had hovered his dark, wolfish eyes over me, and I had quickly moved away from the conversation.

The old Fater must see my mind working, because the tone of his voice softens as he continues. "Juniper, you were taught that we hunt your kind. And we do. But have you ever asked yourself why? How all this killing began?"

I know exactly how the killing began. With your dogs murdering one of the very best of us. He actually thinks I'm going to believe his lies. How did these fools survive this long? He sees my face harden against him, but he seems to take my animosity in stride.

"The Leadership lies, cheats, steals and lives off humanity while hiding behind some Frankensteined idea of evolution. They think that if they cobble together enough rationalization, no one will see the blood between their teeth. But we would not be lambs to the slaughter. So, here we are." *Yes, here we are.* I casually glance at the big, dark-haired Fater. As he was trying to restrain Charlie earlier, I caught a glimpse of a knife tucked into the back of his belt. *He's two steps away now. If I can get there quick enough, take him by surprise…*

I stare back into the old man's face. Focusing on him will lower the guards of the others. His voice grows more emphatic:

"But despite the indecency of the current system," he drones on, "it has always operated under a strict set of rules, a governing construct that believes in stability over conflict—commerce over violence. There are barbaric exceptions to this, such as the Carrion Ring or the Gathering, or even the lengths at which they've gone to suppress *us*." *Even this babbling fool knows the truth about the Gathering. How did I allow myself to be so sheltered?* "But for better or worse, these practices have been agreed upon by the Leadership as a whole. Despite its atrocities, the Leadership is still a republic, and thus the mechanisms are in place to change such evils, if the will to do so were there. But something has changed. Something vital. And the hour has never been more grave. The time has come to act."

I couldn't agree more. I gently slide onto the balls of my feet, preparing my body for the fight of my life. I take a deep breath.

"You didn't answer my question," Charlie says. "Who *are* you?"

"My name is Victor Mason," the old man says, "and I do not intend to harm either of you."

CHAPTER 47

JUNIPER

I feel shell-shocked as I stare at the old man. "You're not Victor Mason," I say. "That's not possible… You're—"

"Dead?" the old man calling himself Victor Mason offers. "Yes, I am. Very much so. This ragged version of a once-great man you see before you is merely a ghost. Having as much blood on your hands as I do is a corrosive thing. Trust me. I still see the faces of every soul we've lost. And I will until the day I die. It has to end."

"I…I don't…I don't understand," I stammer. My head has begun to throb, and it feels as if something inside me is unraveling. *He has to be lying. It's just not possible.*

I watch him watch me. He's gauging my reaction. *Why would he tell such a bizarre lie? What could he possibly hope to gain from it?* He moves toward a wide glass table surrounded by chairs. "Do you mind?" he says. "These old bones exact a mighty vengeance on me if I don't bring them to port at any possible opportunity." He sinks into a chair, gesturing for me and Charlie to join him.

"We'll stand." My voice is firm, but I feel the brittleness at my core and it enrages me. *I need to be strong right now.*

"Suit yourself," he says. The other Faters stay standing, perhaps afraid we'll bolt for the door after whatever we're about to hear next. I brace myself as the old man's face grows grim. "Juniper, I'm afraid the world that you know is on the brink of extinction."

I feel molten anger pour into me. "Is that supposed to be some kind of threat?"

"Not from us, Juniper, if that's what you're thinking," *Victor Mason* says. "We have reliable intelligence that Trevor De'Vant intends to move against the Leadership very soon. On a global scale."

"The Code forbids a single ruler. That's ridiculous."

"Trevor's intent is the complete extermination of the current system. A republic means sharing, cooperation. Trevor wants rule. Control. He wants what many Chapters had before the Leadership swept away the 'less civilized' factions within our world: he wants complete domination. A feudal society—with him as a king—where humans, and the weak among our kind, live beneath the boots of their superiors or drown in their own blood."

"No lone Winder is that strong," I say. *So, this is their plan: capture one of the Leaders, pretend to be one of my heroes, wean me to their side, fill me with dark conspiracies, then maybe release me back into Thessaly as some rebel-minded Manchurian Candidate. I've given these people too much credit. They may be half-decent assassins, but this is just pathetic.*

"Trevor is not alone," Victor says. "He has many allies. Strong allies. He represents a faction of Winders sick of hiding among the human world; they want a world of masters and slaves, and they're preparing to strike. This plan has been in the making for quite some time."

I find myself grinning, against my better judgment. I have little faith that Charlie and I will escape this place with our lives, so I do not intend to allow my enemies to think they've even remotely outsmarted me. Almost laughing, I say, "How could you possibly know any of this? It's not like Trevor would just announce some maniacal plan to you."

The old man doesn't grow frustrated at my defiance; his face only shows a solemn, confusing *empathy*. "Someone very close to Trevor had been working with us for almost a year. Someone close to you as well."

I can feel the color in my cheeks get sucked pale.

I try and hold down my next thought with chains and ties and barricades, cornering it with whips like a mad elephant. But it's no use.

"*Elijah*," I hear myself say, barely above a whisper, as if the solution to some impossible equation has suddenly become clear.

Victor Mason gives a somber nod. "He was very brave. I fear we shall not see his equal again any time soon."

Why am I even listening to this?! But I can't turn away. *Could it be…* It was Elijah who introduced me to all those incredible thinkers, those dynamic *human* minds, subversive scholars, silently building inside me a fundamental rejection of the basic premise of the Leadership: that we are superior; that we are owed the Earth by evolutionary design. *Was he always a traitor?* "Elijah was our Prime…" Words come out of me, but I don't feel any connection to them. "He would never betray— I knew him. He…" But it suddenly makes too much sense. *You killed him, didn't you, Trevor? You tortured and killed Elijah, and you enjoyed every second of it. Then you spoke his name with reverence in the Council Room. You fucking monster.*

"Elijah cared for you very much, Juniper. He wanted to bring this information to you himself." Victor's voice grows careful—delicate—measured. "But when he discovered that your father was working with Trevor, he chose not to test your loyalty."

"My father?" My throat clenches tight. Trevor always said, *In battle, find what your enemy cannot live without and control the spigot.* My father is a perfect candidate for coercion: sad and guilty—tied to his vices like a fiend. *You've made a meal of my father, Trevor. I know you have.* But something doesn't make sense.

"I don't understand," I say. "Why aren't you celebrating the assassination of the entire Leadership? Wouldn't that be a fortuitous case of your work done for you?"

"Elijah's attempt at striking a treaty between our two sides was very close to succeeding when he was murdered. We believe the killing finally has a chance to end. But a system led by Trevor… We are barely able to eke out a stalemate with the American Chapter as it is. Imagine legions of foreign Enforcers descending on us, hunting down all who do not fall in line."

"What do you want from me and Charlie?"

"I suggested a suicide vest for you. Would you be into that?" Tristen says to me with a sardonic smile. I look at her. It takes everything in me not to strike the overconfident cow.

Victor gives Tristen an impatient look. "To so brazenly go after you—a member of the Council—he must fear your voice a great deal," he says. "For now, I simply intend to keep you from Trevor's gasp until we can decide how best to stop him."

"How does he plan to destroy the system, like you say?" I ask.

"We don't know exactly. Not even Elijah knew the answer to that. He said it was odd: that Trevor's decisions and orders had come sporadically, in fits and starts. He said he felt that many were involved but that none had the whole story."

"Then how do you plan to stop him?"

"We must be vigilant."

Victor Mason turns to Charlie, who has remained silent for quite some time.

"Tristen tells me you have the makings of a very powerful Winder, Charlie. You'll need to learn to control such power. And we could use your help. Trevor is a mighty enemy; many will die before this race is run. We're going to need all the strength we can find."

All eyes land on Charlie. And that's when Charlie totally loses it.

CHAPTER 48

CHARLIE

"ALL RIGHT!" Words tumble from me like an avalanche. "It's been *really* fun chatting with all of you, *BUT I WOULD LIKE TO GET OFF THE RIDE NOW!*"

I turn to Juniper. "*I don't know you.*" I point to Victor Mason: "I don't know you!" I wheel around on Tristen: "I DEFINITELY don't know you! This isn't my war. You're not my people. I have no people!"

"Charlie, calm down," Tristen says.

"*DON'T TELL ME TO CALM DOWN!* You lied to me! I find out I'm part of some fucked-up time-traveler war, I learn I killed my best friend's parents, I watch the only person I trusted in your psychotic world get murdered right in front of my eyes, then I nearly die bringing him back, only to find out he's some kind of homicidal child-killer—"

"What did you say?" Juniper looks suddenly distressed. "...You saw Aeman die?"

"Ask *her!*" I point to Tristen. "She did all the stabbing and throat-slitting!"

Juniper spins on Tristen, eyes blazing. "Did you kill my brother?!"

"You're not listening," I say. "I wound it back. He never died, okay? I watched him run away. Stop interrupting me!"

Juniper's eyes fill with tears. I couldn't be more at a loss. *I don't need some misconstrued emotional bullshit right now. These people are crazy, and I need to get the hell out of this funny farm.*

"I promise you, Juniper," Victor Mason says, "he was not the man you think he was."

Juniper's face quivers with rage. "He was my brother!"

"He's alive!" I yell. "Are you all deaf?! HE'S ALIVE!"

"He's not, Charlie!" Juniper spits out. "There's no winding back death. If their heart stops, the person still dies. But if they get wound back, it's even worse. They suffer. It's a slow, agonizing deterioration. You wouldn't wish it on your worst enemy."

My mind is a sloshy pool of shit. Diseased. Nasty. Hateful.

Images flash through my mind: I see my mother's crumbled, decaying body as she reaches for me from her bed, desperate for help that will never come. I hold her head as she vomits into a plastic bucket. I help her back into bed. This morbid cycle continues until it stops. Until she's gone.

"…No…" The word bleeds from me. My knees go wobbly. Juniper turns to me, seeing me stumble.

Tristen moves toward me, but Juniper heads her off. "Stay back!" She slashes at Tristen, then turns back to me. "Charlie, what is it?"

"…*My mother,*" I whisper so quietly, I almost don't hear it myself. I see me as a young boy by her side, trying not to seem scared. Her thin fingers reach out and gently touch my cheek. She's wasting away, and I don't understand why. I don't understand her agony is all my fault. I clench my eyes shut, but now I see her dashed apart in the car wreck. Then she's reassembled before my eyes. She smiles at me, then she recedes almost to a single point of light, until she disappears.

"I wound her back. The car crash… I watched her die. I thought I saved her. She was in so much pain…that was because of me…"

I see it dawn on Juniper what I'm saying. "No, Charlie…" she says.

A young woman enters the room and rushes to Tristen. She whispers something to her. Tristen pulls her phone out and examines something on her screen. Then her eyes smash into mine. I see something strange pass over her expression. Tristen takes a step in my direction. "Charlie… Where's your cell phone?"

I feel myself absently pat my pockets, even though I know it's not there. When Tristen and I flopped onto Aeman's couch—which feels like a million years ago right now—her weight was causing my phone to gouge into my thigh, so I pulled it out and set it next to me on the couch. In all the commotion, it'd either slipped between the couch cushions or fallen onto the floor. "Why?" I ask, but I can feel the dread building in me before she even answers.

"Because right now it's moving rapidly toward New Jersey," Tristen says.

I turn to Juniper, and as quietly as I can possibly communicate, while still remaining clear, I say, "*Create a distraction.*"

"…What? Why? What's going on?" Juniper asks.

"*Right now! Do it right now!*" I hiss at her.

Juniper doesn't ask another question; instead, she turns and punches Tristen savagely in the face. And in the moment of chaos, I dig into Time with everything I got…

THE WORLD BEGINS TO SLOW DOWN UNTIL EVERYTHING COMES TO A COMPLETE STANDSTILL. ALL IS FROZEN AROUND ME. TRISTEN'S HEAD IS SNAPPED BACK, HER BODY IS SHAPED LIKE HALF OF A PAREN-THESIS. HER TWO THUG SIDEKICKS LEAN FORWARD, ATTEMPTING TO COME TO TRISTEN'S AID. VICTOR MASON'S EXPRESSION SEEMS LASER-FOCUSED, IN REACTION TO THE VIOLENCE, BUT THERE'S SOMETHING ELSE IN HIS EXPRESSION THAT MAKES ME FEEL UNEASY. I CAN'T PUT MY FINGER ON WHAT'S DIFFERENT ABOUT THE OLD MAN, AND I DON'T HAVE TIME TO FIGURE IT OUT. JUNIPER SLOUCHES FOR-WARD IN A PETRIFIED LEAN, FALLING FROM THE MOMENTUM OF HER SWING BUT NEVER LANDING. I LUNGE AND SCOOP UP JUNIPER'S FROZEN BODY. I THROW HER OVER MY SHOULDER AND HEAD FOR THE DOOR. MY FACE IS ALREADY BEADED WITH SWEAT AS I CHARGE ACROSS THE ROOM, TOTING JUNIPER LIKE A SACK OF POTATOES.

"CHARLIE?" A VOICE CALLS OUT TO ME. I FREEZE IN PLACE, MATCHING THE WORLD AROUND ME. I TURN, WITH JUNIPER STILL SLUNG OVER MY SHOULDER.

VICTOR MASON STANDS STARING AT ME. *THAT'S WHAT WAS OFF.* HE'S NOT FROZEN WITH THE REST OF THE WORLD. AND I HAVE NO IDEA WHY. BUT TRUTHFULLY, I REALLY KNOW SO LITTLE ABOUT THIS CRAZY WORLD, THIS COULD BE A TOTAL NORM. THERE'S NO OWNER'S MANUAL! BUT SOMEHOW, IT FEELS SIGNIFICANT. LIKE IT'S A SECRET BETWEEN ONLY US. I WAIT FOR HIM TO COME AT ME, BUT HE NEVER MOVES.

"Do not leave here, Charlie. Please. Only death waits outside these walls for you and Juniper. You're not ready."

I don't listen to anything more. I heave out of the chamber. My body is sopping wet by the time I chug through the maze of office cubicles. The building looks like a land inhabited by mannequins. I begin to stagger as I reach the elevator. I pry the doors open with my hands. Luckily, the elevator car has not been called to another floor. I step into the elevator. Then my hold on time releases, and things begin moving normally again. As the doors ding shut, I collapse, my back to the elevator wall, and Juniper slides down into my arms. She breathes out, releasing the air she's been holding in her lungs. She looks at me, then at her sudden change of scenery with a mixture of shock and awe. Last time she checked, she had just punched Tristen in the face. "What… What just happened? How did we get here?!"

"I'll explain later," I say.

We race down the alley, twisting through every possible side street, trying to throw off anyone attempting to follow us. I don't have my cell phone, so they can't track me. *But they know where I'm going! I just have to get there first.* Then my legs start to jelly. Juniper reaches out and clutches me before I smash face-first into the concrete. I'm too heavy for her. I fight to stay on my feet, but it's so damn hard to think, let alone put one foot in front of the other. I used too much energy getting us out of there. *I have to learn how to regulate my energy output, dammit.*

Juniper pulls me into the shadows and props me up against a dirty brick wall. My body's so weak, I can barely hold my emotions in. I'm shivering. I want to disappear. Is there a world where I can cease to be flesh and bone? I'll be the moisture, the rain, swirling endlessly, changing with the seasons—ice, water, gas—nothing more. Juniper can be the gravity, pulling all things toward her. She can even keep her indifference. Gravity doesn't play favorites. She looks me hard in the face, and for a brief moment, all of her tough, guarded defenses disappear and I see how frightened she really is. And I want to take all her pain away. But then I watch her shove her fear down again, swallow it. They killed her brother. Her own people are hunting her. I can't imagine what she's going through. And even in this horrible moment, in my tortured, dismal reality, I'm struck by how powerful her presence feels to me. She's surrounded by darkness, but still she burns like a relentless star. *Could I ever be that strong? No, I don't think so. But I better try.*

"Charlie… What happened back there? I don't understand," she says. She looks more scared than curious.

"You tell me your secret first," I say.

"What secret?"

"How did you take out those Enforcers in Aeman's loft?" *I need to know what weapons we have at our disposal. I have to stop them.*

I can see her questioning whether she should reveal it to me. It's painful for her. Then I see her decide to trust me, and I'm thankful for it.

"Every wind releases a sonic burst. That's why we hear a ringing sound. But the ringing vibrates at a frequency only Winders can hear. Much like a dog whistle…"

"Got that part."

"Right. So. I've discovered that landing multiple miniscule winds upon each other in rapid succession exponentially amplifies the sonic impact. It takes a great deal of practice and precision, but if done properly, it can be quite…" She gets lost in her thoughts for a moment, and her thoughts seem unfriendly. "…I don't think I can do it again. It was…terrible."

I felt her die, Charlie. That's what she said.

"Your turn," she says. "How did we—"

"I have absolutely no idea," I say quickly. "But I figured if you can do it with pillows, you can do it with people."

"What?"

"Time to go," I say, already moving. She follows as I race toward a man parking his motorcycle on the street, outside the alley.

"Where are we going?" Juniper calls after me as she tries to keep up.

"They're going after my family!" I tell her.

—

We're flying over the George Washington Bridge on the stolen motorcycle. Juniper holds on to me from behind. She's never been on a motorcycle before. I can tell by the reservoirs she's digging into my sides. She's scared, but she doesn't let me know she is. This reminds me of when Ducky and I used to ride Todd Schwartz's dirt bike behind the mall, back in seventh grade, only ten times faster.

It took only a small stoppage of time for me to get the keys from the owner as I bumped into him, but I can still feel it. At least the ride is allowing me time to recover. I tried to move as little as possible as I reached into his pocket. Teleportation is kind of the opposite of being inconspicuous. Juniper heard the wind but thankfully didn't ask how I did it. It's not that I'm trying to hide anything from her; I just can't think of anything but Ducky and Grams right now.

"We have to be careful, Charlie," she yells into my ear. "We got lucky the first time. Trevor won't underestimate us again. Whoever he sends after us will be formidable."

And now it dawns on me that I'm dragging Juniper into a dangerous situation that she doesn't need to be in. She has her own battles. Saving my family isn't one of them.

I slow the bike.

"What are you doing?" she asks.

"I'm letting you off. This part doesn't have anything to do with you."

"If you try and stop this motorcycle, I will throw you off of it."

"What?"

"Go!"

What the hell is wrong with this stubborn girl?! Even in this desperate situation, she can still annoy the hell out of me.

"I have my own reasons," she says. "Okay? Now drive."

I don't have the mental energy to fight her right now. All I can think about are Ducky and Grams and the supernatural torpedo I've inadvertently sent their way.

I push the bike to its limits. Juniper doesn't complain. She just holds on to me tighter, if that's even humanly possible. But I don't mind the pain. It's the only thing that makes sense right now.

CHAPTER 49

JUNIPER

Charlie and I burst in through the front door of the miniscule tenement house.

I'm glad he didn't press me for my reason for coming with him, because my tank of justification was empty. I just knew—as surely as I know anything—that I couldn't let Charlie face this alone. And…if I'm being totally honest—the kind of honest only people staring down death can be—for some unfathomable reason, I feel safer with Charlie than without him.

All that being said, I'm so annoyed with him right now, I could crack in half. I told him to take a second to survey the outside of the house, check for danger, for possible threats, but did the cretin listen to me? Absolutely not. So, now we're barreling blindly into what is very likely a deathtrap.

The first thing I notice is the feeling of invitation. Charlie's family home so contrasts the impression I had from the outside that I feel strangely off balance. One more thing I've misjudged. Why did the world feel so black-and-white before? Maybe I was simply ignoring the colors I didn't want to see.

"Grams! Ducky?! Where are you?" Charlie sprints around the house, searching.

"Charlie, wait!" I call to him as he disappears down a hall.

The front door was left wide open, as if the house itself was locked in an open-mouthed expression of horror. If there are Enforcers inside this house, both of us are in very real danger. I need to figure out what we're up against. It won't be second-tier Enforcers this time. This time, it will be someone Trevor trusts to be precise. I shudder at the thought. Charlie needs to listen to me.

"Charlie!" I call out again, but he doesn't answer. Then I take a full breath for the first time since we entered. If they haven't struck yet, I don't think they're here. Tactically, it makes no sense for them to wait. Charlie's family must have been out when they arrived. I didn't see any suspicious cars anywhere on the block as we approached. I force myself to settle and focus.

Take in your surroundings, Juniper. On the wall I see early photos of Charlie and a young, handsome teenager. *Ducky*. I see photos of the two boys next to an older woman, who I assume must be "Grams"—solid and smiling, holding the two boys in her arms with an adoration I have almost no memory of ever experiencing. I have memories of my mother, and feeling loved, but sometimes I wonder if they're actual memories or if my mind is doing its best to fill in the gaps to keep me from probing too deeply.

Then I see a photo of Charlie as a little boy sitting on a grassy hillside next to a gorgeous, slender woman. Shoulders slightly sunburnt, with freckles lightly peppering her cheeks and nose, Charlie's mother leans against her son with the easy love of a best friend. The resemblance is unmistakable, complete with the tiniest of smirks at the corner of her mouth—the same expression I have witnessed infuriatingly on Charlie several times since we met.

The thing I cannot turn away from, however, is the glowing smile on Charlie's face. Joyous. Unencumbered. There seems to be very little of the freedom I see in the child in this photo still left alive in Charlie, the man. I think about what he's been through: losing his mother; growing up sad and haunted. I've seen what winding back death looks like. As children, we were shown what happens if that mortal wall is breached, or if a Winder is careless or desperate enough to *wind out*. Nightmarish images. A spike of anger jumps inside me at the thought of any child having to witness that kind of wreckage firsthand. The force with which Charlie's mother would have been torn away from him must have felt vicious and very personal.

And no one was there to explain anything to Charlie. He had his foster family, but raising motherless children is a Herculean endeavor. Just ask my father. But from the delicate grace in Grams's smile, and the panic I can hear in Charlie's voice as he searches the house for her, I imagine his foster mother did her very best. And for the briefest of moments, I feel envious that Charlie actually had someone who cared, someone to hack away at the fortress he was constructing around his pain like a cavity-ridden tooth, black and malicious at its center, an infected abscess, the kind that, if not lanced away, will eventually inhabit its host.

And then my eye catches on something in the reflection of the photo, and my stomach free-falls. Terror pulses inside me. *No*, I think. *Please no...* I spin around and am bulldozed by the abominable scene before me.

"Oh, God...Charlie! Charlie, come—" I can't even complete my sentence.

In front of me, hanging by her arms, stretched out by ropes in some kind of suspended crucifixion, is *Grams*. Her head slumps down like a dead bird.

Charlie charges in, sees Grams and looks like a man in a drunken stupor, staggering, mind cascading away from the maddening image. He rushes to her, tripping over himself, attempting to hold up her legs.

"*NONONONONO!*" Charlie is inconsolable.

I race into the kitchen, grab a sharp knife from a drawer, then return and cut the ropes. Grams's body crumples into Charlie's arms like an understuffed scarecrow. Charlie's eyes swell and burst. I dive between him and Grams, checking for vital signs. I find nothing. I begin pumping the old woman's chest. I pinch her nose and breathe air into her lungs. Still nothing. All Enforcers are trained in emergency medical techniques, including CPR. But it's been a long time and, from what I can tell from Grams's condition, probably unnecessary, but Charlie needs something right now, and I can't think of anything else to do, so I continue on and on, unable to look at Charlie and his grief.

I plug her nose again and lean down, but this time, as I'm about to cup my mouth over hers, I see her throat catch and lips part slightly, and I freeze. Charlie's glassy red eyes snap up when he hears me stop. But I don't have any answers yet. I lower my head onto Grams's chest, and sure enough, I hear the quietest heartbeat I have ever heard.

"She's alive," I say. I watch her chest gently rise and fall. Charlie reaches out to her but hesitates, as if he's terrified of hurting her accidentally. He delicately runs his hand over her silver hair, then he bends and kisses her forehead.

"...I don't understand... Why...why is this happening?" Charlie sputters. "Why would anyone do this?"

"They must consider you a threat," I say, because I can think of nothing else but the stony-eyed truth. *Why does my capacity for tenderness feel so vaporous?* I want to reach out, put a hand on him, tell him no one should have to live in a world this cruel, that I'm truly sorry my brother stole him from whatever innocent existence he was living, and pulled him into this horror show—though something in me believes Charlie would've always been found eventually.

"A threat? A threat to *what*?!" he demands.

"...I don't know, Charlie. Maybe everything. I've never seen anyone do what you seem to be able to do."

"It's my fault."

"No, Charlie, it's not. None of this is—"

"All of this is my fault," Charlie says. To himself mostly. He doesn't seem to hear me.

"Her heartbeat is very faint and her breathing is weak. She needs medical attention right away." My eyes fall on something pinned to Grams. A piece of paper. A note. I pull it off. But before I can read a single word, Charlie snatches it out of my hand.

I read over his shoulder. The note reads:

Dearest Charlie,
Give us a call. Ducky would love to hear from you.

CHAPTER 50

CHARLIE

I rush to the lemon-yellow landline. Juniper follows me into the kitchen. I call my cell phone. It rings once, then someone answers...

"Hello?" A deep voice smiles through the phone at me.

"Who is this?"

"Charlie, is that you?" There's something in the voice, something cold and bloodless—as if I were speaking to a spider instead of a man.

"I'm so glad Grams passed along the message."

In the background I hear Ducky scream. *At least I know he's alive.*

"Ducky's telling you to hurry quick. You're missing all the fun."

"Don't touch him!" If words could be flames, I would scorch the Earth.

"Come to the safest place, Charlie. Come alone. I will know if you don't. And so will Ducky. See you soon."

The line goes dead.

CHAPTER 51

JUNIPER

"Charlie, what did they say?" He doesn't answer. Charlie dials an emergency number, speaks to an operator briefly, then hangs up and heads for the door.

"Where are you going?" I ask.

"An ambulance is coming. I need you to stay with Grams. Please. He said I have to go alone."

"Who did? Who was on the phone?" He keeps moving. "Charlie, stop! It's obviously a trap."

"It doesn't matter. He has Ducky."

I grab his arm. My eyes pierce into his. He doesn't seem afraid, which frightens me. "Don't, Charlie. Please. We'll figure something out. We have to be smart."

"I hurt everyone around me, Juniper. I won't let Ducky die for me. Or you."

Charlie pulls free. He looks like he wants to say something more, but then he says, "Goodbye, Juniper."

Then he vanishes before my eyes. Only a thick ringing remains in his wake.

I stand there, frozen. *Oh, my God...*

He's a Thane.

Charlie's a Thane.

That's how we escaped the Faters. He actually stopped time. I thought it was only a legend. How could—

And suddenly, something becomes horribly clear to me: It won't be some random Enforcer waiting for Charlie, or even one of Trevor's lieutenants. It will be Trevor himself. He must know Charlie's secret.

I can't let him go. He doesn't know Trevor. He doesn't know what he's up against. Outside, I hear one unsuccessful attempt to kick the motorcycle's engine over.

"Charlie!" I call out. Ten more seconds and it will be too late. *He's in so much pain. Will he listen? It doesn't matter. You have to force him to.*

I throw my body into motion. A wild dash. As I reach the front door, I hear the bike's engine roar to life. I have maybe two seconds. I open my mouth to scream for him, and that's when something cold and metal cinches around my throat, nearly yanking me off my feet. I grab frantically at the noose around my neck, but I can't get my fingers under it. Then a steel-toed boot smashes into my stomach like a sledgehammer. I collapse, wind knocked out of me. My blotchy, tilting mind pulls at time…

THE EDGES BLUR, THEN I FEEL MY WIND BLUDGEONED AWAY. The noose releases from my throat and I fall gasping into a fetal position. I look up into the leering face of…Gael Falcón. Trevor's lieutenant steps smoothly through the doorway. He holds a Glock with a suppressor twisted onto the end in one hand, and a long stainless-steel staff, with a metal loop at one end, in the other hand. He considers me with a lethal indulgence. He slips the steel staff into a holster on his back, then crouches down in front of me, his cruel corpse eyes cut into me like hatchets.

"My apologies, mija," Gael Falcón says, "but that road is not for you. My Teacher would like a private audience with your young friend."

CHAPTER 52

JUNIPER

I scramble backward away from the assassin. Air squeaks back into my lungs as I force myself up. My thoughts feel soaked in glue. Gael is not just an Enforcer; he's the tip of the spear as far as combat is concerned. I spent years training as an Enforcer, but Gael has spent most of his lifetime, and Trevor only selects the most powerful to be his lieutenants. I felt the brute force of his strength as he tore away my wind. I might've had a chance if I hadn't been caught so off-guard. Now I feel weak from having my air cut off and my wind pulled apart. But there's always a way. Always a solution to every problem. I'm just thankful Grams is still hidden in the other room. I need to buy some time, allow my mind to catch up.

"Are you just going to shoot me? Where's the fun in that? Kind of cowardly, don't you think?"

Gael Falcón smiles. "I wouldn't mind a little fun. It's Aeman's baby sister, after all. Maybe I start with your skin and slowly work my way in. But what to do with your little bones? That'll be the real dilemma. What do you think, pobrecita? Wind chimes?"

Thank you, Aeman. Thank you for having such good friends.

Then I see his face change. His smile falters. "Perhaps I should not repeat mistakes. I've always enjoyed playing with my food, but you wriggled away once already, didn't you? My Teacher was not happy with me. No. Better to just kill you and be done with it." Gael Falcón shrugs, "Sorry, mija."

Gael raises his gun, and I hear *ringing* cut through the air. I know I've dodged in some direction, and he wound me back—

either left or right, but the thought hasn't hit me yet. So, I don't know which way I'm going to dodge yet. But Gael does.

"So…which way did I go?"

Gael smiles. Adrenaline prickles my skin. My stomach trembles. I jump to the right. Gael tracks me with his gun, as if it were stuck to me by magnetic attraction. I brace for the moment where the slug bursts through my body, and I desperately begin fighting for my life. And, oddly, in this tiniest of tiny moments, I find myself thinking about Charlie. *I hope he prevails. Somehow. I really do.*

But the gun doesn't fire. The shot doesn't come. Instead, I hear a whirring sound, then a thud, and then Gael howls with pain.

Gael spins, and I see a knife protruding out of his left shoulder blade. I follow Gael's stunned gaze, to find *Tristen*—the Fater girl—standing outside the doorway. Our eyes meet. The Faters have come for Charlie and me. But I don't see anyone else, other than her, which is strange. What's also seriously strange is that Tristen just saved my life.

Then I feel Gael try to wind. The edges blur, but then his wind crumbles as both Tristen and I raise our minds against him. One on one, he might be able to overpower either one of our minds, but with us together, he's no match. Gael aims at her, but Tristen dodges, the bullet exploding the corner of the doorway. Gael fires again. Tristen runs around the outside of the house. Gael goes to follow, but I slide-tackle his legs. He goes down, but he lands right on top of me. I manage to kick the gun out of his hand, which slides into the hallway.

Then Gael's hands are around my throat, and he's squeezing hard. I attempt to knee him in the body, but he twists his weight over me. He lifts up my head and smashes it back down into the ground, and all I see are splotchy, blood-colored stars.

Gael leans in close. "You know, we killed your papa, mija," Gael says. "Heard his last words were cursing your name. Unless you count the gurgling sound. Or did Trevor say his last words were him begging for his life? I can't remember."

Sorrow and rage swallows me as I struggle to stay conscious.

As Gael pulls my body up in order to slam me back down again, I reach behind him and grab the handle of the knife sticking out of his shoulder blade. I yank it out and thrust the blade toward Gael's throat. He grabs my wrist, redirecting the knife and pushing it slowly back toward me. I fight to hold him off, but I'm too weak, and the tip of the blade sinks into my shoulder. I shriek from the pain.

"His death was quite boring," Gael says as a thin line of drool falls from his mouth and hits my chin. "Just like yours will be, mija. Must be in your blood."

"I highly doubt it," a voice says behind him.

Gael Falcón turns to face a shotgun pressed point-blank to the side of his face, held by *Aeman*.

"Hello, old pal," Aeman grins at Gael. "'Always assume someone that hates you is following you.' One of the first things Trevor taught us. You've gotten lazy."

Gael's face burns red. "Aeman, you will not—"

Aeman pulls the trigger. The blast blows the lower half of Gael's jaw off. Blood and bone shrapnel hit me. Gael rolls off my body, blood gushing from the cavernous wound that used to be his mouth.

Aeman doubles over laughing. "What was that, Gael? I couldn't quite make that out."

Gael crawls, aimless, destroyed. His face looks horrific, like a half-mad, dying insect.

"Wow! Gael! Seriously, you've never looked better!"

"Aeman…" My voice sounds like it's being sifted through stones, due to my throttled throat.

"Just a second, sis," he says. "He's trying to get away."

As Gael toddler-crawls across the floor, Aeman points the shotgun at one of his hands and blows it away in a splatter of red gore. Gael rolls onto his back, choking on the blood that begins filling up his exposed throat.

"Please tell my father I said hi when you see him in hell," Aeman says. Gael gags his last breath, then his manic slot-machine eyes click to a stop—no fortune found. Aeman gives Gael's head a little clonk with the shotgun to see if he's really dead.

Aeman looks at me for the first time. His expression is complicated. He knows that I know he gave me up to Trevor. But that's not what I'm thinking about right now. I watch him realize that I'm aware of the horrible fate that lies ahead for him. He sighs. "Raw deal, huh? I was supposed to live to a hundred."

My heart hurts, despite everything he's done, knowing I'm going to lose him. "Who told you that?"

"I told myself that, actually." Aeman smiles, but I can already see the slightest trace of the hollowness that will soon overtake his face. Then his expression grows serious. "I need to tell you something."

The seriousness in his face frightens me a little. It's a foreign look on him. "What?"

"It's gonna be a hard one to hear, but I think you deserve to know…" He's going to tell me about my father's betrayal of the Leadership. I wonder how long he's known—how long he's kept it from me?

But then he hears a tiny noise from the living room.

Aeman swiftly turns his shotgun, facing…

Tristen, who points Gael's fallen pistol at him. A standoff.

"Aeman, please…" I attempt. "She saved my life."

"Well, she didn't save mine," Aeman says, glaring at Tristen. "How would you weigh the odds, La Femme Nikita? Do you give it to the sneaky girl who already killed the boy once, or do you give it to the boy who's already dead and has nothing left to lose?"

"Killing you once was good enough for me," Tristen says.

There's a thick, deadly beat. Then Aeman starts to lower his weapon. Relief washes over me. Tristen lowers hers as well. When she does, Aeman yanks his back up and pulls the trigger.

Tristen tries to dodge, but she takes the brunt of the shotgun blast in her thigh. She lands hard on her side, raises the gun and pulls the trigger, blowing a wide hole in the side of Aeman's neck. Blood spurts from the wound. Aeman drops to his knees. He holds the wound, which is pumping a red ocean out between his fingers.

I leap up, despite my fatigue and pain, and rush to him. He pushes me back.

"…Nope…stay back," he says, his voice wet with blood. "…Don't get any on your pretty white clothes."

"Aeman—"

"This is a better death than what I got comin'. …You know that." He's right, of course. This death is a mercy compared to the brutal deterioration he has in store. He tries for a smile but can't quite get there. Then, all his bravado seems to seep away. He turns to me, and I see a vulnerability in his eyes I haven't seen for such a long time. *"I'm sorry… Wanted to be an Enforcer again… Don't know what I am if I'm not… Guess I'm nothing now, anyway."*

"Did you kill all those people they say you did? Did you kill children?" My words come out in a shaky whisper.

Aeman's energy has dramatically waned. His voice is a gargled horror, but he manages: *"…I'd rather not think of that…right now…sis…"*

"Aeman, I…" I want to forgive him, to tell him that the coldness of our adolescence wasn't his fault, that our father had an atrophied heart, that we deserved far more love than we received. I want to tell him that Father saw my mother's face echoed in his—that it reminded him of all he'd lost instead of what he still had. I want to tell him that I understand the pain he's been through—that in the depths of his despair and loneliness, an evil man stepped in to fill the hole at the center of him. There's so much I want to say, so much I *need* to say, but I can't bring myself to continue. I stare at Aeman, helpless, finding myself the torchbearer of that same chilly distance he'd clawed himself away from.

"Need to tell you…" His voice is growing quieter as the life in his eyes begins to fade. I lean in.

"What, Aeman? I'm listening."

This seems to focus him for a moment. He looks me in the eyes. *"I found her."*

"Found who?" I have no idea what he's talking about.

"…She's alive. In…Westchester."

"Who is?"

"Mom."

I can't feel my body. Everything around me seems hazy, warped. It can't be true. My father told me my mother was dead. Could he have told me such a horrific lie? Did Aeman know it was a lie and didn't tell me? *"She got out, Juniper… Dad helped her disappear…*

knew they'd kill her if they found out. Told us she was dead…but I never believed it… Looked for her for so long… And then…"

"You spoke to her?" I ask, still finding it impossible to believe.

"…I couldn't," Aeman's voice sounds so weak now. *"Didn't want her to see…who I've…become. But you find her, Juniper…if you want."* He hacks an awful red cough and spits it on the ground, blood dribbling down his chin. *"Tell her…I missed her so much."* Suddenly, Aeman raises the shotgun to his mouth. I flinch back in horror. But the gun doesn't fire. It slowly drops from Aeman's already-lifeless hands. He's gone.

My head sags as tears slip down my cheeks. He was a traitor and a coward, but he was still my brother. And his last act was saving my life.

Now I'm completely alone in the world. *No…I'm not. My mother. Alive.* It just doesn't feel real. Why would my father tell me she died? Maybe Aeman was wrong. It doesn't matter. If she is alive, she obviously didn't want to be found. This thought fills me with anger. But what relationship could I have had with her, anyway? She's a human. Our lives would've been based around lies and deceit. It all feels insurmountable. I shove these thoughts away from me, knowing I won't find any answers right now. I hear a groan behind me.

I get up and make my way to Tristen, who's losing a lot of blood from her leg. I yank the cord off of a fallen lamp, grab a cloth placemat of the table and use them to bind Tristen's wound. She screams as I cinch it down. She grits her teeth through the pain, but she doesn't complain. She knows what I'm doing is the best chance she has of saving the leg and hopefully her life. Somehow, there's an unspoken acknowledgement that death has been traded and bartered between us. Stalemate. Even. Her wound looks terrible, and I feel so fatigued, but I need to make it right, fix what Aeman did—I just don't know if I have enough strength left to perform the bulky wind. Also, Aeman will be wound back from death a second time. It won't be pretty. But I know I can't let this girl die in front of me. Not now. I focus my last dregs of strength and pull at the fabric of time…but my wind barely begins before it is shut down. My face snaps toward Tristen, steeped in confusion. *She's blocking me.*

She gives me the faintest of smiles despite her grave situation.

"Not our way," she says. Her tone is firm and nonnegotiable.

"There's an ambulance coming," I say. "It should be here soon."

She reaches her hand out, extending her phone and car keys to me.

"There's a tracking device on Charlie's phone," she says. "Don't let him die, Juniper."

I take in Tristen's feelings for Charlie. I don't know how to process them, since I hardly know how to process my own complicated feelings.

"Charlie's foster mother—"

"I saw her," Tristen says. "I'll make sure she gets help."

I can just make out the sound of an ambulance approaching in the distance. Finally, I give Tristen a little nod—a silent promise. I take her phone, which I see doubles as a tracking device. The schematic and mapping system are quite elaborate. In the center I see a tiny red flashing dot: *Trevor.*

I race out the front door and hit the button on the car keys, hoping it will help point me toward the vehicle Tristen brought here.

The headlights flash on a sleek red vintage sports car parked nearby. I'm not good with car names, but it looks fast. *So, not everything is just bread and water with the Warriors of Fate, huh?*

CHAPTER 53

CHARLIE

I make my way through the disemboweled industrial park, listening to everything at once. My guts are a bag of snakes. The only chance I have of surviving this is the element of surprise. He has my friend. My family. Once again, Ducky's staring down death because of me. *Nope. Stop feeling sorry for yourself! Time to man the fuck up!*

Moving in the shadow of a long, crumbling wall, I approach the broken building where our safe is. The Safest Place. My heart speed-bags inside my chest. *Breathe, man. Breathe. This is all gonna end real quick if you pass out from lack of oxygen.*

I enter from the side of the structure facing the forest, move aside two faded-orange construction cones, and creep up the exposed wooden steps.

The second I heard the voice on the phone, I knew it had to be Trevor—the sound of a man who answers to no one—a man that could put such fear into someone as strong as Juniper. But it would've been so much easier to have brought a bunch of men and gunned us down at Grams's place. No, he wants this to be personal and unwatched. I just don't know why.

I reach the second floor and duck behind a concrete pillar. The tank-like safe stands at the far diagonal corner from where I'm hiding—maybe a hundred feet away. Silence. No movement. Just the acrid smell of dog fennel and rusted iron. I scan for any possible hiding places among the surrounding buildings. Or maybe I'm wrong—maybe it isn't personal at all, just another day at the proverbial psychopathic office—maybe I'm going to step out of the shadows, hear a *POP* from somewhere nearby, and then oblivion.

Okay, the only bad move right now is a stupid move, and since there are no *smart* moves at the moment, I'll just have to try and make the *least stupid* move. So, what is that, exactly?

I hear a faint, muffled cry. I search frantically in all directions. My head feels like a periscope attached to my neck while my body is submerged in a dark ocean of fear. I listen hard... Nearby power lines hum... Somewhere, a collection of crows chatters like drunken club girls... A breeze whistles through the cracked wall, spitting loose dust and gravel across the jagged floor. *Shit. Everything sounds like it's coming from everywhere at once. Was it really a cry I heard? Maybe it was just—*

The cry comes again. This time, I zero in on the sound's origin. The hair on the back of my neck prickles. Without a doubt, the muted moan is coming from *inside* the giant safe. *Oh, God... oh, God...it's a trap. I know it's a—* The cry comes again, and now there's a pained quality to it. *No choice.* I run. Straight across the open, exposed floor. I hold my breath, waiting for the attack. It will come. Any second. Any goddamn second! But to my surprise, I make it to the safe unmolested.

I grab the handle; feeling chips of crumbling metal flake off under my grip. The dense door squeals open, revealing Ducky curled up, bruised and bloody—his mouth gagged. I kneel down and rip the gag off. Ducky's red bloated eyes dart around. His quick, gasping words border on hysterical. "...Charlie... He said he came for you. He said he was looking for *you*... He...he made me tell him things...Charlie... I'm sorry I brought him here. I don't know why. He said I had to pick a place you would know..."

"It's okay, Ducky. It's all right." He doesn't seem to even hear me.

"I didn't know where else to go. Thought at least you'd be on your own turf...maybe the shit in the safe might protect you. I'm so sorry... Oh, God, Charlie, Grams!" Ducky dry-heaves onto the ground. Nothing but greenish bile comes up. I want to tell him that Grams is alive, but I can't risk anyone hearing. Seeing Ducky like this makes me want to kill. To destroy. But I need to be smart if I'm going to get us out of here.

"*Ducky, listen to me,*" I whisper. "*We have to get out of here right now, and you have to be really, really quiet. Do you understand?*" Ducky nods, tears flowing freely from his eyes. I rip the bindings off his hands and legs. He follows me, staggering and half-blind from being stuck in the darkness.

A snapping muzzled gunshot, fired from somewhere close by, hammers Ducky off his feet. He screams and lands hard on his back. Blood pumps from his shoulder, soaking his shirt. But this is what I've been waiting for…

I lunge my will into action and TIME SLOWLY BEGINS TO SPIN BACKWARD. DUCKY SWIPES BACK UP TO HIS FEET, LOOKING LIKE DRACULA RISING OUT OF HIS COFFIN IN SOME OLD BLACK-AND-WHITE MONSTER MOVIE. A PLUME OF BLOOD AND BONE, HAVING EXPLODED FROM HIS SHOULDER, RUSHES THROUGH THE AIR BACK INTO HIS BODY. ONCE DUCKY IS WHOLE AGAIN, I FLEX EVEN HARDER AND GRIND EVERYTHING TO AN ICY STANDSTILL. I CAN FEEL THE PRESSURE OF TIME YEARNING TO RUSH FROM MY GRASP, HEATING UP INSIDE ME LIKE A BLACKSMITH'S FORGE OVEN. I STEP CLOSE TO DUCKY, AND THERE, SUSPENDED IN THE AIR, TWO INCHES FROM WHERE IT HAD IMPACTED DUCKY'S SHOULDER, IS THE *BULLET*, FLOATING, FROZEN IN SPACE.

I BEND MY MIND AGAIN—COAXING—PULLING—AND SLOWLY THE BULLET STARTS MOVING THROUGH THE AIR. I FOLLOW BESIDE THE TINY PROJECTILE AS IT RETREATS TOWARD THE WEAPON THAT SENT IT. IT'S SO SMALL, BUT IT FEELS LIKE PUSHING A BOULDER UP A HILL. THE BULLET KEEPS MOVING, UNTIL… *NO*…

TO MY DISMAY, THE BULLET FLOATS OUT THROUGH THE HUGE OPENING IN THE COLLAPSED WALL, SAILING INTO THE BROKEN-DOWN EXPANSE. I CAN'T FOLLOW IT ANY FARTHER ON FOOT. SWEAT ERUPTS ON MY FACE AS I CONCENTRATE, HOLDING TIME AT BAY. THE TENSION STARTS TO CHOKE ME, BUT I DON'T LET GO. I *HAVE* TO KNOW WHERE IT CAME FROM. I HAVE TO KNOW WHERE THE DANGER IS. I WATCH AS THE BULLET GLIDES INTO THE NEIGHBORING BUILDING, DISAPPEARING INTO THE DARKNESS. I CAN'T SEE WHERE IT GOES, EXACTLY, BUT AT LEAST I KNOW WHICH DIRECTION THE ATTACK WILL BE COMING FROM.

IT DOESN'T MAKE SENSE. WHY SHOOT DUCKY? TREVOR HAD EVERY

CHANCE TO KILL HIM ALREADY IF HE WANTED TO. HE PROBABLY WANTS ME TO WATCH HIM DIE. WHAT AM I DEALING WITH HERE?! WHAT DOES THIS LUNATIC HAVE AGAINST ME?

MY STRENGTH FINALLY BEGINS TO WAVER. THE BULLET REVERSES BACK OUT OF THE ADJACENT STRUCTURE AND BEGINS SAILING BACK TOWARD ME—AND DUCKY.

IT STARTS TO SPEED UP, AND I REALIZE I WON'T BE ABLE TO HOLD IT MUCH LONGER. I PICK UP A HEAVY PIECE OF STEEL PANELING OFF THE GROUND AND I HOLD IT UP INTO THE BULLET'S PATHWAY. Then I release my stranglehold on time. Sound comes barreling back. It's strange: you don't notice the complete absence of the wind blowing until it returns. The bullet ricochets off the metal chunk I'm holding with a deafening *CLONG*.

Fatigue guts me like a fish. I drop to one knee, fighting for breath. I move to Ducky, making sure he's still unshot.

He stares at me, bug-eyed. "How...how the hell did you do that?!...Y-y-you...you were here...and n-now you're over *there*... Charlie? What the—"

Dark laughter erupts behind me. "Very good!"

I turn and see a tall, broad-shouldered, densely built man striding through the broken doorway I entered through just moments ago. *Jesus, he's fast. I didn't even hear his footsteps.* For someone who appears to be in his early sixties, he's scary agile. Trevor wears all black, the outer layer of which is an expensive leather trench coat. *What is it with villains and trench coats?* From his coat he withdraws a large handgun with a silencer twisted onto the end of it. I stand between Ducky and the approaching panther-like assassin.

"I had to see for myself," Trevor says. "Incredible."

"That's him, Charlie! That's the motherfucker that killed Grams!" Ducky howls, stepping out from behind me.

"Let him go," I say to Trevor. "He doesn't have anything to do with this."

Trevor looks impassively at Ducky. "Go," he says.

Fury burns on Ducky's face. "I ain't going nowhere, you piece of shit!"

Trevor looks at me and shrugs, then raises the gun.

"No!" I step in front of Ducky, holding my hands up.

"Truthfully, you killed him yourself, Charlie. First rule of the Code is no normal human can know of our existence, and you just let it shine like a beacon. You should apologize to your friend."

Now or never, I decide. *Can't let too much time elapse. Now I know where he'll be coming from. If I can wind it back, Ducky and I can haul ass in the opposite direction.*

I YANK AT THE FABRIC OF TIME. BUT AS THE EDGES BEGIN TO BLUR, TREVOR RAISES HIS HAND, and my wind sputters and dies. I'm stunned by the sheer force of his simple gesture. It feels different than what I've experienced with Juniper or Tristen—less elegant or precise somehow—more like a hammer. Regardless, I attempt to gather my will again…

"Don't bother," Trevor says, smoothly. "You used up too much power. Now I've got the edge. Aeman should've taught you better. You're unarmed. I'm trying not to take that as an insult. What? You thought you'd take me down that easy? Just stop time, maybe steal my gun; kill me with my own weapon? Should've saved your strength."

"You killed an innocent old woman? Are you that much of a coward?" I need Trevor to think Grams is dead. That way, no matter what happens to me, she'll be safe.

"Oh, that was only decoration. To be honest, I've always wanted to hang someone like that. I miss my days as an Enforcer. I was good. There's so little time to indulge in art these days. And wouldn't it have been difficult to recreate the same sense of urgency with only a note?"

An inhuman snarl bursts from Ducky as he rushes forward. Trevor calmly raises his pistol and fires, just as I tackle Ducky to the ground. His head smashes into the filthy cement floor. The violent *thud* is chilling. Ducky's unconscious. I check his wound. The bullet missed his heart by inches but still ripped a sizable hole in his chest. Blood spumes up beneath his dark grey T-shirt. He lies motionless.

"Ducky!" I shake him frantically. I put my head against his chest and hear a far-too-weak heartbeat. *I have to get him out of here.* Then hot, tubular metal singes my skin as the freshly fired silencer is placed behind my ear. I wait for the coming abyss. Part of me welcomes it—gone from this world where I've caused so much pain to the people I love.

Swallow that crybaby bullshit, Charlie! Blubber and bawl on your own damn time. Right now, you have to save Ducky. Ducky is all that matters.

"What do you want from me?" I'm surprised by the evenness in my voice.

"I thought that was pretty obvious."

"You could've killed me already. So, what do you want?"

Despite the gun, I slowly turn to face the leather-clad creature standing above me. My defiance seems to land on Trevor in a strange way. All at once, his expression transforms from the malignant stare of a diseased shark into one of…contemplation… maybe even…*kindness.*

"You are more than all of this, Charlie. All these childish little sympathies. Don't you think it's time to put the toys away?"

Red hate scorches to the surface of my face. Trevor takes my indignation in stride.

"You cannot defeat me, Charlie. I know it requires a great deal of power and focus for your little freeze-frames, and I won't allow it." *The fact that he knows more about my abilities than I do does not bode well for me.* "I know that look in your eye. I recognize it. You feel lost. You want answers. And you deserve them. But if you want the *truth*, you have to take it like a grown-up. Because I tell you, unequivocally, human beings will never be able to comprehend you. They'll never understand what you're capable of. Their tiny, tepid hearts will drown in jealousy, and even the ones that you love will come to loathe you for being their superior. It won't be your fault; it won't even be *their* fault; they just won't be able to help it. They despise difference, Charlie. They castrate the exceptional. Right now, you're angry and confused, and I understand that. You want blood, but you will die trying to find it here today."

Trevor reaches out, offers me his callused hand. "Let me be your Teacher. You have so much to learn—so much more than a sad charlatan like Aeman could ever hope to teach you. The world is a very dangerous place, but believe me when I tell you *control* is

the only salve for the savagery that surrounds us. I offer you ultimate power—the chance to help quell the chaos, and live up to
your own very exciting potential."

"Go to hell, dick!" *Definitely not one of my better comebacks.*

I lurch to my feet. Trevor shakes his head. "You have no reason
to hate me. I am not your enemy. *Man* is your enemy. They are
but emotional anchors tying your godlike feet to the ground. *Can't
you see that?* This *thing*," he says, gesturing toward Ducky's bloody
form, "is no more related to you than a locust to a king. They are
only creatures to us, Charlie. Nameless. Formless. Passing through
dimensions of time that we are masters of."

"So, you butcher them without any feeling?"

"Of course. If I have to." He says this as if such a thing should
be painfully obvious. "Every brutality that has transpired on this
planet has been the result of *men*. I merely seek to curb the carnage.
I'm here to protect, Charlie. I promise you. Not to destroy. The
swarm *must* be kept at bay, because the swarm is mindless."

I take a step back, allowing my body to slide into a neutral
fighting stance.

"They kill everything. Try to make a difference in man's tragic
destiny and you will die trying. We gave them Joan of Arc. Jesus
of Nazareth. Lincoln. Malcolm X. Even Gandhi was one of us. All
desperately trying to save humanity through 'peace.' But there's
only so many times you can wind someone back if their minds are
relentlessly bent on destruction. Yet *still* they tried. And every one
of them was slaughtered for it. They can't be saved. Your grief is
unfortunately wasted on a lower life form."

He takes in the pulsing fury on my face, but his expression
actually seems to double down on kindness. "I swear I was once
like you, Charlie. I was in so much pain. I was alone."

"I'm not alone—"

"Yes, you are." He cuts me off as his eyes drive into me. And
for some reason, I can't seem to shield my emotions. I feel raw.
"You're holding on to their world so tight, but you'll never really
be a part of it. We can't be. People you've called friends… People
you've loved… Your *mother*…"

He sees my surprise.

"Ducky told me. I'm sure you loved her a great deal. And I'm sure you believed she loved you. But she didn't really *know* you. How can you love someone you don't really know?"

Whether I like it or not, the truth of this statement bores into me.

"Even in our greatest of intentions, we will always be imposters in their world. And that hurts. It feels monstrous. But I have a secret that no one you've ever known or loved could have told you: *the pain isn't real.* You've been taught you're supposed to hurt and cry and mourn. But that's in *their* world. A place where you will never be able to survive, no more than you can live underwater. But you don't have to try to live in their world—with *their* pain—and *their* sorrow. Accept what you are and let their strife slide off of you. You've been living a lie, Charlie. A painful lie. But the second you release their hold on you, you will be free in a way you cannot possibly imagine. No pain. No guilt. No weakness."

A life without guilt? Without pain? Could I ever deserve such a thing? He's offering an escape hatch to a vessel I have felt plummeting toward destruction since I was ten years old. *But he's a monster. A murderer.* But what if he's right? What if I've been torturing myself all these years over events that never really belonged to me in the first place? What if I'm like Mowgli from *The Jungle Book*— refusing to accept that I'm not a wolf or a bear or a tiger, and putting everyone I *thought* was my family in danger because of it? *What's more selfish? Caring? Or not caring?*

Trevor must sense my struggle, because he takes a tiny step toward me and says, "I'm offering you guidance, guidance that you know you need, but also perhaps…companionship. Friendship. We're both orphans, Charlie. Castaways. I'm not perfect. I won't pretend that I am. I'm ugly in many ways. Not all. But perhaps, together, we could try to be something greater. We could help each other." The vulnerability in his eyes is startling. There is genuine loneliness there. He's not lying about that. He sees me wavering and smiles warmly. "You were made for so much more, Charlie."

And that's when I see it. Behind the outstretched hand. Under the friendly tones and offers of brotherhood. It's there, naked and grasping—some malformed thing, scarred beyond recognition, terrified of the world and out for blood. Now I see the silver in his tongue. I see the scales beneath his skin ripple with his true intentions. And I see what he really wants.

"How would I help?" I ask, and watch as he unconsciously runs his tongue over his teeth.

"You are something new, Charlie," he says. "A next step in our evolution. True peace only comes with control, and you could be such a vital part of achieving that control. Help me end the fighting. This war. Together, we could realign the Leadership in a way that would bring an end to so much bloodshed and pain. Please." *He sees me as a weapon.* "The last man with your ability turned his back on his gifts and caused so much pain and death."

"Victor Mason? We've met," I say. "He gave me a different version of this speech."

The mention of Victor's name seems to throw Trevor, but he quickly recovers. He searches my face for the truth of my statement. He doesn't like what he finds there.

"A very old man with very old ideas," Trevor says. "So, now you see you've reached a line in the sand. Don't you, Charlie?"

"I guess so," I say. I raise my hands up in surrender and start walking toward Trevor. "Guess it's time to die. I'm ready."

With a reluctant sigh, Trevor raises his gun. As he does, I slide low and hook a kick into the back of Trevor's knees with every ounce of strength in me. Trevor pitches into the air, inverted. I clutch Trevor's arm as he falls. *Like Juniper taught me, keeping physical contact is going to be vital in this fight.* I use my grip on Trevor's arm to spike the bulky killer face-first into the ground. But a millimeter before his face impacts...

TREVOR WRENCHES TIME IN REVERSE. WE'RE TOUCHING, SO HE WON'T BE ABLE TO MUTATE HIS ATTACK BASED OFF OF INFORMATION I DON'T HAVE. The second time moves forward, I snap a leg out, kicking Trevor's wrist as he raises his gun. The pistol goes flying. Trevor spins like a hurricane and backhands me across the face. The blow blots my sight with red and purple stars. I stagger back but quickly gain my bearings. We stand facing each other, two fighters at the ready. I'm too far away for contact. I've lost any advantage I had.

"This is your last chance, Charlie," Trevor says. "Do not throw your life away for what are effectively plow horses. You'll never be one of them."

My eyes drift to Ducky, lying wounded and dying—the best person I know—an unlikely survivor from a shipwrecked childhood, relentlessly phoenixing out of the kind of damage that would swallow a lesser spirit. I have brought him to this point, and I will not abandon him. Not here. Not to this hateful beast. I glance at our safe—a treasure trove of proof that I am not so different from those I have loved and lost. No one can take that away from me. Ducky was right—I'm fighting on my own turf.

"I don't care what I am," I say. "I'll never be like you."

Trevor's cold stare penetrates through me. I see him make a decision. His thin lips purse like two snuggling leeches, and then I watch his nurturing mask fall away.

"Pity," he says. "Very well. I want you to know your death will be a dismal one. I think I'll go with murder-suicide. Poor little baby, home from soldier camp, can't face the real world."

My eyes go wide and Trevor chuckles.

"Oh, I know a lot about you, Charlie. Ducky just talked and talked. Can't say *he* enjoyed it all that much, but I personally had a blast. Now, where was I? Oh, yes. Murder-suicide. Sad wannabe soldier boy hangs his foster mother, beheads his best friend like a terrorist, and then takes his own life. So tragic. Now, I know what you're thinking: the beheading and suicide have to look *just* right, or people might not believe it. Well, I want you to know I plan to keep doing it until I get it perfect. You have my word."

I swing first and hard. My fist plummets toward Trevor's face, but just before I connect, he effortlessly dodges ever so slightly to the side. Then he uses the full force of my swing against me, bringing his knee up for a staggering blow to my stomach. I didn't *see* him wind, but I know he did, because a definitive *ringing* stings the air.

I plop onto my belly, gulping for my stolen air. Trevor confidently wolfs around me in a circle as I crawl back to standing. Once on my feet, I jackknife a kick toward his head, but he calmly ducks under my leg, smiling—a cat playing with its prey.

I hear the *ringing again.*

I let the momentum of my kick take me into a spinning round-house. My foot swings at his face like a battle-axe. He steps back, leaving just enough room for my kick to pass within centimeters of his cheek before he sends his own leg up, savagely crushing into my face.

Blood spurts from my mouth and I crash to my knees. Trevor grabs me by the back of the neck and sledgehammers his massive fist into my face. The vicious blow rocks me to my atoms. I'm stunned—floating there like a meaty balloon. Then, still holding me by the neck, HE WINDS US BACK TOGETHER TO RIGHT BEFORE HE STRUCK ME, then he releases his hold on time. As time moves forward, he clubs his fist into my face even harder (if that's human-ly possible). I feel several teeth break off and slide down my throat. I start to choke. HE WINDS US BACK AGAIN. He delivers another crushing blow to my face. WINDS IT BACK. Hits me again. I gasp, fruitlessly, only breathing blood at this point. He repeats this tor-ture over and over. I'm being waterboarded with my own blood. He smashes his fist into my face again, but this time he doesn't wind it back. I moan in agony and flop onto my side. My torturer looks down at me and crows laughter. I can barely make out his blurry image.

"Terrible isn't it? It's a little trick I've sometimes *gifted* to my most stubborn students. In the physical world, only the last hit counts, but we wound together, so your mind believes your face is pulp right now."

Trevor bends down and picks up his fallen gun. Blood and saliva spew from my mouth and nose to the ground. I hock the rest of the soppy-sick miasma from my lungs, then attempt to get up. Trevor plants his heavy foot firmly on my back. His boot feels like the entire world. I splat down onto my stomach.

"I have a strange feeling as I'm killing you, Charlie," Trevor ruminates. He crouches, pressing a knee into my spine. Then he threads his fingers through my sweaty, mottled hair and yanks my head back. My entire being arches in pain. I want to fight back, but my muscles feel liquefied.

"See, I know that somehow, you're the next step to my own

evolution." Trevor smashes my head into the hard, concrete ground. The blow splits the skin above my eyebrow. I'm close to vomiting. "And yet how can you be my Darwinian replacement if *I* am in fact killing *you*? Doesn't quite make sense, does it? Perhaps you were actually a step back. Perhaps I'm doing our kind a great service by destroying you."

Trevor presses the titanium tip of his gun against my teeth. He taps the enamel with the metal barrel, sending spikes of pain straight into my brain.

"Knock-knock. Time to open up," Trevor says, tapping even harder against my teeth, trying to force the gun into my mouth.

"CHARLIE, PLUG YOUR EARS!!" Juniper's voice cracks through the air.

Trevor's knee twists deeper into my spine as he turns toward Juniper, and I jam my fingers into my ears.

Juniper stands at the edge of the structure, about fifteen yards away. She mashes both her fists into balls, focusing all her energy, and suddenly THE WORLD AROUND US BEGINS TO FLICKER AND PULSE AS JUNIPER'S STACCATO RAPID-FIRE WINDING RIPS THROUGH TIME. TREVOR SHRIEKS, ARCHING IN AGONY, DROPPING TO BOTH KNEES. HIS BODY BEGINS TO CONSTRICT.

ALL AT ONCE, TREVOR LETS OUT A KRAKEN-LIKE ROAR AS HE LASHES OUT VIOLENTLY IN A BACKHANDING MENTAL *SLAP!* Juniper's winding is suddenly pulverized. She gasps.

"YOU DARE RAISE YOUR MIND TO *ME*, GIRL!!! YOU CHILD!!!"

Blood leaks from Trevor's nose, rushing down his face and into his mouth. He smiles, dark blood coating his teeth. The sight is grotesque.

"Foolish little bitch. Welcome to the adult table." Trevor raises his hand, and despite the massive effort I can see Juniper exerting to block his wind, Trevor is just too strong. BLOOD RUSHES BACK INTO HIS NOSE. AGAIN, TREVOR AND I ARE TOUCHING, SO I PERCEIVE EVERYTHING AS HE REWINDS TIME UNTIL THE EXACT MOMENT JUNIPER SLIPS OUT OF SIGHT. MY SOUL WRENCHES AND TWISTS INSIDE ME, CLIMBING MY SPINE WITH IRON SPIKES AND GRAPPLING HOOKS, WORKING ITS WAY OUT OF MY GUTS AND INTO

MY THROAT, INTO A HOWL OF ANGUISH, BECAUSE I KNOW *EXACTLY*
WHAT'S COMING. Trevor releases time a split second before Juniper
appears.

I want to scream, to stop her somehow from taking that last
fatal step—push back the beautiful, fiercely intelligent girl who
tries a little too hard, who's a little too abrasive, who lives inside her
head and the incalculable fathoms that exist there, whose smile is
hard-earned but decimates legions when it arrives—the green-eyed
girl who I can tell has been hurt far more than she's been held,
and who has been loyal to a cruel, antagonistic world that doesn't
deserve her. But most of all, I want to tell Juniper Trask *Thank you
for saving my life again.* But I can't. There isn't time.

Juniper lands as she starts to call out to me, "CHARLIE, PLUG
YOUR—"

Trevor turns and fires.

NOOOOOOO!!!

My wail is sucked into the void. Soundless. Lost to itself.
Stretched to some rootless tapering flashpoint, then discarded. And
in this briefest of moments—this nanothought—I thank Ducky, and
Aeman, and Grams, and Ducky's parents, and all the kids at Lazarus
who still have scars from an angry boy who never stopped swinging
at ghosts, and I thank my mother—my beautiful mother—I thank
them all for not hating me too much and allowing some soggy scrap
of karmic luck that somehow has wriggled through my clogged and
cringing spirit—I thank them, because, in this moment, Trevor has
fully taken his focus off of me.

I yank at time like I'm in a stagecoach aimed off a cliff. And
bit by bit, the white-hot bullet racing toward Juniper BEGINS TO
SLOW DOWN IN THE AIR. AGAIN, TREVOR AND I ARE TOUCHING, SO
NOW *HE* IS PERCEIVING AND PUSHING AGAINST *MY* WIND. I FEEL THE
BLUNT FORCE OF HIS MIND BASHING AT MY EFFORTS, BUT I ALSO
FEEL A NEW FEAR IN HIM, A GROWING DESPERATION, BECAUSE I *AM*
MANAGING TO SLOW IT DOWN. BUT IT'S NOT SLOW ENOUGH. THE
NOW-CREEPING BULLET REACHES JUNIPER. I DOUBLE MY EFFORT.
THEN I TRIPLE IT. *I AM WILLING TO DIE WITH MY BACK AGAINST THIS
BOULDER IF I MUST. WILL TREVOR RISK THE SAME?* THERE IS A LIMIT
TO HOW MUCH ENERGY ONE CAN THROW AT TIME. AEMAN CALLED

IT "WINDING OUT." *HERE WE GO.*

ABOVE ME, TREVOR'S EYES BLAZE WITH FURY AND CONCENTRA-
TION AS HE THRASHES AGAINST HIS TEMPORAL FOE.

THE BURNING-HOT BULLET MOVES EVER SO SLOWLY UNTIL IT
GENTLY TOUCHES THE DELICATE SURFACE OF JUNIPER'S FOREHEAD.
LAYER UPON LAYER OF SKIN, BLOOD AND MUSCLE ARE SHREDDED,
SHUCKED OFF, THEN CAUTERIZED, AS THE SIZZLING FOREIGN
OBJECT WORMS ITS WAY INTO JUNIPER'S SKULL. TO MY HORROR,
HER EYES POP WIDE WITH FEAR. IN AN EFFECT MUCH LIKE THE
BLURRING EDGES OF A BEGINNING WIND, A KIND OF LOCALIZED
BUBBLE FORMS, WITH TREVOR AND ME AT THE EPICENTER—BOTH
OF US YANKING AT TIME LIKE TWO CHILDREN GRIPPING THE SAME
BALL AND WAILING FOR POSSESSION. TIME CRUMPLES AND COL-
LAPSES INSIDE THIS BUBBLE, AND WHEN IT REACHES JUNIPER, HER
LEGS BUCKLE AND SHE FLOATS TO HER KNEES. BLOOD LEAKS OUT
OF THE EDGES OF HER EYES. TWO CRIMSON LINES STREAM DOWN
OUT OF HER NOSE. HER MOUTH INVOLUNTARILY GASPS LIKE A
FISH… IT LOOKS HORRENDOUS… SPASMING, SHE STARTS TO FALL
FORWARD… THIS IS THE END…

BUT IN THIS GLACIALLY MOVING MOMENT, THIS BRUTAL STALE-
MATE, I FEEL A GENTLE VOICE OPEN ITS EYES INSIDE MY HEAD:

(She's kind of a square, isn't she, Charlie?)

Yeah, and she's proud of it.

(She's smart.)

I know.

(Does she like you?)

I think so.

(You think so?)

Okay, okay, I know so.

(So?)

So, what?

(Don't be stupid.)

You're a ghost. Ghosts can't call people names.

(Don't be a jackass.)

…

(Do you think I'd like her?)

Yeah. I think you'd love her, Mom.

(Good.)

Mom?

(Yes, Charlie?)

I'm so sorry.

(I know.)

I love you.

(I love you more.)

I need to let you go.

(It's about time, kiddo. You're going to be all right.)

I'll miss you.

(I'll never be far.)

And then it opens. Some space inside of me. Some reservoir. A dam breaks, and a tremendous battle cry begins screaming out of the dark place where I've kept eight years of molten rage—a fire that's been building inside me for almost half my life. It started in that car; it grew as I watched my mother die for the second time; it grew as I fought those skinheads in front of Grams's house; it grew in Camp Lazarus alongside the cruelty I witnessed on a daily basis; it grew as Aeman left me for dead and Tristen betrayed my trust. But it's mine. All of it. It belongs to me. So, I release it all…because Juniper's heart has not stopped yet.

THE BLOOD ON JUNIPER'S FACE RETRACTS. SHE'S PULLED UP TO HER KNEES, THEN TO HER FEET.

THE BULLET SLOWLY EXITS THE WOUND. THE SKIN SEALS BEHIND IT.

THE BULLET HURTLES BACK TOWARD TREVOR'S GUN.

I FEEL TREVOR FIGHT AGAINST IT. FURIOUS. BUT HIS STRUGGLES ARE FRUITLESS. THE BULLET CONTINUES ON ITS COURSE UNTIL IT FINALLY SLIPS INTO A TINY STORMCLOUD OF SMOKE PROTRUDING FROM THE TIP OF TREVOR'S GUN BARREL.

AND THEN EVERYTHING COMES TO A COMPLETE *STILLNESS*.

THE GLOWING LITTLE SLUG HOVERS, PINK AND RAW, AT THE VERY TIP OF THE GUN'S BARREL.

I'M VAGUELY AWARE THAT MY FACE IS A BLOODY MESS. QUIVERING WITH FOCUS AND FATIGUE, I REACH UP AND GUIDE TREVOR'S HAND, AIMING HIS PISTOL INTO THE BOTTOM OF HIS OWN CHIN. AND SINCE WE'RE IN CONTACT, TREVOR PERCEIVES IT ALL.

BOTH TREVOR AND I TREMBLE WITH EXERTION, THE VEINS ON OUR FACES NEARLY BURSTING FROM THE MENTAL AND PHYSICAL WAR WE'RE WAGING. THERE'S AN AGONY IN TREVOR'S EXPRESSION AS HE STRAINS AGAINST A FORCE AND POWER HE WILL NEVER WIELD HIMSELF.

"So much…for ultimate power." I say.

TREVOR'S EYES, BLISTERING WITH MADNESS, FIND MINE. HIS WORDS COME OUT HAGGARD AND DISTORTED AS HE RAGES AGAINST THE STILLNESS I'VE IMPOSED, SWEAT GUSHING DOWN HIS FACE.

"…*Foolish boy… We…are just pawns in the game, Charlie… Pawns and pawns and pawns… It can't be…stopped…*"

TREVOR ROARS ONE LAST FIGHTING EFFORT, THEN I RELEASE MY GRASP ON TIME AND SHIFT ALL MY ENERGY INTO BLOCKING HIM. Trevor's eyes slacken to faraway points as blood, brain and bullet erupt out the top of his skull.

Trevor's big, lifeless body slumps to the ground next to me. The aftershock of such a tremendous energy loss feels like I'm being torn apart from the inside. The world flickers before me. I see images of friends and foes and family and then someone else: a face appears above me, haloed and silhouetted, and I realize I must be a ghost myself.

The face is calling to me. *Pleading.* It seems curious to me that someone so distant should seem to care so much about me. I take a breath, and as the cool tendrils of air fill my lungs, I realize I can't actually remember the last time I took a breath, and right now, I can't remember the last time something felt so amazing.

Life rushes back to me. The face above me is Juniper. Kneeling over my body. I can tell by her frantic tone that I'm in bad shape. She holds me in her warm arms, cradling my head.

"Charlie...Charlie...you're going to be all right...please. Are you okay, Charlie?"

With the very last bit of strength I have left in my trampled body, I lean up and kiss her. The kiss is meaningful, and full, and very, very needed. I feel it everywhere, even tingling behind my toes. After a long moment, our lips detach, and we stare at each other. She sits back in shock, having no idea how to react. Then, all at once, the dark realities of the last forty-eight hours suddenly pour back into me.

"No...I'm not okay," I manage to say. "...None of us are. People shouldn't be able to do these things, Juniper. This power. We can't be trusted with it."

Juniper doesn't know what to say. She doesn't necessarily disagree, I can tell. Not after everything she's experienced recently. But still...

"Charlie...I..."

"Help Ducky. Please. He's hurt."

Juniper looks at Ducky, then back to me, wanting to say something, but she just can't seem to. She goes to him. I force myself up, inch by shaky inch, into a hunched sitting position. I wonder if I look even half as terrible as I feel.

"He's still alive, but he needs a doctor right away," Juniper says.

I can hear vehicles approaching now. I pray it isn't Enforcers coming to finish the job. *Why would they wait?* At this point, I couldn't fight off a kitten attack.

Several members of the Warriors of Fate climb the steps to the floor where Juniper, Ducky and I occupy the small space at the center. They see Trevor's dead body. No one says a word. Tristen is not with them. *Don't know why I thought she would be.*

As they rush toward us, a singular feeling overwhelms me. I know dwelling on this is pointless; I know I had no choice, but still, it sits inside my belly like an abscess:

I just killed a man.

He almost murdered Grams and Ducky, and he was very much in the process of slaughtering me and Juniper…but none of these facts seem to wash away the stain that's forming. I feel it soak into the fabric of me. I will never again have not killed this man, whether his death was justified or not. Somewhere amidst my battered face, I feel hot tears soak the corners of my eyes, then run down my cheeks. My instincts are telling me my body is ground meat, but as I glance down at myself, I know I have survived. But it means nothing if Grams and Ducky don't.

With Juniper's help, and care, the Warriors start to carefully lift Ducky. I can feel Juniper's eyes on me. She's worried.

I grab hold of my heart and force myself to my feet.

CHAPTER 54

JUNIPER

I'm not safe. I feel it. I shouldn't be here. This isn't my home anymore.

The Warriors let me leave. Victor wasn't sure, but the girl, Tristen, vouched for me. *Why? After all my family has done to her. No time to think about that now.*

As the elevator ascends toward the upper floors of Thessaly Tower, I can't shake the feeling that I'm actually slipping *down* the esophagus of some carnivorous, cold-blooded beast. As if, long ago, some serpent-eyed titan hunched above us, unhooked its jaws, rolled back its scaly eyes and slowly swallowed my home, top down, floor by floor, soul by soul—a paralytic rabbit entering a python—and we have been subsisting in its steamy entrails ever since—all of us, every single one of us, soaked in blood, hands at our sides, boiled like frogs in the guts of this pernicious monster of our own making.

I continue to slide upward. I check the number. I'm almost to the floor of my chamber. *If I can lie on my bed for just a moment, maybe curl up with Vic, everything might be okay.* Exhaustion tugs temptingly at my eyelids. *If I could just close my eyes, put my face against my cool pillow, breathe in the scent of my sheets, then maybe, just maybe, when I open my eyes again, the last forty-eight hours will have been no more than a twisted, anxiety induced nightmare. Or maybe I'll wake up and I will actually be five again, and my mother will be there, and my brother and father will still be alive, and I'll have a chance to say just the right thing to make my mother want to stay with us; I'll know the perfect combination of quirky-little-sister advice to make Aeman feel loved and valued and enough. And my father—*

The elevator *passes* my chamber's floor and my mouth clanks open like a sprung door. The floor number hit my destination, then charged ahead. Unabated. Continuing higher. *No. No. It's happening too soon. I'm not ready yet.* My body locks in place—a girl-shaped sculpture with an apoplectic pulse bashing inside its throat. Someone must have redirected the elevator from the outside. I try and slow my breath. *Focus. Focus!* But in my mind, the swooshing glide of the elevator becomes a deafening *slurping* sound, and I know without a doubt my digestive journey, my pterygoid walk, is far from over.

Of course they already know I'm here. The stupefied look on the face of the cropped-haired girl in the lobby had spoken volumes. Careening across the marble floor in her smoke-grey power-pantsuit, the girl had nearly stumbled when she saw me. She must've called. She hadn't looked familiar, but how many people did I really even know at Thessaly? I had felt a pang of guilt at that thought but figured I could address my hermitic tendencies later. I hadn't stopped. Hadn't even slowed. I just kept moving.

Now that perpetual motion has turned against me.

Where are they bringing me? Who else did Trevor have working with him? Am I about to die? They wouldn't dare assassinate me inside Thessaly—would they? I can't fathom such audacity, but perhaps I'm about to pay for that miscalculation with my life. *God, why did I come here?! This is suicide! Why did I make it so easy for them?! Stupid girl! Trevor was right: I am a child seated at the adult table.* Then my reason for coming swells in my chest, and I steady my breath. I feel my feet on the elevator floor. My leg muscles flex, then loosen, finding balance. *They won't take me easily.* Adrenaline gushes into my body, pumping into my limbs. I get into the most advantageous stance for attack. This will not be a moment of defense. I will draw first blood. I will tear at the face of my killers, whoever they might be.

I feel the almost undetectable slowing of the elevator, and I prepare for battle. Fists clenched. Rocking onto the balls of my feet. The elevator stops. The arrival bell pings, slanting my posture like an unsprung cat. I hold my breath. Beat. Beat. The shiny brass doors start to peel apart. Beat. Beat. *How did I ever think this place was a home? This monolithic stockyard.* Beat. Beat.

The portal opens...and...

What I see in front me is completely confusing. A dozen thirteen-year-old girls (I approximate their age based on height, breast size and the presence of acne), all dressed in Enforcer training tunics, stand in two disciplined lines outside the elevator. They collectively *flinch* upon seeing my violent posture.

"...M-M-M-Miss Trask?" the redheaded girl at the front of the right line stammers at me. The girl behind her gives her an annoyed nudge, and the momentarily stunned spokesman of her line snaps to attention, deciding she's more afraid of her peers than she is of me. "We're supposed to bring you to the Council Room, Miss Trask."

I don't answer, and I don't let my guard down. My body is still quivering like a struck drum.

I look around at the girls lined up before me. They present a bouquet of expressions ranging from hostile to awestruck to enamored but all falling firmly under the category of *We Want To Be You Someday*. I've never really thought about what the impact of me becoming a Leader might have on...well...anybody, really. But here I am, solid proof to these twelve girls that such power is within arm's reach.

I don't like their stares, their eyes, their vibrant Technicolor expectations. Especially the goofy redheaded girl in the front, with her hair pulled back and parted in an identical style to my own. Then I notice she's not the only girl in the bunch to have adopted my hairstyle. *Ridiculous*. I know I should take it as a compliment, but my God, don't these little idiots know the sky has fallen? *No, I suppose not*. Still, a gaggle of groupies is the last thing I need right now.

"Why?" I direct my question at the redhead, my tone far from friendly.

I see the girl swallow. "...Why *what*, Miss Trask?"

"Why are you bringing me to the Council Room?"

The girl helplessly glances at the others for support. No support comes. "I don't know, Miss Trask," she says. "We were not informed. 'Questioning is—'"

"'Questioning is the doorway to treason.' I know that one." I cut her off. I don't blame her for kneejerk-reciting Trevor's axioms on cue. I have so many of his little blurbs of wisdom rattling around inside my head, it's a wonder I ever have an original thought of my own. But hearing this wide-eyed preteen parroting Trevor's worldview right now makes my skin crawl. That was me once. I remind myself that no less than two days ago, I was basking in the very ascendency these progeny are currently worshipping. *So, I'm a hypocrite. Whatever. I'm a hypocrite that needs to survive right now.* I stride confidently through the middle of the two lines, causing my escorts to jump out of the way. They have no choice but to fall in line behind me.

When the giant door to the Council Room whisks open, the adolescent tribe doesn't follow me in; they know they're not allowed. And as I enter, the memory of them gets instantly obliterated as I see several members of the Leadership Council rushing at me at once.

Hands are on me before I can process their intentions. Maya Steele places her long, sleek, dark-knuckled hands on either side of my face and looks deep into me with her big amber eyes, and I'm suddenly stunned by the level of concern I see there.

"Oh, Juniper, thank God you're safe!" Maya says. "We were so afraid."

I don't speak. A flabbergasted expression fills my face—a look I imagine magicians must get bored of. I look over her shoulder. Behind her I see the entire Leadership Council (minus Trevor and my father), all with their own brand of fear/worry/relief on their faces. Even repulsive little Gordon Tang looks as close as I imagine he gets to concern. Benjamin Acosta, the elder statesman, steps forward, his gaunt face even more hollow-looking than usual.

"Dear girl, you are one of us now," Benjamin says, "and therefore, you deserve nothing less than pure honesty. No use prolonging… Juniper, your father is dead. I'm so sorry."

I am in the lion's den, and I do not know the rules. The overriding of the elevator was an act of capture, whether they would admit it or not. I have to be smart. They've brought me here for a reason. *"You know, we killed your papa, mija."* Gael Falcón's voice slithers inside my head. But there is zero reason that I should already know this, so my reaction must seem authentic. But I don't have to fake anything. Just hearing someone say it aloud floors me with the finality of it. I choke back tears of rage. I'm about to speak when Maya gets there first…

"I don't know how the monster thought he could get away with it," Maya says through clenched teeth.

They know! They know about Trevor! I can't believe it. They've pulled apart the dark, treasonous web themselves and discovered the truth without my help. Why did I underestimate them? They are considered the best of us for a reason. Relief washes over me in a vindicating surge. I'm red-eyed and disgusted; my words tremble out. "Trevor—"

"Has gone missing." Maya cuts in. "Trevor, as well as his lieutenant, has disappeared. We're trying to remain hopeful, but right now we have to expect the worst."

No. Blood drains out of my face. *No!*

"These terrorists will not rest until we're all gutted and hung. We have to strike *now!*" Gordon Tang hisses.

"He left a note, Juniper," Maya says.

"*Who* left a note?" I ask, the hair on the back of my neck already cactusing like crazy.

Maya looks to Benjamin, who speaks evenly: "I'm afraid your own lab tech, Daniel Fin, betrayed you. Betrayed all of us."

"...Daniel?" My voice quakes.

"Daniel Fin's suicide note was a vile manifesto of treason." Maya's dark tone ripples my skin like an icy breeze. "It seems he desired a seat on the Council, which he believed you stole from him, ludicrous as that sounds. While his intentions seemed mostly bent on chaos and disruption, his intended plans for *you*, in particular, Juniper, were more than a little disturbing."

"Disgusting," Benjamin Acosta mutters.

"We feared desperately for your safety," Maya says.

"What do you expect?" Gordon Tang snorts ruefully. "The little cretin sat in front of a goddam screen all day long with a full-bodied woman strutting back and forth—"

Maya wheels on Gordon: "I will tear that repugnant tongue from your diseased mouth if you utter one more lecherous syllable at this girl, Gordon!" The toadish man swallows the rest of his comments.

"Your father's personal guard was compromised as well," Benjamin states. "Jeffrey Gates had apparently been working with Fin for some time. It was a systematic, coordinated attack. While the three Enforcers Fin had enlisted made an attempt on your life, Mr. Gates drugged your father with a lethal amount of fentanyl citrate.

Mr. Gates was executed this morning."

Jeffrey? They killed Jeffrey. He was practically family. I can't remember a time when he was not with us. I feel nauseous. My cheeks burn. And then I think of my father. *Did he know about Trevor's plan to have me killed? Would I have just been found stuffed into some filthy sewer, a bullet wound in my face? Had he drowned himself in enough drugs, drink and women that he barely remembered he was still part of a family—like a petrified tree that ceases being wood, stops being a tree, becomes stone? It's a process called permineralization and people aren't immune to it. But then why is he dead? Why would they kill him?*

How could you help Trevor after all he did to your family, Father? Your wife, your son, your daughter—not one of us left unscathed. I'll never understand that kind of weakness. Then a thought hits me. Benjamin Acosta said *fentanyl. Or did my father die by his own hand?* I can definitely see Trevor taking credit for something my father could have easily done himself. What if he woke up to the truth of what he was doing? But he knew it was simply too late. I suppose I'll never know. The thought fills me with sadness. My father was terribly flawed, and compromised and selfish, but he was still my father, and I will miss him. Or perhaps the idea of him. But I suspect I'm going to miss all of it. The man he could've been, and the man he was.

I look around. I don't know whom I can trust in this room. Maya's fierce defense of me feels unearned; I barely know her. I almost trust Gordon Tang more, because no one with ill intentions toward me would be so openly salacious. Perhaps Benjamin Acosta's austere grace is simply a front for some deeper diabolic plan. And Virginia, Trevor's paramour, hasn't uttered a word. I meet her grey eyes for a moment. Victor Mason said that Trevor had many followers, but he also said that Elijah had come close to a treaty. Which means he must have had some on his side as well. Was Virginia more loyal to her lover or to her only child? I know nothing. I feel utterly out of my depth right now—a wounded bird waddling amidst invisible cats. I take a step back toward the door. "Please excuse me," I say, "I have to check something in my lab."

Now Virginia speaks. Her expression turns oddly delicate. "I'm afraid your lab, for the moment, is being considered the scene of a crime, Juniper. It's pesky business, but everything's being scoured for signs of sabotage and terrorism. It's just a precaution, but an important one, given the circumstances. I hope you understand."

"Of course," I say. "Makes sense. …How did Daniel—"

"The creature burned himself alive," Gordon chortles. "His note said it was a symbol of protest." I feel emotion start to well up, imagining the horrible things Trevor most likely did to Daniel, trying to get to me. But I shove it down; I refuse to cry in front of these predators.

"Did you have any inkling of Daniel Fin's mental instability, Juniper?" Benjamin asks.

"No…I…I didn't. Daniel…always seemed…"

"The poor girl's exhausted," Maya says, coming to my rescue. "Now is not the time to press her for information. It's time for us to come together as a Chapter. If Trevor has, in fact, been slain, we will need to elect two new Council members, not to mention…a new Prime. May our rituals and traditions serve as steadfast anchors during these turbulent times. Perhaps, later, Miss Trask will give us all a full recounting of her heroic escape. But right now, I think the greatest gift we might give our young heroine would be a good night's sleep. How does that sound, Juniper?"

"Yes…thank you," I say. I nod to Maya and the rest of the Council, then I turn and walk out of the chamber.

I make my way back to the elevator, enter, then I simply stand there. The doors close around me, but I haven't selected a floor yet, so nothing moves. I close my eyes, thinking I might just fall asleep standing up, hide away in the center of this steel cocoon. Then I open my eyes—focusing on what I came here for in the first place—and I press the button.

They've been inside my chamber. Everything's moved. It's subtle but ubiquitous. A chair's angle altered, the bedsheets left slightly uneven, a drawer pushed a little too far in. I even found Vic huddled in the far corner of my closet, clearly not excited to hear the door opening. Thankfully, he's okay, and is now eating greedily. I don't have many sentimental keepsakes; I've never really seen the need. But there are a few things... I take a silver ring of my mother's (which was given to my mother by *her* mother). My mother...*I can't think about that now. I need to save Aeman's revelation for later. Right now, I need to stay focused.* I take a little carved wooden turtle Aeman bought me as a child, and I take a postcard my father sent my mother before I was born, with a poem written in cursive on the back:

> *The saddest birds fly north*
> *Cold wind, pelted plumage*
> *Unknown fathoms below*
> *A silence like darkness*
> *Lost, but for your laugh*
> *Cherry blossom tendrils*
> *Baked upon your hot skin*
> *Drift up—show me the way*

Everything has been touched, no stone left unturned. The thought of Trevor, or one of his goons, with their hands on any of these things makes me want to burn all of it. They've been everywhere that was once mine, but what frightens me most is that I can tell these things weren't placed back with the meticulous eye of someone attempting to convince *me* that no one has been in here. The job was *just* sloppy enough to be meant for someone else who might be looking to see if anyone has been in here. Someone other than me. Which means that I was not expected to return.

My eye catches on something else. The vanity at the far end of my chamber has a mirror. Something has been written on my mirror. I walk to the glass and see handwriting that looks remarkably similar to my own. At least, someone has made a valiant effort to make it look like mine. Written on the mirror in fine, faux-Juniper print is one sentence:

AT LEAST I HAVEN'T BEEN FIRED YET.

Anyone else reading this might suspect it to be the scribblings of an anxiety-ridden eighteen-year-old girl who has just been made a Leader. An encouragement to myself: *Look on the bright side: at least I haven't been fired yet.* Only, I didn't write it. So, who *did* write it? I have a theory. I move quickly to the nightstand set against the right side of the bed. I slide the skinny, stilted oakwood table counterclockwise, then reach over and pull the side of the wooden drawer, which unhinges, flapping down and opening like a little drawbridge. I reach inside the little secret space and my hand catches on the exact prize I was fishing for. I pull out a thin white pistol with a pearl handle. It's a beautiful weapon. The gun was given to me the day I became a Leader. "An elegant weapon for an elegant calling," Benjamin Acosta said as he handed it to me at the ceremony. So much has changed since then.

As I hold the weapon in my hand, I notice that the clip has not been pushed all the way in. My heart begins to beat faster. I let the clip fall into my hand, but I am not concerned with the bullets. What sparks my mind is whatever is blocking the clip from sliding home. I turn the gun right side up and something slides out into my hand. *A flash drive.* Daniel's final gift to me: our research, encrypted, just like I had asked. *"At least I haven't been fired yet."* Very clever, Daniel. I have not fired this pistol yet. Not even at the private practice range for Council members. The gun is too new. I feel suddenly choked with sorrow. *I'm so sorry, Daniel. You were better than all of them.*

I replace the clip, slide the pistol into the back of my pants, slip on the ring, and pocket the postcard as well as the tiny wooden turtle. Aeman told me, when he gave me the little cartilaginous-shelled gift on my seventh birthday, that the turtle was lucky.

I have a feeling I'll need it.

One last stop.

CHAPTER 55

CHARLIE

The machines wheeze and hiss as they fight to keep Ducky alive. He's hooked into the various apparatuses from all sides, making it look like they're building a Ducky-shaped robot. His heart monitor beeps…beeps…beeps… I drift up to the edge of his bed. I want to take his hand, but I don't. He looks unbearably vulnerable. So weak. The brilliant, charming kid who's always had my back, who called me a brother when he had every right to despise me, who stood by my side as I clawed my way out of childhood, flailing and faltering, losing far more often than I won—that selfless kid—the only family I have left—is lying prone in a hospital bed, fighting for his life, and as usual, it is entirely my fault.

If I could trade places with you, Ducky, I promise you I would. I'm all out of tears. Rage burns behind my eyes. I hold my breath. There is no sound but the machines.

"Your friend will survive." Victor Mason's voice speaks softly behind me. I didn't hear him enter. I glance at him, then focus back on Ducky. "That was very dangerous, Charlie."

"I had to try and help them."

"Your foster mother is recovering fully at the hospital. We'll have to get word to her that you two are safe before she tears the place apart." Normally, the thought of innocent bystanders facing off against a raging Grams would make me smile, but I suddenly feel like I may never see her again. As if Victor can hear my thoughts, he says, "We have people placed all around the hospital, but she doesn't seem to be in any danger. Trevor would not have broadcast any information about your existence, and both his lieutenants are dead. I believe she's safe."

"She won't ever be safe as long as I'm in her life."

Victor doesn't show that he agrees or disagrees with me.

"Know that you saved many lives today, Charlie. Hopefully, we will find our way toward peace with Trevor gone."

"I don't think so," I say.

"What makes you say that?"

I turn to him. "Trevor's last words. He said, 'We're all just pawns in the game. Pawns and pawns and pawns.' And then he said 'It can't be stopped.' That doesn't sound very peaceful."

The old man gets lost in thought—his face grows cloudy and unsure. Then he seems to come to some kind of realization.

"You're certain he said 'pawns'? Those were his exact words?"

I nod. "Yep. Hard to miss. He said it like five times." I would've thought the whole *It can't be stopped* would be the more worrisome part. His tired sagging face seems to droop even further.

"…The Carrion Ring," Victor says in what is almost a whisper. "I believe I might have been very foolish, Charlie. You see, Trevor was actually quite a small man, if you can believe that. There are far worse than Trevor in this world, I'm afraid. Trevor was driven only by power and cruelty. He cared about nothing. Real power comes from protecting something you care deeply for. Something you love. You and your surprising success are a shining example of that."

"I wouldn't call anything that's happened a success."

"There are those who would protect their way of life by means that they have honed for a thousand years. A way of life they believe the Leadership stole from them. If what I fear is true, we may not have seen our darkest hour. In my heart I hope I'm wrong. I need to think on it." Now his tired eyes focus on mine. "Will you join us in our cause, Charlie? Or will you be leaving us? We could most definitely use your help. You have a rare and amazing gift."

"We both do," I say, calling out the truth that we each know. "Not that I'd call it amazing. Kindness is amazing. Generosity. Risking your life when you *don't* have the option to take back all your stupid mistakes whenever you want…that's what *amazing* is. We're just playing bumper cars."

Victor just smiles a sad smile, not commenting. Finally… "There will be great need for courage in the coming days. You've lost so much, Charlie. Experienced so much more pain than any young man your age should ever have to. Perhaps you can help keep others from such a fate. Not to mention I know it would make Tristen quite happy if you stayed."

I cannot help my incredulous reaction. "That girl has done nothing but lie to me from the first moment we met. Why would I care about her happiness?"

"She risked her life going after you alone the way she did. I could've wrung her neck. She also saved Juniper's life by mere seconds, according to Juniper's telling of it—not to mention your foster mother."

I have no idea what to say to this. I had grown quite comfortable with the idea of Tristen as a backstabbing, selfish user. This new twist on her character leaves me feeling uneasy.

"Juniper…" I'm not sure what I'm even trying to say.

Victor sees my struggle. A knowing expression spreads across his face, which is super annoying. "As if you need more on your plate," he says. I'm about to say something back—something to shoot down whatever mischievous dementia-ridden-old-man thoughts he has pinballing around in his foggy brain—but just as I open my mouth, I hear the *clip-clip-clip* of Tristen entering the room behind me on her crutches.

Her leg is heavily wrapped. The shotgun blast did considerable damage, but the bone is apparently intact. Not that I care. She makes eye contact with me and Victor in turn. Victor turns back to me.

"I hope to talk again soon, my boy. Please think on what I said." Then Victor smiles and exits the medical wing.

Left alone, Tristen and I contemplate each other. I remain stone-faced.

"I was just checking on your friend," she says.

"Victor says he'll be all right."

Tristen looks over at Ducky. "It's difficult to get close to people outside our world. I've tried a few times. It's never gone very well."

"I don't consider myself part of your world," I say.

"Maybe not. But it considers you part of it regardless."

Pissed, I walk past her, heading out of the room.

"Hey, Charlie…" Tristen begins.

I stop and turn back to her. She swivels on her crutches to face me.

"How many times did you have to wind us back in the park?"

My cheeks flush a little. I had been pursuing her with reckless abandon, manipulating time to win her over, and she had known what I was doing the whole time.

A beat lingers between us.

"Maybe six times, " I say. "Little embarrassing."

"I suppose I could've played harder to get," Tristen says.

"Then there's the fact that you were there on purpose just to use me."

"Then there's that…"

A quiet, less-harsh moment passes between us.

"See you around, Charlie."

I feel like I want to say something, but whatever it is, it dies before release. I turn and continue walking.

I find Juniper at the end of a long corridor standing with her body almost pressed against one of the floor-to-ceiling glass windows that face out toward the city. I watch her for a moment. Outside, the salmon-belly sky bleeds down to the horizon, where it pools and glows. Thessaly Tower rises up in front of Juniper.

My footfalls are soft and speechless as I start down the hall toward her—an old habit. I spent half my childhood trying to remain unnoticed and unannounced, hoping that if I took up less space, perhaps someday that extra space might add up to fill the tremendous vacuum left at the center of Ducky and Grams's lives. *Ducky…Grams…* Tristen's words from the bar echo in my head: "*Sometimes, things that should scar us don't end up leaving as big a mark as we deserve. And that ends up hurting more. But then we go on.*" As a kid, I felt like a ghost haunting my own life. I thought I was crazy. But now I know I was never crazy. And there's a responsibility that comes with that. *No more whining. No more tiptoeing. It doesn't work.*

I land next to her without a single thought of what I'm going to say. She looks stunning in the raw pink light. Sad but beautiful. We've both lost so much. Something about that binds us together. But on top of losing her father and brother, she's also dealing with a different kind of loss from mine. Hers is all twisted up in home and faith and disillusionment, and I can't begin to touch any of it.

She hasn't looked at me, and suddenly I feel like an intruder. Maybe she doesn't want me here. I want to retreat, but I have no place to go.

"It's so ugly," Juniper says. I follow her gaze to Thessaly Tower. "It's ostentatious. Unimaginative. Even the gargoyles are predictable." I watch three slow breaths wax and wane within her lean body. "Why did I feel like I lived in a palace? What made me think that?"

Now she turns to me and her emerald eyes glitter with emotion. She looks so lost. I want to take her in my arms, wrap her up in whatever patchwork tenderness I have left inside me. But I don't know if that's what *she* wants, and I'd sooner throw myself off this building than make her think there's another person in her life asking something of her that she doesn't know how to answer. So, I simply stare back at her like a peeled potato, damp and naked. The moment passes, and she faces back out the window again.

The second she turns away, I realize what an idiot I am. *She wanted me to say something. I'm doing everything wrong.* The silence between us feels deafening.

"You went back," I say. The sound of my own voice spooks me a little.

"Yes."

"I heard you brought back a little girl with you."

"And a cat."

"Oh…cool. I like cats. My mom was allergic, so we never had one. But Grams had a big old ginger Maine Coon for a bunch of years. Used to take baths with Ducky when he was little. Loved the water. Super weird cat." *I'm rambling. Oh, God, organize your thoughts.* "Who's the girl?" I ask.

"Her name is Sofia. She didn't belong there."

"Victor asked me to join them. He thinks it's going to get worse."

This last thought seems to land heavy on Juniper. Her gaze drifts slightly downward, away from the only home she's ever known. Her eyes dance back and forth, her brow furrows, and suddenly I feel awed watching this brilliant girl's mind chew on an idea. She turns to me, and this time, the shaky vulnerability has been traded in for a starchy, congealed determination.

"You don't have to be a part of any of this, Charlie," she says. "You can leave. Wait for Ducky to get better and then just go."

I meet her stare, the pendulum of my gaze drifting from her left eye to her right and then back again. In a few words, she has summed up the recurring thought that's been ceaselessly bashing around inside my brain since leaving the medical wing—*Take Ducky and get as far away from this place as possible.* Away from the Warriors of Fate. Away from the Leadership. Away from the terrible potential irrevocably seeded inside me. *Away from her.* But the second she opens that door, I know I'll never walk through it. And now *my* brow is furrowing, and now she gets to watch *me* think. *A far less impressive spectacle, I have no doubt.* Finally, I say, "…I spent most of my life feeling like I was the cause of so much pain. Then I grew up and learned that it was all true. Maybe this is a chance to actually help people."

"But it isn't even your fight," she says.

"Is it yours?" I leave my eyes on her; I don't turn away. Not this time.

Juniper doesn't answer. We stand in silence. Then she's facing out once again. The crimson glow at the horizon has been gulped down by the west, and Juniper's face has already taken on a slightly shadowed quality. I hear tiny beads of saliva pop on her lips as she gently parts them to speak.

"My mother was normal," Juniper says. "Human, I mean. …I don't remember her very well. But I remember her being very loving and very sad." Juniper's words float in the air before me like gossamer balloons, unmasked and unbearably fragile. I can tell she wants to stop. Whatever this is, she doesn't think she can say it directly to another person. Fear pushes back at her with its many, many hands. But with everything I can summon inside me, I gently will her to continue. And after exactly five heartbeats, she does.

"My father adored her. He lived for her. But he couldn't tell her his secret. The secret to why everything always seemed to go extremely right for him and not for her. She was not a pet, not a woman to be coddled. She was headstrong and ambitious but also crippled with insecurity and doubt. It started just after I was born. They thought it was postpartum depression, but it lasted. She resented having to be medicated; she thought it made her seem defective. My father agonized over the irony that regardless of how powerful he might be, there was nothing he could do for her. And she refused to be helped. She also never understood the bond between my father and me. My abilities were groomed nearly from birth. At least I have no memory of not knowing I had them."

"How could he tell that you—"

"I could hear the ringing," she says. I offer a tiny nod of understanding. She swallows, then continues. "My father told me my mother killed herself when I was five. One day, she was there; the next day, she was gone."

"I'm…I'm so sorry, Juniper." I want to yank this memory from her psyche, pull apart the pain.

"After that, my father lived in this…perpetual state of self-medication. The cruel irony is his abilities grew exponentially after losing my mother. There's some kind of intrinsic tie between the depth of our emotional worlds and our abilities. Like our wells of power can only be filled as deep as we've dug them with our pain. I've been studying the limbic system of Winders. It seems the neurons in our hippocampus—" She catches herself burrowing under the pain and stops short. "Before Aeman died, he told me he found my mother. That she's still alive. And I know this sounds awful, but part of me wishes she'd stayed dead—that he'd never told me. Because I don't know what to do about it. She's human. We can't live in the same world. Not really. My father tried it, and look what happened to him. We can't save people, Charlie. I don't think our powers were meant for that."

"What the hell are they meant for, then?" I ask.

"…I don't know… I don't think anyone does. The Leadership says the world is ours by evolutionary right, that in nature no animal refuses to use its natural advantages against another animal: bigger teeth, faster legs, bigger brain… They say morality is only what the survivors say it is. As a child, I imagined *evolution* to be some kind of elegant metamorphosis. Caterpillar into a butterfly and all that. But it turns out it's just a pretty name for the millions of deaths that allow for one species to slowly become something new. It's all shit, Charlie." Her voice catches, but she rallies and pushes forward. "We don't change. The world changes, and we just die or we don't. Humans have never been able to perceive our powers, and for thousands of years, it's made us nearly unstoppable. Then *you* come along, and you seem to be more powerful than all of us, and yet normal humans can see what you do. *Why?* There's probably no answer. No morality. Just chance…" She breaks off, fighting to find her next words. "…I do believe you're important, though, Charlie. Maybe there's a reason that you're here at this exact time."

And then she says something I don't think I believe: "Maybe you're meant to save us from ourselves." But from the look on her face, I know some part of her believes it.

Several more heartbeats tumble through the air between us. Then something unexpected happens: the right corner of my mouth twinges upwards ever so slightly and I smile. It's small, and half-buried in the debris, but it's there all the same, stomping at the edges of my sorrow, and I can no longer be silent as I stare at her lovely face. "Well…you're definitely the smartest person I've ever met. So…if you're telling me we have a chance, maybe I'll let myself believe it."

Juniper takes in my scrawny confidence. It doesn't seem to displease her. "What are you going to tell Ducky and Grams?" she asks.

"Haven't quite figured that out yet."

Fresh pain seems to strike at Juniper's center. Tears brim in her eyes. But this time, she doesn't fight it. "…Everything I've ever known is gone. I'm all alone, Charlie."

"You're not alone."

Juniper can't make eye contact with me. She stares out.

"Do we stay or do we go our own way?" I ask her.

A faraway look permeates her face. "I don't know," she says.

Somewhere far on the horizon I see the blinking lights of a traffic helicopter coasting through the sky.

"Would you come with me?" I ask.

Juniper turns to me. She knows I mean it.

"Yes," she says. "That's the only thing I do know."

"Then we'll figure it out. Together," I say.

Here we are, two shipwrecked kids being asked to dive into shark-infested waters with nothing but blood-soaked life preservers to keep us afloat. The space between us is pulpy with connection. I have never felt pulled toward another person like this before.

"Okay," she says, as simply as a word has ever been spoken. Our eyes linger. I hold my breath. Then Juniper gently slips her hand into mine. And despite the fear, despite the anger and confusion clawing away inside me, searching for my limits like demented bloodhounds, Juniper's hand feels soft and warm. And somehow—for now—that's enough.

Acknowledgments

This book would've been half of what it is without the help and guidance of my brutally honest agent, Joshua Bilmes. Thank you for your belief that I could get to something halfway decent in the end, and for your patience along the way.

Karen, your badass editorial instincts are felt on every single page. Thank you so much for making my story better.

Lisa, I couldn't be more grateful for your careful attention to detail. Even the tiniest choices were given their due.

Big thanks to Brady and everyone else on the JABberwocky team.

I also want to thank my little sister, who was the first person to read and give me notes on this Sisyphean boulder. You're the best, sis.

I spent a year workshopping the first draft of this book with an amazing group of writers I met through Talia Bolnik at The Hatchery in Los Angeles. The Hatchery will be missed. Fuck you, pandemic.

Two people I have to thank, who threw some serious love and encouragement at me and this book, early on, when I really needed it: Joe Loya. *Quadrants homie*. And Gloria Fan. Your support meant the world to me.

I want to thank my lovely wife who put up with me endlessly talking out every aspect of this book along the way, and for not giving me too much shit as I came to bed just as the sun was coming up once again.

Finally, I want to thank the woman who sat me down in a chair and forced me to read *The Secret Garden* when I was ten. It's been a long journey since then, and I've had a book with me ever since. Thanks, Mom.

Ryan O'Nan is an award-winning screenwriter, actor and director. He has written on such series as Marvel's *Legion* on FX, as well as the edgy teenage drama *Skins, Queen of the South* on USA, and *Wu-Tang: An American Saga* on Hulu. Currently, Ryan writes and produces on *Big Sky* on ABC. On the film side, he wrote/directed the hit indie film "Brooklyn Brothers Beat the Best" which was released theatrically by Adam Yauch's (Beastie Boys) company Oscilloscope Laboratories, where it received several awards. Ryan has been featured in both *Filmmaker Magazine* and *Creative Screenwriting Magazine*. As an actor, Ryan is best kown for playing King George on the series *Queen of the South*. He lives in Los Angeles, California with his wife and three cats: Bosco Beanbag, Fantine the Bean, and Amelia Wolfman. *Winders* is Ryan's debut novel.